The Off Season

A Novel
by
Stephen M. Heck

The Off Season
© 2021 by Stephen M. Heck

ISBN: 978-1-7373734-0-7
Library of Congress Control Number: 2021940407

Printed in the United States of America

Cover and Book designed by SeaGrove Press
Ronald Thomas Rollet, Publisher

SeaGrove Press
638 Sunset Blvd
Cape May, New Jersey 08204
seagrovepress@gmail.com

Dedication

To my mother, the first person who saw I had a book inside me.
Thanks, Mom.

Acknowledgments

The person at the top of my thank-you list is my wife, Janice. She listened to every word, changed some and never complained about my infatuation with characters that lived in my head. Just when I thought I'd thrown in the towel she threw it back.

Ronald Thomas Rollet, thank you for your guidance and professionalism. *The Off Season* wouldn't be a reality without you. Nor would my book be what it is without Koren Cowgill, Scott Griffith, Jane Kashlak, Christine Cote, Jim Gannone and Devin Loring.

Special thanks to those who chipped in early with suggestions and encouragement. Among them are Tom Loftus, David Schwartz and Judi Salasin.

And thanks, Keira, for lending your name.

PROLOGUE
THE END OF EVERYTHING

"This is the place. What do you think?" Randy said, tucking his dress shirt into his suit pants. In doing so, his hand crossed his stomach. He realized he was getting soft, had been for years, though it no longer mattered. The decades-old battle with his waistline was finally over. Tonight he was retiring the gray pinstripe.

"Wow," the limo driver said. "I couldn't afford a restaurant like this."

"I can't afford this place either."

As the driver approached to open his door, Randy pulled himself from the limo and stepped onto the bustling sidewalk, sensing the city's rhythm was out of whack. People hailed taxis, hustled their way to subway entrances, leaned on car horns, got pushed along the pavement wedged within hordes of commuters and tourists.

Today was different. A number of pedestrians slowed and raised their heads.

The Black Sky had plunged New York into a city of cold darkness.

"Something's very wrong," the driver said.

"No kidding. By the way, I won't need you to pick me up later."

"I thought this was a round-tripper."

"It's one-way."

"Mister—"

"Collier."

"Sorry, the work order just says Randy," the driver said. "What do you think about this friggin' sky? Those don't seem like normal storm clouds to me."

"They're not storm clouds."

Randy heard a scream above him and quickly glanced up. The body crashed onto the concrete with a squishing thud, maybe twenty feet from the men.

The driver shouted, "Oh my God!" He winced as he kept his distance from the dead body, its blood and guts oozing.

"Eleven," Randy said.

"What did you say?"

"Here's a couple of C-notes for you. Go have some fun."

The driver held the bills without looking at them. "Some guy just fell from a window."

Randy walked through the stained glass door of the Zagat-starred restaurant. The maître d', attired in a jet-black tuxedo, met him inside and said, "Welcome to L'Orange, sir. Do you have a reservation?"

"Trimingham."

The maître d' peered down at the podium. "Ah, there it is, six o'clock. We have a nice table ready for you."

"Thank you," Randy said, folding five one hundred-dollar bills into the man's hand. The maître d' made brief eye contact with the cash and deftly tucked it into his inside breast pocket. "I'd like your best table," Randy added.

"Yes, sir." The maître d' motioned to a man wearing a black vest over his white dress shirt. "Andre."

"I'm dying in this getup," Randy said, while removing his jacket and blue tie. "Find a home for these." He extended them to the surprised maître d'.

"Sir, normally a jacket and tie are required in the dining room. However, if it's for your health, we can certainly make an exception."

"I feel better already," Randy said.

"Pardon me for asking. Have you dined with us before?"

"No. But I did see a review. Said the food's pretty good."

"Yes, quite. I'm wondering if we've met before. Do you live in the city?"

"Uh-uh. I'm Randall Alistair Trimingham III, of the London Triminghams. My father used to summer here. Maybe you met him, Randy number two."

"No sir, I don't think I've had the pleasure."

Andre was stationed a few feet from the men awaiting his next prompt. A subtle nod from the maître d' brought Andre closer. "Escort Mr. Trimingham to table eight."

Andre raised his eyebrows. "This way please."

As the duo passed elegant patrons, Randy noticed many staring at them. "Casual Friday, folks," he said with a smile.

Andre stopped at a table beneath a mural of Cezanne's *Still Life with Apples and Oranges*. "It's actually Thursday, sir."

"You and I know that but let's not tell everyone else."

Andre laughed as he pulled out the table. He turned and stared through the glass-paneled doors leading to the restaurant's courtyard, where the live orange trees were shrouded in darkness. "It's like midnight out there."

"Yeah. We need to get this show on the road."

"Yes, sir. Colette will be your server this evening."

"Andre, wait a second." Randy reached into his wallet and peeled off five twenties.

Andre slipped the bills into his pants pocket. "Thank you, sir."

"You're welcome. Tell Colette to scoot over here. I'm hungry. And Andre, you've got a wine steward on duty I assume."

"Certainly. Brian is a Master Sommelier."

"What's the difference?" Randy asked.

"Brian was certified at Le Cordon Bleu in Paris."

"Cool. Ask him to drop by."

A tall thin woman with high cheekbones, her long brown hair pulled back, approached the table. "My name is Colette and I'll be taking care of you. Would you like to peruse our wine list before Brian comes to see you?"

"You can leave it."

She placed it near Randy and offered him a menu. A Runner breezed by and handed Colette a small crystal bowl containing Beluga in a gold tin. A gold spoon rested on a bed of ice chips, which she positioned in front of Randy. Another staff member brought a bottle of Ciroc centered on a small crystal tray, with the bottle surrounded by ice and etched drinking glasses. "Thank you, Charles." Colette whispered, as he moved away.

"What's all this?" Randy asked.

"Caviar and vodka," compliments of the maître d'. "Charles will be back shortly with spring water and tumblers." She quickly scanned the dining room. "Where did he go?"

Randy waved toward the maître d' and mouthed a thank you. "Fish eggs, right?" Randy said quietly. "Do you guys eat this stuff?"

"I've tasted it," she said. "Once."

Andre shook his head. "I never tried it but I'm sure it's delicious. Excuse me, I'll go check on Charles," he added.

"Will anyone be joining you?" Colette asked.

"Just me for now, but let's keep the other table setting. I'm an optimist." Randy put the menu down without opening it. "I like your outfit."

She blushed. "Thank you. The orange vests are a tad bright but, well, L'Orange," she said, adjusting her black bowtie. "Brian will be here in a second—oh, here he is. Charles will bring the water."

Brian's snug-fitting shirt and vest hinted at his fitness. He had short-cropped hair and sported a ready-made smile. "Good evening, Mr. Trimingham. Are you interested in ordering from our wine cellar? I would be happy to assist you with your selection."

"Have you got anything that'll knock my socks off?"

"Pardon?"

"Come on, Brian. You already know my name, so you can guess I'm part of the fictitious Trimingham clan. Recommend a special wine."

"We do have a 1986 Chateau Lafite-Rothschild, which would pair well with our meat selections."

"How's it taste?"

"It is magnificent." Brian peeked at the maître d' who was watching them.

"That's an interesting hunk of jewelry around your neck," Randy said. "Looks like you scored a silver medal in the Olympics."

"It's actually—"

Suddenly, staff members began yelling. "Help, is there a doctor here? I think he's dying! He's in the men's room!"

"Twelve," Randy said.

Brian spun toward the commotion and headed in that direction.

Colette returned to the table. "I'm sorry, but an older gentleman got sick. Not from the food, I can assure you." She fanned herself with her hand. "It's stuffy in here today. I'm told someone is checking the AC and ventilation. Did you have a chance to study the menu?"

"Don't need to. I want the biggest steak your kitchen has. I want it Pittsburgh rare. When I bite into the thing I want to feel the crunch and then get a mouthful of blood. Can they do that?"

"We have a wonderful Steak au Poivre, that's with cracked peppercorns. I'm sure our chef can pan-sear the filet to your liking."

"I don't want any peppercorns. Make that two orders and include a heaping mound of mashed potatoes with gravy."

"Two filets?" she asked.

"I'm expecting someone to join me."

"That's nice. Did you want to order any hors d'oeuvres?"

"It would just get in the way."

"Oh, alright. I'll leave a menu for your friend."

A moment later Brian reappeared. "Did you decide on the wine, sir?"

"What happened with the sick guy?"

Brian stood silent for a couple of seconds. "He's being rushed to the hospital."

"I didn't see the EMTs take him away."

"There's a rear entrance."

"Brian, I'll take a bottle of that 1986 stuff you mentioned on one condition."

"What would that be?"

"Have a drink with me. I'll do the swirling-in-the-mouth thing and then you have a glass. Deal?"

"I don't know, sir."

"Call me Randy."

"Yes, sir."

"Off you go," Randy said. "Bring three glasses with that, please."

Colette brought two tumblers to the table and placed a large bottle of Evian alongside them.

"Wasn't a guy named Charles supposed to bring the water?" Randy asked.

"I don't know where he disappeared to." She twisted the cap and was ready to pour.

"No thanks. I'll wait for Brian. He's bringing me a Lafite something-or-other. Colette, can I ask you a personal question?"

"If you answer one for me first."

"Sure."

"How did you get by the maître d without a jacket? Frank's a stickler for that."

"I gave him five hundred dollars."

Colette laughed. "I didn't know he had a price."

"My turn. Would you have dinner with me this evening?"

"You mean after I'm off work?"

"No," Randy said. "You bring the meals and then take a seat across from me."

"I couldn't possibly."

"Suppose this was the last day?"

"The last day of what?"

"Of everything."

Colette fidgeted with a button on her vest. "Thank you, but I can't."

Randy shifted his gaze to the floor and pointed. "What do you see there?"

"The carpeting? They just cleaned it this morning," she said.

He rose and stood next to her. "Now check it out."

"Not sure what you mean."

"What do you see on the carpet?"

"Nothing. My shadow is all."

"What do you think of mine?" he asked.

"Your shadow?" Colette shifted her feet and sidestepped for a better angle. "Hmm. I must be standing in the wrong spot."

"Let's switch," Randy said, exchanging places with her.

"You—you don't have one. You're not a vampire, are you?"

"I used to have a Shadow but the thing yanked itself away months ago and is now blocking out the sun with thousands or millions of other Shadows."

"I don't understand."

"I should have done something. My Shadow warned me and I didn't do a damn thing."

"I'm sure you're mistaken about this," she said.

"I wish I was. You did notice the sky is closing in on us, didn't you?"

"The news people said something about temperature thermal inversion. I think I heard that right. One newsman called it a black sky."

"The sky is falling, literally. It's a solid mass of Shadows sucking away our oxygen. I'm aware of a dozen people dying around me today."

"Oh my." Colette glanced over her shoulder. "Frank is signaling me. Other tables to take care of—sorry, gotta run."

"Colette," Randy said. "See it for yourself. Go outside and look at the sky, really look at it."

"Maybe I will. I could use some fresh air."

Randy saw the maître d' heading in his direction, pausing to ask patrons if everything was fine. One man stood up, loosened his tie, and shuffled to the restroom.

"Mr. Trimingham, is everything to your satisfaction?"

"Yes. Did you have something specific in mind?"

"Well, I'm aware you asked Brian and Colette to join you."

"I did."

"I'm sorry, but we couldn't allow that."

"I think you can." Randy said, still standing. "Come with me." He gently nudged Frank's elbow and guided him across the room.

"What are you doing?" the maître d' asked.

"Showing you something."

Both men stepped outside. Colette stared upwards.

The night air was still. Numerous emergency vehicles, their light bars flashing, motors idling, were parked along Fifth Avenue. Sirens wailed in the distance. Traffic lights blinked red. A woman, carrying an infant, ran screaming across the intersection. Two men fought at the hotel entrance a few doors away. People gathered in clusters; some gawked at the street chaos while others pointed to the sky.

A bearded man, his hair disheveled, his t-shirt ripped, passed the trio on the sidewalk. "It's getting cold," he said. Frank unbuttoned his tuxedo jacket and handed it to him.

The blackness now hovered near the antennas atop the Empire State Building.

"What time is it?" Colette asked.

"Just after six," Randy said.

"How could it be so dark?"

"Like I told you. It's them."

Colette shuddered. "I'm scared."

Frank glared at the sky. "What the fuck is that?"

"Shadows," Randy said. "Colette, do you think our steaks are ready?"

"Um, I'll go check," she said.

"Will you join Colette and me for dinner?" Randy asked the maître d. "Give you half my steak."

Frank nodded. "Colette, tell Jean-Claude to fire up three more. I'll invite Brian and Andre."

They turned to the front door, and a gunshot echoed behind them.

"Unlucky thirteen," Randy said.

The restaurant lights shone unusually bright as The Black Sky descended.

Excerpted from *Shadows: The Other Side*

A novel by David Farmer—Winner of the 2016 Bradbury Award for Best New Science Fiction Writer.

Chapter One

Five years ago my life changed forever. Forever doesn't last as long as it once did. Give forever a moment and it'll change again.

It was the off-season in Wildwood, New Jersey and the tourists had returned home, leaving the area as a quiet sanctuary for the locals.

The Wildwoods were comprised of four separate communities on an island closely bordering the mainland and connected by three bridges. North to south were North Wildwood, Wildwood and Wildwood Crest. Jutting into the Back Bay was West Wildwood, an island unto itself without an ocean beach and almost forgotten.

October weather could be most anything in the Wildwoods. Mother Nature would deliver a seventy-degree day followed by a string of forty-degree days packed with gusting winds. Nor'easters loomed. I didn't allow the weather to deter my daily five-mile stroll. I was like the postman—neither snow nor rain.

I walked the famous two-mile-long boardwalk noting the nearly deserted beach, the steel-gray ocean, the rattle of shuttered storefronts, piers with dormant carnival rides, and colorful motels awaiting a fresh coat of seasonal paint.

All the days were much the same for me—until they weren't.

Moving at a brisk pace, I heard a clanking sound to my right and saw a man harnessed near the top of the Great White rollercoaster. His hammering distracted me and I collided with the woman. She lost her balance and fell to the hardwood planks, bracing her fall with one arm. A white paper bag she'd been holding ended up on its side and some of the contents spilled out.

"Oh no," she said, reaching for the candy from a kneeling position.

"I'm sorry. I wasn't watching where I was going. You okay?"

I bent to help her as she gathered the candy.

"Darn, I love these things." she said, raising her arm to me. I tugged as carefully as I could and pulled her up. "Thanks, I'm fine," she added, as she stuffed candy in her coat pocket. "These licorice wheels are so good."

"Where'd you get them?"

She motioned with her finger. "Fudge Kitchen. It's like the only place open today."

"I'll buy you more."

"No thanks. I can wash the dirty ones off at home. Anyway, most of them stayed in the bag." She reached in and pulled a black wheel. "Want one?' she asked.

I shook my head. "I'm good. I still want to get you more."

She ripped off a piece of the candy, placed it in her mouth and began chewing. She stopped eating and stared at me. "Oh my God! David Farmer! You're him, right?"

Uh-oh.

"I am."

"I absolutely loved your book. Those shadows scared the living daylights out of me. I read it like five times."

"I'm glad you liked it."

"It gave me goosebumps."

I glanced at the sleeping rollercoaster, the ocean roiling off its pier. "I was watching the guy on the coaster when—"

"That's Jason," the woman said. "He does maintenance for the outfit that owns the pier."

"Yeah, I've seen him before."

"He lives right over there," she said, pointing past the southern end of the boardwalk.

"Nice place," I said, turning to look at the high-rise condo where I also lived, just down the hall from Jason Bell.

"You have to have a few bucks to afford that place," she added.

"I guess so. You sure you're all right from the fall?"

She flexed her arm. "Still works. Wow, David Farmer, what an honor to meet you."

I nodded and smiled.

"I'm Kate, by the way," she said, pumping my arm.

"If you're okay, I'm—"

"You look different than the book jacket," she said. "Let's see, you've got a moustache for one thing and your hair, you let it grow. Cool, I like it."

"I'm in a bit of a hurry," I said.

"You kinda look like a later George Harrison, you know, when he was alive. Oops, I hope I didn't offend you. Sorry."

"No problem."

"Mr. Farmer, when is the sequel coming out?"

"I'm retired."

"Oh no, that's too bad. The thing is I still pick up your book and flip to a page and start reading again. I get scared every time, you know what I mean?"

"Yes."

I was scared, too.

"It sold millions of copies," she said. "I saw you interviewed back then on *60 Minutes*. They said millions were sold, I can't remember how many."

Kate was a pleasant enough fortyish woman, with features that would offend no one. Her brown bangs covered her forehead atop equally brown eyes.

"How did you ever think of that plot?" she continued.

I'm not sure I did.

I shrugged.

She laughed. "Oh, how silly of me. You're not going to tell me your secrets."

I realized she was going to be a problem. "I should get going."

"Before you go could I ask you a personal question?"

No.

"Sure."

"Are you just visiting Wildwood, like a vacation maybe?"

I hesitated. "I live in the area."

"That's wonderful!" Kate said. "Can I ask another personal question? I promise it'll be the last one."

"Alright."

"In that interview I saw on TV, your wife was sitting next to you. She's very pretty. Is she here with you?"

After I ruined my marriage, I pulled away from women. No girlfriends, no dating, no prospects. I was fully prepared to go it alone.

Nothing is ever always or never. Things still happened sometimes just because they could.

The previous night my attractive neighbor knocked on my condo door. She said she wanted a little sugar, but said those words with a wink. I knew little about Cecily Slade and less about her husband Dennis, but after her visit I was anxiously awaiting her return. She was gorgeous, a few years older than me, her body blessed with curves Mae West would admire.

I had intense sex with this woman. Lovemaking had eluded me for too long and I reacted on instinct. I didn't need a GPS.

"We're divorced," I said to Kate.

"I'm so sorry to hear that. I apologize for asking."

"It's okay."

"I'm kinda surprised I didn't see that online when I was checking to see if there was a sequel. Then I wouldn't have been so careless to ask. You know, there's not much out there about you."

"I'm a private person," I said.

"Oh, so I won't bother you. If we see each other again and you don't wanna talk, we won't talk."

At that moment, a specter from my past, something that hid itself for years, something I prayed would never invade my life again, unexpectedly returned. There it crept along the boards—right behind Kate. I hoped I was mistaken. I peered up at the sky. Maybe there was a flock of birds causing a shadow. Seagulls, airplane, something.

Nothing.

This wasn't a shadow. It was a Shadow.

"What are you looking at?" she asked.

The Shadow grew as it crawled toward Kate. Dreadful thoughts powered back from across the years.

"Mr. Farmer, you okay?"

"I thought I saw something." The something I saw was now spreading behind her like a massive bloodstain. My fear escalated as the thing inched its way up her body, covering her legs in darkness.

"Kate," I stammered.

"Is something wrong?"

I froze for a second.

"Something is wrong," Kate said with increasing apprehension.

The Shadow steadily evolved into human-like shape. An outline of hands slithered toward her throat.

I reached out with my right arm, swiping a glancing blow to her shoulder,

"Mr. Farmer—"

The Shadow vanished.

"Something there?" she asked, straining to see sideways.

I could've confirmed that yes there was indeed something there, something I once conjured up in a disastrously popular novel, something that could swallow her whole.

But it would make no sense to her since it barely made any sense to me.

"A—wasp. Big ugly one."

"Where'd it go?" she asked.

"It went away."

"Thanks, I guess." Kate might've been wondering about her favorite author.

"I've got to be somewhere," I said.

"Me too. But that was weird wasn't it?"

"What?"

"The wasp. I never saw it. I probably shouldn't say this but you looked like maybe you saw a ghost."

"No, I don't like bugs."

"Me neither. By the way, don't worry about me making a nuisance of myself. Some people get all goofy around a celebrity, you know?"

"I know."

"Your secret is safe with me. If we see each other again, I'll give you a little wave and keep on moving."

I started to inch past her when she reached out and touched my arm. "Why haven't you written another book?"

The ocean hummed against the shoreline in a jagged rhythm. I was no longer writing and that was the simple fact, though the reasons were as far from simple as the Land of Oz was from where I presently stood.

"Kate, if I had the answer, I'd tell you."

I watched her walk away, Shadowless. They were more interested in me, in showing they were back. It was starting all over again.

Kate continued in the direction of my condo. If Kate was going in that direction I'd be moving in another.

I headed down the stairs, stepped on the beach and heard a furious squawking. Numerous seagulls swooped as a man and boy were tossing bread, flipping pieces into the air, many of which were snagged on the fly like a first baseman grabbing an errant throw.

It was unusual to see anyone on the beach on a blustery autumn day. The man stood on tiptoes attempting to see beyond the whitecaps to where the boy was pointing. I heard the man say, "It's a dolphin. Too cold for sharks." They trudged toward the boardwalk while the birds battled on the sand for the final crumbs.

As we passed each other the man said to me, "There's a dolphin out there. Looks like it's in trouble."

I wasn't anxious to see an injured dolphin. I gazed toward the condo and saw Kate in the distance. It was difficult to see if she was facing me but then I saw an arm raise and swing back and forth. That gesture convinced me to take my time getting home.

I plodded toward the ocean, toward the dolphin, and saw what the man meant. There it was, perhaps fifty feet out and rolling on the waves, making slow progress toward the beach. It was colder by the waterline and I flipped up my sweatshirt hood, debating whether I wanted to see this unfortunate creature.

Authors are curious people by nature, even those who lay dormant like Rip Van Winkle. The object appeared again, in shallow water, heaving in and back with each swell.

I couldn't help myself. I approached the churning waves, close enough for the breakers to soak my Reeboks, and suddenly backed off.

This was not a dolphin.

Bobbing towards me with alarming certainty was the body of my next-door neighbor, still wearing the same leopard-print blouse I helped remove last night—her lifeless body floundering in the sea foam, coming to rest at my feet.

Chapter Two

I was mesmerized. Cecily's body lay sprawled out in the sand facedown, her head at a ninety-degree angle twisted towards the incessant Atlantic, reddish bruises evident on her neck. I'd lived one door away from her for years and we barely spoke a word other than neighborly greetings—hello, how are you, nice weather we're having.

Then, without warning, I'm in my bed with her last night, the last night of Cecily's life.

It didn't compute.

Death stole her beauty. It was sad to observe her scraggily hair, her shriveled skin and its discoloration. This woman was married; she was someone's daughter; she was loved. Now, she was dead.

I couldn't help but feel responsible.

"What the fuck?" a voice said. "That's Cecily!"

I snapped out of my reverie and saw Jason suddenly at my side, reaching into his jacket pocket.

"Jason," I said with no words to follow.

"Did you call 9-1-1?" he asked.

"No."

Jason tapped the numbers on his phone. "I'm reporting a dead body on the beach a few blocks south of Adventure Pier." He hesitated. "Yes, I'm sure she's dead. She's purple." Hesitation again. "Jason Bell. Get somebody here."

"What happened?" he asked me.

"I don't know," I managed to say.

"I can't believe she's gone." He made the sign of the cross and bowed his head. He shoved the phone back into his pocket and glared at me. "Why didn't you call?"

"I don't own a cellphone."

"Figures."

"What does that mean?"

"Fits your profile," he said. "You don't talk to your neighbors except Maggie. It's like you can't be bothered."

I let the comment pass and bent down toward Cecily when he grabbed my arm. "Don't touch her. Leave this for the cops."

"I just wanted a closer look at her neck," I said, pulling my arm from his grasp. "Those marks."

"Looks like a broken neck. Know anything about that?"

"Why would I?" I asked.

"Here you are. There she is."

This wasn't the time to discuss his hostility towards me. "You were on the coaster," I said. "You've got a good view from up there. Did you see anything?"

"Yeah, I saw you knock her down."

"What?"

"Kate. You practically trampled her," Jason said. "What were you running from?"

"I don't know what your problem is but save it for another time. It's disrespectful to Cecily."

"Another time, then."

Sirens wailed in the distance.

"Finally," Jason mumbled. "What the hell? There's police cars from both Wildwood and the Crest, and that's a state trooper's cruiser. This is liable to be a turf war."

Two uniformed officers jumped out of the first car and ran in our direction slowed by the soft sand.

The first cop panted as he arrived. "You gentlemen found the body?"

"He did," Jason said, pointing to me.

The second cop joined us and leaned toward the first one. "Ted, the M.E. is two minutes out." He glanced behind him. "Soon this place will be crawling. We'll have every local and their uncles here."

The first cop nodded and turned his attention to me. "I'm Officer Bronson. Your name, sir?"

"David Farmer. I live in the Crest Castle Condos."

"And you, sir?" he asked Jason.

"Jason Bell. I live on the same floor with him and—her."

Bronson held up his hand. "You called it in. Let me write this down." He pulled out a tiny top-spiraled notebook and jotted information. "Did either of you touch the body?"

We shook our heads.

Another contingent of police reached the scene and one crouched for a closer look—but avoided contact with Cecily.

Others were milling around. I listened to their comments.

"M.E. just pulled up. You know how she is."

"Yeah. Don't even breathe on the corpse," said another.

"State is here, too. They own the ocean."

"Who's next, the frigging Coast Guard?"

"Wouldn't be surprised. Maybe she fell off a boat."

"Mr. Farmer," Officer Bronson said. "Do you know the deceased?"

Jason turned and started to walk away.

"Where are you going?" Bronson asked.

"Get my tools. They're on the pier."

Bronson motioned to another cop. "Go with him. We'll need him back here."

"Forget it," Jason said. "I'll just wait until this dance party is over. If my tools turn up missing I'm blaming you guys."

"Mr. Farmer," Bronson said, returning his attention back to me. "Did you know her?"

"Her name is Cecily Slade. We're neighbors. Her husband is Dennis and they live in unit number 7F, seventh floor, next-door to me."

"And what were you doing when you found her?"

"Walking the boardwalk, like I do every day."

"You spotted her from back there?" he asked, peering over his shoulder. "It's a long way from the boardwalk to the water."

"I was going to head back along the beach."

"I see. What is your occupation?"

"I'm retired."

"What field?"

Jason snickered. "He's a big-time author."

I peeked at him. He smiled in return.

"Officer Bronson," I said. "Can I leave now?"

A bulky woman in a white lab coat and blue gloves joined us at that moment. A small group accompanied her, also in lab coats with "Coroner" printed in bold blue letters on the back. The woman stared at Cecily for a few seconds. "Anyone touch the body?" she asked Bronson.

"None of us and both of these gentlemen say they didn't."

"Good, now back everyone off my crime scene. This isn't a sandbox. Set up a perimeter and the only people I want here are my crew and the detectives when they arrive."

"Yes, ma'am."

Officer Bronson motioned to one of the cops. "Goddard, you know the drill. Move 'em out."

"This way guys," Bronson said to us as he plodded toward the boardwalk, stopping about halfway.

"One more thing, Mr. Farmer. When is the last time you saw the deceased?"

I tried not to flinch. "Yesterday."

"Where did you see her?"

"We passed in the hallway. Said hi to each other."

"Thank you."

I thought he was ready to dismiss me but then Jason asked, "Officer, did Dennis call in a missing persons?"

"That's not for me to say."

"I'll ask him later," Jason said.

The cop raised his eyebrows, and then looked my way. "You can leave now. We'll be in touch if we need more information."

"Bye-bye," Jason muttered.

I wanted to avoid walking back with Jason. Up until now I figured our relationship was working; we ignored each other's existence. The good old days.

"Gentlemen," said Bronson. "I'd prefer you not say anything to Mr. Slade. We'll send someone shortly."

I headed to my condo and turned to see if Jason was following. If he was I might be sprinting home. I'd forgotten he had to fetch his tools.

I was surprised he was still standing where I'd left him—next to Officer Bronson, talking to the cop with animated gestures and pointing in my direction.

Chapter Three

There are three David Farmers—and I am all of them.

First up was the blend-in-the-crowd original, then the flawed celebrity copy, and finally this present loner. I braced for the potential new model, improved or otherwise.

I can't help but feel disappointed in them, in me.

Cape May was an elegant Victorian town located at the southern tip of New Jersey. Horses pulling carriages clopped down streets lined by colorful Bed & Breakfasts and hauled passengers along Beach Avenue to relax in the cooling ocean breezes—a tourist's dream.

People believe there are ghosts in Cape May. Such information drifted in the salt air and could be picked up at restaurants, on the promenade, in local taverns. If you bought the rumors, ghosts haunted more than one B & B.

There was a time I demanded proof of the paranormal—see it, smell it, touch it. That was before I experienced Shadows.

I didn't stay current, didn't read newspapers, didn't hunch over a computer Googling every other thing, didn't listen to the radio unless I was in the mood for oldies. If my TV was on it was likely tuned to The Weather Channel.

Local news came from Tommy. I didn't think a real estate guy could be so plugged in. I was wrong. A life-long resident, he knew every property and what its true worth was. On the island this was a valuable commodity. He knew the flood zones, and more importantly, which properties should've been included or excluded. Tommy understood the depth of decay the ocean's salt air brought to every dwelling and which buildings were the most infected.

He was a local bigshot and if you wanted to buy or sell property, Tommy was your man.

He sold me my place. The building and the condo itself were new. I might've been the easiest sale he ever had. As soon as I saw the condo I loved it. As soon as I looked out the patio glass slider I loved it even more. The sparkling blue water urged me to buy the unit.

I liked Tommy, which was saying a lot since I was no longer the mix-and-mingle type. With the publication of *Shadows*, I'd gained an overabundance of dubious friends. They latched onto my success in the same manner I hung onto others who were movers and shakers in the literary realm.

My ex-wife, Marcy, disliked the pretentious world we stepped into. I think what she disliked the most was the ease with which I adjusted to that crowd and became one of them.

She likely wouldn't approve of my present limited roster of friends. There was Tommy—and then—Tommy.

I met Thomas Finch, successful realtor, chronic snoop, and class clown I was sure, in one of the boardwalk bars. The best thing about Tommy? He knew of the previous David Farmer, the once-famous author, and didn't care.

I parked my Cannondale Bad Boy 1 against an old-fashioned light pole, locked the chain and stepped inside.

"There you are," he said, as I plopped next to him on a barstool at The Atlantus Tavern. The Atlantus sat on a corner in the Washington Street shopping area and was named after the famous sunken ship off Cape May's coast. Tommy's ever-present Phillies baseball cap rested atop a head of slicked-back hair in the Johnny Cash style.

"I thought you might not show," he said.

"Why not?"

"I heard about your grisly discovery on the beach this morning," he said.

"Where'd you hear that?"

"Grapevine. Why don't you just search for coins like everyone else?"

"Lower your voice," I said. I nodded to the bartender. "I'll take a double Maker's on the rocks."

"You trying to forget what happened to your girlfriend?"

"You're an idiot," I said, shaking my head. "She's not—wasn't—my girlfriend."

"Maybe not, but I've heard you describe her. I thought you might be planning to elope."

"I don't know why I put up with you."

"Sorry, didn't know you were taking it so personally."

I raised my glass in his direction. "Cheers."

He brought the mug to his mouth but didn't take a swig. "Cecily Slade was beautiful. I got a gander at her myself when I showed you your condo. I remember your exact words, '10.5 on a one-to-ten scale.'"

"She was my neighbor, that's all. And married, too."

"The pretty ones always are."

"Anyway, she's gone and I don't know what happened. Drowning? Suicide?"

"Try murder," Tommy said.

"You serious?"

"I hear things."

"Did your source tell you they talked to me on the scene?" I asked.

"That's basic stuff. Who you are, where you live, your favorite color, that sort of thing. They're sending in the first string next."

"I don't like the sound of that."

"You're not a suspect—yet. They'll interview you later today, tomorrow maybe after the coroner's report. Your place, so it'll be nice and comfy for you."

"Oh, boy."

"Just be your normal sleepy-eyed self."

"I want to stay out of the news," I said.

"Hey, her death could be inspiration for you. Like for a book—I see it now, the big comeback."

This was sensitive ground, even for Tommy. He was my only friend in a world of nearly seven billion people. Didn't say much for me. But, friend or not, this was a subject we avoided. I stared at him, turning on my barstool.

"Relax, I'm kidding," he said.

"You know I don't like talking about that part of my life." I said, and drained half my bourbon.

"Gotcha. Wanna talk about Cecily Slade?"

I peeked at the other bar patrons and leaned toward Tommy. "Ssshhh, you're going to wake the dead."

He laughed so hard he sputtered and coughed. "I can't believe you said that. You and your wacky sense of humor."

"You talk too fucking loud."

"Okay. I'll whisper this. You thought she was hot. I get that, but hopefully you didn't sleep with her, or the police will wonder about you."

"I didn't sleep with her." We looked at each other. "Well—maybe I did."

"Not last night I hope."

"Yeah, last night."

"Lovely. Don't tell anyone else," he said.

"Who am I going to tell? Anyway, it doesn't mean anything. People sleep with each other all the time."

"You might be the last person to see her alive."

"If she was murdered, second to last," I said.

"The two detectives working the case are pretty smart, especially the woman. I hear she's like one of those little terriers. Once she grabs onto your pant leg, forget it."

"Meaning?"

"If they catch you lying you move to top of the list. Dum—da—DUM DUM."

I might've laughed if I had something to laugh about. "You think everything is funny."

"I'm thinking about you," Tommy said. "Was there anyone else around when you found the body?"

"Jason Bell, my neighbor down the hall was there."

"You've mentioned his name in the past. I got the feeling he's not your favorite person."

"I'm not his, either."

"What was he doing there?" Tommy asked.

"Hammering away on that big rollercoaster."

"Now, I remember him. You said he paints and repairs the pier rides."

"That's him. He showed up at my side when I found Cecily. He was in a bad mood."

"Why?"

"Because I was there."

"Doesn't anybody like you?" he asked.

"It works for me. I don't have to send out a bunch of Christmas cards."

Tommy smiled. "What did Jason say to you?"

"I think he accused me of killing her."

"Seriously?"

"Kinda."

"That's not good," Tommy said. "He could say something to the cops."

"I think he already did. He was bending the cop's ear when I was walking away."

"Could he have something to do with Cecily's death?"

"Um—maybe—it's possible. No, I don't think so. He's a jerk but he's not a murderer."

"Something to think about. Was anyone else around?" Tommy asked.

"No." I'd almost forgotten my encounter with Kate. "Wait, I did bump into a woman just before on the boardwalk and spent a minute or two talking to her."

"You talked to a stranger?"

"She recognized me. Turns out she's a fan."

"What did you talk about?"

"Nothing," I said.

"C'mon, Dave. This could be important."

"How do you figure?" I asked.

"A theory is popping into my head."

"Mainly, we talked about my book. She was scared by it."

"What did she look like?"

"Like everybody else," I said.

"My man, you're an author. Authors notice details."

I did notice the ice was overwhelming my drink. I took a sip before the whiskey got too diluted. "I'm not an author."

"Once an author always an author," he said. "It's in your blood."

"Beer is in your blood. Have another."

"Talked me into it. One for the road then," Tommy said, waving to the bartender.

"Last one for me, too. I gotta bike home."

"You and your bike," Tommy muttered.

"Don't you like my bike?"

"Get a car already. Comes in handy on rainy days. Now, tell me about this woman."

"I literally walked into her."

"Hmm. Do you think it was a coincidence?" Tommy asked.

"Sounds like you've been watching too many cop shows."

"Maybe she knows something," he said. "Could be a reason she was out there."

"She was buying candy."

"Or checking out the scene of the crime. Her and Jason—any connection there?"

"Oh yeah, way too much TV."

"What was her name?" he asked. "I assume you at least got that."

"Kate."

Tommy nodded and I thought he was going to say something. Instead, he grabbed hold of his mug and guzzled nearly half the glass before setting the remainder on the bar. He stared at it for a moment. "Ah, that's good stuff." He reached again and polished off the beer with a huge gulp.

"Thirsty, are you?"

"I've gotta get going," he said, and lifted himself from the stool. He signaled to the bartender, flashed me a wink and said, "Put this on my father's tab."

Tommy squeezed my shoulder and leaned close to my ear, and then disappeared out the door. It sounded like he said, "Be careful out there."

CHAPTER FOUR

Eleanor Roosevelt said, "With the new day comes new thoughts and new strengths." She wasn't describing me. I struck out on both possibilities—same old thoughts—same old weaknesses. Worse yet, I greeted each day with a persistent apathy. You might think a man approaching forty years of age, with a best-selling novel under his belt would have reasons to be happy.

Shadows: The Other Side was a product of another era, by another author. Couldn't have been me. I could barely scribble my name in this new strange land I inhabited. There was solid evidence, however. Inside my nightstand drawer, dust-laden and sleeping peacefully, was a hardcover first edition of the book bearing my name in outrageously large font. It was a clear declaration I was responsible for what followed.

Not that I didn't have help, someone to share the blame with. JJ, my agent, proved to be an unholy accomplice. It unfolded in plain sight, in clear view of my star-struck eyes though I saw nothing out of order— blinded by the glitter of fame. JJ steered the fortunes of *Shadows* through an obstacle-ridden process with suspicious ease.

The fix was in.

Though my fame wasn't merited, what other options were there but to embrace it? Reject that success? JJ would've killed me. I might've killed me.

At first I reveled in the success of *Shadows*. It more than went to my head: it went to my soul. Eventually, my enthusiasm waned and I got tired of the tours, the cities, the hotels, the restaurants, the hookers, the buying public and their innocuous questions. Most of all, I got tired of myself.

As did Marcy. She and our son, Josh, moved from our New York City condo to the other side of the world—Montana. Her parents had retired to the Big Sky State years earlier.

Marcy received a generous slice of money at our divorce. I didn't fight her. I kept my lawyer under wraps. Marcy could have whatever she wanted. She was willing to settle for less but I defied legal common sense and insisted on more. I set the whole divorce racket back by centuries.

I walked to the glass slider and pulled it open a couple of feet. Fresh air.

Sitting on the sofa I garnered the strength to call, grabbed the landline handset and punched Marcy's number. The knowledge I'd been the one to screw up our marriage was always left unsaid but it was there, sitting before us, as enormous as a supertanker.

Marcy answered on the second ring.

"Marcy, it's me. How are you and Josh?"

"We're fine David; how are you doing?"

"I'm okay. I wanted to say hi to Josh, if you don't mind."

"Of course I don't. He's outside. Give me a minute."

I touched the speaker-phone option and placed the handset on the cushion so I could pour a few fingers of bourbon while I was waiting.

"David, you still there?"

I reached and snatched the phone. "Still here." I said, turning off the speaker.

"Seriously, are you all right? I worry about you."

"I'm doing just fine."

"But you don't sound happy," she said.

"I'm smiling right now."

"That's good to hear."

It would be even better if it was true.

"Are you writing?" she asked.

"No."

"I think you should."

"I don't want to start things up again. You remember as well as I do how everything spun out of control."

"That part of your life is over."

I wish.

"I'm not ready yet," I said.

"Alright. I won't push it."

I debated whether to mention Cecily's death. While it was unlikely this particular news would create a ripple in Montana, Marcy could trip over this nasty piece of information online.

I took the plunge. "I found a dead body on the beach."

"Oh my God, David! What happened? Where—?"

"The waves washed it up and I found her while I was walking. It apparently was some type of accident."

"You said her. It was a woman?"

"Actually it's my next-door neighbor."

"How terrible for you." There was a second or two of quiet and then muted voices on her end of the connection. "Not now Josh, I'm talking to Daddy."

"Don't worry," I said. "The police will do their thing and figure it out. This happens every day somewhere."

"The police? That sounds like you're saying it might not be an accident."

Dang.

"I wouldn't jump to any conclusions," I said.

"She was your neighbor? So you knew her."

"Just to say hi."

"It's a shame it had to be you."

"What do you mean?" I asked, with my defense mechanism kicking into gear.

"I hope you don't get dragged into it."

"I didn't do anything."

"I'm talking about the press," she said. "If they get wind of this, they might try to dramatize it."

"That's why I'm telling you, in case it makes the news."

"I'm glad you did. Is there anything I can do?"

"No."

"What was her name? I want to follow this."

"Cecily Slade," I said.

"Okay. Always remember I'm on your side, and don't mention anything to you-know-who. Bye, David."

A second later, you-know-who was on the phone. "Daddy, what aren't you supposed to tell me?"

"Um—about the shark."

"You saw one?"

"I thought I did—but it was a dolphin."

"That's too bad. A shark would be cool."

"Sharks don't like the cold water in New Jersey so they stay near Florida."

That didn't fly. "They're in Cape Cod, too," Josh said. "And that's way up north. I learned about them on The Discovery Channel."

"Oh. Then I guess they might be around after all."

"Sharks would be fun to see," Josh said.

"There's other fun here. There's Ferris wheels and merry-go-rounds and—"

"Merry-go-rounds? That's for babies."

"I forgot you're grown up."

"I'm going to be nine years old. You haven't seen me in a long time."

Ouch.

"What have you been doing?" I asked.

"I've been riding a horse, a real horse!" he said. "Mommy walks with me but I was in the saddle by myself. His name is Skylark. He's a palomino."

I pictured Trigger, Roy Rogers's horse. "What's a palomino?"

"It means he's all gold except for his tail and his mane. They're white."

"Mane?"

"Oh, Daddy. You don't know much about horses. I could teach you."

"I have a lot to learn. Where did you ride Skylark?"

"On a real ranch. It belongs to Mr. Kessler, but Mommy said it's okay to call him Brian, like she does."

"That's nice. He's a friend of Mommy's?"

"Yes, and he lets us stay at his ranch sometimes."

Yeah, I bet.

"Good for you. I'm happy for you and Mommy."

"Will you come and visit?"

"I sure will. A couple of people are stopping by soon so I have to go but ..."

"What?"

"I have something to tell you first."

He was waiting for me to find the words I was searching for. "I love you," I said, choking back tears.

"Me too, Daddy. Goodbye."

Telling Josh I loved him was almost painful since I was aware my actions contradicted my hollow words. Even if Josh didn't see it, I did. I loved my son but wasn't there for him. Were there any words to explain that?

Marcy and Josh were riding the plains with a cowboy as I sulked two thousand miles away—all because I failed at being a husband. I had no right to feel envy or jealousy.

I was envious.

I was jealous.

I rolled onto my side and settled into the cushions. There, in the quiet of my living room, I lay there listening, listening to the ocean breathe.

CHAPTER FIVE

During the summer, Cape May and the Wildwoods overflowed with tourists. I often stood on the seventh-floor balcony of my condo and watched the vacationers basking in their beach chairs, wading in the shallow ocean water or battling waves farther out.

Looking north, I'd see the crowded boardwalk in the distance where games of chance, amusement piers and food stands served the tourists. I would almost hear the recorded message playing nonstop from the blue and yellow trams. "Watch the tramcar please."

A late October breeze swept across the balcony. I was dressed in a t-shirt and shorts, gazing at the Atlantic. I checked the beach and couldn't help but think about Cecily. It was just over twenty-four hours ago and her death was fresh in my mind.

I noticed uniformed police officers walking below me. One stared up in my direction.

"Mr. Farmer," he shouted.

I cringed at the mention of my name but the winds mangled his next words.

"What?" I yelled.

He cupped his hands to his mouth. "We'll be right up."

Crap.

Opening the door, I recognized Officer Bronson. He was bookended by two people in plainclothes.

"Hello, Mr. Farmer," Bronson said. "I hope we didn't catch you at a bad time."

I had the feeling it wouldn't matter even if it was.

"This is Detective Cho and that's Detective Faraday," he added.

Faraday was a tall man, a few inches over six feet, and looked as though he could play center in any pickup basketball game at the local outdoor courts. With his lean appearance I got the impression there were athletic muscles buried under his sports jacket. When we shook hands I was certain of his strength as his raw energy powered its way into my fingers.

Detective Cho was a petite woman, obviously younger than her partner, and the gray blazer fitted her perfectly, as did the white blouse it partially covered. The detective's well-coiffed black hair was cut short with every hair in place—almost every one. Her hand tamped down a couple of renegade strands, which spiked at the top of her head.

"Breezy out there," Cho said. "Mr. Farmer, you were the one who found Mrs. Slade's body, is that right?"

"Yes."

She glanced at Bronson and quietly said, "Thank you, Officer. We'll take it from here."

When he left, Detective Cho motioned toward my living room and asked, "May we come in and sit?"

"Certainly. Can I get anyone anything?" I said, backing out of their way.

"No, thanks," Cho answered without consulting Faraday. The two detectives sat in chairs near the sofa where I claimed the cushion farthest from them. "This is a very nice home you have, Mr. Farmer."

"Thank you."

She smiled at me but it didn't put me at ease. Terrier, that's what Tommy warned. I reminded myself of a Mark Twain quote, "If you tell the truth, you don't have to remember anything."

The truth would be difficult.

"We'll get right to it, Mr. Farmer," Cho said. "How well did you know the deceased?"

"Cecily and I barely knew each other."

"Cecily?"

"That's her name. I call her husband Dennis. No problem, right?"

"None."

Faraday busied himself jotting notes in a spiral-bound pad, which he balanced on his left leg.

Cho stared toward the slider. "Beautiful view," she said.

"Was it an accident, or suicide maybe?" I asked.

"Excuse me?" Cho said.

"Cecily—accident?"

Her eyes shifted from the glass door to me. "We're waiting for the final report from the lab. You were about to tell us how well you knew Mrs. Slade."

"I knew her only as a neighbor. I said hi to both of them. We'd see each other in the corridor or parking garage, wherever."

"Was that the extent of it?"

"Yes."

"Were either of them ever in your home for any reason?"

Well, there was that one time.

"No."

"Were you ever in their home?"

"No."

"Ever meet either of them for social reasons—perhaps a restaurant or a bar?"

"No. I don't get out much."

"Your encounters were cordial?'

"Yes."

"No neighborly disputes?"

"None." I said, trying to keep up with her.

"Yet, I understand you've lived here nearly three years."

"That's right."

"All that time and no disagreements. Very commendable."

I understood the reasoning for telling the truth, for following Twain's recommended course of action, but he likely never slept with a woman for the first time only to find her dead body the next morning.

"Detective," I said. "Your focus on personal relationships makes me wonder if she was murdered. I feel like you're interrogating me."

"As I said, we're still waiting for the Coroner's findings. In the meantime, I think it's prudent to gather as much information as we can."

"Of course," I said.

"What were you doing when you found the body?" she asked.

"I walk five miles every day. I mentioned it to the cop."

"You walked on the beach?"

"The boardwalk—but I saw something from the beach."

"Oh yes, Officer Bronson did make a note of that," she said.

"A guy and a boy were feeding seagulls and the guy mentioned he saw a dolphin in distress. They left and I went for a closer look. That's when I saw—the body. I don't know who those two were but maybe you should try and talk to them."

"We already have. Mr. Bell pointed them out to the officers on the scene."

"That was nice of him," I said.

"You and Mr. Bell are friends, I take it?"

"We're more like neighbors."

"Officer Bronson mentioned something about sensing possible friction between you and Mr. Bell. Friction—yes, that was the word he used."

"Jason doesn't like me."

"Why not?"

"You'd have to ask him."

"We might. Did you notice anything unusual about the body?" Cho asked.

"Unusual in what way?"

"Anything strike you about her clothing?"

"I have no idea what you mean," I said.

"Did you recognize what she was wearing?"

Uh-oh.

"I didn't notice."

"She wore a striking animal-print blouse. Had you seen her in it before?" she asked.

"I—I can't be sure."

"Mr. Farmer, I assume you need keen observation skills in your profession."

"Oh, you think I'm a writer."

"We're detectives," she said, bringing her hand to her mouth as if stifling a laugh. "That was my little joke. I read it in the report and then checked online. My goodness, you wrote a best-selling novel five years ago."

"I did."

"As a matter of fact, the local bookstore still has a few copies on the shelf," she said.

"Heavily discounted, I'm sure."

"I'll have to purchase one." Cho paused and stared at me with soft hazel eyes. "So, had you seen her in that blouse before?"

"I think I already said no."

"You were a bit uncertain but now you've cleared that up. Thank you."

I glanced at my watch and then noticed she was staring at me. "Are we keeping you from something, Mr. Farmer?"

"I've got a few more minutes."

"We'll move this along as quickly as we can. Did you ever witness any interaction between Mr. and Mrs. Slade that would give you cause for concern?"

"Concern? Do you mean for her safety?" I asked.

"Yes."

"I heard bickering from time to time, like every other married couple."

"Recently?"

"Maybe a week ago. I heard them from the hallway."

"What were they, as you said, bickering about?"

"I don't know."

"Were there accusations? Threats?"

"I couldn't hear the words."

She nodded. "Let's move on then. Have you ever seen or heard either of the Slades arguing with any of the neighbors?"

"I don't recall anything at the moment, but why are you asking me?"

"Your observations might help us," she said.

I felt a bead of sweat form on my forehead and dabbed it with my finger. I glanced to my left and looked out beyond the balcony rail. Clouds rumbled across the darkening skies.

"I assume you want to help us as much as you can," she added.

"Sure."

"What can you tell us about Mr. Slade?"

"Nothing, really." I thought briefly about my next sentence and decided to go with it. "Dennis has a surly nature."

"Surly?"

"Yeah—disagreeable, unfriendly."

Faraday put down his pen and looked at me. "We know the definition of the word. Do you have examples?"

The guy speaks!

"Well, he had a problem with the ex-major leaguer, Jackson," I said.

Cho leaned forward. "Mr. Rodney Jackson from down the hall in—I think 7C—is that correct?" she asked.

"Yes. Everybody calls him Hot Rod from his baseball days. He was with the Chicago White Sox and—well—he's kind of a party guy. Lots of people coming and going from his place. Loud music."

"How does this relate to Mr. Slade?" Cho asked.

"Dennis complained to him about the hip-hop music, and especially the women."

"Oh?"

"Dennis thought they were prostitutes."

"You overheard this discussion?" she asked.

"I heard it from a reliable source."

Maggie's as reliable as they come.

"Who told you?"

"I'd rather not identify the person."

"I guess we'll have to find out on our own as we speak to your neighbors, although it would be better if you told us in the spirit of cooperation."

"Margaret Callahan. She's in 7D."

I could feel the Maker's staring at me from the kitchen countertop. "I think I'm overtired with all this happening. Are we almost done?"

Cho smiled. "How was the relationship between the Slades and Mr. Bell?"

"Fine," I said.

"They all got along?"

"I guess so."

"How about Mr. Zdenko?" she asked.

"What about him?"

"How did he interact with Mr. and Mrs. Slade?"

"I'm feeling a bit uncomfortable with these questions. They're not very objective."

"We're almost done," she said. "What about Mr. Zdenko?"

"You might already know there's two Zdenkos. Twins. Vedra is the larger one and lives here fulltime and Nikolai is a regular visitor. They're from Albania. As for getting along with everyone, he does. Big as he is, that's a good thing."

I smiled at my little joke but Cho didn't display any reaction while Faraday concentrated on his note-taking. I reminded myself what Tommy said. The detectives were smart, especially the woman. I was talking too much.

"We done?" I asked.

"Almost," Cho said. "How well do you know Mrs. Callahan?"

"She's a widow, a very nice lady and keeps to herself."

Well, she is a nice lady.

"And Miss Montrose, the doctor? What can you tell us?"

"I barely know her. That's all. I've got things to do." I stood and moved one step toward the front door before noticing they were still seated.

Faraday turned his head toward me. "Sit down, please."

Cho looked his way and whispered, "Artie." She rose from her chair and slowly walked to the door. Faraday closed his notebook and slid it into the side pocket of his jacket. He trailed us by a couple of steps.

Walking alongside me, Cho asked, "Where were you last night?"

"Here, watching TV."

"Watch anything good?"

"CNN. Catching up on the news."

"Was anyone with you?"

"I was alone."

"Thank you so much for your patience and cooperation, Mr. Farmer," Cho said, as I opened the door. "You've been most helpful."

That's what I was afraid of.

CHAPTER SIX

When I was seven years old in central New Jersey my parents began taking me "down the shore." It was never phrased any other way. Wildwood was our most popular summer overnight destination. The advantage Wildwood offered was the magnificent boardwalk and the amazing pier rides carrying me halfway to the sky. That feeling never left.

With the heavy tourist activity Wildwood was busier, noisier, more crowded than its neighboring communities. When the time came, after my stay at Rosewood, I needed to find a home and bought a condo in the largest building in Wildwood Crest, the Crest Condo Castle. Locals called it *3Cs*.

The Crest featured a more sedate environment and my intent was basic—to blend in with the scenery, to live in virtual anonymity.

I didn't do so well.

After my meeting with the detectives, I needed to clear my head and trekked toward the boardwalk. The wind gusted as the afternoon sky turned the color of charcoal. Pulling up my jacket collar against the autumn chill I walked up the ramp to the wooden surface.

I didn't want to see either of them again that day. Maybe I should've stayed home.

I glanced at the Great White coaster to my right looming like a fossilized brontosaurus on the pier. And, there was Jason at work today as he was yesterday. He was belted to the skeletal body welding its struts.

And there was Kate, dead ahead.

Go home, Dave.

Too late. Kate smiled at me and offered a subtle wave. "Hello there."

"Hi." I said, already working on excuses to about-face and head home.

"You're out walking again," Kate said. "You must log a lot of miles."

"Yeah, but I'm still in the same place."

There was a brief silence and I prepared to fill it with my good-bye speech.

"I have something to tell you, Mr. Farmer."

"What?"

"I'm being followed," she said.

"By whom?"

"I don't know. It might not be a person."

I saw Jason making his way down the side of the coaster.

"I don't understand," I said.

"I think it's them, like from your book."

"Them?"

"When I turn to look—well—there's no one there."

"You sure—"

"Shh. Here comes Jason," she said.

He stepped over an unraveled spool of wire and strode toward us. I sensed Jason had something on his mind.

I might have flinched at his up-close-and-personal look. He was cloaked in a thick orange welding vest. His green safety goggles and protective earmuffs were stuffed under his fluorescent yellow helmet, which he dropped on a bench. He was still clutching his welding torch like Wyatt Earp.

"Hi Kay," he said.

Kate barely managed a reply. "Hi Jason."

He glanced at me. "Farmer."

We stood quietly. They exchanged knowing glances. What they knew I couldn't be sure. I felt like an outsider in this trio, as though I joined a conversation in midstream. All that was missing was the conversation.

In one second I would have been out of there. My feet were antsy and my tongue was a beat slow as Kate announced, "I have to be going. Bye guys."

I detected a frown on Jason's face, although this could easily be his default expression. We both missed Kate's presence I was sure.

"Fixing the coaster?" I said.

"I see you and Kay are friends."

"Only from seeing her on the boardwalk."

"Getting to be a habit. Yesterday. Today."

I noticed a burn mark on his left arm. "That looks like it hurts," I said, pointing to the scar.

"Part of the job."

"I gotta be going."

"How do you know her?" he asked.

"I don't know her. And how is that your business?"

"I'm concerned about her."

I shrugged.

He added, "After Cecily's death it's not safe for a woman out here."

"You think her death was suspicious?"

"Maybe murdered on the pier and thrown into the ocean."

"Or an accident," I said.

"Yeah, and maybe you believe in Santa Claus."

"Well, I did get a nice bike last year."

"Dennis was right. You are a character," he said.

"You and Dennis chat about me often?"

Jason grinned. "He thinks you may know something."

"About what?"

"About what happened to his wife. He says that you and Cecily were friends."

"I don't know where you're going with this but I don't like the implication," I said.

"I'm not implying anything. I'm telling you what Dennis thinks."

"Look, the next time you and Dennis want to talk about me—don't. I don't know how Cecily died. Got that?"

"Don't get excited."

"I'm going," I said.

"Okay, but leave Kay alone."

"What the fuck did you say?"

"Someone's been following her, scaring her."

"It sure as hell ain't me."

"She's my friend, Farmer. I won't let anything happen to Kay—like what happened to Cecily."

I was tempted to take a swing at him. My last punch years ago connected with one of the orderlies at Rosewood and that did me no good since he walloped me with the metal end of his broom. That episode earned me a further extension, not to mention a cracked rib that dogged me for months.

But reflexes being what they are, I took one step closer to him. He did the same and raised his welder like a ray gun from a science fiction movie.

"Won't do you much good without a power source," I said.

"Guess you're right about that," he said with a fleeting smile.

Our feel-good moment lasted all of two seconds as he added, "I'll be watching you, Farmer."

I turned and headed back toward the condo. I passed by the Convention Center to my left and saw the huge red and blue poster advertising a recent oldies concert.

At first I was so engrossed in the poster I didn't notice her. She was standing in front of the building's wall of glass.

Kate smiled at me, but I kept on walking.

Tommy phoned that evening and asked to meet for dinner at Nino's, an Italian restaurant on the boardwalk. I wheeled past several closed businesses and chained my bicycle to a bench outside the restaurant.

Inside, Tommy was already seated and his hand beckoned me.

"You're late," he advised, as I sat across from him in a red-cushioned booth.

"Hello to you, too."

"Find any more dead bodies?"

"That's not funny," I said.

"No, I suppose not."

"Why did you invite me?"

"Where did that come from?" Tommy said, feigning insult. "Why would you think I have an ulterior motive? Maybe I'm just hungry."

He motioned to the waitress as she passed nearby. "Sweetheart, fix us up with a bottle of house Cabernet." Tommy removed his cap and dropped it on the seat next to him. "You're mixed up in some shit."

"No kidding." I put my hands in front of me like I caught a fish this big. "Lots of crazy stuff has been happening."

"Anything I haven't heard about?"

"You know about Cecily and me of course. Then Jason pointed me out to the police as a prime suspect. And earlier today those two detectives treated me like I'm public enemy number one. Then I got Kate telling me she's being followed. And, oh yeah, my ex-wife is dating Roy Rogers."

"I warned you about the detectives. How did you think the interview went?"

"Pretty well," I said. "Cho tried to rile me but I don't rattle. I aced it."

Tommy shook his head. "You better be right."

"You heard something?" I asked.

"Not really. But my guy has big ears. The detectives plan on seeing you again."

"Shit. I was mostly truthful."

"Next time they'll turn up the heat."

"I'm not telling them I slept with Cecily. That's like admitting I'm guilty."

"Let's talk about this when the time comes. I'll be your coach."

"Thanks—I think."

Tommy smiled. "You said that woman, Kate, is being followed?"

"She didn't finish telling me everything because Jason showed up acting like he was the cavalry coming to her rescue."

"Those two have something going," Tommy said.

The waitress arrived holding a bottle of red. This wasn't the kind of restaurant where you did the winetasting by swishing a sip around your tongue before nodding approval. Protocol was simple here. She poured it; we drank it.

"What did you mean about your ex dating Roy Rogers?" he asked.

"Why are you interested?"

"I'm nosy."

"Marcy and my son are staying at some guy's ranch in Montana."

"Ah. Riding off into the sunset?"

"You're not making me feel better," I said.

"I'm working on it. That's why you're here tonight in this culinary haven. I'm going to give you something to make you happy, so happy you'll be forever grateful."

"Tommy, what the hell are you talking about?" I asked.

I thought I saw movement out of the corner of my eye and glanced in that direction only to discover I was right. Through a partially-curtained window I saw her.

"Tommy. That's Kate!" I half-shouted.

"Who, where?"

When I looked again she was gone. "Son of a bitch, Kate's stalking me!"

With that outburst we were now the center of attention. Diners stopped in mid-bite, pasta dangling from utensils.

"Sorry, my bad." I muttered to the widely scattered group.

"Forget her," Tommy said, pushing my wine glass closer to me. "Take a slug of this. You'll feel better."

"I need something more potent."

"I have a surprise for you," Tommy said.

The waitress returned to our booth. "Have you gentlemen decided?"

"Do you have Maker's Mark?" I asked.

The waitress looked puzzled. "Is that the name of a wine?"

"Bourbon," I said. "Whiskey."

"Give us another minute," Tommy said to her. Then he looked at me. "Bourbon. They have wine, red or white."

As she walked away, he rummaged through the side pocket of his sports jacket, first one side then the other. He came up empty and then delved into an inside chest pocket. His hand emerged holding a tiny box covered in silver wrapping paper. He raised it up with a theatrical flourish, like a magician, and spiraled it down to the table. All that was missing was the abracadabra.

"Happy birthday!" he said.

"What is that?"

"Open it," he said. "It won't bite—much."

I picked it up like I was saddled with a grenade. I was careful not to shake it. Fumbling with the shiny wrap, I pulled the lid off a black jeweler's box and there inside was a single piece of folded white copy paper. "Huh?" I said.

I unfolded it a few times to get the darn thing open. I was staring at ten numbers, side-by-side without any spacing.

"What's this?"

"A surprise birthday present, me to you. I shopped and I shopped but what do you get the guy who has nothing?"

"So you got me—what?"

"Keira's phone number," he answered with an air of self-assurance.

"Who is Keira?"

"Keira Donaldson. She works at the local newspaper. And I'll tell you this as fact—you've never received a better birthday gift and you never will."

"Uh, my birthday is months away."

"That's what makes this such a surprise."

CHAPTER SEVEN

A piece of paper with a phone number.

Keira.

It was typical of Tommy—everything dramatic—a most unlikely best friend for a man living under the radar. I blended in with the crowd, even if no crowds were evident. David Farmer—average height, average build, middle-aged, didn't remind anyone of Tom Cruise, nor the Elephant Man. If I had a distinguishable feature, my unruly mop-top hair might qualify. Kate wasn't far off the mark when she referred to George Harrison. I looked like a Beatles reject.

I hadn't dated a woman or made love in many years, with that one startling exception. And like the bicycles you never forget how to ride, I didn't forget when Cecily knocked on my door.

Years ago on book tours, my publicist prepared frenzied timetables that only a man braced by amphetamines could handle. I drenched myself in booze and drugs—too much money, too much ego, so little judgment.

I was weak. Women came on to me and I allowed it, encouraged it. I was swallowed by a sense of entitlement as if all this was a reward and the natural byproduct of fame.

I had it all—everything—except humility. Drugs were now a lowlight of my past while whiskey helped me stumble back from more than one gloomy trip down memory lane.

I wasn't sure I fooled the detectives, especially Cho, who appeared to analyze my every response with her eyes. Could she have already suspected I'd been with Cecily? There was always the possibility someone on my floor spied and tattled. If I were to guess I would bet on Maggie Callahan, whose life seemed lonelier than mine.

I was afraid Cho suspected I wasn't telling the truth. Now that the lie regarding Cecily was out there I would need to support it. I was married to that statement. It was important for me to find out if Cho knew.

"Maggie, it's Dave," I said, wrapping my knuckles against her door.

She opened it fully. "It's so nice to see you, Mr. Farmer."

"Maggie, how many times have I asked you to call me Dave?"

"A hundred and twelve?"

We laughed. "May I come in?" I asked.

"Certainly, uh, Dave, come in and pardon my attire but I wasn't expecting company."

Perhaps she wasn't anticipating anyone, but Ms. Margaret Callahan, like a Girl Scout, was prepared for any contingency. She wore a cream-colored pantsuit and was weighed down with ten pounds of jewelry. Her necklace, a rainbow mix of gemstones, could slow a racehorse.

"I have a quick question for you," I said.

"The quick question can wait until we're seated like civilized people," she said with a smile.

I entered her home and saw vases Chinese emperors might envy. "That vase over there," I said, pointing to a blue-green floral-patterned vase, perched on an ornate pedestal. "Is that new?"

"Oh dear, no. It's an antique. I bought it at an auction house in New York City."

I sat on her sofa and assumed she'd be sitting next to me. However, she remained standing and said, "I feel awkward calling you by your first name."

"I call you Maggie and you don't get all frazzled. Because we're friends, right?"

"Of course," she said.

"Then let's not get bogged down in formality. From now on, it's Dave to you. David if you want to mix it up a bit."

She nodded.

"Okay, that's settled," I said, patting the sofa cushion. "Have a seat and let's be civilized."

"You have a funny sense of humor," she said.

"I look at it this way—if you're going to have a sense of humor, funny is the best one."

She laughed. "You are a card! May I get you a cup of tea? I have a pot of Darjeeling all ready."

"No thanks."

She sat down and turned to face me. "I'm glad you're here. I don't get much company."

"I don't know why."

"I'm the oldest on the floor so maybe that's it."

I shook my head. "Age has nothing to do with it. Satchel Paige said how old would you be if you didn't know how old you were."

"I don't know who Mr. Paige is, but I like that. I'd be thirty-eight."

Time to get down to business.

"Maggie, there were a couple of people in the hallway earlier and I was wondering if they were with the same Bible-thumpers that came to my door. Did they bother you?"

"Bible-thumpers? No soliciting is allowed in our building."

"They must've sneaked in the back door."

"No. They didn't come here."

Let's try this again.

"You know, I was sure I saw two people at your door," I said.

"Maybe you saw the police."

"Police?"

"Detectives actually. They were asking about poor dear Cecily." She then lowered her voice as though the place was bugged. "They wanted to know if I had seen her recently."

"And had you?"

"All the time, same as you."

"Huh?"

"She's our neighbor. We often see her." Maggie said.

I smiled. "Of course."

"Didn't the detectives stop by your place?" she asked.

"I'm out walking a lot."

"Oh. The woman detective was very polite, such a refined lady. I think she's of Asian descent and so pretty."

"When they asked you about Cecily did they by any chance ask if either of the Slades visit you?"

"Heavens no. Why would they ask that?" Maggie said.

I was handling this conversation as poorly as the one with Cho and Faraday. "I saw a TV show and that's the kind of questions detectives asked."

"Well, now that you mention it, they did want to know if I saw Cecily visit anyone else on the floor recently."

Crap.

"And had you?"

I held my breath.

"Why, yes I did," she said with a slight smile.

I glanced down at the carpet and then checked to see if my laces were still tight; anything to avoid meeting her eyes.

"Less than a week ago," she said. "I was bringing my trash to the chute, and saw Cecily going into Mr. Zdenko's apartment. He's a nice man don't you think?"

"I'm sure he is." I felt a wave of relief. "I should be going back now. It's getting late."

"Before you go, dear, I'd like to tell you a little story if you don't mind. Won't take but a minute."

I'd already completed my task. Much like *007*, I had infiltrated, assessed the situation and secured the information I needed. Mission accomplished.

"Sure," I said.

"My husband, Harold, you may have heard me speak of him. He died several years ago—God rest his soul. We owned a highly successful restaurant in Cape May, did you know that?"

"I think you said."

"Our restaurant was first-class and very popular even if I do say so myself. It was a high-end operation with the finest china and cutlery. It's gone now, sad to say. There's a condo building in its place. I can't bear to even look at it—such memories."

She paused as if trying to remember where she left off. "My Harold was a good man, a smart man. But he had his other side. When you crossed him you were on his shit list, pardon my French. Liquor licenses back then were difficult to obtain. If you didn't serve alcohol you were at a disadvantage. Well, the cops and the politicians knew that. So what did they do? They jacked up the cost, not just for the license but the kickbacks to get on the list. You had to be on the list so the city bosses could vote you a license. And, don't you know, you would get turned down if you didn't pay bribes? You had to pay off this one and his brother.

You paid the cop on the beat. He'd hand it off to someone else, taking a cut himself. That was the way it worked."

"Probably similar to today," I said.

"At first, my Harold resisted and then came the city inspectors. Health violations, threats of closing—intimidation if you know what I mean. So we had to pay. We could afford it mind you—don't get me wrong. We were doing quite well. But, Harold learned something from that experience. He disliked the police for the rest of his life. They were part of the corrupt machinery. Do you see where I'm going with this?"

Not a clue.

I shook my head.

"All right then," she said. "Let me get to the bottom line as they say. Harold didn't hold the police in high regard and that rubbed off on me. To this day I think twice before telling them anything. Now, in the future, if you want to know if I told the detectives something, like the time I saw Mrs. Slade stay with you for an hour the night before her body was found, just ask me."

CHAPTER EIGHT

A day passed without incident—no Kate sightings, no Jason, no detectives. Just me and my Maker's. I was thankful for the respite.

Life on the seventh floor of my condo was quiet. Maggie passed me in the hallway and flashed me a wink, which caused a touch of discomfort. We shared a secret.

Dennis Slade hadn't returned after the funeral, which I didn't attend. Maggie did pay her respects at the funeral home and casually mentioned that Cho and Faraday sat in the back row. I wasn't looking forward to seeing them again and I certainly did not want to see Dennis.

I spotted Zdenko and Nikolai, often outside in the parking garage enjoying a smoke. Vedra Zdenko offered wide smiles and enthusiastic waves while his brother stood zombie-like. I stayed clear since their black cigarettes soiled the air worse than Chernobyl.

Hot Rod Jackson hosted another rouser of a party amped with rap music and dancing, although it sounded more like mongooses battling a nest of vipers. He apparently wasn't mourning the loss of our neighbor.

Dr. Gail Montrose, two doors down the hall, was divorced and put in long hours at the hospital. She often slept there—the grueling work schedule keeping her away from home. When we finally bumped into each other in the elevator she asked me if anything was new. When I mentioned Cecily had died, she didn't flinch and indicated she'd heard the news.

Then something out of leftfield happened. She asked me if I wanted to have dinner and drinks with her sometime soon at her favorite watering hole, as she called it. I didn't know if I was more surprised she asked me for a date of sorts, or that she had a favorite watering hole. I accepted without thinking, and later felt uneasy with my response. I was more than comfortable in a tavern setting but less so sharing dinner with a woman.

I was going to have to get over that.

Tommy and his crazy behavior. The average person might just tell someone a friend's phone number. Not my buddy. Everything was over-the-top theatre.

Two nights later, we were rummaging like rats in the real estate building's basement. Yesterday, Tommy advised me he needed to find some decades-old files buried downstairs.

He only wanted someone to hold his hand while he was working, I was sure.

"What am I doing down here?" I asked.

"Well, so far you're just standing there daydreaming."

"The lighting is piss-poor."

"It's a basement," Tommy said.

"I should be home with my new bottle of Maker's."

"We're looking for files, maybe a huge Pendaflex folder."

"I never heard of Pendaflex," I said.

"Seriously?"

"Seriously."

"It's probably green and overstuffed. There should be a label indicating the Emlen Physick Estate."

"The what?"

"Dude, you live this close to Cape May and you never heard of it?"

"Oh, is it that giant mansion on Washington Street?"

"Finally, it dawns on you," Tommy said. "Hey, did you call Keira yet?"

"Ten to one you already know I didn't. My guess is you checked with her."

"What the hell are you waiting for?"

"Tomorrow," I said.

"Call her."

"Yes, Dad."

"Here's the sucker," Tommy said, holding a thick file.

He blew dust off the folder and I waved my hand in front of my face while backing off. "What the fuck?" I said.

"Relax. It's been on the shelf a while."

"You don't have any whiskey here by any chance, do you?"

"What was that sound?" Tommy asked.

"What?"

He held a finger to his lips and shook his head. "We shouldn't be down here," he muttered.

I heard a footfall on the stairs.

Another. Then another.

Closer.

Tommy's eyes bugged out. He crouched while grabbing my shoulder taking me with him. We were behind a desk encrusted with even more dust. Tommy then peeked over the desk and rose slowly.

"Don't say a word," he whispered.

I heard him tiptoeing away.

There was silence lasting a few seconds.

"This is silly," I mumbled.

Then came the scream. It was Tommy and he shouted, "Make a run for it!"

Without thinking I jumped up and there was Tommy laughing uncontrollably, standing alongside an attractive blond woman who was smiling. If I read her right, she felt sorry for me and the practical joke my friend was having at my expense.

"You are a dickhead," I said to Tommy, who was now calming down.

"Oh, what's da matter, wittle baby got all a-scared?"

The woman shook her head. "Don't let Tommy get to you," she said in the most pleasant voice I'd heard in years. "He can't help it. He's just an idiot."

Tommy held up his hands in mock surrender. "You'll both thank me years from now when you tell people how you first met. Dave, I'd like you to meet Keira."

Tommy was a goofball, pure and simple. Yet, I was glad he was my friend.

After talking to Keira and getting the okay to call her, I biked along a near-deserted Ocean Drive bordering Cape May Harbor, heading east toward home.

The sky darkened and the rising moon climbed over the distant buildings along the Atlantic. As I pedaled over the rickety bridge, I glimpsed a couple of fishing boats moored in the Intracoastal Waterway. Cape May disappeared behind me and I glided by the salt marshes to my right, where herons and egrets foraged for food. Across the street was Two Mile Landing, its restaurants and marina empty and cloaked in darkness.

I rarely biked at night although I did sport numerous bright orange reflectors on my Cannondale.

A jeep approached slowly in the opposite direction and I was surprised that the driver, a young man, had not zipped up the jeep's soft-top. He must be freezing I thought, despite being protected against the chilly night with a denim jacket. Instinctively, I glanced his way and saw a menacing Shadow hovering behind me as another vehicle was directly on my tail. I panicked.

There was no time to react. The car was a split-second from colliding into me. I veered sharply as it rumbled passed, but I was propelled into the air. My bike and I had no options as to where we would touchdown. Fortunately, the marshes were saturated with a high-tide water level that cushioned our fall. While in the air I twisted my body and released my grip on the bicycle. We landed side-by-side.

It could have been much worse. The marshes provided a spongy cushion, and while crashing caused a pain in my shoulder, I knew it wasn't serious. I worried as much about my bicycle. It was nearly submerged in the flora with only the handlebars visible in the reeds.

I peered down the street searching for the offending vehicle but it had sped away, indifferent to my status. I grabbed my bike, yanked it from the swampland, carried it to the road and determined it was still functional.

A vehicle pulled up and I noticed it was the young man in the jeep. He had u-turned and double backed.

"You okay?" he asked, hopping down from his seat.

"I think so," I responded while taking inventory. I flexed my right knee and swung my shoulder and said, "I'm good."

"That car, it hit you?"

I hesitated. "Yeah."

"And it just kept going. Maybe a drunk driver."

"Did you see the driver?" I asked.

"I didn't notice. I wasn't paying attention until I heard you yell."

"Yell? I don't think so. I'm sure I didn't."

"You had other things on your mind," he said. "After you screamed, whatever, I turned around and by that time the car was long gone."

"Thanks anyway," I said.

"One more thing, mister. It was strange."

"What was?"

"I could you see you clearly when you looked at me and then—well, when it happened I turned and it was like a fog surrounded you. I swear you were inside it." He gazed around the wetlands and added, "Though it seems to have lifted mighty fast."

"Fog, huh?" I said, pulling a chunk of undergrowth from the bike chain.

"I should call 9-1-1." he said, reaching into his pocket.

"Don't bother. We're fine."

"Okay, but you must be shook-up. That was a scary accident."

Thinking back to a few minutes ago I recalled I was driving carefully on the shoulder of the road providing ample room for passing vehicles. And, while the incident occurred in a virtual heartbeat, I could swear I saw a Shadow *before* I saw the car.

"I'm fine but can you give us a ride to that big condo over there?"

"Us? Oh, you mean your bike. There's room in the back." He stared at the huge structure ruling the eastern sky. "The 3C building? You live in that place? Sweet."

He delicately placed my Cannondale behind the seats as I clambered into the passenger side. I stared at the marshes and could see the outline of my splashdown.

Accidents happen I thought, and sometimes they don't.

CHAPTER NINE

I never liked Halloween, especially when I was a kid. The holiday was intended to be spooky. I didn't like spooky.

The free candy wasn't motivational enough nor was the handful of coins collected at the end of an evening. I stopped trick-or-treating. My mother didn't understand and I was too embarrassed to explain myself. The scary decorations in the neighborhood were bad enough. Watching all those people in costumes was terrifying. Who were they?

What if the masks weren't really masks?

Many years later, my experience with Shadows reinforced the thought things really do go bump in the night.

The Condo Association was holding its annual Halloween party this evening. I intended to pass it up for a relaxing night at home with my Maker's and TV. Costumes no longer frightened me but I wasn't eager to brush elbows with people in any type of party setting.

My shoulder was still barking at me but I gulped a few aspirin and the pain subsided. Maybe I would use the shoulder as my reason for staying home. Mrs. Plimpton, our community social director, liked to hear excuses for failures to attend her events. Somewhere along the line our paths would cross and I'd make something up. She may have intimidated others but I made a game of it. Last year I told her I was a Seventh-day Adventist.

Or, I could attend—with Keira. I'd be less awkward with her at my side and this year I was a little curious what my neighbors were speculating about Cecily's death and my finding her body.

I was asking a lot of myself—a date and a party in one night. However, I wanted to see Keira. The worst she could do was decline. Then, it would be CNN and Mayberry reruns.

I normally avoided making phone calls, except for pizza deliveries. I tapped in her number on the landline.

"Hello," the lovely voice said.

"Keira?"

"Yes. Dave?"

"It's me," I said.

"I'm glad you called. Tommy said today was your birthday. Is it?"

"No, it's a couple of months away."

"Figures. Tommy," she said.

"Yeah, Tommy."

"About last night," Keira said. "I didn't know what Tommy was up to, the way he tricked you into meeting me."

"No problem. I'm getting used to his unbridled nonsense."

She laughed. "He's an acquired taste."

"What are you doing tonight?" I asked.

"It's Halloween."

"That's why I'm asking," I said. "There's a Halloween party at my condo and I thought you might want to go with me."

"Us girls normally need advance notice. Tommy warned me. He said your social skills might be a bit rusty."

"I'm trying to shake off that rust."

"A Halloween party could be fun. I don't know—I've got a lot of candy already set up for trick-or-treaters."

"Bring the candy along. We'll eat it."

"Is this part of the shaking-off process?"

"I have no idea what it is," I said.

She giggled. "Are you a celebrity by any chance?"

"Not anymore."

"Pardon me for even bringing it up but Tommy was kind of cryptic when I asked him what you do. He got my curiosity going. He hinted you were famous at one time but didn't tell me your last name."

"Farmer."

"Farmer? David Farmer. I know that name," she said. "Give me a second."

"I wrote a book."

"Yes, now I got it. You wrote a best-selling horror novel."

"I don't really like talking about it," I said.

"Oh. Whatever your reasons, I respect them."

"So, can you make the party tonight?" I asked. "I could send a cab to pick you up."

"Cab? I saw your bike yesterday at the real estate office but—what—you don't own a car?"

"Not anymore."

"No problem. Where and when should I meet you?"

"The party is here at the Crest Castle at six, in the ballroom. You can't miss it. Follow the trail of balloons and pumpkins. You might want to wear a costume. There's a tough woman who heads our social committee and she insists everybody wear one."

"What are you wearing?"

"See if you recognize me when you get here," I said. "Use the parking area under the building and take the stairs to the first floor. Just tell the security guy, Farmer—passcode 9917. That will cheer him up and he'll let you in."

"Will do. I'll throw something together and meet you."

I had a date and I was euphoric—for a fleeting moment. My brain reminded me I could screw this up in a big hurry. Killjoy.

At six o'clock I ducked under the orange and black balloons and entered the ballroom. I didn't readily spot Keira in the crowd. I did notice a vampire, a matching pair of hillbillies, an overweight Spider-Man, a frizzy-haired clown, a couple of hippies, and a wide assortment of crazies. Mrs. Plimpton approached me. She was something out of *Gone with the Wind* in antebellum attire, clutching a feathered Stick Mask, which she held over her face.

"Oh finally, the mysterious man from the seventh floor," she said in a high-pitched voice. "You live next to Cecily, and you found her body—most unfortunate."

"Yes, very."

I shied away from the "mysterious man" reference. I wondered how many others shared that opinion.

"I'm so glad you could make it," she said. "Last year you didn't come for religious reasons as I recall."

"That was a phase I was going through. I'm good now."

"Um, alright. But where is your costume?" she said with a hint of concern.

"This is it. Don't tell me you don't like it."

"That's just a sweatshirt and jeans."

"Look what my shirt says—'Lost and Found in Cape May.'"

"So?"

"Mrs. Plimpton, don't you get it? I'm a tourist."

She lowered her mask, tilted her head back and laughed. "You're fooling with me. Well, I'll let it slide this time, if only because some of us haven't had a chance to get to know you. Enjoy yourself, Mr. Farmer." Mrs. Plimpton then shuffled away.

"You handled that smoothly," the clown next to me said. I recognized Keira's voice. "I bet you get your way a lot, don't you?"

"Hi, Keira," I said, hugging her as though we'd been separated for years.

"Wow, you must love clowns."

"Nice outfit," I said.

"Oh, this old thing? Left over from a college bash many years ago. I added a fresh coat of paint, and voilà!"

Her head craned, taking in the room—costumes dancing now, *Monster Mash* playing over the PA system, punch being guzzled. "You know all these people?" she asked.

"I don't know three-quarters of them even out of their loony outfits. But I know him," I pointed and waved.

A huge person in a green rubber suit with shredded shirtsleeves and purple shorts advanced. Vedra Zdenko, attired as The Incredible Hulk, in what had to be the greatest example of type-casting ever, bounced in our direction. Tagging alongside him was another hulking figure, this one clad in baggy pants, torn black coat, bow tie, straw hat, and sporting a big red nose, similar to Keira's.

"My brother Nikolai is the W.C. Fields, remember him? Say something," Zdenko said to Nikolai.

The brother clasped Keira's hand, bowed and said, "Ah, my little Chickadee."

"Hello Mr. Dukenfield," Keira replied with a curtsy.

The use of Fields' actual name confused the two brothers, who glanced at each other.

"Oh, is joke," Zdenko said. "I am not understanding but is funny."

I was about to explain when he blurted, "Mr. Dave, who is this, the Bozo Clown?"

"I'm Dave's friend, Keira."

"You have wonderful costume. I am also friend of Dave. I am V. The name is short yet I am big. You figure," he said with a hearty laugh.

"I heard you went home for a visit," I said.

"Yes, I see friends and I come back." If Zdenko was a novelist, his book might end on page twelve. He added, "I am feeling bad about Mrs. Slade."

Zdenko took a stride toward me and put his massive hand on my shoulder. I could imagine my clavicle snapping if he applied pressure. "Is terrible you find her. You are upset." But his sentimentality dissipated quickly as he added, "Please we go. We want to try punch. They say it is with booze."

In tandem, they headed towards the bar.

I said to Keira, "That Hulk guy—that was Vedra Zdenko. He lives down the hall from me. His slightly less bulky brother lives in the Atlantic City area. You threw him with that Dukenfield comment."

"I guess they didn't know."

"Well, they're Albanians," I said.

"And they're quite large."

"Probably steroids."

I felt a tap on my shoulder. A voice said. "Steroids? Evil shit, dude." I turned and saw the hand was covered in a black batting glove and belonged to fellow seventh-floor resident, Rod Jackson. He was dressed in a Chicago White Sox jersey. "When I was in the bigs, everyone was bulking up. I tried it a few times, who didn't?"

"Did it help?" I asked.

"I stopped. They were cracking down with piss testing. See these?" he said, pointing to his biceps. "All natural muscle—no juice. If I did use it regular, I would've lasted more than a few years—dig?"

"Dig."

"You okay, dude. When you said steroids you musta been talking about those two fucking giants. I saw them walking away from you. I was coming out of the elevator like an hour ago, and those two were outside waiting—Dumb and Dumber. I could barely squeeze by them. You think they would move the fuck over."

Jackson gave me the impression he was already sampling the punch. "Is that your original baseball jersey?" I asked.

"This thing is the real deal. Still fits from my playing days. I got all my shit. I got the whole uniform somewhere. All my mitts, spikes—even got a couple of bats."

"Hoping to start a softball league?" I asked.

"Softball, ain't that some shit. Bunch of old fat-belly white guys." He shifted his gaze to Keira. "Who's this?"

The greasepaint and lipstick accentuated her frown. She glanced at Jackson and said, "*This* is Keira."

"Cool. You with Dave?"

"I'm with Dave," she said without emotion.

A moment of silence ensued and we stared at each other—clown, ballplayer and me.

"I gotta get better booze," Jackson said. "Where'd that bar go? I could use another scotch." I indicated the bar setup near the entrance although I assumed Jackson had already made a pit stop. "Yeah, that's it," he said. "Knew it was somewhere. See ya later."

"Delightful man," Keira said as Jackson left. "So far, your neighbors are—interesting."

"We're a fun bunch."

I scanned the ballroom, taking in all the residents.

"Who are you looking for?" Keira asked.

"I can't tell who anyone is."

Then, I saw a sight that surprised me, and scared me worse than any childhood Halloween fears. Dennis Slade entered the ballroom, and Mrs. Plimpton might be less than thrilled with him also as he was wearing street clothes. A black leather jacket covered his hefty torso as he glared at the happy residents who enjoyed themselves in the holiday spirit just hours after they lowered his wife's body into the ground. Dennis Slade stormed past the hillbillies, super heroes, and almost trampled a dancing skeleton.

He was now on a collision course with me.

It couldn't be—had to be my imagination. I sidestepped to my right praying I was wrong but he adjusted his stride to his left.

"Do you know this guy?" Keira asked.

As Dennis neared, I noticed a dark-colored tie poking out from under his jacket and paired with a white shirt. Funeral clothes. There was no mistaking his intent now and nothing for me to do except to wait it out and hope the tornado whirled past me.

No such luck. He parked his body in front of mine, his face inches away. He smelled of tobacco, and cologne that failed to conceal the distinct aroma of liquor. Whisker stubbles advertised he hadn't shaved in days.

At first his lips appeared to form a smile, but that rapidly morphed into a snarl. I retreated a couple of feet as Keira stepped aside.

He leaned forward as if to whisper but instead screamed, "You know what you did!"

I was rooted to the floor and didn't flinch.

"You!" He shouted directly into my face. "You are a fucking bastard."

There was nothing I could say.

With those words he about-faced and stomped back toward the door. As he approached the Zdenko brothers I saw Dennis shove The Incredible Hulk away from the table. I thought for a brief moment Dennis was going to spoon himself a glass of punch. But instead, he lifted the entire bowl over his head, like Atlas holding up the planet, and allowed it to drop, the glass shards flying, splattering the floor with crimson.

Chapter Ten

I had sex with a woman exactly one time in the last five years. As if that fact wasn't enough to dissuade me, Keira witnessed Dennis Slade screaming in my face followed by the punchbowl crash. I wouldn't forget the incident and was sure she wouldn't either.

Cecily Slade saw me as a target on that last night of her life. She had sex on her mind and guessed I would be a willing participant.

How right she was.

Not that I recognized signs from women desiring sex. While some guys simply needed a facial expression to tip them off, I needed Cecily to wave a banner with four-foot-high letters declaring her intentions. She kind of did.

When Cecily knocked on my door, I was in my zero-sex-for-five-years slump. It was more than a slump; it was a lifestyle. She asked if she could borrow a cup of milk. She wasn't even holding a cup.

Then came the four-foot-high letters. As I opened the fridge, she snaked her arms around my waist from behind, sliding one of her hands down the front of my shorts. My penis reacted on instinct and swelled. When I turned to face her, she was already falling to her knees while undoing the zipper. Seconds later I exploded into her mouth.

She peered up at me and whispered, "Okay, your turn."

Cecily wasn't searching for love. She was just searching.

Prior to the Halloween party, I hoped Keira would sleep with me. After Dennis Slade's outburst, I realized it was unlikely, even when she accepted my offer to come up for a drink.

"What was that all about?" she asked in the elevator.

"He thinks I slept with his wife."

"Why does he think that?"

"She had a way of coming on to guys."

"With you, too?"

"Hard to believe, isn't it?"

"Not at all," she said. "So, you did sleep with her."

I nodded.

As we arrived at my floor, Keira added, "Still, I feel sorry for Mr. Slade, his wife dying like that."

"Me, too."

She could've pressed the "down" button to the parking garage and I would've understood, but she followed me instead to my home. I fumbled with the key card, dropped it, and before I could react she retrieved it.

The things you notice.

As Keira bent down, I glanced to my right and saw the slimmest opening in Maggie's door. While I couldn't see her eye, I could bet it was squeezed into that crack. This was a sight to observe. A clown unlocked my door and entered my place with me in hand.

Once inside Keira asked, "Where's the bathroom?"

"That-a-way," I said, pointing down the hall.

I poured myself a glass of Maker's, and gulped down half the contents and headed to the sofa. The confrontation with Cecily's husband rattled me.

Guilt can do that to you.

A different Keira returned from the bathroom. Gone were the red pajama bottoms, the red and white flannel shirt, the cherry-colored straw, the heavy makeup. In its place were black panties, matching bra and nothing else. She washed away the makeup and now sported a natural complexion that brightened the room. Her blonde hair splashed to her shoulders.

I was in awe.

"I hope you don't mind," she said. "The rest of my clothes are in my car."

I was breathless and wondered if I could speak—to say something clever, something romantic, something. "You're beautiful."

"Thank you," she said, while approaching the sofa where I sat with my glass cradled in my hands.

"Shouldn't you offer a girl a drink?"

"I was just about to. You don't like bourbon by any chance, do you?"

"If you cut it with water I might."

"I think I have a bottle of white wine hiding somewhere."

She sat next to me and tucked her legs. "I'm fine with the bourbon."

I started to get up but she touched the back of my hand. "That was some party," she said.

Uh-oh.

"Your neighbors are—how should I put it?"

"Different?" I said.

"Very. I'm usually pretty good on reading first impressions. The Incredible Hulk seemed nice but he and his brother gave off bad vibes."

"Probably because you never saw giants dressed up in costumes."

"Worse than them was the baseball player. That guy is arrogant and chauvinistic. And that man with the punchbowl. That was friggin scary."

"Don't worry. I have a couple of normal neighbors, but they're smart enough not to attend these things, which is what I normally do."

"Why did you go to this one?" she asked.

I wanted to see you naked.

"To see my neighbors in crazy outfits."

She laughed. "That's funny—you didn't even wear one."

"I got an exemption from Mrs. Plimpton, our social director. Now, let me get you that drink."

I walked into the kitchen and removed a tray of ice cubes from the freezer and filled the glass before adding an ounce or two of Maker's. I dropped one cube in my glass and refilled it.

"Here you are," I said, handing her the drink and sitting next to her.

"Thanks," she said. "What should we drink to?"

"To our first chapter."

"Ooh. I like that," she said, tapping her glass to mine. "That reminds me. Can I ask you a personal question?"

Not about my book, I hope.

"Sure."

"I'm intrigued by your book. I looked it up on my cell and read the synopsis. It's about creepy shadows that kill people, right?"

"Kinda."

"There's a lot of ghost stories out there, but shadows, that's unique. How did you think of that?"

They helped me.

"Sometimes you just go where the story takes you."

"Okay. But, did you start out by writing about shadows?"

"There must be something else we can talk about," I said.

"Sorry, I did it again. You don't want to talk about your book. You tell me whenever you're ready."

"I don't want this to get weird—my not talking about the book. How about we try this another way."

"Okay."

"I'm going to tell you my life story and satisfy your curiosity."

"Oh, goody." She sipped her drink. "Yikes! So, this is what bourbon tastes like."

"Want me to get the white wine?"

"No. Tell me your story."

"I was born in a log cabin in Kentucky—no wait—that was another guy. I was born in north Jersey and later lived in New York City. I was married and worked a crappy job. Then I wrote a novel that sold like crazy and I traveled the country on book tours, where I kind of slid off the rails. My wife divorced me.

"Fast forward to present. I have no job and live off the success of that book. I live a quiet life and walk five miles every day. The end."

I made no mention of Shadows. Any news regarding them might send her running for the hills.

"Did you and your wife have children?" she asked.

"One boy. They live in Montana. Now you know everything about me."

"I doubt it but I'm hoping to learn much more."

"Eventually."

"Do I get to ask another personal question?"

"Okay," I said. "On one condition."

"What?"

"If I get the answer right, you have to see how I decorated my bedroom."

"Um, maybe. What was it like to be a best-selling author?"

"Insignificant," I said.

"Come on. I read that 60 Minutes did a segment on you. That's big."

"Same show they also ran a piece reuniting *Gilligan's Island* cast members. That's not big; that's sad. Bob Denver was even wearing that stupid hat. I was a momentary curiosity. It was as fleeting as a NASCAR lap. And for that I'm grateful."

"What about a sequel?"

Fuck, no.

"You're sneaking in an extra question," I said.

"It's logical you'd want to write another."

"Logic has nothing to do with it. My life went haywire and I don't want a repeat. There's my logic."

"I think I touched a nerve with my prying. Sorry."

"You can make it up to me," I said.

She smiled. "How so?"

"Check out my bedroom and give me decorating tips."

Chapter Eleven

I spent three years at Rosewood, a mental institution for the criminally insane. Shadows were responsible for my incarceration just as if a Shadow itself struck the man sitting next to me with that broken bottle years ago at a New York City tavern. I wasn't crazy before I arrived at Rosewood and wasn't crazy when I left. The long stretch in the middle—that was the time I could've slipped into crazy.

In the early months, it was hell. By the end of my stay, it was home.

At first, I wanted out. I silently rebelled at the sameness of institutional life. I didn't like being trapped in the controlled environment and adhering to a heavy therapy schedule. But as time passed I saw things differently. I developed a dependency on the staff. I got comfortable.

Dr. Stuart Sanderson and his group struggled to achieve the lofty goal of curing me. The legal system dumped me into their lap and they were as stuck with me as I with them. They would be my jailers, my confidantes, my friends.

When I met Dr. Sanderson, I didn't like him. It was that scraggily beard, which I immediately branded as a prop. It was his persistent habit of answering my questions with questions. Much of the first few months, he and I danced around each other with neither of us landing a solid punch.

Yet, I found myself looking forward to my sessions with him though we weren't always alone. Occasionally, a Shadow would slump itself into the chair next to me, and sometimes drift over to the shelves and scan the massive books. On one of those occasions I blurted, "Go away."

Dr. Sanderson smiled at me and calmly said, "I assume you weren't speaking to me."

"Sorry about that."

"Is there one here now?" he asked.

"It's checking out your library."

The doctor didn't bother looking away. "Not very interesting reading, I'm afraid."

Dr. Sanderson amazed me with his talent. He knew his way around a psyche and coaxed me into filling silences with my ramblings about Shadows. Sessions were often intense and sometimes marked by long silent lulls. I fell asleep during one and Dr. Sanderson woke me by tossing a piece of wadded up paper that caromed off my cheek. When I opened my eyes he was laughing and I couldn't help but join him.

He explained that I used the Shadows as a reason for my failures, so I could offload the blame for bad behavior. My core issue involved having character flaws, which left me vulnerable to my wayward creative nature. I bought his theories.

Eventually, the Shadows disappeared altogether. No sign of them anywhere. I began to think the whole experience was a product of my imagination, the invention of a malfunctioning brain.

He wasn't Sigmund Freud—just a normal human being, like I used to be.

Then came the day I was dreading. The doctor advised I was ready to be released. I didn't jump for joy—I panicked.

"No," I said.

"No to what?" he asked.

"I'm not ready."

"You are ready, Dave. We've done all we can for you. You'll take it the rest of the way. Trust me, please. You are strong and you can cope with anything."

"I might have to return." I said.

"Here, you mean?"

"The outside world isn't a good place for me."

"You don't belong in this place anymore. They pay me to decide when the time is right. I asked you a second ago to trust me. More importantly, I want you to trust yourself."

"Where will I go?"

"You told me you love the ocean, the Cape May area. Rent a place there, buy a place. Wouldn't you enjoy seeing the ocean every day?"

Despite Dr. Sanderson's well-intended efforts, he didn't cure me. Couldn't. Could not possibly. I prayed, yes prayed, the Shadows would be gone forever.

Forever didn't take.

Keira slipped off her bra and panties. She pulled back the covers and lay on the bed. I was thrilled.

Thrilled. Anxious. Nervous.

I tried not to think and began undressing.

Don't think.

So, naturally I did, adding pressure to what should be my most pleasurable experience in many years.

Ready, set, go.

I climbed on top and saw she'd already closed her eyes as I started sucking on the nipples of her full breasts. Minutes later she pushed me aside, reversing our positions, and smiled down at me while straddling my rib cage. Keira touched her wet lips with a long shiny fingernail and dabbed my lips. I licked her finger and played with it like a lollipop. She withdrew it, leaned into me, and substituted her tongue instead. When I entered my tongue into her mouth she clamped her teeth carefully but nearly consumed it.

Much of what followed was a blur. I remember a strand of Keira's golden hair becoming stuck in the corner of her mouth. I recall an earring dropping to the bed only to have her arm reflexively sweep it away.

I slept until the early-morning sun climbed over the distant horizon beyond the bedroom balcony, casting a pale orange glow in the room.

Keira stirred. "What time is it?" she mumbled.

"Too early," I said. "Go back to sleep."

Seconds later I listened to her rhythmic breathing in sync with the sound of the breakers lapping against the shoreline. I was fully content hearing those sounds fold into each other.

Until I heard a noise by the glass slider.

I lifted my head up from the pillow. The Shadow stood there, inside my bedroom, the outline of its hand tapping something against the glass. As I got out of bed, the Shadow dissolved and an object fell to the floor. I retrieved it.

Keira's earring.

I couldn't sleep after that.

I still had the earring in the palm of my hand when Keira woke again. "I guess you're staying awake?" she asked.

"Yeah, enjoying the sunrise."

"What do you have there?" she asked, noticing my hand.

"I found this on the floor."

"I'm glad you did. My mother gave me the earrings last Christmas."

Keira rose from the bed, grabbed my t-shirt from the bedcover, and moved toward the slider. "Oh my God!"

I hustled out of bed, stepped into my boxers, and went to her. "What?"

"Would you just look at that sun! The pinks and yellows bouncing off the water, coming right to us. I'm jealous. You see these sunrises every day."

"Anytime you want, I can arrange it."

"You like my shirt?" she asked, whirling like a ballerina.

"I should like it—it's mine."

"But it looks better on me."

"It would look even better lying on the floor," I said.

"You just want to see me naked."

"You say it like it's a bad thing."

"I hope you care more about me than my body."

I laughed. "You and your body—they're a package deal."

Staring at my boxer shorts she said, "Speaking of which, I see *your* package is alive and well again."

"I think it wants to talk to you. Come a little closer."

"Not now. I'm starving. What do you have for breakfast?"

"Cheerios."

"You're joking, I hope," she said. "I'm thinking eggs, bacon, stuff like that."

"I don't have stuff like that."

"Don't tell me you eat cereal every morning," she said.

That's when I heard the doorbell ring. As much as I disliked ringing telephones, doorbells were worse. I put a finger to my lips urging Keira to be silent. Maybe the intruder would go away.

No such luck.

I heard a feeble voice speak my name. Zdenko? I jumped into my jeans. "Stay here, okay? I'll get rid of him and be back in a flash."

"Get rid of who?" I heard her mutter as I walked away.

I opened my front door and was unprepared for what I saw. Zdenko was a huge man and as such cast a large shadow. But this was not the man, even though his voice suggested otherwise. This was a Zdenko-Shadow. It hovered at a height nearly a foot taller than me. In place of its face was a quivering dark hole leading to a near formless throat. The vacant shape blocked my doorway.

"What the fuck?" I stammered.

Keira's voice drifted from down the hall. "David, is everything alright?"

Wrapped in my robe, she stepped from the bedroom. From her straight-line perspective she could only see me and not the hallway to where the Shadow was now dissipating.

"Wait," I said to Keira.

"What's wrong?" Keira hurried to me. At first, I extended my arms to shield her from the apparition until I realized it was gone. She leaned against me and peeked around the door frame. "Who was here?"

I hesitated. "What?"

"I heard you speaking to someone."

"Oh. That was—Zdenko." My wheels turned and I tried to offer an explanation.

"Where did he go?" She stared into my eyes as if imploring me to explain how a 300-pound mountain of a man could be gone so quickly. "David."

"I like the way you say my name."

"Where the hell did he go?"

"To the store," I said. "Asked if I needed anything."

"At seven in the morning."

"Wawa is open twenty-four hours a day."

"And what did you tell him?"

"I said I was good."

She glared at me as if I were speaking a foreign language. "I didn't hear you say that."

"You were in the bedroom."

She squeezed passed me into the empty hallway and glanced toward the elevator, then the door to the stairs, and finally moved to the street-side window and peered down. "Then what?" she added.

"What do you mean?"

"Where did he go? He wasn't in the hall. I was here in seconds. The floor indicator over the elevator wasn't moving. What did he do, jump out the window?"

"He's The Incredible Hulk, not Superman." I sensed she wasn't happy with that response. "He went down the stairwell."

She turned to me and shook her head. Reentering my condo she touched my face with her fingers.

"Something just happened here," Keira said, walking toward the glass slider. She glanced left and right down the beach. "No sign of him anywhere."

"He's fast for a big guy."

Keira spun back to me, and stopped short. "This smells fishy."

"I don't smell anything."

"Don't be patronizing," she said harshly.

"I was trying to lighten the mood."

"Well, don't."

I walked forward and gave her a hug. She hugged me in return and the faint odor of yesterday's perfume drifted in the air. I backed off a step and kissed her cheek.

"Now, what do you want for breakfast?" I asked.

"What are you talking about?"

"You wanted something to eat. Remember?"

She grunted. "Something is very wrong here," she said. "And you acting like you don't know a damn thing isn't helping. But I know one thing."

"What's that?"

"You look like you've seen a ghost."

CHAPTER TWELVE

Seeing the Zdenko-Shadow frazzled me. If I hadn't experienced Shadows before I might've sworn off whiskey.

I heard the Shadow speak my name, which was a new wrinkle. Even though the voice was weak, up until this morning they'd been silent. The tapping of Keira's earring on the slider was a first, as was taking the shape of another person. None of this was good.

They were evolving.

Keira said, "David, we need to talk about what happened this morning."

Her plaid clown-shirt was back on, though left unbuttoned.

"Something bothering you?" I asked.

"Do me a favor, please?"

"Sure."

"Step outside in the hallway, wait ten seconds and ring your doorbell."

"I'm shirtless—and barefoot," I said.

"Then put on something."

"Nah, I'll live dangerously."

I shuffled into the hallway as Keira closed the door behind me. I counted down. "Three, two, one, blastoff." I pushed the button.

Keira opened the door.

"Howdy, Miss. Is this the residence of the once-semi-famous-writer, David Farmer?"

"Yes it is, sir."

I entered and looked around my condo. "Nice digs."

"Here's the thing," she said. "I went to the bedroom and heard the bell ring."

"That's where I do my best ringing."

"I'm serious. I didn't hear it earlier."

Crap.

"You're saying you didn't hear the doorbell when Zdenko was here?" I asked.

"Exactly. I didn't hear it and didn't hear him speaking to you."

I took her hand and led her to the sofa. "That's easy to explain. You didn't hear Zdenko because, for one, he was out in the hallway, and two, he was whispering to not wake anyone. As for the doorbell, I recall we were laughing at the time and the door to the bedroom was closed."

She was quiet for a moment. "Oh, it was closed? I don't remember that."

"It's a habit from my childhood. My parents used to argue all the time. I couldn't sleep."

"That's a shame," she said. "But you heard the bell."

"I wasn't certain, so I checked."

"And it's normal for Mr. Zdenko to ask if you need something from the store?"

"No, it's not. But he saw the light under the door and guessed I was up. Sometimes he's just too nice. I'll have to talk to him about checking with me so early."

"Oh," she mumbled, nodding her head.

I quickly added, "Your inquisitive nature is every bit as adorable as the rest of you."

"Maybe I'm curious because I work for a newspaper."

"I don't want you to worry. You could get acid indigestion—right about—here," I said, touching the area between her breasts with my finger.

"Where?" She placed her hand over mine and guided me to her nipple. Her hand then slid down my chest and into my boxers. We kissed and I steered her to the bedroom, closing the door behind us.

After our second round of sex, Keira stretched her body as if warming up for a gymnastic event. "Now I'm really hungry."

"Even if I had food, I can't boil an egg."

"What do you eat in a typical day?"

"Lots. Cereal, sandwiches, pizza, ice cream, potato chips." I headed to the fridge, opened it, pushed the milk aside and latched onto a carton of orange juice. "Only a few days past expiration."

"Do you have anything of substance in the cabinets?" she asked.

I opened the first one and announced the good news, "I've got peanut butter. I've got bread."

"Peanut butter? Um, probably not. Let's toast the bread for starters."

"Soon as I get a toaster."

"How about jelly? Got any of that?"

"What kind of establishment do you think I'm running here? Of course, I do. You want a PB&J sandwich? Coming right up."

After washing down the sandwich with OJ, Keira said, "Pardon me for saying, but you're a minimalist. Very little in the way of wall décor for example. You could use a woman's touch."

"For sure. I could also use help in decorating this place."

She smiled. "I think you'd feel better with a picture here and there, maybe a couple of plants to add life. You joked about decorating the bedroom but it needs it. You have nothing on the walls, the nightstands, anywhere. Just one lonely little lamp."

"Great sales pitch. You've got the job," I said.

"If I'm overstepping, please say so. I can be a bit forward."

"You're fine," I said. "I used to live a flashy lifestyle, wasting money like I'd always have it. Today, I have less of everything and am the happier for it. More stuff equals more clutter equals more problems. And I hate it when things break."

"Like toasters?"

I pulled on a cabinet door from under the sink. "There she is," I said, pointing to a toaster. "Crapped out on me."

She laughed. "You're hopeless."

"Keira, my turn. How about I ask you personal questions?"

"Seems only fair," she said.

"Do you have any boyfriends, or manfriends, whatever you call them these days?"

"No, I don't. Next question."

"Do you have any husbands?"

"I did once. We divorced long ago and we still like each other."

"Do you ever see him?" I asked.

"Yes, I do. He lives in the area."

"You don't work together, do you?"

"God, no."

"You said you're a reporter or something?" I asked.

"I work for the weekly county newspaper and get my share of bylines. Hey—how about a feature on a best-selling author living right here in Wildwood Crest?"

"Sounds great as long as you're not referring to me."

"Spoilsport."

"Keira, that book I wrote—it's nothing I'm proud of. I caught lightning in a bottle. It wasn't a work of art and I had help writing the darn thing."

"Oh?"

"JJ, my once-upon-a-time agent, was dissatisfied with the ending so she got behind the wheel and drove the manuscript to the finish line. I barely hung on for the ride."

"I'm sure you're being modest," she said.

"Even if I was, I've buried that whole experience."

"Got it. Mum's the word—for now."

Keira had a hell of a story perched right in front of her fabulous blue eyes. The best ingredients—famous author, adultery, murder, crashing punchbowls.

Shadows. There were enough elements to craft a sensational article.

Would anyone believe it? Oscar Wilde said he could believe anything as long as it was incredible.

He'd believe my life.

CHAPTER THIRTEEN

With Keira gone to her job in Cape May, I turned on the TV to check the weather. A storm was tracking in our direction. A Nor'easter, forming along the South Atlantic coast, might find its way to the Wildwoods.

"Cool," I said to myself, inviting more trouble.

I grabbed my sweatpants and threw on a hooded jacket and made for the boardwalk. A chilly wind greeted me as I trekked north along the water's edge. The ocean churned on my right and to my left sat a string of rainbow-colored motels. When I reached the south end of the boardwalk, I hopped up the wooden stairs and immediately spotted her leaning against the metal railing with the beach sprawled out behind her.

"I was waiting for you," she said.

"Hi, Kate."

"Don't be upset, Mr. Farmer. I said I wouldn't bother you, but I had to see you."

"I'm not upset." I said.

She peeked down the boardwalk and tugged at her collar, adjusting it against the wind. "It's happening to me, like in your book."

"What's happening?" I asked.

"The Shadows."

"What are you saying?"

"Remember when I said your book scared me?"

"I remember."

'I'm getting scared all over again."

Me, too.

"What do you mean?" I asked.

"I ..." She hesitated and scanned the boardwalk again.

"Why do you keep doing that?"

"What?"

"Looking every which way," I said. "Are you waiting for someone?"

"Mr. Farmer, have you ever had the feeling you're being followed?"

"Someone is following you?"

"Something is. I'm being watched. It's gotta be a Shadow. What really scares me is it's happening more often. That means it's going to kill me."

"Nothing is going to kill you. I made all that up."

"But I'm being followed," she said.

"Is the Shadow here now? Can I see it?"

She shook her head. "You know *you* can't. It's following *me*."

That's when I saw it. The Shadow stood on one of the boardwalk benches, a few feet away, teetering as though the wind could carry it off. From that perch I almost expected it to climb the railing and drop to the sandy beach.

"Kate, do you see that?" I asked, pointing in the direction of the Shadow.

"What? Those kids playing?"

A few boys were kicking soccer balls on the beach, and the Shadow was directly in our sightline. You couldn't miss it—unless it wasn't there. She clearly didn't see it. The thing faded as I stared at it.

"Those boys, is that what you mean?" Kate asked again.

"Yeah, I thought I recognized one of them."

She shuddered and dabbed at her eyes with anxious fingers. I reached out and hugged Kate, encircling her body with my arms. I rocked her back and forth. I told her it would be all right. She likely didn't believe me, but the trembling abated and I released her.

"I love your jacket pin," I said, hoping to calm her. "Beautiful seahorse with that shiny pink eye."

She smiled. "My mother gave it to me. I absolutely adore it."

"You should," I said. "Well, I've gotta get going."

"Mr. Farmer?"

I waited a few beats but she didn't continue. "Did you want to say something else?" I asked.

"How can I make the Shadow leave me alone?"

What answer could I give her? I was hoping she was wrong. They were my Shadows.

"Kate, get yourself some rest. You'll be fine."

"Do you really think so, Mr. Farmer?"

I can't be certain.

"I'm certain of it."

As I walked away and glanced over my shoulder, I saw her watching me. She lifted her hand ever so slightly and I couldn't be sure if it was a good-bye wave. But I kept going.

Later, returning from my walk, I spotted Gail Montrose in the parking garage. Gail was my neighbor down the hall, next to Jason Bell. I knew very little about her, except that she apparently was separated from her husband.

"The elusive Dave Farmer," she said.

"I've been called worse."

"That was one brutal shift. The hospital is killing me with these hours. What were you—out walking?"

"Every day."

"How about you and I head over to the Crest Tavern this evening?"

"The favorite watering hole you mentioned?"

"The beer's cold. You game?"

"I suppose so."

"Well, don't sound so excited," she said. "I hate to twist your arm."

"I don't have a car."

She indicated her BMW. "Got you covered. Knock on my door—let's say around six. Deal?"

"Deal."

For no valid reason, I felt conflicted after agreeing to a date with Gail. Keira and I were off to a great beginning of what could be a serious relationship.

It was mind-boggling for me to score two dates in two days after a five-year hiatus. Maybe it was this sudden flurry that had me confused. Keira and Kate—combined with Cecily's visit.

"You heading up? I'll share the elevator with you," Gail said.

Just as the door closed, I noticed Detective Cho getting out of a car. I could take a guess as to the driver.

When Gail and I arrived on our floor we parted and I hurried to my condo to pour a finger of Maker's.

The doorbell rang. I gulped the whiskey and placed the empty glass on the kitchen counter.

"May we come in, Mr. Farmer?" asked Cho, as I opened the door.

"Okay."

Cho and Faraday walked past me with barely an acknowledgment. I sensed they were here on serious business.

"May we sit?" Cho asked, as she sat on a chair. "Mr. Farmer, we need to speak with you again." Then she turned to Faraday who claimed the couch for himself. "Artie, how did Mr. Farmer answer the question regarding if Mrs. Slade was ever in his home?"

He pulled a notebook from his side pocket.

Faraday flipped through the pages. "Wrong date," he muttered. "Oh yeah, I got it. Mr. Farmer said, and I quote, 'No.'"

Jerk.

I sat on the arm of the easy chair, hoping they would see this as a signal our meeting would be brief.

"Mr. Farmer, you're a very successful author, aren't you?" Cho asked.

"Not really."

"Don't be modest. Your book was on The New York Times Best Sellers list for seventeen weeks. I would call that a success."

"What's your point?"

"You live in a beautiful condo—one that would be considered a mansion in my home country of Indonesia."

"Compared to my place, too." Faraday said.

"Enough talk about my mansion. If you have something to say, say it."

"Some people conceal the truth to preserve their lifestyle," Cho said.

"I've lost my patience with your rehearsed production."

I was about to stand up when Cho said, "Cecily Slade was here with you the night before she died."

"And what's your point?" I said.

"You didn't tell us the truth."

I smiled. "Tell your partner to read the full quote. Your question concerned whether I'd invited either of the Slades into my home. I hadn't.

Cecily dropped by of her own accord."

Faraday grunted. "Just when we thought you wanted to help us."

Jerk, The Sequel.

"Cecily asked to borrow something and I let her in."

"How long was she here?" Cho asked.

"Maybe an hour."

"My, what was she borrowing that took so long for you to find?" Cho asked.

"It was pretense. She came by to see me. Cecily and I had sex. It was the only time and she initiated it."

"I don't care who started what," Cho said. "I care you didn't tell us. Why didn't you?"

"I thought you might get the wrong idea."

"And what idea would that be?"

"Probably the one you're getting now."

"Did you kill Cecily Slade, Mr. Farmer?" asked Cho.

I shook my head. "No. I liked her."

"What was it you liked about her?"

I paused.

"Well?" she asked.

"It's true I didn't know Cecily very well, but she was always pleasant. She wanted to have sex with me and I was good with that."

"What time did she leave?"

"Maybe around six; it was just getting dark."

Cho and Faraday exchanged glances.

"Where did she go?" Cho asked me.

"Not sure."

"Home? She's right next door. Perhaps you saw if she went there."

"Now that you mention it, Cecily stood outside her door when I last saw her."

"Then what?"

"She turned to look at me and smiled."

"Was her hand on the doorknob?"

"I don't—yeah—I think it was."

"Did she say anything?" Cho asked.

"No."

"Was anyone else was in the hallway?"

"No, there wasn't."

Cho got up from the chair and walked to the side of the sofa where she leaned against the wall, cocked her head, her ear an inch or two away. "Are these walls soundproof?" she asked me.

"Sometimes I can hear muffled voices if they're shouting."

She turned to me. "Did you hear any arguing that night?"

"No. Of course, I didn't do what you just did."

"Of course."

Cho nodded to her partner and he shoved the notebook in his pocket.

She bent down and retrieved her handbag from the floor. When she straightened up, she focused on me. "Mr. Farmer, Detective Faraday and I will be speaking with you again. I suggest from this point forward you don't let semantics get in the way."

There was no hint of a smile as she added, "Don't get up. We'll let ourselves out."

Chapter Fourteen

Following the punchbowl episode at the Halloween party, I steered clear of Dennis Slade. Prior to stepping into the hallway, I looked and listened. If I heard him at his door, or heard his voice in the hall, I stayed put.

I sometimes cupped my ear to the wall, as Cho had, straining to hear any signs of life.

It was a hell of a way to live.

I grabbed my one pair of Old Navy khakis, added a clean red tee, and was about to venture over to Gail's when I speculated as to why I agreed to this date. My relationship with Keira was off to a rousing start and I didn't want to jeopardize that, though it was way too early to set boundaries.

Gail offered me something Keira couldn't—a perspective on my neighbors' possible involvement with Cecily. As a suspect, I wanted to take a proactive approach and determine who else deserved to be in the spotlight.

At my door, I paused and then detoured to the kitchen, where the Maker's waited for me. I poured a splash into a tumbler and guzzled it.

I opened the door, scanned the area, and headed down the hall.

"Right on time," she said.

This was a well-dressed version of Gail I hadn't seen before. Designer blue jeans were adorned with a yellow rose sewn onto the left-front pocket. A white silk shirt was partially hidden by a blue denim jacket emblazoned with white stars on the sleeves. Her close-cropped auburn hair appeared freshly curled.

"Wow, you look great," I said.

"Thank you. You clean up pretty good, too."

She drove us to the popular Crest Tavern on Pacific Avenue. The crowded restaurant surprised me since this was the off-season. The barstools were all occupied and additional drinkers endured standing room only. However, we snagged the last booth.

"I'm not going to ask about what happened between you and Dennis at the Halloween party," Gail said from across the table.

"Good."

"Though I'm dying to find out," she added with a wide smile.

"What did you hear?"

"We're short one punchbowl."

"No comment," I said.

"Ah, your legend is growing."

A waitress stopped by. "Can I get anyone a drink?" she asked.

Gail promptly said, "Hendricks dirty martini with the biggest olives you've got."

"What's the dirty reference?" I asked.

"Olive juice," Gail said. "Trust me." Then she glanced at the waitress. "Make that two."

After the woman walked away, Gail and I stared at each other for a moment.

"You don't get out much, do you?" she asked.

"I'm out every day."

"Not walking or jogging. I mean out socially with human beings."

"They're the worst kind of beings," I said.

She laughed. "Which surprises me since you're a famous writer."

"You read my book?" I asked.

"No offense, I don't have the time. Jason told me. His exact words were Farmer's a bigshot author."

"Jason," I mumbled.

"What's up with you and him anyway?"

"No clue."

Gail shook her head. "That's two not in your fan club—Jason, and now Dennis."

I shrugged. "What can I say?"

The waitress brought the drinks, glasses filled to the rim, a toothpick sprouting from the surface spearing three submerged olives. "Are you ready to order yet?" the woman asked.

"No," Gail said. "In a few minutes,"

My shoulder protested when I reached and lifted the drink. A few drops sloshed down the side of the glass. "Oops," I said, tasting the martini.

"How do you like it?"

"I used to love martinis though it's been a while," I said. "There was a bar in Manhattan near my apartment where they served them with salami-stuffed olives."

"That's worth a try. So, you lived in the big city. How did you wind up in the boonies?"

"I took a wrong step and fell off the edge of the earth."

"I bet that is one great story," she said.

"Uh-uh. Boring and full of bad turns."

"Doesn't sound boring to me. We'll have to order a second martini."

"No way."

"It's not your go-to adult beverage I take it."

"I'll have bourbon now and then," I said, picking up the menu. "So, what do you recommend?"

"Scallops in any form. They're off-loaded fresh every day. Did you know Cape May is the fourth largest fishing port in the U.S.?"

"I heard that somewhere," I said. "Gail, do you mind if I ask you a personal question?"

She smiled again. "Go ahead and get it over with."

"Word is that you're separated from your husband."

"So that's what Maggie thinks, huh?"

"Well, she might've mentioned something."

"Not much gets by her," Gail said.

"She wasn't very specific."

"Let me help. I've been liberated."

"Liberated?"

"Divorced. Finito. It just turned official and I guess the news hasn't crossed the hallway yet."

I laughed. "You know, I can't recall ever seeing your husband."

"That was part of the problem. Me working long hours and him disappearing to who-knows-where doing who-knows-what. I shouldn't say this, but he had a thing for Cecily. It wasn't totally his fault. Cecily knew what she was doing."

"I'm sorry I brought it up."

"He—smelled of her perfume." She paused. "I don't want to talk about him anymore."

"I shouldn't have asked."

"No problem. You were just being nosy." She raised her glass. "Here's to people with big noses."

She giggled at her toast and I raised my glass to hers. "You've got a sense of humor," I said.

"In my line of work, it helps."

"You're a doctor at Cape Regional?"

"I'm part of the oncology team. That means I log plenty of hours and deal with my share of sadness."

"The stress must be tough."

"No argument there."

The gin scorched my throat but Gail gave the impression she was sipping Perrier. There was a practiced symmetry in the way she swirled the alcohol, removed the toothpick and slid an olive into her waiting mouth.

"With that schedule, do you get any time to know our neighbors?" I asked.

"You are the curious one, aren't you?"

"I'm a writer, remember?"

"I smell an ulterior motive but I'll play along. I chat from time to time with our mutual friend, Maggie," Gail said. "And I keep my eyes open."

"How well did you know Cecily and Dennis?" I asked.

"You sound like those two detectives."

"They saw you too, huh?"

"Oh, yeah. Asked a bunch of questions and went on their way. Later as I was locking my door, I noticed them waiting at the elevator when that pretty lady left your place. Your friend used the stairs and I saw the tall one jot a note in his book."

"Why does that not surprise me?"

"What do you mean?" she asked. "Nobody said it was murder."

"They're making a list, anyway. I'm there with an asterisk."

"Why would that be?"

"I'm her neighbor for one."

"And for two?"

I hesitated. "There is no two. They live next door to me. Suspicion by proximity."

"Everyone is fair game," she said. "If she was murdered I'd take a hard look at her husband. Dennis has a serious temper. I saw it firsthand."

"Oh?"

"I heard him arguing with Cecily in the parking garage one night—about a week ago. I came home from a shift and was beat to hell. I pulled into my spot and they were walking in the next aisle. He was shouting at her."

"What did he say?"

"When I opened my car door I heard him yell, 'If I catch you one more time! I swear—'. When I shut my door he clammed up quick."

"Then what?" I asked.

"Like I said, I was wiped and just wanted to sleep. But she got in the last word—told him to go fuck himself."

"I hope that didn't come back to bite her."

Gail asked, "What's up with your shoulder?"

"What?"

"That's the second time you rubbed it."

I hadn't noticed, but it was still stinging from the accident. "Fell off my bike," I said.

"Really? You don't strike me as the clumsy type. Would you like me to take a look at it—maybe back at my place?"

"That's a nice offer, but I'm fine."

"Alrighty then." She downed the rest of her drink. "So, what happened with you and the bike?"

A car and a Shadow double-teamed me.

"A car clipped my bike in the dark and I ended up in the marshes off Ocean Drive."

"That's scary. Did you call the police?"

"The driver kept going and I didn't get a plate number or anything. I was too busy flying through the air."

"I'm glad you're in one piece."

"What's your read on our other neighbors?" I asked.

"You're not looking for a killer, are you?"

"No, we're just talking."

"Oh, my," Gail said. "You *do* think Cecily was murdered. And you're wondering if one of our neighbors did it."

"More like I'm thinking out loud."

"More like you're writing another book."

"God, no."

"If we're going down this road, we both need another drink." She waved to our waitress, holding up two fingers.

I was about to protest but—

Sure—what the hell.

"Our neighbors then. What do you think?" I asked.

"That baseball player, Jackson, is a loud-mouth conceited jerk. All that hip-hop racket, all the women, in and out. He fancies himself a ladies' man. I noticed the way he looked at Cecily. Not looked—leered. I bet he tried to hook up with her."

"Could be. Did he try with you?"

"Let's just say he struck out. And I'm not sure about Vedra Zdenko."

"How so?"

"I do the basics with him like hi, how are you. Nothing else. He said to call him V, or was it Z? I can't do that. Who calls someone by a letter?"

"He's Albanian," I said.

"And I'll tell you something else—women know if a guy is sneaking a peek. V or Z, whatever, his eye contact is for shit. I'll never lean over in front of him unless I'm wearing a turtleneck."

"He's not bad."

"You're a man. How would you know?"

"Fair point."

"Then there's the Bells," Gail said. "Jason and Melissa and their two young girls."

"I can't remember when I last saw his wife or the kids."

"Jason told me they're staying at her Mom's place in Court House."

"I don't know how the guy can afford to live here. His job can't pay a whole lot," I said.

"Melissa comes from money. Her grandfather started that taffy place on the boardwalk—the store with the orange-striped awning. She keeps him on a budget of sorts. Pisses him off. Then he sees you walking around like you own the joint while he's out there busting his ass—all his words, by the way."

"Fucking guy talks about me a lot, doesn't he? Pardon my French."

"Don't worry, I speak French."

"I didn't do a thing to Jason," I said.

"I guess he's jealous. Not your fault. But, the guy kinda likes me."

"Well, stand in line. He's got a thing for a woman named Kate. He's protective of her."

"Protective?"

"He acts like her bodyguard. I was talking to Kate on the boardwalk and he came way the hell over from the rollercoaster to butt in."

"I don't know this Kate person," Gail said. "As for me and Jason, don't get the wrong idea. I'm not in the market for a married man."

Gail was being forthright and I considered pushing the envelope. Maybe there was something else to learn. I clasped my hands in front of me and leaned forward on my elbows as the second martini arrived. "And what do you think of the guy living next to Dennis?"

She hesitated. "Oh, you mean you. Fishing for compliments? That's not fair. I might have to ask your opinion of me."

"I think you're a nice lady—okay—your turn."

She laughed and said, "Alright, you asked for it. I see that guy as a loner and a square peg in a round hole. His past may be chasing him and he's putting distance between it and the present. For a young guy—what are you like thirty-five?"

"Close enough."

"With a best-selling book on his résumé, he looks like he's got the weight of the world on his shoulders. He's preoccupied—always worried about something but never figuring out what it is. His introversion likely causes others to read him as arrogant. How am I doing so far?"

"I'm not an introvert. I just stay in my own lane."

"Same difference," she said.

"You sure you're not a psychiatrist?"

"Could be. Right now, for example, I'm getting strong vibes from you. There's something deep on your mind."

"Yeah. I'm trying to figure what to order for dinner."

Chapter Fifteen

I was a dutiful Christian for much of my childhood. My parents sent me to a Catholic grammar school, high school, and influenced my decision to attend Seton Hall University.

I believed everything the nuns and priests said. If they wanted me to slide over on the classroom seat to accommodate my guardian angel, I did. Fear of going to hell kept me a regular at Mass. The Church had a tried-and-true program that fostered blind acceptance.

It was comforting.

I breezed through the elementary grades like a Stepford student. Yes, Sister, and yes, Father, flowed easily from my lips. In fifth grade, Sister Matthias spotted my writing talent. I'd written a short story about the Gino Robbins Gang, a group of criminals. The twist was they were crooks who were likable. She read it to the class and I wasn't all that embarrassed. I wrote numerous stories after that, mostly murder mystery or sci-fi, and my mother told me how wonderful they were. Mom was a biased critic of course, but her compliments put me on Cloud Nine. Maybe I'd be the next Bradbury.

As a high school kid, I had to step it up a notch to attain good grades. Teachers fell for my snow jobs; the difference being I was now consciously trying to fool them. Blessed with an excellent memory, I was built for tests—could memorize everything while learning nothing. That strategy, bolstered by essay-writing ability, near-perfect attendance and compliant Catholic manners all translated to success—until college.

At Seton Hall, things went haywire. My buddies and I often ditched classes and hopped a train for New York City. We developed a routine starting with a cab ride from Penn Station to Greenwich Village and then hoofed it from there. We'd zig-zag our way to Little Italy on through Chinatown, barhopping at the places that didn't card us. Manhattan made us feel like citizens of the world.

We'd return to the campus in South Orange around midnight. Those daytrips represented the most effort I exerted during my abbreviated college career.

If New York wasn't the current diversion, we played stickball in a nearby park, shot hoops in the school's gym, scarfed down Italian-style hotdogs at Jimmy Buffs, frittered away the semesters drinking beer and

Jack Daniels in our dorm rooms. I remember my first taste of bourbon—like turpentine. Never again, I thought.

Like forever, never didn't take.

Springtime was for baseball. I'd sit in the grandstand to watch the Seton Hall Pirates compete rather than head to Corrigan Hall where the History of European Civilization was on display. I failed this course and failed it again during the summer makeup.

Months fused together and I was content with my lack of responsibility—living day-to-day with no endgame in sight. Maturity crawled forward but I was disinterested. No place to go and all the time in the world to get there.

During my sophomore year, the inevitable caved in on me—I washed out. I'd learned virtually nothing, except which came first, the chicken or the egg. According to Professor Northrup's assertion to his Philosophy 101 class, it was the chicken. In Northrup's world, actuality ruled over potentiality. The simplicity of this revelation boggled my mind, causing a blast of realization. I found myself on the wrong side of that theory. Just like the egg, I, too, was all about potential.

I saw my first Shadows at Seton Hall—exactly when I can't say. It might've been the morning I was shooting foul shots alone from a rack of basketballs in the gym. As I retrieved a ball from under the hoop, there was my Shadow on the nearby wall—but something was wrong. I brought the ball over my head and the Shadow didn't copy that movement. I two-handed the ball to it as though passing to the open man. It didn't flinch and the ball caromed back to me. I told myself what just happened—hangover.

Or, it could've been the time my friends and I were in the Student Union Center watching the World Series. The three of us sat side-by-side on a large sofa and shared a flask of dark rum. When I dropped the container to the floor, I noticed my Shadow was twice the size of the other two. I checked out the overhead fluorescents—bad angle—had to be. When I looked down again, all was right and proper; the shadows were of equal size. My heart raced but I calmed myself with another swig of rum.

Hangover? Trick lighting? Often, I added two plus two and got five.

Those events scared the crap out of me even with my attempts to rationalize them. I urged myself to have another drink, maybe with a Xanax. If nothing else, I'd zonk out.

The Shadows removed all doubt of their presence, often walking alongside as I made my way across campus. There'd be one on each flank moving out of step with me. The sun's location or even its absence didn't matter.

There was no denying it. No booze to blame. Shadows existed or I was going crazy.

Why me? There were others available to frighten.

Then, Brad gave me something to consider.

I hated all my classes, except one, English Literature. The instructor was a man in his thirties with a penchant for bright-colored sweaters. The nameplate on his desk read Dr. Bradley Araway, but he liked to be called Brad. He assigned the class a project.

"I want you to write the best short story of all time," he said. "Keep it under 1,000 words. I've got a life. Best story earns an A for the semester."

"Can you do that?" someone asked.

Brad laughed. "I'm an English Lit. Professor. The things I can do."

It was my A for the taking. The story was titled, "The End of Everything." Years later I polished it up for my *Shadows* novel.

"Where did you get that crazy-ass idea?" Brad said to me after class.

As a lapsed Catholic, I shaded the truth. "Out of the blue." I wasn't about to tell him Shadows invaded my life.

"C'mon, you got it from somewhere. What—did you see dark clouds flying too low and wondered what they were up to?"

"Uh-uh."

"You were out walking and your shadow was messing with you."

Yes.

"No."

"Listen," he said. "I've been doing this a while. Anyone can get a clever idea but that's the end of the line for most. You can write. I said short story; you could've written about anything and you jumped into the horror genre with a tale that made my teeth chatter. I kid you not."

"Does that mean I get an A?"

"Hell, yeah. But you gotta promise to keep writing. I want a shout-out when you get published."

"What published?" I asked.

"Your book. You're gonna to be a fucking Rockstar."

"I don't—"

"You wrote this story for a greater purpose. Now follow up. You've got the best reasons in the world to take a crack at this—fame and fortune."

"I'm not that good," I said.

He laughed. "Nobody's that good until the buying public tells them otherwise." Brad pointed out the window. "Hey, look! Isn't that Dave Farmer parked outside in his Maserati? And that's Cameron Diaz with him." Brad smiled at me. "How's them for reasons?"

I couldn't help but glance toward the window.

"Sounds fairytale-ish," I said.

"Dude, life is the most wonderful fairytale of all. Am I getting through?"

"I'm listening."

"What I found especially interesting in your story was the fact that your Randy Collier character had earlier interaction with the Shadows, right?"

"Yeah."

"What if it was true?" Brad asked.

"What's true?"

"Picture this," he said, his hands framing a scene. "The Shadows and a human join forces. Like making a deal with the devil. The guy serves as a front man. That's the direction your story could've gone before you decided to end the world. Maybe you should take a run at this other storyline and flesh it out—a novel maybe."

"Um—I'll give it thought."

"I'm serious and I'm published, short stories, a few essays. My agent is one of those balls-to-the-wall types. Makes Hilary Clinton look like a Girl Scout. She's got an office off Central Park and if you put a manuscript together, I could hook you up."

"Really?"

"Really. You'll eventually remember where you got the idea for *The End of Everything*," he continued. "It'll happen, probably when you're not thinking about it, not thinking about anything. Like you said, out of the blue, which is where your next flash of brilliance is hiding. Ever hear of Dee Hock? Of course, you haven't. He's the founder of Visa. Brilliant man. His advice was to make an empty space in any corner of your mind and creativity will fill it."

"I think I know what you mean," I said.

"Let's be certain. We need one of those Mr. Spock Vulcan mind-melds. Focus on that clock over the blackboard."

Huh?

He raised his hands toward my face and stopped inches short, pulling them back. "I'm kidding about the mind-meld. But not about anything else. Keep that head clear, Farmer. Air out your psyche. Leave it wide open like a barn door. Let any old fucking thing come tumbling in."

"Um, okay."

"I sure hope you're getting all this," he said.

"You're saying I can make a boatload of money."

"By George, I think he's got it."

I added two plus two and got Shadows. They were here for a specific reason, though it would be years before I understood their menacing intentions.

The End of Everything was just the beginning.

Chapter Sixteen

After flunking out, I returned home to live with my father. I didn't expect him to take my news well. I tried to soften the impact by making one of his favorite foods—a grilled cheese and tomato sandwich.

He came in from work and placed his thermos on the kitchen counter. "What are you doing home?" he asked.

"Making you dinner. I bought a can of vegetable soup, too."

"This ain't spring break, is it?" He was spoiling for a fight. My parents divorced three years earlier and he still carried a grudge against life.

"I flunked out."

He shoved his thermos into the sink where I heard the glass liner shatter. "When did this happen?"

"It's been happening for nearly two years," I said.

"You always got good grades in school."

"College is different."

"College or you?"

"What do you mean?" I asked.

"You've gotten lazy. Last summer, you shoulda made more money for school."

"I got a job."

"Yeah," he laughed. "Part-time stocker at ShopRite. You woulda made triple working at the power plant. You had an in with me."

"That's heavy work."

My father made a fist of his thick, calloused hand. "You're soft. What about all the money I spent for this higher education of yours?"

"I'll pay you back," I said.

"Fat chance. Did you manage to learn anything that would give me hope you can support yourself."

I wasn't about to mention Shadows. While I hadn't as yet understood their purpose, I realized they had the potential to change the world.

Potential.

"The chicken came before the egg," I said.

"What?"

"I learned that in Philosophy."

"Bullshit," he said. "A year and a half shot in the ass."

"I'll get a job."

"Damn straight you will."

Turns out my father knew a guy who knew a guy and I got a job with a small landscaping company, mowing lawns and trimming hedges for a guy named Shaky Sam. Sam was afflicted with Sydenham's Chorea, a nerve disorder causing involuntary muscle movements. His body twitched and jerked as though grooving to a tune only he could hear.

He coped by downing a few cold ones at a bar, which he did regularly with the aid of a straw. The glass stayed on the bar's surface with Sam hunched over. After a few beers his hand was steady enough to bring the glass to his lips without cracking a tooth.

Shaky Sam saw how I could be of use to him. I spoke limited Spanish and he supervised a crew of Mexicans. His constant spasms combined with a stuttering problem confused the group. The Spanish I memorized in high school allowed me to communicate the basics to his men. I filled in the gaps with sign language.

Sam normally drove to any nearby tavern to drink his lunch, often inviting me to ride with him.

"You don't need to tell your father about our lunches," he'd say.

"Why would I?"

"Anyway, they're not just bars. There's food there. I'll buy."

Sam's car was equipped with a unique steering wheel, courtesy of knobs fixed at the ten-and-two positions. He normally handled the road well, as he drove me to and from work each day.

One day, on our way to lunch, he right-turned onto a street where another vehicle was stopped at the traffic light. Sam misjudged the turn and side-swiped the other car. He then pulled us over to our side of the road and went to speak to the other driver. I watched from the front seat when I saw Sam sprinting back. He hopped in and floored the accelerator, informing me the other guy was from Poland and spoke broken English. Sam had agreed to follow the man to his brother's house where we could sort out the accident with the man's brother serving as an interpreter.

That didn't happen. We drove off at racecar speed to the tavern.

"You know," Sam calculated from his barstool, "I think the accident was 65% my fault and 45% his." I didn't bother to correct his math nor did I ask him how our Polish friend was at fault.

This accident was a boon for me. Sam presented an unspoken bribe by promoting me to his assistant, a job that previously didn't exist. It was totally unnecessary as I had no inclination to share the hit-and-run incident with anyone. I accepted his offer.

I patrolled the neighborhood and directed the workers to their next property. No longer did I have to handle a noisy hunk of machinery. My hands stayed relatively clean as I coasted through each day.

That's how I met Marcy.

She saw me walking the streets with a clipboard, checking with the workers, and guessed I was their supervisor. She came to the front fence and motioned in my direction. "Are you part of the lawn service group?"

"Yes, miss."

"One of the men cut my mother's trumpet vine. Please make sure they know the difference between a plant and a weed."

"Will do. Sorry."

Marcy leaned against the fence. "I didn't mean to be rude, but my mother is upset and wants someone to be aware."

I was now aware that I wanted to know this young woman. Marcy didn't have the classic beauty that adorned the covers of celebrity magazines. Her allure was more subtle, blessed with a natural warm smile. I couldn't define the specific quality that gripped my heart. She radiated goodness.

In the coming weeks I made it a point to be more visible on her street with the guys, gesturing to this yard or that one, waving my hands as if I were directing traffic. Marcy's yard received special attention and no more trumpet vines met with a premature demise.

I remember that sweltering day. Marcy walked out to the street and flagged me down. "You work so hard," she commented.

"Thanks, I'll pass that on to the crew."

"Would you like a glass of iced tea?"

I don't like iced tea.

"I'd love one."

Marcy and I sat in her kitchen and spoke about nothing in particular for an hour. By the time I left that afternoon I'd made a date with her, which was followed by another, and another. We saw each other regularly for a few months before I asked her to marry me.

I learned an awful truth about myself. I was a decent sprinter, but didn't handle long distances well. With Marcy, our relationship got out of the gate in good form, but as time passed, I couldn't last the distance.

During the first couple of months of our marriage, Shadow sightings increased. They were toying with me, living in the corners of my eyes and disappearing when I turned my head.

One day I said to a Shadow, "Fuck off."

Marcy entered the den at that moment.

"Who were you talking to?" she asked.

"No one."

"You said fuck off."

"Oh, that."

"Not to me, I hope," she said with a laugh.

"Did you see the fly? Big sucker."

"You were talking to a fly. Perfectly normal."

"We should buy a flyswatter," I said.

"There's one in the utility room. You ready for dinner?"

"I'm not hungry right now."

"You say that a lot. You're eating less and drinking more. I wonder if there's a correlation."

"I'm not drinking much." I pointed to my desk. "That bottle there is a week old and still half full."

"David, I love you. You should always be honest with me. You're going through more than a bottle a week."

"That can't be," I said.

"You need something to do with yourself. We're still newlyweds and you should be happier. You're preoccupied and I wish you would tell me what's bothering you."

"What you really mean is I need a job."

"Well, you can't stay with Sam forever. That landscaping business is on its last legs."

"Thanks. I'm the one running the business."

"You know what I was thinking?" she asked.

"I'm afraid to ask."

"On our honeymoon, remember we were walking at Elbow Beach and you started talking about shadows. You joked that our shadows were following us and that was a great idea for a horror novel."

I was testing the waters.

"I remember."

"You should," she said with a smile. "You kept bringing up the book idea for five days."

"I did not. We spent most of our time in bed, as I recall."

"I'm talking about the book," she said. "I'm teasing."

"What's going in that pretty little head of yours?"

"Write the book. You can do it."

She didn't realize I never stopped thinking about writing it, every day, every hour. They wouldn't let me stop.

"I've got news for you, Marcy. I already started the book."

"Oh great! I'm so happy. When did you start?"

Maybe tomorrow.

"Couple days ago."

Writing was my best skill, possibly by default as I had little else in inventory. I could write anything with creativity and style. I didn't need Brad's compliments but I kept them close by. They stuck in my brain, reinforcing what I'd already known. Throw any topic at me and I could field it like a like a Gold Glove shortstop. And now I had help—the Shadows.

I understood they wanted me to tell their story. It was more than a sixth sense. I felt them rummaging around in my head. I heard their fractured whispering.

Writing *Shadows* could've been fun. The fun lasted a few chapters, and then took a fearful 180-degree turn. There the Shadows were—on the wall moving independently of me, hovering alongside as I typed, invading my psyche. I got their message—keep writing, Farmer. Don't stop.

I wrote scared.

During the writing of *Shadows*, days would sneak by when I barely spoke, barely ate. Scared or not, I wrote with maniacal urgency. Sometimes I'd write all day, go well past midnight and crash on the sofa, too often accompanied by excessive drinking. Marcy offered mild protests, which I ignored.

"Don't talk to me now." I'd say.

"When can I talk to you?" she'd say.

I was in a zone.

Marcy never wavered in her support for me. Despite my erratic behavior, my mood swings, she was my assistant, diligently listening to every chapter I read aloud, making suggestions, asking for clarification, yet always complimenting, always upbeat, always moving the project forward.

She had no idea how it hurt me not to be the man she deserved. I faced the truth. I was damaged goods.

Marrying Marcy was the highpoint that should have sustained me for the rest of my life. Damned if I didn't make a mess of it.

Like Shaky Sam's faulty calculation, the math was a bit fuzzy when applied to my marriage. Assigning blame, I'd estimate the fault as 100% mine and 10% hers—for using bad judgment in saying yes to my proposal.

I wish I could've told her what I was going through with the Shadows. What chance was there she'd believe me? Even I didn't believe at first. However, it wasn't just a matter of belief. It was possibly a matter of life and death. I wasn't certain what the Shadows were capable of.

Then they provided a hint.

One morning after a long night of bourbon-soaked writing, Marcy came into the den. "David."

I struggled to sit upright on the sofa and smoothed out my crumpled shirt. "What time is it?" I asked.

She sat on the swivel chair at my desk. "Time for a talk."

"Oh?"

"See the bottle?" she asked, her finger aimed at the empty bourbon bottle alongside my laptop.

"Yeah, I see it."

"Guess where I found it this morning?"

"Right there?"

"No. It was sticking out from under your body," she said.

"Here, on the sofa?"

"There, on the sofa. I have a question. Was it more comfy than sleeping with me?"

I stared at her as she waited for a response. I glanced up.

"David?"

I couldn't speak. A horde of massive Shadow-spiders crossed the ceiling, stopping over Marcy.

CHAPTER SEVENTEEN

Dinner with Gail was fun and she was right-on regarding the scallops recommendation. I considered adding them to my limited regimen of food. She provided insight to my neighbors' possible involvement in Cecily's death, though Gail wasn't fooled by my flimsy approach for information. Too often, women spotted my intentions a mile away.

Following yesterday's encounter with Kate and later with the two detectives, I wanted to see Keira. She offered better solace than bourbon.

I punched her number into the handset.

"Cape Banner, this is Jim, can I help you?"

"I'd like to speak to Keira."

"Hold on," he said.

In a few seconds I heard her voice. "This is Keira Donaldson."

"My name is David Farmer," I said. "I have a breaking news story to report."

"Great. Whatcha got?"

"How's this for a headline, Wildwood Crest man buys new toaster?"

"Hold page one, Jimmy," she shouted.

"You didn't really yell that to him, did you?"

She laughed. "You didn't really get a new toaster, did you?"

"Well, I thought you might pick one up on your way here. I'll pay C.O.D."

"I can't now. Jimmy and I are the only ones in the office."

"No problem." I said. "How about I come over there and take you to lunch."

"Are we walking or am I riding double on your bike?"

"I have another idea, I come over there and you take me to lunch."

"That works," she said.

I pedaled my Cannondale toward Cape May. *The Cape Banner* was located just off Beach Avenue, a five-mile ride from my condo.

The colorful Bed and Breakfasts stood side-by-side across the street from the ocean, showing off the Victorian architecture for which Cape

May was famous. The B & B's were decked with wrap-around porches sporting numerous rocking chairs. These gorgeous buildings lined up like century-old crayons in their box.

An approaching ridge of gray clouds slid in from the south.

As I neared the western end of Beach Avenue the gazebo was ahead to my left, nestled against the beach, while the historic lighthouse towered across the cove in front of me. I leaned right and swung in behind a small motel to the newspaper office.

Inside, open floor space was difficult to find. A couple of unoccupied desks, an ancient copy machine, stray chairs and Bankers Boxes provided obstacles for anyone daring to navigate the room.

"Is Ms. Donaldson in?" I asked at the desk, where a young man focused on his laptop computer.

He peered up at me. "Huh? Oh, yeah, nobody calls her that." He turned his head and announced, "Some guy here to see you."

Keira appeared from behind a door. "David. Come on in."

I maneuvered my way to her tiny cubicle where I squeezed sideways past a filing cabinet and almost tripped over a sizeable carton on the floor. The only guest chair was stacked with papers and file folders while the modest swivel on the other side of the desk belonged to her.

"This place is worse than my condo."

"We're downsizing, rearranging things."

"Does anyone actually work here?" I asked. "Or do they just phone it in?"

"We've been cutting back."

"Hopefully you've got tenure."

"I'm okay, especially with that new toaster exclusive you called in."

"Can you go to lunch?" I asked.

"Can't be too long. Jimmy and I are holding down the fort."

"You've already lost the fort. I'm just glad you didn't take an arrow during the siege."

"Ha-ha," she said, smiling. "You up for a nice walk on this cloudy autumn day?"

"Sure."

Once outside, we headed to the Washington Street Mall, the popular shopping area a couple of blocks in from the beach. During summer, the Mall was packed, and tourists wandered in and out of the stores clutching bags of t-shirts, souvenirs, fudge and taffy.

"Those clouds," Keira said. "Feels like a storm brewing."

"Weather Channel says it's a couple of days away."

"There it is," Keira said, pointing to a corner restaurant. "Ever been there?"

"Nope."

The Atlantus Tavern was named for the famous sunken ship off Sunset Beach in Cape May Point. The concrete ship, Atlantus, transported troops home from Europe at the end of World War I. It was saved from salvage and brought in for use as part of a ferry dock, but broke from its moorings during a storm in 1926. The ship sank off the coast and was still partially visible while digging itself even deeper into the sandy muck.

The restaurant was dark. Not gloomy dark but just the natural color scheme. The long wooden bar to my right was a polished black cherry complimenting the equally dark well-varnished massive staircase, which bisected the bar area from the main dining room. The bar crowd was all male, regulars I assumed for this November day.

I detected the enticing odor of charred meat wafting from the kitchen.

"They could use some lighting in this place," I said, as we sat in a bar booth.

"No way. I wouldn't tamper with the charm."

"It's got character, I'll say that."

"So, what's up?" Keira asked.

Well, let's see—there's a Shadow that's making a nuisance of itself. It climbed on Kate and may be stalking her. It arrived at my door looking much like Zdenko. The thing showed up in my bedroom, holding your earring. Oh, and it was there when my bike and I went airborne.

"Nothing."

"Yesterday when I left your place, I saw a tall man and a woman by the elevator. Official types. Were they the detectives you mentioned?"

"That's them," I said.

"They question you again?"

"Of course."

"Do they know you slept with Cecily?" she asked.

"I'm sure they do by now. I left it out of the first interview."

"So, who told them?"

"Probably Dennis. Now they think I'm a liar."

"Why did you lie?" Keira asked.

"Technically, I didn't. Detective Cho asked me if I ever invited either Dennis or Cecily over and, well, you know what happened."

"David, you're talking to me now. That's a lie in anyone's book."

"I thought you were on my side."

"You were afraid of what they would think."

"I figured one bad behavior would imply worse behavior."

She reached across the table and touched my hand. "I can buy that," she said. "I hope you learned something from this."

I scratched my head as if studying a Rubik's Cube. "I learned it's best not to get caught lying."

She playfully slapped my hand. "Do you think Cecily was murdered?"

"I get the impression the detectives think so."

"What do you think happened?" she said.

"She wasn't going for a midnight swim."

A beefy man with graying hair walked to our table. He was dressed in crisp blue jeans, black fisherman sweater, and black cowboy boots accented with a silver toe rand. "Hi Keira," he said. "Good to see you again."

"Oh, Mick. This is my friend, Dave."

Mick extended his hand and I did the same.

Keira said, "Mick owns The Atlantus."

"Nice place," I said.

"Thanks. First time here?"

"Yeah. I really love that staircase—the rails and steps are so shiny."

Mick and Keira exchanged glances. "Nancy takes good care of it," Mick said.

I nodded. "She's doing a great job. Give her a raise."

Mick smiled. "Can't do that. She's been gone a long time."

Keira turned to me. "Nancy is a ghost."

"Oh," I mumbled.

Mick laughed. "I've seen her but I don't expect you to believe that."

You'd be surprised what I can believe.

"Enjoy your lunch," Mick said. "I gotta go—helping in the kitchen today. Good to meet you, Dave, and Keira, thanks for dragging in a new customer."

As Mick walked away, I asked, "You've dragged in other people?"

"A few. An occasional lunch with an advertiser. I came here with Tommy once or twice."

"My Tommy?" I asked.

"The one and the same. I didn't have to drag him. He practically lives here. That stool in the corner by the window—that's his. Regulars don't sit there. Saves them from moving when Tommy shows."

"A sign of respect." I said.

"Everybody likes Tommy. He's got a way about him. When you first meet him, it's like you've known him for years. Plus, half the people here probably used Tommy to buy or sell a home, rent a property, whatever."

"Like me."

"Like you."

A waitress stopped by, "May I get anyone a drink?"

"Ginger ale," Keira blurted.

"Make it two," I added. As the woman left, I said, "I hesitate to ask but what's this about Nancy?"

"She's a local legend. Last year, I did a piece for the newspaper on her and The Atlantus. In 1932, there was a crowded wedding celebration upstairs and, of course, there was drinking. Nancy was eight years old. The guests formed some sort of Conga line and danced around the room bumping into Nancy. She fell out of an open window and her head hit the pavement.

"Terrible. Now she haunts this place?"

"No, she lives here. There've been lots of sightings, even though Mick only uses the upstairs now for storage. And the bathrooms are there."

"And Nancy?"

Keira nodded.

"Have you seen her?" I asked.

"No, but Tommy has."

The waitress placed the glasses of ginger ale on the table. "May I take your order?" she asked.

"The Caesar Salad," Keira said. "No anchovies."

"For you, sir?" the waitress asked.

"Cheeseburger, medium rare, and fries."

Keira sipped her soda and waited for the waitress to walk away. "I'm sure you know there are many ghost sightings in Cape May. B & B's, for example."

"Sure, it's a profitable industry for enterprising businessmen," I said. "Trolley tours, horse and buggy romps. Books. Souvenirs. If I owned a B & B, I might gin up a ghost or two to help the occupancy rate."

"You sound like a cynic," Keira said. "There are things in this world that can't be explained with logic and tangible proof. I'd be disappointed if you didn't believe that."

"I can't have you all disappointed," I said.

"Seriously, you do believe?"

I nodded. "Yeah. Why are you looking at me like that?"

"Nancy is up those well-varnished stairs you like so much," Keira said.

"Is that why you brought me here? To chase ghosts?"

"What's the matter?" she asked. "Are you afraid of what you don't know?"

I'm more afraid of what I do know.

"I gotta take a leak," I said, standing up.

"Oh, good."

I climbed the first few steps and turned to see Keira smiling at me. The waitress brought the food and I wondered if I should've ordered bacon on the burger. When I resumed my climb, a man wearing a brown fedora stood motionless at the top of the stairs. Everything about him was off. I thought he was shivering, unsteady on his feet. He wore an oversized long dark coat and baggy dark pants. I guessed he'd dropped a lot of weight. His hands were hidden by the coat sleeves, which were too long.

The hat was cocked well over his forehead, covering part of his face. He kept his head down as he started moving on the stairs—directly toward me.

I pushed myself against the railing leaving room for him. Instead, he adjusted his path and walked straight at me.

"Excuse me," I said, sidestepping the man at the last second.

I continued to the top step and noticed the upstairs room was spacious and dimly lit with barely enough light to illuminate the signs on the bathroom doors—*Sailors* and *Mermaids.*

"Hello, Nancy?" I whispered to the empty room. Round tables covered in faded sheets dotted the floor while chairs were stacked in the corners. I had the sense of dust and decay.

I stood there. I gave the girl a chance. Nothing.

As I turned to walk back to Keira, the man in the fedora stood a few steps below me. He moved toward me again, his head still looking down.

I backed up and entered the men's bathroom. The door's creaking hinges cried out for WD-40. I slipped into a stall, pulled the door shut and sat on the closed lid of the toilet.

The men's room door opened with a loud screech, and a shape crossed outside my stall.

My heart pounded as I waited for any familiar bathroom sounds—the flushing of a urinal, a running faucet, the soap dispenser, the sound of the creaking door signaling someone's exit.

Nothing.

I wondered if I was alone. I pushed open the door to my stall, leaned out and peeked both ways. No one was there.

Out of the corner of my eye, I detected movement in the mirror, which reflected the figure by the door, wavering in the still, musty air.

With the hat and clothes gone, a wisp of foggy haze slowly dissolved, too.

Chapter Eighteen

"You were gone awhile," Keira said when I returned to our table.

"The darn soap dispenser was clogged."

"Oh, I thought maybe you saw a certain little girl."

"Sorry, no sign of her."

"I knew that was a long shot. But did you notice anything unusual?"

I could've said there was a Shadow upstairs and I watched it vanish into thin air. I could have said that. "I wonder if it's too late to add bacon to this cheeseburger." I took a sizeable bite. "Hmm, good as is."

"That doesn't mean anything," Keira said.

"Huh?"

"The fact you didn't see any sign of Nancy. She's up there and she saw you."

"I have an idea," I said.

"I hope it's a good one."

"Let's drop all talk of ghosts and talk about us instead."

"Oh, that is a good idea."

It was evening when I stepped onto the elevator following a walk along the beach. I arrived at the seventh floor and hesitated before entering the hallway.

With no sign of Dennis Slade, I almost tiptoed toward my condo.

"Dave."

A woman's voice, thank goodness.

"Can I see you?" she said.

I turned and saw Maggie Callahan standing in her doorway.

"Come in, please," she whispered. "I have something important to discuss with you."

"I hope everything is alright," I said, walking inside.

"As my Harold used to say, things are hunky-dory."

Maggie wore a gray blazer buttoned over a pink blouse and navy-blue slacks. "Are you going out?" I asked.

"Heavens no. Why do you ask?"

"You look nice."

"Thank you, Dave. That's the best compliment I've had since—I don't know when."

"I call 'em as I see 'em," I said.

"Do sit down, please. May I get you something to drink?"

I sat on the sofa. "I'll have a bourbon neat, water back."

Maggie smiled. "You probably think I don't know what that means. I helped tend bar in the restaurant Harold and I owned. Neat was in a shot glass and water back meant a separate glass as a chaser. We had our own variation, using a crystal tumbler for the whiskey, and for the water we had tiny silver pitchers for pouring in a drop or two."

"You know your stuff."

"But I don't have any whiskey," she said, with a laugh.

"I was kidding."

"I know. I do have a kettle of tea on the stove, and I might have some beer leftover from the summer."

"No thanks."

"I have a proposition for you," she said, smiling.

"I'm all ears."

"Harold said that, too. You're a lot like him," she said, sitting on the opposite side of the cocktail table.

"I'm honored. What's the proposition?"

"You and I would make a great team."

"You're not thinking of *Dancing with the Stars*, are you?" I asked.

"Of course not. I can't dance a lick. I mean like those two detectives."

"I'm not following you."

"Do you watch *Law and Order* on TV? They always pair a male and female together. See what I mean?"

"No," I said.

"You and I can solve Cecily's murder."

I almost fell off the sofa. "What?"

"You look surprised," she said.

"No one even said she was murdered. It could've been a freak accident."

"If it walks like a duck and quacks like a duck. The detectives think there was foul play. Dennis thinks she was murdered, so does Jason, so do you."

"How do you know what I think?"

"A little birdie from down the hall told me. You mentioned it to her."

My big mouth.

"That was me thinking out loud. I could be wrong."

"You're not," she said. "I've been thinking about this ever since Dennis made such a scene at the Halloween party. He was out of line. I heard what he did—smashing that punchbowl was dreadful."

I wasn't sure if Maggie's ire was directed at the vulgar language Dennis screamed at me from point-blank range or the loss of the bowl itself.

"Maggie, you told me that you know Cecily was at my place just before she died. So, it's understandable Dennis would be angry with me. Even I get that."

"However, Dennis is the prime suspect. It's normally the spouse that did it."

"Or the butler."

"Oh my, you are a rascal, aren't you?"

"At the very least."

"I'm not only talking about what Dennis did at the party. What's worse is what he's likely telling the detectives."

"Which is?" I asked.

"You killed his wife."

"There's nothing I can do about what he says."

"That's where my brainstorm comes in."

Oh, Lord.

"What exactly is this brainstorm?" I asked.

"You're going to love it. We partner up, put our heads together and investigate what happened to Cecily. I have a nose for this sort of thing. Remember when someone stole that bottle of expensive champagne from our clubhouse? I had Mr. Caruthers from downstairs pegged right from the start."

"Petty theft is a lot different than murder."

"But the criminal mind is the same," she said. "Why was the crime committed? What is the behavior afterwards that points to the perpetrator? I can connect the dots."

"Cho and Faraday are already doing that," I said.

"I bet we're as smart as those two detectives."

"I bet we're not."

She shook her head. "You haven't heard the best part of my plan."

And I don't want to.

"Tell me," I said.

"Dave, you like parties, don't you?'

"Maybe if there's enough to drink."

"I'm going to throw a dinner party here and invite all our neighbors, stir up the pot and flush out the killer."

I sat there—stunned.

"You like the idea?" she asked.

 "Not especially. Does this work on those TV shows you watch?"

"Yes. An episode of *Murder She Wrote* ended with the crime being solved at a dinner party thrown by Angela Lansbury."

"The actress?"

"Her character in that series. It was famous back in the 90s, you must've seen it. There are reruns all the time."

I shook my head. "No."

"Anyway, she was terrific and won awards for her role. Harold said I look like Angela Lansbury. That was sweet of him to say." Maggie stopped for a moment. "Now, where was I?"

"You were planning to wreak havoc on all our neighbors."

She laughed. "Oh, the dinner party. I'll have it catered with all kinds of goodies. There will be plenty to drink, don't you worry about that, and then when the alcohol is flowing, you and I will deviously steer the conversation in the direction of Cecily's death. We'll sit back watch the sparks fly. You know what they say, loose lips sink ships."

"I'm not sold on this idea. If one of them is a killer, this could be dangerous. You'd be taking a big risk," I said.

"You mean we'd be taking a big risk."

"I'm not sure I want to be here for this."

"You have to," Maggie said with a big smile. "We're partners. And bring that pretty young lady you've been seeing."

I could hear the bourbon calling my name from across the hall.

Here I come.

"I should be going," I said.

"Of course, dear. But when you think about it, you'll see I'm right."

"Then why do I sense this will go horribly wrong?"

"Don't worry. Just stick with me and follow my lead."

I rose from the sofa and Maggie added, "One more thing. I overheard Dennis threaten Cecily a few days before she died. It's bothered me ever since. I don't know if I should say."

"I think your partner has a right to know."

"I was going to mention it to the detectives, but I decided not to. You remember I told you Harold's opinion of the police."

"The kickbacks scheme for your restaurant's liquor license."

"I'm still carrying a grudge in Harold's honor. They have their investigation and we have ours."

"Maggie, tell me already," I said.

"I wasn't eavesdropping mind you, but I heard him through their door."

"That's a thick door," I said. "Where were you?"

"I'd slid my trash down the chute and heard him raise his voice."

"What did he say?"

"Remember when I told you earlier that the murderer is usually the spouse?"

I nodded. "Yeah."

"He told her that if she ever did it again, it would be the last time. And that's a direct quote."

"If she did what?" I asked.

"I didn't hear that part."

Chapter Nineteen

Life is simple, but we insist on complicating it. Not my words. Confucius expressed that thought 1500 years ago. My life was complicated and threatened by something the Chinese philosopher would never be able to explain.

I was part of a bewildering mystery—Shadows.

My former agent, JJ, must've been involved with them. It made sense. My novel was going nowhere. That changed when JJ jumped into the front seat, her foot planted on the accelerator. Suddenly, the wheels of progress spun at dizzying RPMs. Closed doors swung open for her. My manuscript was fast-tracked into publication.

At the time I labeled JJ a miracle worker.

Maggie's party plan came out of the blue. I recognized it for what it was—a bad idea. I also suspected that my opinion was irrelevant. Maggie was determined to make this happen. Even Harold couldn't have changed her mind.

I kept a watchful eye on the door next to my place as I crossed the hallway, hoping Dennis wouldn't show. I slipped the keycard into my door, and as if on cue, Dennis opened his. I practically dove into my condo.

My heart thumped as I neared the bourbon on the kitchen counter. I hadn't reached the stage where I'd drink from the bottle, though I was tempted at that moment. I resisted, grabbed a glass and poured an ounce or two, which I immediately gulped before pouring another. I added ice cubes to the second pour.

Then I remembered what I'd intended to do.

I went to the bedroom closet and saw the collection of baseball caps, knit caps, pairs of winter gloves and a solitary scarf, heaped together on the top shelf. Peeking from under the pile was what I was searching for.

I hauled out my laptop with the power cord still attached and carried the computer to the kitchen island where the glass of Maker's sat. I hadn't used the laptop in years but it made the trip with me when I moved to Wildwood Crest. It was, at the very least, an encouraging sign I might write again. Write what? A short story perhaps, a journal, a shopping list—something.

An electrical outlet was built into the side of the island. I plugged in the laptop and turned it on. And waited.

And waited.

The old Dell chugged to life with a struggle, sputtering like a dying coffee machine.

My attention focused on a file—*Shadow Sequel*. I tapped the dusty keys and the file sprung to life, revealing my old notes for a possible follow-up to the first novel. Back then, JJ was lukewarm about a possible sequel. However, I was riding high with the success of *Shadows* and assumed I should be moving forward with another book project. Reading those notes now was disconcerting.

Ideas were undeveloped; sentences were left unfinished; characters names sat there lifeless with nothing to do. I felt like I was visiting a grave.

I swirled the glass, allowing the ice to bounce around in the bourbon, and swallowed half the contents in one sip.

There was another file on the desktop, which also lay dead for years— *Book Review*. Not just any review of course, but THE book review, as published in The New York Times.

I hesitated before reading it, same as I did years ago when the review first made print. JJ had warned me to the hour when I'd be able to read it.

I remembered her phone call.

"Dave, are you sitting down?"

"I got up to answer the phone," I said.

"Get a cellphone. Everybody's got one."

"Why'd you call?" I asked.

"The New York Times. The New York Fucking Times is reviewing our book."

"That's good, right?"

"Good? It's colossal. Stupendous," she said.

"Unless I get a bad review."

"We won't."

"You say it like you're sure," I said.

"As sure as the sun will rise tomorrow."

"Uh-oh. The sun doesn't rise. The earth rotates."

She laughed. "Have I ever been wrong yet? I guarantee you a fabulous review."

"You've been right, so far."

"Spoken by a man who wonders if my streak is in jeopardy. You wound me, sir," she said in a dramatic voice.

"I just think—"

"Don't think," she said. "Don't—fucking—think. That's my job. I'm more than your agent. I'm your guru, your spiritual healer, your mother, your cosmic tour guide through this hostile universe."

"Wow. Does that even fit on a business card?" I asked.

"You wanna do something useful while we wait for the hoopla that goes with being a best-selling author?"

"What?"

"Lose a few pounds. Get that little chip on your front tooth taken care of. I want you photogenic. I want cameras to fall in love with you."

"Yes, mommy."

As JJ promised, the review was favorable, unbelievably favorable, written by Nellie Hagerstrom, whose name appeared below the bold 16-point headline, "Casting a Giant Shadow."

Following the review, events transpired rapidly. *Shadows* sold like gangbusters. Book-signing tours were arranged almost overnight. They assigned a publicist to travel with and keep me on schedule. Freddy was a glad-handing back-slapping ever-smiling sidekick. He was a decent guy.

I didn't like him.

I viewed the guy as an impediment to the fun I was entitled to. Being on the road, I experienced a freedom and exhilaration I hadn't felt since college. The thought crossed my mind that I'd mess things up again.

My concern was justified.

Despite the fact Marcy and I had an active sex life and despite my lofty opinion of her, despite all logic and sensibility, and despite knowing the ramifications of bad behavior, I did the worst possible thing for which I offer no excuse. I slept with every woman who was willing.

I was immature, disrespectful, crazed on fame. I was an idiot.

Freddy lost track of me as I ditched him at every opportunity. He left frantic messages at my hotel room, sounding like he'd been out running a four-minute mile.

I'd been out gallivanting.

Freddy squealed on me. We were on the Chicago leg when I got the call.

"Dave, this is JJ," the voice on the other end of my hotel room phone said.

Crap.

"It's nice to talk to you," I said. "The schedule is hectic but all's going well."

"Cut the shit," she said. "You're a fuckup."

"I—"

"If I get one more call from Freddy, I'm coming out there and cutting off your balls. Got that?"

I paused, thinking I might punch Freddy the Tattletale.

"Got that?" she screamed, almost piercing my eardrum.

"Got it," I said.

"There's a lot riding on this promotional tour, far beyond what your feeble little brain can fathom."

"I—"

"Quiet," JJ said. "New city—new slut. Your dick is now officially out of service till you get home. Speaking of, you do remember Marcy, don't you?"

"Don't go there," I cautioned.

"You're left-handed, yes?"

"Yes."

"That hand is now your girlfriend for the next few weeks. And stay out of the fucking bars. There's a goddam minibar in every room. Drink to your heart's content. Cue up a movie, tell Lefty to get to work, collapse on the bed, whatever. And when Freddy calls you in the mornings, jump out of bed, clean yourself up and put on your game face."

I started to answer before I realized she'd already hung up.

Sitting at the kitchen island with the computer screen staring back at me, I recalled the words, courtesy of the Grateful Dead,—"what a long strange trip it's been."

I flipped on the TV to catch up on the weather, anything to distract myself. The storm Brenda graduated from tropical-depression status to a hurricane, simmering off the east coast of Florida. A high-pressure system from the northwest stifled Brenda's progress, shoving it eastward where it could miss the coast entirely—or not.

My life was one big storm. In part, I blamed myself for my experiences with the Shadows, which led me to Rosewood, which led me to the Wildwoods, to Cecily and her sudden death.

It all started with the fucking book. JJ was to blame, also. There was still enough blame leftover for another culprit. Nellie.

I always wondered what she saw in my novel to give it such a sterling recommendation. I wrote the book. I liked my book—but didn't think it was nearly as good as Nellie wrote. Her enthusiastic review heaped so much praise on *Shadows* that the reading public was swayed into buying the book. If The New York Times loved it, then it must be good.

I Googled my early big fan.

Popping up on the screen first was Nelly, a rap singer. What the hell? The autofill feature suggested N-E-L-L-Y and I went along. Try again.

N-E-L-L-I-E H-A-G-E-R-S-T-R-O-M. No autofill this time. She was described as an author with one novel on her resume, *The Other World*.

I clicked on a link and read a sample portion. Her book was a scant 157-page novel about an invasion of extraterrestrials on a planet that may or may not have been Earth. There was one particular sentence in the synopsis that caught my eye, "In plain sight, the aliens walked among them."

The writing was proficient and book sales were modest. I surmised the novel garnered enough attention to land her this book-reviewing gig at The Times.

A photo of Nellie's face showed blondish hair sitting atop a somber expression.

I returned to the search-engine page and scanned the other options on display. There was a Wikipedia entry in her name. I assumed there would be one for me. Whether I would ever possess the nerve to read it would be another wonder for another day.

The site indicated that Nellie Hagerstrom self-published her book, and also identified her as a graduate of Seton Hall University, where I lasted almost two years before drifting off into the trembling hands of Shaky Sam.

Seton Hall.

Hmm.

Brad Araway?

Hmm.

Then I saw another entry that grabbed my attention. She was a founding partner of an organization called The Phantoms Society. Those words were boldly highlighted and when I clicked on them, I read this message, "The Phantoms Society is dedicated to the investigation of paranormal sightings." Then it listed four "founders" of which Nellie Hagerstrom received top billing.

The Phantoms Society. I wanted to learn more.

The final piece of relevant information regarding my favorite critic was this, "She currently resides in Delaware."

Curiosity. Even though it is said to have killed a cat, not everyone knew the punch line, which was that satisfaction brought it back.

I was more than curious.

Chapter Twenty

The internal operation of the eleven-story Crest Castle was of little concern to me. My basic needs were being met; the heat and air conditioning worked, and I didn't fall through the floor. Beyond that, I didn't worry about the nuts and bolts of keeping the tallest building in Wildwood Crest on its feet.

We had a Home Owners Association for that. It was comprised of too many members, one representing each floor, as though each were an individual state. Our seventh floor rep was Jason Bell.

Somewhere along the way, Jason and I went wrong. He wasn't crazy about me before I bumped into Kate on the boardwalk. Afterwards, I sensed a deeper undercurrent of resentment. The man spent so much time maintaining the pier rides I speculated he'd been affected by the well-known corrosive properties of salt air.

An impromptu HOA meeting was scheduled for today. I didn't attend past residents-invited condo meetings. A few were held each year and I skipped every one.

However, this time was different. Maggie, always in the know, spilled the beans and told me about the guest speakers.

My phone rang and the caller ID indicated it was my favorite news reporter.

"Keira?"

"Hi David, how are you?"

"Now that you're on the phone, pretty darn good. Come on over and bring a bottle or two of wine."

"Yesterday you wanted me to bring a toaster. What is this? I have to bring something every time?"

"Forget the wine, just bring you," I said.

"I want to talk about Cecily's death."

"What about it?"

"I have a cousin who works at the police department. I called him asking for information regarding the coroner's report."

"Really? I wouldn't think he'd be allowed to say anything," I said.

"He's not. Greg and I have been like brother and sister all our lives.

We'd tell each other about childhood sweethearts. He held my hand through my divorce."

"Sounds like a good man."

"He is. He's also the Public Information Officer for the department."

"But he can't tell you anything, right?"

"Right," she said.

"But he told you something."

"That's why I'm calling."

I scanned the kitchen, hoping the bottle of Maker's was in reach. It was currently in hiding.

"Hang on a second," I said.

"Uh, okay."

I laid the handset on the island and opened a cabinet door.

Ah, there you are.

I pulled the bottle down and placed it on the granite counter. I heard a distant tinny voice coming from the phone. I picked it up. "Did you just say something?"

"Yes, what are you doing?" Keira asked.

"I'm getting out the Maker's."

"You need a drink? Now?"

"Why not?" I asked.

"Seems odd to me—you needing a drink in the middle of a phone conversation with me."

"It's not a big deal. I'll wait till we're done."

I heard her take a deep breath. "Maybe it's me," she said. "This could be the wrong time to raise a red flag about your drinking. Never mind, I'll drop the subject."

"You're not saying I drink too much?" I asked.

"I'm not saying it—yet."

"Let's talk about your cousin," I said.

"I was before you ran to the bourbon."

"I tried to train it to run to me, but no luck."

She hesitated. "This isn't a joking matter. My ex was an alcoholic. I'll never go through that again. He scared me."

"I'm sorry to hear that."

With my free hand, I lifted the bottle and slid it back into the cabinet.

"Tell me what your cousin had to say."

"Oh, okay," she said. "At first he's like no comment, which is typical for him until I push a little."

"Then what?"

"You can't tell anyone. Swear?"

"Swear."

"The coroner's report says this is a homicide."

"I kinda figured," I said.

"The two detectives are assuming Cecily knew her attacker and they're proceeding from that premise. Thus, they're focused on your building, on your floor."

"It could've been anyone from anywhere," I said.

"Not likely in the off-season, especially at night. They're pretty certain Cecily went willingly."

"How did she die?" I asked.

"He wouldn't say. Our cousin bond extends only so far. Information will be released to the public in a few days. They'll word it carefully without any mention as to the specific cause of death. But …"

She stopped talking.

"You going to finish that sentence?" I asked.

"Some in the department are looking at you for this."

My heart skipped a few beats. "For killing Cecily?"

"Greg said it as a caution. You know, to be careful if I'm dating you," she said.

"Suddenly I don't like your cousin as much."

"He's being protective. Forget that. The point for us is that you're a suspect. You being with her the night before is reason enough. Then, of course, lying to the detectives didn't help."

"It wasn't exactly a lie," I said.

"Let's not revisit that again. You have to be careful with those two. Be honest and don't be cocky."

"I like the way you say cocky."

"Settle down," she said. "David, one of your neighbors is a murderer. You think it's her husband?"

"Maybe."

"You're living right next door to him. That's creepy."

"Does that mean no more visits, no toasters?" I asked.

"I'm not going away, but I am concerned. I don't want anything to happen to you."

"Don't worry," I said. "Even if Dennis killed Cecily, that doesn't mean he'd want to kill me."

"It means exactly that. The Halloween party is still fresh in my mind, too. He made a beeline for you, practically foaming at the mouth. I'm glad he wasn't holding a gun."

Me, too.

"He's been okay since," I said.

"Really? Have you spoken with him?"

"Um—not in words."

She grunted. "What else is there?"

"Fair point," I said. "I'm going to a condo meeting on building security this afternoon."

"Good. Listen carefully and sit by yourself. I don't trust anyone."

"I'll sit with Maggie."

"One more thing. Can I ask you for a favor?" she said.

"Sure."

"Leave that bourbon alone for now."

"Will do."

"Let me know how the meeting goes," she added.

We hung up and I checked my watch. Time to head downstairs.

I arrived at the ballroom with an uneasy feeling. My gut expected the worst. Numerous folding chairs dotted the floor. I checked out the empty seats and selected one off by itself but Maggie wasn't having it.

"Dave," waved Maggie. "Over here, sit with us."

Huddled along with Maggie was the seventh-floor contingent—Vedra Zdenko, Nikolai Zdenko, Jason, Hot Rod, and to my dismay, Dennis Slade, who flashed a menacing grimace. The sensible alternative would be for me to bolt from the room.

Across the aisle, on the other side of the room, sitting quietly in the last row of seats were the guest speakers Maggie told me about, Detectives Cho and Faraday. I didn't see a notebook in Faraday's hands.

I approached my neighbors as Maggie sprang from her seat and grabbed my arm, dragging me to a chair next to hers. I sat on her left while Zdenko and Nikolai were seated on the opposite side. Hot Rod, Jason and Dennis formed a trio behind me.

"Hi guys," I said before taking my seat.

Dennis didn't say a word, didn't look at me. Hot Rod nodded as if uncertain who I was. We'd just spoken to each other at the party, not that he was in any condition then to recall it.

Jason said, "You're always out there walking and yet here you are in the same place. If you walked in a straight line you'd be passing through South Carolina about now."

"Shouldn't you be up there sitting with the other board members?"

"Always the wise guy," he said, making his way to the front table where the other HOA reps were sitting.

"Mr. Dave," boomed Zdenko's voice alongside Maggie. "Hello, and you know my brother, Nikolai."

Leaning forward, I smiled at Vedra Zdenko. "How about dropping the mister and just call me Dave."

"Yes, of course—Dave. And you call me V."

"Okay."

"I ask this before," he said.

I nodded.

"My name is Albanian," he added.

"Very cool."

Why did I start this?

"It means I am good worker and good friend."

"Suits you to a T," I said.

Zdenko said to his brother, "Is American expression."

Nikolai stared at me for a moment and shook his head.

The HOA president tapped a gavel on the tabletop and stood. "Attention, everyone. As you know, this is a special meeting to address the issue of security. For months now, the board members and I have been kicking around ideas to increase safety. We'll have something solid to propose in the coming weeks that hopefully won't add much to the monthly maintenance fees.

"First, however, we have a special visitor today, Detective Daiyu Cho, who would like to speak to us about security." He waved his hand. "Detective, would you like to join us up here?"

"No, sir. I don't have the loudest voice. I'll be better heard where I am," she said walking to the middle aisle. She wore brown slacks and a tan blazer buttoned over a pale yellow blouse.

"I am Detective Daiyu Cho with the Wildwood Crest Police Department. I am here with my partner, Detective Arthur Faraday."

Many in the crowd turned toward him. Out came the notebook.

Cho continued, "I want to thank Mr. Billings and the entire board for their long-standing invitation to attend one of your meetings. With the recent death of Cecily Slade, Detective Faraday and I thought this would be the appropriate time for us to visit. Regarding Mrs. Slade, the coroner's report is not yet conclusive, though we are proceeding as if the cause of death is suspicious."

That's not what Greg says.

"We applaud the steps your representatives are considering in the area of future safety and we want to add a few cautionary measures for the present circumstance."

Cho roamed the room, making eye contact with many of us, a crowd of perhaps forty year-round residents.

"We have placed our business cards on the table by the entrance. Take them with you, please. There are multiple phone numbers for you to use. There is always 9-1-1 for an emergency of course, but there is a separate number to better reach an intermediary for Detective Faraday or myself. Call that number if you see anything suspicious. We'll respond promptly. A vehicle you don't recognize, a stranger in the parking garage, a new face in the building, these are reasons to contact us. We can be discreet. We can also be effective."

Cho pointed to where I was seated. I was puzzled until I realized she wasn't pointing at me.

"Yes, Mr. Slade," Cho said.

Dennis got to his feet. "Detective, I have something to say."

This cannot be good.

"My wife was viciously attacked and—"

"Mr. Slade," Cho interrupted. "We don't know that as a fact."

"Maybe you don't, but I do. You're dragging your feet while Cecily's murderer is still loose."

I heard a chair slide back, and twisted my head to see Faraday coming to his feet, pocketing the notebook in his sports jacket.

Dennis must've heard the sound, too. He glanced to his side in time to see Faraday staring at him.

Dennis returned his focus to Cho. "Some maniac killed my wife and tossed her into the ocean like a piece of trash."

"That's enough, Mr. Slade," Faraday said while striding towards him.

Dennis held his ground. "You two have gotten nowhere, and now this nonsense. Watch for a strange car. A new face in the building you say. I say don't bother. Cecily was murdered—probably by someone sitting right here in this goddam room."

CHAPTER TWENTY-ONE

It was chilly on my balcony, standing there thinking about Nellie Hagerstrom.

From seven floors up, the Atlantic spread out like an endless blue-gray carpet rolling over the ocean floor. Standing there in a long-sleeved t-shirt, I was almost hypnotized by the cadenced rhythm of the waves sweeping against the sand. The early afternoon sun struggled with dirty clumps of ashen clouds, which were pushed by a southerly breeze.

My reverie didn't last as I adjusted my gaze from the partially-obscured sun to the asphalt walkway below where I detected movement. Bundled in drab clothing, hopping from left foot to right and back again, blowing the cold out of her hands, was Kate. She lifted her head and peered up at me, squinting against the reemerging sun.

"Mr. Farmer," she yelled, cupping her hands to her mouth. "It's still happening." She then checked the beach both north and south. "Could you come down, please?"

"I can barely hear you," I shouted.

"I'm still seeing them. Please come down."

I'd planned on taking a walk anyway so I pointed north and said, "I'll meet you outside the convention center in a half hour."

"What?"

"Convention center," I screamed. "Half hour."

"But Mr. Farmer, I'm—"

"Later."

"Alright." She lowered her head and shuffled away.

I wanted to get in touch with Nellie for a few reasons. We had things in common. My book for one. She was a dormant author with exactly one novel to her credit, same as me. Seton Hall was another bullet point.

Combining this with the mention of a Phantoms Club in the online bio, I felt a measure of urgency. If there was such a thing as a sixth sense, mine was stirring.

I called Keira.

"David, how was the HOA meeting?"

"Cho and Faraday were there."

"Oh, Greg didn't tell me that," Keira said.

"You're not the only one with contacts. You got your cousin; I got Maggie."

"Good. Between the two we got it covered."

"Speaking of Maggie, she wants to have a party for the seventh floor. Wanna go?"

"Is it somebody's birthday or something?" Keira asked.

"Maggie thinks she's in an Agatha Christie novel. She wants to flush out a killer, I kid you not."

"What are you talking about?"

"When I see you I'll explain," I said.

"Okay. Did the detectives talk to everyone?"

"Cho delivered a nifty little speech. She told us to be alert for any strangers."

"She didn't say Cecily was murdered, did she?" Keira asked.

"Not in those words. She kinda danced around it while Faraday sat quietly in the back—until Dennis accused us of murder. Then Faraday took a run at him."

"Oh my God. Dennis accused who of murder?"

"He didn't mention names but he meant me."

"That's terrible." she said. "I'm coming to see you. Want me to bring anything?"

"No. Are you still at the newspaper?"

"Yeah, why?"

"Feel like doing some investigative journalism?"

"Sure," she said.

"Remember that Nellie Hagerstrom person I mentioned?"

"The one who wrote the review."

"I want us to find her," I said.

"By us, you mean me?"

"Damn, you're good."

Keira laughed. "Why do you want to find her?"

"I owe the woman. She helped launch book sales and thanks to Nellie, I met you."

"How did you come to that conclusion?" Keira asked.

"Simple logic. Nellie tells the world my book is good—in the friggin' New York Times yet. I get famous for a while, get myself all screwed up, get divorced, move down here and meet you. Don't you think I should be grateful?"

"It's simple logic, I'll grant you that."

"Then do that reporter thing," I said. "Get an address, her phone number, her favorite color."

"I'm on it."

"Here's a head start. I read online she lives in Delaware and belonged to a group called the Phantoms Club in college. They apparently investigated the paranormal."

"After I find her, then what?" she asked.

She might know about the Shadows.

"I'm not sure yet. Let's just find her first."

"Got ya."

"One more thing," I said. "There's a lonely bottle of bourbon sitting in a cabinet all by itself with no one to talk to. I know just what to say to it."

She laughed. "You didn't have to tell me but I'm glad you did."

"I also have a frozen pizza from Acme. You coming by?"

"Of course. I'll bring whatever info I find regarding Nellie."

We hung up and I reached for the Maker's.

I sat in my favorite chair, clicked on the TV and took a sip. Then another.

I woke up in time to learn that Brenda was now a Tropical Storm, steering for the Carolinas and points north. I noticed the empty tumbler beside me on the end table, and past that, the dimming sky off the balcony. I glanced at my watch—almost four o'clock.

Kate.

I threw my hooded sweatshirt over my head and hurried to the elevator. The door opened but—I heard something—a voice? Maggie?

Music leaked from under Hot Rod's door. It was a litany of thumping and sputtering—rap.

However, that wasn't the sound I'd heard.

I knocked on Maggie's door. "Maggie?" I said. "You okay?"

I pressed the doorbell and could hear the chimes inside. "Maggie," I said, raising my voice. Nothing. I gripped the door handle but it was locked.

"What's wrong?" Vedra Zdenko said, entering from the stairwell. "I see you are ready to jog."

"I heard a strange sound from Maggie's condo. She didn't answer when I called her name."

Zdenko took a stride towards the door.

"It's locked," I said.

"I try," Zdenko offered. I thought he was going to employ a different tactic, maybe rip the handle apart, but instead he yelled, "Maggie, this is V. Open the door."

I wasn't sure he realized how loud he roared but I was pretty certain the seagulls outside the building scattered.

"Is not good. I call the manager, yes?" Zdenko asked.

I saw a gray blur along the inside bottom of Maggie's door.

"Get the manager here now. Can you break in?" I asked.

Another door opened behind us. Jason Bell stood in his entrance, his Australian bush hat clutched in his hand. "What the hell's going on out here? This crazy fucking music and you two screaming at the top of your lungs."

I went to answer but Zdenko beat me to it. "Dave say Maggie called for help."

"Call the manager," I said to Zdenko, "We need a key, pronto."

"I got one," Jason said. He ducked into his condo and seconds later emerged holding a key card. "Maggie's. She gave a spare to my wife in case." He inserted it and the LED light switched from red to green. Jason grabbed the door handle and pushed. We stepped inside.

There, partially collapsed on the beige carpet, her head propped against a plush sofa, lay Maggie, body twisted, hair disheveled, her pink robe rumpled.

My eyes caught a glimpse of a formless shape scurrying its way through the closed slider and then gliding beyond the balcony into the night.

"Maggie," Zdenko said, shoving Jason and me aside. He knelt on the floor beside her. "You okay?"

She opened her eyes as I moved closer. "I think so," she muttered.

Thank God.

I reached down for her, wedging my hand under her shoulder. "Let's get her on the sofa," I said to Zdenko.

We lifted as gently as possible. Once seated, Maggie brought her hands to her hair and began fussing with it. "I must look a sight," she said.

"You're fine," I said. "What happened?"

She craned her neck. "Where is it? Where is that accursed thing?"

It drifted into the night.

"There it is," she said, pointing toward the coffee table.

I turned quickly.

"That infernal vacuum cleaner," she said laughing. "It attacked me— or maybe I just tripped over the darn thing."

"You're okay, then?" Jason asked.

Maggie peeked over Zdenko's shoulder and said, "Oh, Jason. I didn't see you back there. My, my. Three gentlemen to the rescue. I'm a lucky lady, and embarrassed as all heck."

"I'll be heading out," Jason said. "I'm glad you're alright, Maggie."

"Thank you for helping," she said. After Jason left, Maggie added, "I feel foolish."

"I fall down, too," Zdenko said. "This happen yesterday. I drink the vodka."

Maggie laughed again.

"Maggie," Zdenko said, getting to his feet. "I make you tea?"

"Heavens no. You've done enough, thank you."

"I go now," Zdenko said. "I am happy you are fine."

As he walked out the door, Maggie whispered, "I wanted to talk to you alone."

"Sure."

"I don't quite know how to say this without you thinking I'm crazy, or senile."

"No way I'll think that," I said with a smile.

"Maybe you should sit down."

I sat next to her as she adjusted the robe, tugging it over her knees. "What did you want to say?" I asked.

"I saw—something."

Damn.

"Something?"

"I can't describe it. The—whatever it was—was watching me from over by the sliding door." She paused, and then continued, "I think I saw Harold. There, I said it. He—it—floated toward me. Then I fell over the dang vacuum. Thank goodness I didn't get a heart attack."

"Harold? Did you recognize a face?" I asked.

"It didn't have a face. It—oh, I can't be certain what I saw. Now I really feel foolish."

I patted her hand. "Can I tell you a secret?"

"Yes, please do," she said.

"From time to time I see things I can't explain. They're tricks of the eye. It happens to everyone regardless of age."

"To you?"

"Yeah, and I'm only twenty-one."

She chuckled. "You don't fool me. I hope you won't mind but I checked your age on my computer. You're thirty-seven."

"I feel like fifty-seven. Satchel Paige, the old time pitcher, said something like how old would you be if you didn't know how old you were? I'm pegging you at thirty-nine, like Jack Benny."

Maggie laughed. "You have a knack for saying the right things."

"I've gotten enough things wrong in my life."

"You might've been right about a trick of the eye. My Harold would never frighten me like that."

"I'm sure he wouldn't." I said.

"It was so nice of you and Mr. Zdenko and Jason to come to my rescue. It makes a gal feel safe."

"You would've been alright even if we hadn't shown up," I said, trying to believe it.

She nodded. "You're probably right. But, I have a question for you. How did you know?"

"How'd I know what?"

"That I fell. Did you just happen to be outside my door and hear me?"

"I was on my way—"

Kate!

Chapter Twenty-two

I left Maggie's condo and hurried to the elevator where I pushed the down button over and over as if that would speed it up.

As twilight gave way to the invading darkness, I hustled toward the convention center in a steady jog. I hit the boardwalk running as the few people wandering about exited via the wooden ramp. The cold ocean gusts helped shove them away.

I strained my eyes searching for Kate as I arrived at the building. She was nowhere in sight.

Something felt wrong.

"Kate," I yelled, standing at the building's glass entrance. I pulled on the doors but they were locked. "You here?"

I turned and scanned both directions on the boardwalk and listened. Nothing.

"Sorry I'm late," I said into the night.

To the right of the front entrance, a walkway stretched alongside the building to its rear. I peered down the long cement path and heard the rumble of the Atlantic.

"Kate?"

I wondered if she decided to use the public restroom.

I walked a few steps, glancing right to a view of the deserted beach and the distant Crest Castle reaching up into the half-moon darkness.

I continued to the back of the building and noticed something lying on the concrete floor. At first I thought it was a pile of clothes.

No, no.

I approached, dragging my feet like a man being lead to the gas chamber.

The body was wedged up against the side of the building. I lugged myself alongside my number one fan. I could now confirm this was indeed Kate. I hoped she was just asleep or unconscious. Crazy, the things I hoped.

"Kate?" I whispered again, crouching to her.

Kate's torso angled to the left, her face twisted in the opposite direction as though the head had received a command the rest of the body hadn't heard.

The reality set in. Kate came to me asking for help and received none.

I did this.

I stared into her face, which was flush against the concrete. Her mouth was open and a mottled blue-purple bruise covered her neck.

Since I didn't own a cellphone, I sprinted back to the boardwalk. A group of teenagers laughed and smoked in the adjacent parking lot. There were four boys, which meant four cell phones.

After a quick lesson, I phoned the police. Then I made another call.

One of the boys said, "Two calls, two bucks."

They all laughed.

"The police are on their way," I said, handing the phone back. "You'll need to stay here and wait."

"I ain't waitin'," the boy said.

"You'll be leaving the scene of a crime."

"What crime?"

"They'll tell you."

"We didn't do anything," the boy said.

"Maybe you saw who did."

A police car arrived and two officers headed in my direction.

"David Farmer, right?" one of them said.

"Yeah."

"I'm Officer Bronson. We met when you found that other body on the beach. Where's this body?"

"What body?" one of the boys said.

"You know these kids?" Bronson asked me.

"No, but they let me use a cellphone to call 9-1-1."

Bronson turned to his partner. "Keep them here. I'm going with Mr. Farmer."

I motioned to the walkway. "At the end."

I heard a buzz and Bronson spoke into the radio on his shoulder. "Yes, I just arrived. I'll be at the body in a moment." He hesitated. "Yes, ma'am," he nodded. "Yes, ma'am."

"That was Detective Cho and she asked that you wait here for her."

A familiar car pulled up near the parking lot railing. The horn honked. Tommy bounced out of the vehicle and trotted up to the boardwalk.

Tommy's hair spiked sideways from under his Phillies cap.

Bronson stood between me and Tommy. "Sir, what is your business here?" Bronson asked.

"He's my lawyer," I said.

Bronson pointed to his partner, "Goddard, no one leaves." Bronson headed onto the cement walkway.

"Thanks for coming," I said to Tommy.

He put his arm on my shoulder and we walked a few feet away. Sirens filled the night air as other police vehicles arrived.

"You said on the phone you found a dead body." Tommy said.

"Kate, that woman I told you about."

"Damn. Do you need a lawyer? 'Cause I can get you one."

"I don't think so," I said.

"Kate's the woman from the boardwalk; the one stalking you," Tommy said.

"She's not—wasn't a stalker. I should never have said that."

"You flipped out when she followed you to that restaurant."

"I overreacted," I said.

"Whatever. Can you tell how she died?"

"I think her neck was broken."

"Like Cecily," Tommy said. "And you found them both. That's a coincidence, right?"

"What the fuck's wrong with you?"

"Sorry," he said. "It was reflex. The cops will have an even more knee-jerk reaction. Maybe you should get a lawyer."

I noticed the Medical Examiner's van pull up and the same woman made her way to the boardwalk. Officer Bronson met her.

I heard Bronson say, "Looks like the same M.O. as the other one. I'm thinking—"

"Don't spoil the ending for me," she said. "Do you even know what M.O. stands for?"

Bronson stood silent as she walked away.

"No lawyer," I whispered to Tommy.

"We'll table that for now. Those detectives are going to ask what you've been doing for the last few hours."

"Let's see, watching TV, drinking, napping and, oh yeah, picking Maggie up off the floor."

"What the hell?" he said.

Daiyu Cho arrived at that moment and crossed to Bronson. They whispered to each other as she glanced in my direction.

She thrust her hands in her navy-colored peacoat and moved over to me.

"Mr. Farmer," she said. "Let's take a walk, please."

I stepped in behind her as did Tommy.

"Not you." She turned with her finger poised like a dagger at my friend.

"That's Thomas—" I started to say.

"He stays," Cho said. "Now, come with me."

As I walked alongside the detective, I noticed for the first time that I was a head taller than she was. I guessed she'd been enjoying a quiet night at home when she received the report. Her hair wasn't as neatly combed and the wind did its best to tangle it. Instead of her normal business attire, she wore blue jeans and a pair of white sneakers. Her coat mostly obscured a yellow sweatshirt.

We headed slowly on the walkway, towards the ocean, towards Kate.

"Who was that back there in the baseball cap, your lawyer?" she asked.

"A friend. Why, do I need a lawyer?"

"Have you done anything to warrant a lawyer?"

"No, I haven't," I said, as we reached the crime scene. Caution tape was in place and a chalk outline bordered Kate's body.

"Wait here, please," Cho said to me, ducking under the tape.

The M.E. was kneeling beside Kate's body. Cho walked around Kate, which caused the M.E. to look up.

"Hi, Vera," Cho said.

"Oh, Detective Cho. Nasty night for this business."

Cho nodded as she removed a baton-like object from her coat pocket. "Would you mind?" she asked.

"I already did that but go ahead."

Cho gently leveraged the torso, and raised the legs, enough for her to peek under. "Thank you, Vera. I'll touch base with you later."

"You know how to reach me," the M.E. said. She got to her feet, smoothing out her lab coat. "Who is this man with you?"

"David Farmer. He found the body."

"Same guy?" the M. E. asked.

"Same."

Cho asked me, "Mr. Farmer, did you touch the body at all?"

"No."

She looked at the tiny group gathered a few feet away. "Officer Bronson, escort Mr. Farmer to the front of the building and stay with him."

Bronson touched my elbow as Cho added, "Mr. Farmer, please wait for me there. I'll be along shortly."

"Sure," I said, taking one last glance at Kate, who should be home relaxing on this chilly night. However, thanks to me, she lay dead surrounded by strangers.

Tommy approached me as Bronson and I returned to the boardwalk.

"Everything okay?" Tommy asked.

"Nothing is okay."

"I've been thinking about this. I know a good lawyer who owes me a favor."

I shook my head as Cho was suddenly standing next to me.

"Give us a moment," Cho said to Tommy, who backed away.

Cho watched him and then shifted her attention to me. "You knew this woman quite well, I take it."

"Why do you say that?"

"I saw you cringe when I moved her body," Cho said.

"I met her a few days ago. She read my book and recognized me."

"And what's the extent of your relationship?"

"There is no relationship," I said.

"What's her name?"

"She told me Kate. I don't know anything else, her last name, nothing."

"I see." Cho hesitated. "Your friend over there is worried about you. He keeps staring at us. Do you think he'd be upset if we took a ride together?"

"I don't know about him but I might get upset."

She smiled. "It's nothing for you to worry about and strictly voluntary."

"Am I getting the third degree?"

"Pardon?"

"The one-way-mirror thing at the police station and the good-cop bad-cop routine. I'm casting your partner in the bad-cop role."

Cho laughed. "No one falls for that anymore. I had something else in mind."

"Like what?" I asked.

"Tell me, Mr. Farmer. Do you like cheesecake?"

Chapter Twenty-three

Detective Cho didn't say where she was taking me. At least I wasn't wearing handcuffs.

We headed north in Cho's white Mini Cooper as she kept her eyes focused straight ahead.

"Where are we going?" I asked.

"There's a diner in North Wildwood that serves great cheesecake with strawberry sauce. Sound good?"

"Um, sure, sounds fine. No offense, Detective, but I thought you'd be in a larger vehicle, an SUV for instance."

We've got a department-issued Ford Explorer, which my partner has at the moment."

When we entered the diner, Cho whispered to the hostess and she guided us to the last booth in the far corner, near the back door.

Cho removed her coat and slid it across her seat cushion. "It's always warm in here," she said. "I took the liberty of ordering for both of us. You drink coffee, yes?"

I nodded.

The waitress brought the coffees and Cho tore apart a Splenda packet and dumped in the contents. I opened a creamer and poured it in mine.

I gazed out the window and saw a dumpster sitting behind the outdoor stairs at the edge of the parking lot.

"Detective, why are we here?"

"Don't you like it here?"

"Well, other than we're one foot out the door, I guess it's okay."

"Mr. Farmer, do you believe in coincidences?"

"Who doesn't?" I asked.

Cho laughed. "Detective Faraday says they're too coincidental to be believed."

"You're saying this because I found the two bodies."

"And you knew both of them."

"You think I had something to do with their deaths?" I asked.

"Not necessarily."

"You're either thinking it or you're not." I slid out from the booth. "I'm going home."

"Please sit, Mr. Farmer."

"Why?"

She smiled. "It's a very long walk."

I sat back down. "When I say we're done, we're done, right?"

"Yes, sir."

The waitress approached carrying hunks of cheesecake that would've sated a Little League team.

"Enjoy," the waitress said.

"Yikes," I said, as the waitress walked away. "I might need a shovel for this."

"I like when the strawberry sauce is drizzled on the side." The detective picked up her fork and sunk it into the tip of the dessert. Cho sloshed the cake in the sauce and placed it in her mouth. "Delightful."

I sampled my slice without the sauce-dipping.

Cho stared at me for a moment. "Did you also sleep with Kate Bromwell?"

"No, I didn't. Bromwell was her last name?"

"You didn't know?"

"I told you on the boardwalk," I said.

"Oh yes, so you did."

"Like I said, there was no relationship. We met during one of my daily walks. She'd recognized me and waited for me to come along. At first, she just wanted to meet me, tell me how much she enjoyed my book, how it scared her. But then Kate said she was being followed."

"By whom?" Cho asked.

"I'm not certain it's even true."

"Why do you say that?"

I glanced around the diner. "They don't serve liquor here, do they?"

"No."

I took a sip of my coffee. "Kate came to me this afternoon. I stood on the balcony and she shouted up, saying she was still being followed. She asked me to come down."

"Did you?"

"I was in the middle of something," I said. "I told her I'd meet her by the convention center. Then—I forgot." I lowered my head. "By the time I remembered it was too late."

"May I ask what were you in the middle of?"

"I was reading news articles on the computer. On my way out I stopped by Maggie Callahan's condo."

"Was anyone else there?"

"Jason Bell and Vedra Zdenko."

"What time was this?" Cho asked.

"Late afternoon."

"How late?"

"Maybe around four," I said.

She nodded. "Mr. Farmer, are you writing a book now?"

"No," I said.

"It would be quite normal after that great success."

"Detective, I'm not working on a book. I don't intend to ever write one again."

"Why?"

I hesitated. "My marriage, my life went to hell."

She stared, watching, processing. Tommy had warned me about her.

Maybe I should talk to a lawyer.

"We almost done?" I asked.

"Anytime you want to leave I'll be happy to drive you home. Yet, I do think this informal discussion is helpful."

"To me or you?" I asked.

She poked at her cheesccake and glanced up at me. "You had doubts Miss Bromwell was being followed. Why?"

"She said my book frightened her. My book is about evil Shadows that terrified my main character. Kate may have confused reality with fiction."

"I have to read that book."

"It's in the bookshop in Cape May. Probably be the first one they sell in months."

She stabbed another forkful, chewing slowly. A minute passed before Cho said, "When you talked to Kate on the boardwalk, I understand that Mr. Bell joined in your discussion."

"Jason likes her. He doesn't like me."

"Do you think he was jealous?" Cho asked.

"I gave up trying to figure the guy out."

"A minute ago you said Kate came to you this afternoon and shouted up to your balcony. Was there anyone else who might have overheard?"

"Coulda been, I suppose. I didn't see anyone."

"Let me ask about Cecily Slade," Cho said.

"What about her?"

"Think back to that night when she was at your condo. Did she say anything about being followed?"

"No." Then I remembered. "Wait a second. Cecily mentioned she heard a noise in the stairwell."

"When?"

"She'd heard it before knocking on my door. I remember she even looked back over her shoulder before stepping inside."

"You just recalled that now?" Cho asked, raising her eyebrows.

"Yes."

"Every detail is important and the earlier the better."

"Detective, I want you to know that I'm innocent."

Cho nodded. "My partner and I hear that a lot."

I glanced at my watch. "Time to go," I said.

"Mr. Farmer, I'm curious about one more thing before I drive you home."

I held my breath bracing for the next words as she rose and buttoned her coat.

"You never mentioned if you liked the cheesecake."

Chapter Twenty-four

In the parking garage, I stumbled my way out of Cho's car.

"Careful, Mr. Farmer," she said.

"It's tougher getting out than in."

"My partner was in this car only one time. He crawled out."

"Goodnight," I said.

"Goodnight and thank you," Cho said before driving off.

As I stretched my muscles, I heard a voice. "What was that all about?"

"You scared me," I said.

Keira stood by the entrance to the building. "I called you. When you didn't answer I swung by the boardwalk thinking you might be out walking. I saw the police cars and stopped."

"Let's go inside," I said.

We kissed each other on the cheek and headed up in the elevator.

"I can't believe another woman was murdered," Keira said.

"I found the body."

"Tommy told me. David, this is so tragic for you." She hugged me as the elevator doors opened to my floor.

"Isn't that cozy?" said Dennis Slade.

"Good evening," I said.

"Yeah," he mumbled. "You two coming out of there?"

Keira and I stepped into the hallway; my hand stayed in contact with the door so it wouldn't close. After he was in I pulled my hand back but the door remained open. I saw his finger touching the button inside the elevator.

"I want to talk to you, Farmer."

"What about?" I said.

"You and Cecily."

Fuck.

"Not here, not now."

"Maybe you can fit me into your busy schedule." He pulled his hand back and the door shut.

"That was tense," Keira said.

"His talk with me will be worse."

We walked inside my condo and there it was—staring, teasing, enticing.

Maker's.

"I've gotta use the bathroom," Keira said, heading down my hallway.

I went in the other direction and opened the freezer. I had two ice cubes in the glass when Keira returned.

"For me?" she asked.

"Uh, yes."

"Pour yourself one, too."

"Good idea," I said.

Keira and I sat on the sofa.

"First things first," she said. "Tommy told me about the body. What a horrible thing for you. Tommy said it's the same woman you met on the boardwalk. He said she's a stalker."

"He's exaggerating, as usual."

"What were you doing when you found her?"

I groaned. "I hate to say this. I agreed to meet her by the convention center. She wanted to talk to me about someone following her."

"She was here?" Keira asked.

"She was outside yelling up at me."

"And what happened?"

"I fell asleep. When I woke up I went looking for her."

"Then you found her, called 9-1-1 and Tommy."

"Yeah."

"But you don't have a cellphone," she said.

"There were kids on the boardwalk."

"Good. Do you know how she died?"

"Based on what I saw—a broken neck, like Cecily."

Keira drank the last of her bourbon and placed the empty glass on a coaster. "And then you went where with Detective Cho? I called my cousin, Greg, and he said she didn't bring you to the station."

"She brought me to the Star Diner."

"Really. Did she read you your rights?"

"No. She said it was voluntary and I could stop at any time," I said.

"Tommy says you shouldn't have gone."

"Tommy. He's an expert on everything, I guess."

"What did she ask you?"

"Nothing much. How did I know Kate? What was I doing this afternoon? Do I believe in coincidences?"

"I don't like that question, not at all," Keira said. "She's saying you had something to do with both murders. Did you tell Cho someone was following Kate?"

"I did."

"Okay, good. That's the number one suspect. I wish we had a line on who it was."

Or what it was.

"I feel sorry for Kate," Keira added. "But let's learn something from this. If nothing else, don't go anywhere alone with Cho."

"I'm not stupid. I didn't say anything to incriminate myself."

She shook her head.

"What?" I asked.

"Tommy said Cho would play you."

"That's what he said, huh?"

"Actually he said she'd make mincemeat out of you."

"My buddy."

"Forget him," Keira said. "This is me talking. The detectives have a job to do. They care about only one thing and that's arresting someone— anyone for these murders."

"I get it."

"I hope so. Now, let's talk about your Nellie."

"Alright."

"She was easy to track down, though there isn't a huge amount of personal info available. You know about her book. She's not married. The most fascinating piece of information I found is that Phantoms Club you mentioned. It disbanded right after Nellie graduated from Seton Hall. Nellie and her four friends investigated paranormal incidents throughout the state.

"Cool," I said. "Google had her living in Delaware. Do you have an address?"

"I wouldn't be much of a reporter if I didn't. She lives by herself in a condo community across the bay in Lewes, near the ferry landing."

"I'm gonna call her."

"I figured," she said, handing me a piece of folded paper.

"You done good."

"One more thing, David. Nellie visited Cape May many years ago investigating a ghost sighting."

"Where?" I asked.

"The sources I checked weren't specific. I can dig further or ..."

"I can just ask her."

Chapter Twenty-five

There was no chance I'd sleep well last night, even with Keira at my side.

Kate's death affected me more than Cecily's. I failed Kate. That alone was more than enough reason to be anxious.

Then there was the news story I saw on TV while Keira slept.

"Hi, Sleepyhead," I said to Keira as she woke.

"Good morning," she said. "What's for breakfast?"

"You're funny."

"Oh, that's right. You don't believe in food."

"You can't complain. You never brought me a toaster."

"Wouldn't matter," she said. "I'd have to bring bread and something to spread on it."

The doorbell rang.

"What the hell," I said. "It's eight-thirty."

"Is that Mr. Zdenko again?"

"Better not be." I jumped into my jeans and tossed on a t-shirt while heading for the front entrance.

"I hope I didn't disturb you," Maggie said when I opened the door.

"No problem. I had to get up to see who was here anyway."

She hesitated a second before breaking into a grin. "That almost went over my head."

"I doubt if much gets by you. Would you like to come in?"

Say no.

"No, I have things to take care of, but thank you just the same. I do have a question. What are you doing tonight?"

"Nothing."

"Good. Remember I mentioned I wanted to host a dinner party at my place?"

"Yeah—a flush-out-the-killer party."

She put a finger to her lips. "Well, don't announce it to everyone." She peered over her shoulder. "Now it's even more important to do this, what with last night's—tragedy."

"How do you know about that?" I asked.

"That tall detective came by last evening interrupting *Murder She Wrote*. He asked if you were with me yesterday afternoon."

Crap.

"Of course, I told him you were," she added.

"Come on in. I think we should talk."

Keira shuffled barefoot from the bedroom. Her blouse was tucked into blue jeans though her hair was mussed.

"Hello, Mrs. Callahan," Keira said.

"Oh, good morning. I hope I wasn't disturbing anything."

"You're not," I said. "Maggie, this is my friend, Keira."

Maggie smiled at Keira. "It's lovely to meet you, dear. And call me Maggie. That way I won't feel so old."

"Will do. David, invite her in," Keira said.

"Why didn't I think of that?"

The two ladies followed me to the kitchen.

"David told me you're his favorite neighbor," Keira said.

"Well, he's my favorite."

"Glad that's settled. Anybody for a cup of coffee?" I asked.

Maggie spoke first. "That would be nice."

"Coming right up," I said. "Keira?"

"No thanks, but I could use some OJ," she said, opening the refrigerator. "Oh, I forgot. I will take coffee, after all."

I started the Keurig as Maggie sat on one of the stools at the island.

"Did Dave mention the dinner party I'm throwing for our neighbors?" Maggie asked Keira.

"He did. That's very generous of you."

Maggie smiled. "I'll bet he told you about my ulterior motive."

Keira glanced at me. I offered no help.

"It's okay, dear," Maggie said. "But it is our secret. And now with what happened last night …"

I looked at Keira. "Faraday paid her a visit to confirm my alibi."

"I'm not surprised."

"Maggie," I said. "Did Faraday ask if Zdenko and Jason were also there?"

"He certainly did, and he wasn't very subtle about it, either."

Maggie turned to Keira. "Did Dave also mention he picked me up off my floor yesterday?"

Keira scrunched her eyebrows. "No, he didn't."

"Silly me. I tripped over my vacuum cleaner. Suddenly, three gentlemen came to my rescue."

"You're alright?" Keira asked.

"I am, thank you. Though I may have discovered a new way to meet gentlemen without leaving my home." Maggie laughed.

"Coffee will be ready in a minute," I said to Maggie. "How do you take it?"

"Black is good. The way it was meant to be, my Harold used to say."

"The dinner party," I said. "Tonight? What if our neighbors can't make it?"

"I've dropped a couple of hints already, keeping my options open. I first wanted to make sure you both were available before making it official, and then I'd twist everyone else's arms."

"I'd love to come," Keira said.

"Go ahead and twist away. We're in," I added.

"Wonderful," Maggie said. "It'll be so much fun; don't you think so, Dave?"

"Fun? Yeah—that's just the word I was thinking."

"You're not worried I hope," Maggie said.

"It could get ugly."

"No, no. It only works like that in books and movies."

"And real life," I said.

"You won't have much to do. Just follow my lead."

"I'll try."

"I should be going now. I have so many things to attend to," Maggie said.

"What about your coffee?" I asked.

"I'll take a raincheck."

"Okay. By the way, are you inviting everyone on the floor?"

"Of course, dear."

As Maggie left, I thought about Dennis, his hatred of me for sleeping with Cecily followed by her gruesome death. I thought about Jason, the reserved-just-for-me snarl on his face, his jealousy of my non-relationship with Kate. I thought about Zdenko and his Shadow-appearance at my door. And there was Hot Rod, who barely knew me, whom I barely knew. What I did know, I didn't like.

This dinner party had disaster written all over it.

I inched over to the countertop and the cabinets. All I could think of was one tiny slug of Maker's—or maybe a big gulp.

As I opened the cabinet door, Keira said, "Get me some Cheerios, too."

I passed up the bourbon and pulled down the cereal box as she grabbed the milk out of the fridge.

"What are you thinking?" asked Keira.

"About what?"

"Maggie's dinner party. What did you think I meant?" She said with a smile.

"Just what you said."

"It might be fun," Keira said.

"It won't be. The find-a-killer concept is ridiculous. Maggie's playing with fire and I'm the one that'll get burned."

"Why do you say that?" Keira asked.

"I don't like being with my goofball neighbors, especially if one of them is a murderer. And I sure don't like the idea of provoking them— like prodding a snake with a stick."

"It'll be fine," Keira said.

"Think so? Dennis will be there. Remember his little trick with the punchbowl at the Halloween party? If I were you, I wouldn't hang too close to me. You might catch a glancing blow."

She opened the carton of milk, sniffed, and held it in front of her.

"You can pour this down the drain."

"Sorry."

"I didn't want cereal anyway," Keira said. "I get your apprehension about Maggie's dinner idea but I'll be there as your bodyguard."

"I'll need one."

Keira rose from the stool and crossed over to the other side of the island where I stood. She put her arms around my neck and kissed me on the lips.

"What was that for?" I asked.

"I feel so sorry for you. You found the two women, which is bad enough, but you've got the detectives breathing down your neck, and you've got a bunch of misfit neighbors."

And the fucking Shadows.

"Are you trying to make me feel better or worse?" I asked.

"How are you dealing with this?"

"Well, for one thing, I have a very nice lady friend who's always trying to comfort me."

Keira nodded. "She'll think of something."

"She'd better soon before things get worse."

"Are you expecting that?"

"I got up at three this morning, couldn't sleep, came out here, switched on the TV and caught a newsflash on CNN. My picture was on the screen."

"What?"

"They did a live feed from the boardwalk. They were too late for any real footage. It was dark and there were only a few cops milling around. I'm watching this with my mouth wide open, and then they show a stock photo of me from the good old days as the one who found the two bodies. I should sue fucking CNN."

"Did the newsperson say anything to implicate you?"

"Didn't have to. Linking my picture with the deaths is enough. You should call your cousin and find out who leaked this information."

Keira already had her cellphone on CNN's website. "Here's the article. The headline says, 'Famous Author Finds Second Body on Wildwood

Beach.'"

I opened the cabinet door and latched onto the Maker's.

Keira looked at me.

"Don't say anything," I said.

Chapter Twenty-six

Keira left for work, promising she'd be back at my place prior to the dinner party.

I needed to stretch my legs and dressed for the gray chill outside in a blue windbreaker, my trusty five-mile-walk sweatpants and well-worn sneakers.

Ever since Cecily died, I followed a self-imposed alert to stop, look and listen before leaving my condo. However, I entered the hallway at the worst possible moment—as Dennis left his condo.

I almost dove back inside. Too late. There we were side-by-side, both likely surprised by each other's presence.

"Farmer," he said. "I want to talk to you."

"I'm going for a walk."

"Go some other time."

Crap.

"Where do you want to do this?"

He pointed. "Your place."

I unlocked the door and headed to the kitchen with bourbon on my mind, as Dennis slumped onto one of the stools.

"Can I get you a drink?" I asked. "Cup of coffee?"

"This ain't a social visit." He leaned his ample body against the kitchen island, propping his elbows up on the granite, interlocking his fingers. The leather bomber jacket stayed zipped to his neck.

"You fucked my wife." Dennis said in a calm voice.

This was no time no time for excuses. "I apologize."

My apology served no good purpose. Cecily was gone, leaving him alone with my indiscretion and her infidelity.

"That punchbowl at the Halloween party, I wish I hadn't dropped it," he said. "I probably scared the hell out of everyone. If you were standing next to me I might've bashed you in the skull with the damn thing."

"I understand."

"Where was your understanding when it counted?"

"I wish—"

"You wish what? You wish you didn't think with your dick?"

The Maker's sat ready on the counter. "Dennis, can I pour you a bourbon?"

"I'm not drinking with you."

I left the bottle corked.

"Change your mind?" Dennis asked.

"I'm not in the mood."

"Don't tell me you have a conscience. I know your kind. See a pretty woman and think you're God's gift. Men like you don't care if she's married. You're a selfish bastard, aren't you?"

I didn't respond.

"Aren't you?" he repeated.

This was a dangerous street and I wanted to check both ways before stepping out into traffic. I could get flattened by a bus.

"I screwed up. I'm sorry."

"She came to you, didn't she?"

"Yes, she did."

"You're not the first, you know. Not by a long shot," he said. "There were others. There have always been others, wherever we've lived. She was a sex addict, Farmer—bet you didn't know that."

I shook my head.

"Yet, even with Cecily gone, I don't forgive her and I sure as hell don't forgive you."

"I don't blame you."

"You don't blame me? You don't fucking blame me?" he shouted.

Watch out—here comes that bus.

"That's rich," he continued. "You and her are to blame."

"Is this what you wanted to tell me?" I asked.

"You ain't nothing special. Don't think for one fucking moment that if you and her were together, that it wouldn't happen to you, too. Cecily couldn't help herself. That's the way she was—God have mercy on her soul. And God have mercy on me, too, and I know that it doesn't make any sense, but I still love her."

With those words, he rose from the stool and plodded to the front door where he turned to face me. "I think it would be a good idea if you and I stayed away from each other."

"I agree."

His head nodded faintly. Dennis walked out into the hallway and I heard him open the door to the stairwell.

I once saw a television clip of Lily Tomlin, the comedienne, and she remarked that things are going get a whole lot worse before they get worse. She was right.

Two murders apparently weren't enough on my plate. Nor the return of the Shadows. More horrors were yet to come. How did I know? I just did.

With hours on my hands before Maggie's party, I decided to call Nellie. I picked up the handset just as it rang. The caller ID displayed a name from my past.

Things were now officially worse.

"Hello," I said.

"My favorite ex-author," JJ replied. "The former number one thoroughbred in my stable."

"Someone left the barn door open. I got away years ago."

"It's time for you to come home, sweetheart."

"What do you want?" I asked.

"First, a little love, appreciation, respect."

"That's three things. Skip down to number four," I said.

"Fine. Be that way. I want you to write another book."

No way.

"You're not my agent anymore. I'm a free man."

"Free? You know that's not true," JJ said. "Not for either of us. We're getting back in the David Farmer business."

"I'm living a quiet life here and I don't want you fucking it up."

JJ laughed. "You are so full of shit. Quiet life. I saw you on the news—finding dead bodies. Your life's a mess."

"Whatever it is, I'm not letting you make it messier."

"You're seeing them again, aren't you?"

My heart almost stopped. "I'm done with them and I'm done with you."

"You couldn't possibly be that naïve," she said.

"Stay the hell out of my life. I'm warning you."

"Oh, stop already. I'm going to make you a superstar all over again whether you want it or not."

"I'm hanging up now," I said.

"Don't you dare or I'll be on your doorstep tomorrow."

"You don't even know where I live." As soon as the words left my mouth I sensed I was wrong. JJ was always plugged in every which way.

"When I do show up, I might not be alone."

"It was so much better when you and those fucking things were out of my life," I said. "I hoped never to hear your gravelly voice again."

"I tried to reach out to you before—before that bar incident in the city. Then, I intended to visit you in that facility. But it was so—so depressing. And once you were released, I tried to contact you again. You fell off the grid. You could have called me."

"I could've."

"Let's not talk about who should have done what," JJ said. "It's in the past. I want to talk about the future and get you working on a project or two."

"I'm not that person anymore."

"Sorry, babe. You're always going to be that person," she said. "The public wants a *Shadows* sequel and they'll need one. I've got a wildly successful agency here with a million-dollar view of the Reservoir in Central Park. Come up to the city and we'll do lunch at Tavern on the Green, my treat."

"No."

"You'd make a bundle of money."

I grimaced. "How did that work out for me the first time?"

"Made you rich and famous for one."

"Yeah, I'm still trying to recover."

JJ was silent for a few seconds. I heard a cigarette lighter click.

"Still smoking those long thin cigarettes?" I asked.

"My trademark."

"They're fucking gross."

"You're hostile. However, I could get you back on track. These murders are the perfect setup for us. At one time in New York we used to trip over dead bodies just heading to the local bodega. But Cape May? We are so lucky."

"You're not hearing me."

I heard her blow smoke. "I've got a scathingly brilliant plan," she said. "First, you write a true-life crime drama about the deaths. I have a delicious title ready to go but I'll keep you in suspense for now."

"Don't want to hear it."

"You're smack-dab in the middle of a fantastic story with a birds-eye view. Even I want to see what the hell's going on."

"You probably already know," I said.

"It's not them if that's what you're suggesting. You've got a flesh-and-blood serial killer on the loose. We could do this up so nice. I'll sell it to HBO. It'll be bigger than Game of Thrones. The world will be back at my—our feet. The David Farmer brand will be expanded to a new genre and the world will be ripe for your sequel to *Shadows*."

"No."

"Think about it."

"Okay. I just thought about it—no."

JJ laughed again. "Same old Farmer," she said. "I'm going to have to work on you."

Keira arrived for a pre-dinner drink. I broke open the bottle of cabernet she brought and we sat on the sofa. I poured us each a glass and placed the bottle on the coffee table.

Keira wore dark gray slacks with a long-sleeved purple blouse partially hidden by a light gray unbuttoned blazer.

"You look very stylish," I said.

"Thank you. Are you going like that?"

"Am I overdressed?"

"I wouldn't say that. Those are the same jeans you've been wearing for at least three days. Same sweatshirt. Same dirty sneaks."

"Hmm. I planned on changing. I guess I'll do that now." I hopped from the sofa. "I'll throw in a shower for free."

I retuned and spread my arms wide. "Ta-da."

Keira smiled up at me. "Much better," she said. "Blue Henley, nice. Clean white sneakers, good. Same jeans?"

"I like them, they like me."

She smiled. "That was nice of you to change."

I sat down next to her and sipped my wine. "Dennis Slade stopped by today."

"Here?"

"See that barstool on the right? That's where he sat. He told me just what he thought of me and Cecily."

"What did he say?" Keira asked.

"Basically that he still loves her and hates me. He did all the talking while I kept out of fist-swinging distance."

"Oh, my goodness. Did you resolve anything?"

"What could be resolved?" I said. "He told me to stay out of his way. He also said Cecily had been with other men. She was a sex addict."

"Oh. That's interesting."

"Why?"

"Sex addict," Keira said. "That adds a whole new angle to this. I bet we know something the detectives don't."

"You sound like Maggie."

"Her party should be very interesting." Keira swallowed a mouthful and lifted her near-empty wine glass. "Let me have some more of this."

I refilled both glasses from my seat.

"Don't get drunk," I told her. "I need my bodyguard to be in complete control of herself. You may have to spring into action."

"You mean to defend your honor at Maggie's?"

"That—or defame it later in my bedroom."

She jabbed me on the arm. "You have a wicked mind."

"You bring out the best in me."

She snickered. "Was that it with Dennis?"

"That's it," I said.

"Did you call Nellie?"

"I meant to but I got sidetracked."

"What do you plan on talking to her about?"

Shadows.

"What she's been up to," I said. "Small talk."

Keira leaned over and kissed me firmly. I felt a stirring in my groin. It would've been easy to ditch Maggie's party.

"Keira," I mumbled. "The party."

"Yeah, the party."

"We better get going, or we'll never go." I stood up, held out my hand and guided her to the door.

My alert system failed again. Keira and I walked into the hallway at the same moment Dennis did.

"We have to stop meeting like this," I said to him.

He flashed an angry scowl, which I read loud and clear.

Shut the fuck up, Farmer.

"Hi, Mr. Slade," Keira said.

"Hello. Was that you dressed as a clown at the Halloween party?"

"Yes, that was me," she said.

"I owe you an apology. I'm sure I frightened you with my outburst. That was disgraceful, but I was very upset with this guy and my wife's death."

"I understand, Mr. Slade. You have my sympathy."

"Thank you. This is your boyfriend I take it?"

She smiled.

He shifted his gaze to me, and then back to Keira. "You have my sympathies, too."

Chapter Twenty-seven

We were a mismatched trio entering Maggie's condo and I suspected she was delighted when we checked in together.

"It's so nice to see all of you," Maggie said.

She was decked out with a double strand of gray pearls, draped over a heavily-frilled white blouse. A dark blue skirt dipped below her knees settling inches above a pair of gray leather dress boots.

As I scanned the room I noticed Maggie had rounded up most of our neighbors. Except for an attractive black woman, whom I didn't recognize, the others were all residents. Hot Rod Jackson was tinkering with the stereo system, while that pretty woman stood alongside sipping from a wine glass.

Jason Bell slouched on the sofa, a tumbler lifted toward his mouth. He wore blue jeans sporting a blowout in his right knee and a green t-shirt with a brownish stain center square on his chest. Dennis sat two seat cushions to Jason's left, still in his leather jacket, a pilsner glass of beer in his hand.

Vedra Zdenko cozied up to Gail Montrose at the kitchen island. She perched on a barstool while he hovered over her. Zdenko resembled a bear emerging from hibernation, with his bulky gray sweater and his tangle of black, curly hair. If he leaned any farther he might fall in Gail's lap. I thought of her claim that Zdenko had peeked at her cleavage. Her green turtleneck sweater offered protection.

Absent from the festivities was Janice Bell. Maggie had said the woman was visiting her mother. I could not remember the last time I'd seen Jason's wife.

Our hostess, former restaurateur and current amateur detective, stocked her condo as though hosting a wedding reception, with clusters of food everywhere. Maggie must've had the caterers on standby ready to scramble. On the center coffee table they'd placed a mound of shrimp cocktail, which showed evidence of having been attacked. Side tables were weighed down with crab fingers, crackers, cheeses, and bacon-wrapped scallops.

When Maggie asked my drink preference, I said, "Do you have whiskey by any chance? On the rocks if you do."

She nodded. "I'll check."

I saw Jason staring in my direction, his balding head exposed as the Australian bush hat lay crammed on the sofa at his side.

Hot Rod Jackson walked over to the glass sliding door where he sunk both hands into the side pockets of his dark crimson sports jacket. He stood there alone staring out at the ocean. I knew very little about him and would normally keep it that way, but I reminded myself of Maggie's mission statement for the evening.

Time to mix and mingle.

"Nice party," I said, arriving at his side.

"I don't get it."

"Don't get what?"

"Whatever the hell this music s'posed to be. I almost shut the damn thing off."

"That's Bach, I think."

"What's Bach?" he asked.

"Johann Sebastian Bach. Classical music."

"Whatever. I hope we ain't gotta hear it all night."

The black woman, her hair pulled in tight cornrows, walked passed me and handed Hot Rod a snifter. "Here you go, baby," she said. A spicy odor of perfume drifted in her wake as she retraced her steps.

"Her name's Jetta," Hot Rod said. "Guess I shoulda introduced you."

"Next time."

"She's a money-spending machine. That gold dress she's got on—I paid for it. Cost like it's made a gold."

"She seems like a nice lady," I said.

"She ain't nice as all that." He glanced at his drink. "Hey, this stuff's pretty good. Know what it is?"

"I saw the bottle. You're drinking cognac."

"Hello, gentlemen," Maggie said, as she handed me a glass of what I hoped was whiskey on ice. "Especially for you," she said.

I smelled the contents. "Bourbon."

"Maker's Mark. I saw it sitting on your counter." She smiled and returned to the group.

Hot Rod tapped his glass to mine and downed a generous sip. "This cognac stuff is smooth, man. 'Course I been warmin' up in the bullpen, if ya know what I mean."

There are those who sip and those who gulp their drinks. He was not a sipper and I noticed Jetta kept a constant eye on him.

Time for chit-chat. "So, I'm guessing it was a thrill being a major leaguer," I said to the former second baseman for the Chicago White Sox.

"Guess so. I had one dynamite year, batted .307, and that's when I got the big contract. After that it was downhill. Suddenly I can't hit a curveball. They had to play me 'cause I was making serious dough and I could turn the double play. They pissed me off though when they started batting me ninth. Ninth! Then they brought up that fuckin' Dominican kid with hands like velvet. I was history."

"Too bad," I said.

He moved closer to me and whispered, "Hey man, you wanna know the best things about playing in the bigs? Drugs and pussy."

I checked the room hoping no one overheard him.

Then he added, "Don't get me wrong, I don't do that no more."

"No more pussy?"

"What? I get it. Man, you just screwin' with me."

Hot Rod bumped his fist against mine.

He continued, "Horny chicks in every town, know what I mean?"

"No. Maybe I should mingle a bit," I said. I started to turn away but he snagged my elbow.

"Yo, where ya goin' homie—I'm talkin' to my main man."

"Me? I've never been a main man before."

Hot Rod shook his head and laughed. "You got a crazy sense of humor."

"I try."

He took another mouthful of his drink and said, "I hear you're a book writer. Dude, that is cool."

"It was a long time ago."

"What was the book about?" he asked.

"Shadows. That was the title and that's what it was about."

"Shadows? For real? A whole book about them?"

"The whole book."

"And they paid you for that," he said. "You writin' about shadows and me with one good year and here we both are. Ain't that some shit?"

He startled me with his next comment, which he uttered so quietly I couldn't be certain I heard him right.

"What did you say?" I asked.

"Cecily read your book."

Keira ended a conversation with Maggie and moved a few steps in our direction. I waved her off with a shake of my hand. She veered away and sat on the chair near Dennis.

Good girl, take one for the team.

"Why did you mention Cecily and my book?" I asked

"'Cause man, she had a thing for you."

"How do you know?"

"I didn't hear it on the news. She told me. Exact words out of her mouth, which I didn't like at all, seein' as she was with me."

I wanted to grab my ten-speed and scoot out of town.

"Maybe you misunderstood," I said.

"I heard what I heard."

"When was this?"

"What? Like what day? I don't keep a diary. One night, few weeks ago." Then he leaned toward me and winked. "I know it was night 'cause that's when I do my best work."

Women came and went from Hot Rod's condo as though he was giving away free World Series tickets. Apparently, Cecily was one of his fans.

"You tapped that ass, didn't you?" he said.

"No."

"I just figgered, babe like that, lives next door, digs you. Yeah, it'd be natural you got a piece, that's all I'm sayin'."

"Never happened. Maybe you've had too much to drink."

"What the fuck? Why you gotta say that?" His raised voice had others shifting their attention towards us. I couldn't be sure who heard what, but the sheer volume of his voice produced a hush among the guests.

Just when I thought Hot Rod's short-lived friendship with me was over he flashed a wide grin and declared to everyone, "Ain't no thang, my bad. Me and Dave got us a friendly argument goin'. Anybody here know this guy's a Yankees fan? In Chicago, we hated 'em, always buyin' up the talent. Hey—why didn't those bastards lay out some bread for me?"

Jetta approached him and asked, "What's the matter, baby?"

"Ain't nothin' the matter. Go back where you were."

"I didn't mean to offend you," I said as Jetta headed to a chair.

"You okay. Yeah, one drink too many. Wouldn't be the first time."

I was about to free myself from this exchange when he whispered, "I know why she was murdered."

"Really?"

"That broad was horny as hell. She rolled in the hay with the wrong dude. I'll guaranfuckintee you that."

"Maybe."

"Ain't no maybe 'bout it. Jealousy, man. Guys do some bad shit when they get mixed up with the ladies. Get all possessive, ya know? They don't wanna share."

"You could be right."

"No shit I'm right."

He initiated a handshake by sliding his hand against mine and morphing it into a finger lock and fist punch, but I got confused three quarters through and tried to grab his hand. He snickered and walked away.

Keira arrived at my side.

I took her hand. "My mingling days are now officially over," I said.

"Why? What was that all about?"

"He thinks Cecily and I were lovers."

"He said that?"

"Not in those exact words. But yeah, he did."

"I don't like him," she said. "He was rude to both of us at the Halloween party."

"He was drunk."

"That doesn't make it okay."

"Five minutes ago, we were male bonding and things went to hell." I said. "He shared things I didn't need to know."

"Such as?"

"Baseball players get lots of pussy."

"Stop that."

"He said he slept with Cecily."

"Oh my God, poor Mr. Slade."

"You said that when I told you I slept with her."

Keira brushed strands of golden hair from her shoulder. "David, can I tell you something and you won't get mad?"

"Tell me first."

"Alright. You had a few drinks before you got here. Maybe you want to switch to soda."

"Is this the part where I get upset?"

"Are you?"

"Keira, you're watching out for me. I'm not used to that. Thank you."

She kissed me on the cheek. "You're something," she said.

"Or something else. Maggie made a generous pour so I'll nurse this drink for the rest of the night even though I see bad moons rising."

She reached for my hand. "You'll be fine. Relax."

I nodded my head. "As soon as the food is on the table let's eat and run. Then I'm going home and hide under the covers—hopefully with you."

"What are you afraid of?"

"Take a peek at Jason over there." She turned her head but I gripped her arm. "Don't make it so obvious," I said.

"What was I supposed to see?"

"That man looks ready to beat the shit out of me."

CHAPTER TWENTY-EIGHT

I was glad when Maggie clapped her hands for attention. Hot Rod Jackson's mention of the possibility Cecily and I slept together threw me for a loop. Who else suspected?

"Everyone, please. I'd like to say something," Maggie said, her face radiating a smile that could guide ships safely to port. "I have an announcement to make." She waited a couple of beats and mustered her most dramatic voice. "Let's eat!"

The dining room table offered tight quarters for our group. Folded name cards were in place. Maggie stood at the head and motioned for me to sit on the first chair to her right and Keira fell in alongside me. Things got dicey after that as Dennis sat on the other side of Keira.

Worse, however, was Jason sitting directly across from me with Gail next to him and then Jetta and Hot Rod. Zdenko occupied the far chair at the opposite end of the table from our hostess.

Maggie, still standing, said, "We're all neighbors yet I think we know virtually nothing about each other. We say hello in the hallway or when we get cooped up in that tiny elevator, but that's just being polite. So, I have a great idea. I'm going to introduce everyone and say a few words about each person here. This is exciting, isn't it?"

The group was silent as Maggie beamed at her guests.

"Now, now, no sad faces," she said. "I'll make this as painless as possible. Where should I begin?"

I slumped in my seat.

"David Farmer, this is your life," she said.

"Good grief," I muttered.

"Dave is a very famous author and was once featured on 60 Minutes. Have any of you read his bestselling novel, *The Other Side of Shadows*?"

Maggie butchered the title and I refrained from correcting her. This was Maggie's show—Maggie's rules.

A voice spoke up, "Actually, it was entitled *Shadows: The Other Side* and it was the number one book in the country for four months."

"Thank you, Gail," said Maggie, with a smile across her lips. "Sorry about that slip-up, Dave."

"No problem."

Maggie sipped her wine and put the glass back on the table. She looked at Keira.

I patted her leg. "Good luck, kid."

"And that most attractive woman next to Dave is Keira, his friend. I don't know much about Keira but I do know she's a newspaper reporter, so I guess we should mind our p's and q's. None of us wants to end up on page one."

"We're off the record," Keira said.

"Thank you, dear. Pardon me, Dennis, I'm skipping over you for now. Rest assured, like General MacArthur, I shall return." She then pointed to her left. "That's Doctor Gail Montrose and she's an oncologist at Cape Regional Hospital. She's a life-saving hero. We hardly ever get to see Gail since she's most always on duty."

"Or home sleeping," Gail said.

Maggie smiled. "This is Jason Bell, whose wife, Janice, is away visiting her mother. Jason is employed on the amusement piers. He's an excellent mechanic and keeps those thrilling rides in such good shape. Not only are they always freshly painted but thanks to Jason, the rollercoaster cars don't go whirling off into the ocean.

"And that very pretty woman is Jetta—my, what a lovely name. You're Rod's friend, aren't you?"

"You might say that," Jetta said.

"I'm sorry, hon, but I don't know a thing about you."

"Doesn't matter. I'm invisible."

"That can't be true, dear. Not as beautiful as you are."

Jetta peeked sideways at Hot Rod. "Trust me, some people look right through me."

Maggie hesitated and then resumed. "Next to her is our famous athlete, Hot Rod Jackson. He was a great baseball player with the Chicago White Sox. They would have never won the World Series without him."

I saw his smile vanish. "We didn't get to the Series."

"Oh my, that's a shame. Now, where was I? Yes, Vedra Zdenko, there at the far end of the table." She held up her hand as if shading her eyes from the sun. "Is that you down there?"

"Maggie, please, my name for all friends is V. Is the easy name to remember."

"Mr. … excuse me, V, was a real estate magnate. He's from Albania, not Albany like I first thought. I misunderstood your accent when we met. No matter, V had success in his home country where he bought homes, fixed them up and then resold them. They call it flipping. Is that the term?"

"You are, how Americans say, right in the target. But I have question for you, Maggie. I have accent?"

Everyone chuckled except for Jason who stared at me. I was tempted to wink, but stopped myself.

Maggie continued, "I hope no one thinks this is tedious and I'm almost finished as you can see. I saved Dennis for last. I think everyone knows Dennis recently lost his darling wife, Cecily. She was a wonderful woman, always so pleasant, and they loved each other very much. I don't know if Dennis will recall this, but years ago we had a conversation and he told me how he and Cecily first met. I don't think he would mind if I shared this.

"Dennis worked at the Fulton Fish Market in New York City. That was a back-breaking job, I'm sure. Cecily worked in an office building a few blocks away. They met on lunch at a hot dog stand one afternoon and the rest, as they say, is history. I do have the essence of this correct, don't I, Dennis?"

"It's like you were there," he said as Maggie sat down.

"Maggie," said Zdenko. "Is now your turn. You tell us about you."

"Well, I guess that's only fair. I'll give it a try. For those of you who don't know, I was married to a fine man, and just like our friend Dennis, I also lost my spouse. Harold and I owned a seafood restaurant in Cape May. My Harold was smart and, excuse an old woman for saying so; he was smart enough to take my advice. You may wonder about me today at my age, but back then my brain was sharp as a tack. They say behind every great man is a great woman." She paused and sipped from her water glass. "I loved my Harold." Maggie sat and her eyes glazed over. She inhaled and paused. "That's all I can say."

She then smiled and wagged her finger at Zdenko. "I blame you for this, V." She dabbed an eye with a napkin. "Now, shall we concentrate on the food?" Maggie nodded toward the kitchen.

The caterers brought out plates of salad.

I dreaded the direction Maggie would steer the conversation. I mulled whether to start a discussion about weather, or politics, or the beach replenishment project—anything to avoid the topic that Maggie introduced.

"Isn't it terrible about last night's death of that woman on the boardwalk?" she asked.

To my surprise Keira said, "Her name was Kate Bromwell. She was thirty-three and lived with her mother in Villas."

I slid my right leg sideways and tapped Keira's ankle.

"That's all I know," she said, popping a crouton into her mouth.

"This is supposed to be a resort area," said Jetta. "That's why Rod moved here."

"How do you know?" he asked.

"That's right, I forgot. I don't know a damn thing about nothing."

Jason said, "I find it interesting this is the second death in the same area found by the same person." He glared at me.

"You implying something?" I asked, as Keira touched my arm.

"I'm implying that you show up and people die."

"You've got the sequence wrong," I said. "They died first and then I found them. See the difference?"

Zdenko said, "I see difference. Jason, I do not like you saying this."

"Get real," Jason said.

"I say my opinion," Zdenko added.

Gail said, "I'm surprised at you, Jason. You don't know anything more than the rest of us. Yet here you are accusing—"

"I didn't accuse Farmer of anything. Guy's got a guilty conscience."

"You inferred his guilt—on purpose." Gail said. "You have no basis for that other than your dislike for him."

Thanks, Gail.

"Why are you defending this guy?"

Gail turned to him. "Wait for the facts. We don't know if there is a connection and we don't even know for certain they were both murdered."

Jason looked across the table. "How about you, Farmer, what do you think? Murders?"

"Why are you asking me?"

"You're the famous writer. You must have an idea."

"Let's talk about something else," said Maggie.

Hot Rod then spoke up. "Murder, pure and simple. That's it. This woman got killed right near where Cecily was. This kind of stuff ain't s'posed to happen here."

"That's what I was saying," Jetta said.

Hot Rod glanced at her. "I'm talkin' now. This Kate girl was on the pier at night, maybe she was meetin' someone. Then, that guy murders her. That's how this went down." Hot Rod pushed the salad dish aside and slid his elbows on the table. "What if the killer lives in this building?"

Maggie said, "Mr. Jackson, we don't know that."

Hot Rod asked, "Dennis, do you think your wife was murdered by someone she knew?"

Dennis rubbed his hand over his stubbled face. "Damn right she knew this guy."

"Are you sure?" asked Maggie.

"Certain of it. Detective Cho agrees with me. Someone Cecily knew broke her neck and threw her in the ocean. My wife was a smart woman. Cecily would never be walking on the boardwalk at night alone. She was meeting someone she knew, someone she trusted, and he killed her. Without a doubt in my mind, that other woman was killed by the same person who murdered my wife. Find someone who was friends with them both and you'll find the person who did this."

"My goodness," said Maggie, "that's a frightening thought."

Jason stared at me and said, "You knew Kay, didn't you?"

"Don't screw with me. I'd spoken to her a couple of times. A grand total of ten minutes."

"We should stop this," Maggie said. "It's not an appropriate topic to discuss in front of Dennis."

"I'm okay," Dennis said. "What happened to my wife is the most important thing to me. If anyone has any thoughts, I'd be interested in hearing them."

Not me.

The salad dishes were cleared and I asked, "What's for dinner?"

Jason laughed from across the table. "I have something to add."

Maggie tried to answer my question. "We're having surf and—"

"I saw Farmer on TV last night," Jason said.

CHAPTER TWENTY-NINE

Jason's statement that he'd seen my photo on TV didn't shock me. However, it bothered me. I anticipated someone might mention it. I hoped to be wrong.

I glanced around the table and saw everyone staring at me.

Zdenko asked, "Dave, you were on the TV?"

I took a swig of my watered-down bourbon. "For anyone who doesn't know, CNN ran my picture because I found Kate's body last night."

"But that doesn't mean anything," Maggie said. "You're always out walking or jogging up and down the boardwalk."

"Yeah, that must be the reason, because he's out there walking," Jason said. "It couldn't be anything else."

Keira said, "I don't like what you're suggesting, Mr. Bell."

"Careful he doesn't get pissed at you," he said.

"Be extra careful I don't get pissed at you," Keira said.

I touched Keira's hand. "Jason, if you have something to say—say it to me."

"I was Kay's friend. She had an unhealthy fascination with you. You and that stupid book of yours."

"I wanted to help her," I said.

"I don't trust you, and neither does Dennis."

Maggie said, "Friends, I don't like where this is going. We need to stop before this gets out of hand."

Zdenko said to me, "I do not understand. Jason thinks you kill these women?"

Jason responded quickly. "Think about it, Zdenko. Farmer finds Cecily's body. And then he gets all chummy with Kay and now he supposedly finds her body. Pretty big coincidence."

"Why do you call me Zdenko? I say call me V. And you should not say such things about Dave."

"Well—V," Jason said. "How many dead bodies did you ever find? I'll bet it's the same amount as the rest of us. None."

"Why would I kill Kate?" I asked.

"I'm not sure yet. But you were stalking her, from the moment you met her on the boardwalk. Kay told me she was being followed. There's something off about you, Farmer."

"Maybe it was you following her," I said.

Jason snickered. "You're a jerk."

"Here you are, a married man yet you found the time to know her well enough to call her Kay."

"You sonofabitch!" he shouted at me. "You killed Kay."

We both jumped up at the same time and tried to maneuver around Maggie, who also rose from her chair. I swung at him and my fist glanced Jason's shoulder. He cocked his fist but Hot Rod grabbed his arm from behind. Then, I was lifted off the floor and my chest felt as though squeezed by a boa constrictor. I was spun halfway around and dropped to my feet. Then Zdenko let go of me.

I turned back to Maggie. "You okay?" I asked. "I didn't get you, did I?"

"No, I'm fine."

"I apologize for my behavior," I said.

Keira held my hand, though I had no recollection of when she took it. "David, we should leave."

"Not yet."

Sometimes you do something you know is wrong. You do it anyway. When I threw my punch at Jason, I saw my fist drilling through his skull and exiting out his head's new back door. It was a pleasant image.

"Don't anyone leave, please," Maggie said. "We're going to have dinner together and enjoy the rest of the evening."

Zdenko still stood alongside me.

"Thanks," I said.

He patted my shoulder and headed to his chair.

I remained standing and waited for everyone to sit down. "I'm very sorry. I'm not used to being accused of murder." I then sat.

"I don't accept your apology," Jason said.

"It wasn't directed at you."

"Gentlemen, that's quite enough," Maggie said. "I won't have fists flying over my head again." She turned towards the kitchen. "I'm glad we didn't scare away the caterers."

The caterers brought steaks, lobster tails and bottles of wine to the table.

No one commented on the incident; no one was speaking at all—the wild scene from a moment ago replaced by an uneasy calm.

It didn't last.

Zdenko said to Jason, "You should talk with respect."

"Don't get bent out of shape." Jason said.

"What is this bend out of shape?" Zdenko asked.

Jetta answered. "He's afraid to make you mad."

"I don't want us talkin' 'bout this no more." said Hot Rod.

"I do," Jetta said.

"No, you don't," he said, raising his voice.

"I wish you wouldn't speak to me like that."

"Then don't talk stupid."

Jetta removed the napkin from her lap and folded it on the table. "You're lucky I'm a lady. Otherwise I might tell you to go fuck yourself— Rodney." She pushed back her chair and walked out the door.

Hot Rod picked up a knife and cut his steak. "Sorry, she gets bitchy," he said.

When I peeked at our hostess, I saw she was staring down at her plate—and not eating.

"Maggie," I said, "this food is delicious. The lobster is so sweet."

"Thank you. They're from The Lobster House."

We all ate in silence as I focused on developing an exit strategy. This amateur detective business proved to be punishing work.

No more mixing and mingling for me.

Hot Rod aided the cause by getting to his feet. "I gotta go see how the princess is doin'," he said on his way out.

"I have to leave, too," Gail said. "I'm due at the hospital early tomorrow. Maggie, you're a wonderful hostess. Too bad we weren't better guests."

Jason got up next. "I regret my part in this, Maggie. And Farmer, I'll see you around."

"Not if I can help it," I said.

"Doesn't anyone want dessert?" Maggie asked. "We have fresh-baked apple pie and vanilla ice cream."

"Like they say, I am full to here." Zdenko leveled his hand at throat height. "I go now."

"Then, take some pie with you, V." Maggie said.

"Okay. You twist the arm."

Maggie waved to the caterers. "Cut Mr. Zdenko a huge slice. He's a growing boy."

"Thank you, Maggie, for wonderful time. And Dave, I hope I did not break the rib."

"Even if you did, I've got plenty of good ones left." I said. "Thanks for saving me from myself."

"That is American expression I do not know."

"It means I screwed up."

"I try to remember." He accepted a plate from one of the catering staff and lumbered into the hallway.

Maggie said, "Well, that's good news for the rest of us. We get their shares."

"I'm sorry, Maggie. Some other time for dessert," I said.

"Oh. Then it's just us, Dennis."

"I need to hit the hay, Maggie. I'm beat," Dennis said.

As Keira and I arrived at the door, I noticed Dennis caught up with us. *Crap.*

Maggie stood in the doorway. "I hope you all enjoyed the food."

Keira said, "It was delicious. Thank you so much for including me."

"I'm sorry for the commotion," Maggie said. "I didn't expect this to happen."

I did.

"It wasn't your fault," Dennis said.

"I agree," I added. "Maggie, we'll talk soon."

Maggie closed the door to her condo and there we were again—just the three of us. I debated whether to grab Keira's hand and sprint down the hall to my condo. We could outrun Dennis.

"Jason had some interesting things to say," Dennis said.

"Interesting to whom?" I asked.

"Apparently not you. Could be he was making sense, though."

"He was talking nonsense," I said.

"I wonder."

If Dennis and Jason conveyed their suspicions to the detectives then it wasn't surprising Cho plied me with cheesecake. It would be the one-way mirror next.

Keira, Dennis and I walked down the hallway together.

I unlocked my door and wished myself inside. Home sweet home, scant seconds away.

Dennis moved closer to me. "I know you're mixed up in this somehow. We're going to settle this man-to-man one day."

Keira said, "Mr. Slade—"

I interrupted her. "Why don't you go inside."

"Alright, David," Keira said, and then stepped into my condo. I waited for her to shut the door.

"That sounded like a threat," I said to Dennis.

"You wanna hear a story?" he asked.

"Not really."

"I belonged to the Teamsters. We didn't settle personal disputes with talk. We'd hammer things out like men, maybe in an alley behind a tavern. Two of us would meet there and only one would come back. Catch my drift?"

"Cute story. Now I got one for you—one time a guy pissed me off and then he didn't anymore."

"Are you threatening me?" Dennis asked.

"There's a limit to my patience."

"You are fucking threatening me."

I opened my door and closed it behind me.

Chapter Thirty

After the debacle of Maggie's dinner party, I finished off the bottle of Maker's and headed to bed with Keira.

In the morning I tried to recall if I'd made love to her again but my memory failed. I didn't think it would be wise or prudent to ask her.

Keira suggested a change of scenery would be beneficial for us, for me.

If I had a bucket list, Atlantic City wouldn't crack the top 100. I'd seen enough bright lights in my life, enough empty glitz and phony glamour. Yet, I happily tagged along. After all, Keira had the car, the keys, the driver's license. She had it all.

The blackjack dealer stood with seventeen—house rules. My hand of eighteen won. Keira tapped my arm and I wasn't certain of the message. Was it a signal to quit while I was ahead or a way-to-go, Champ? This was my fifth winning hand in a row and the bettor's axiom preached you bet with a trend. So, regardless of her intent, I was playing again until I lost, and then likely a few more deals, which as I understood was the preferred method of gambling endorsed by all the casinos.

Keira liked to play the slots. On the ride up to AC she mentioned that the machines called to her when she walked past them. While most people might doubt that, I'd seen too much in my life to disregard it.

Keira nudged me again. "What time is it?"

I'd forgotten my watch but pulled back my sleeve and peeked at my wrist. "Nine-twenty," I said.

"Good, I thought it was later."

"Play some more slots," I said. "I'll come find you."

"What about your good luck charm?"

"Huh?"

"Me, silly. How will you win without me?"

"I don't want to win too much. I'd feel guilty if Caesar's had to close up shop because of me."

She wandered off toward a bank of penny slots.

Despite the sizable throng in the casino, I saw the two brothers standing out from the crowd like WWE wrestlers among high school kids. I crouched and tried to blend in with my fellow players.

"Is him—I told you!" boomed Zdenko's voice.

I looked up in time to see them approach. Clad in his shiny red leather jacket, Zdenko said, "Is great to see you tonight, so soon after last night, yes?"

"Great," I said.

"You know my brother, Nikolai." Zdenko edged up behind me, placing his bear-like paws on my shoulders. He squeezed them and I felt his fingers, strong as railroad spikes, kneading into my muscles.

Ouch.

I rotated towards Zdenko and he released his grip. From my seat, I extended my hand, which he swallowed in his.

Nikolai wore a brown corduroy sports coat over a blue turtleneck and faded jeans. He didn't offer his hand but nodded in my direction.

"You like my jacket?" Zdenko asked. "Very soft leather. Want to feel?"

"No, thanks," I said. "You have a thing for red, don't you?"

"Ah, red. It is to mean passion."

Nikolai laughed. "Or blood."

"It does not," said Zdenko to his brother. Then he turned to me and smiled. "This is surprise, meeting you now."

"Oh, yeah," I said.

"Is hot in here," he added, unbuttoning his jacket. A chunky gold chain flopped over his white velour shirt.

The dealer said to me, "Are you in or out?"

I scooped up my chips and tossed him one. "Out, thanks."

I leaned around Zdenko, trying to locate Keira while hoping not to see her just yet. I didn't want this to become a lopsided foursome and I planned to dump the brothers as soon as possible.

Nikolai caught on first. "You're not here alone," he said.

"I'm meeting someone."

"Who—do I know him?" Zdenko asked.

"Friend of mine." I stepped away from them but it wasn't going to be that easy.

"Your friend is late?" Zdenko asked.

I developed a spur-of-the-moment pretense. I stood on tiptoes and said, "I better go look—might be lost."

"Is casino. How he get lost?"

"It's a big place."

"Okay. We go with you," he said.

"Never mind. I'll wait a few minutes."

"Good." Zdenko pointed to a bar. "I drink beer."

He cupped my elbow and ushered me toward the bar. I'd have one drink with them and sneak off. Despite being a six-footer, I felt dwarfed by these two as they walked on either side of me. When we got to the bar I maneuvered myself so I wasn't sitting between them. Zdenko sat to my right and his brother alongside him.

"What brings you boys to AC?" I asked.

"We gamble," Zdenko said.

"Makes sense."

The bartender moved to us. "What'll it be, gents?"

I ordered Jack Daniels on the rocks while Zdenko and Nikolai both agreed on Guinness.

"In Albania we go to Tirana for casino," Zdenko said. "Is nothing like this—is small. No one gets lost."

"Tirana?" I asked.

"Our capital, big city, but not like American cities."

"I wouldn't have pegged you for a gambler."

"Pegged—ha! I know what that means. I am good on American expressions."

"You guys come here often?" I asked.

"Nikolai and me, we like poker. You play with us."

"Can't. Like I said, I'm meeting someone."

"Then we talk."

The bartender set us up and I downed my bourbon in two gulps.

"You are thirsty," Zdenko said.

"Thirsty, yeah, you're right." I motioned to my empty glass and the bartender reached for the bottle again.

Zdenko stared at the overhead TV. "Party was much fun, you think so?"

"I've had better times."

"Jason does not like you."

"How could you tell?" I asked.

He laughed. "Is a shame about our neighbor, Cecily, Mrs. Slade," he said.

"Sure is."

"I speak to the detectives, the tall guy and his Chinese partner."

"They have to speak to everyone who knew her," I said.

He turned to face me. "Jason and Dennis say the women are murdered."

"Why are you bringing this up?"

"They say it was you."

"I'm not talking about this," I said.

"But why they say that?"

"Dennis is grieving and Jason is—just Jason."

Zdenko wrapped his hand around the beer mug and swigged a healthy swig. "Ah, is good. Police in Albania always think worst. If you are dead they say you are murdered."

"Doesn't anyone ever die of natural causes over there?" I asked.

"Of course you make the joke. But police are suspicious like in my country."

"They'll figure things out."

"You were friend of Cecily, yes?" Zdenko asked.

"Not exactly friends."

"She was good woman. Was friendly to me. Friendly to you?"

"Sure."

"Maybe she was nice," added Nikolai. "But her husband, I don't like him."

"You say too much," said Zdenko. "It is better when you are quiet. So, be quiet."

Zdenko reached into his pants pocket and removed a handkerchief, which he swept across his brow. He looked at me. "Do not listen to him."

"Listen to who?"

The brothers whispered to each other.

"It is hot in here, we all walk outside," Zdenko said.

Nikolai lifted himself from the stool, stretching his arms in front of him, his hands locked together. I heard a few knuckles crack. "Yes, it's too hot."

"I've still got some of my drink left," I said.

I was the only one of our trio still seated when Nikolai reached over my shoulder and lifted my glass to his nose. "What is this?" he asked.

"Bourbon."

"Smells bad," he said. "Want me to finish it for you?"

No.

"Help yourself," I said.

He drained the glass in one swallow.

"It tastes worse than it smells," Nikolai said.

"Next time I'll order something you like."

"We go," Zdenko said, as they shuffled from the bar. "Fresh air is good."

I checked and couldn't locate Keira. I threw five dollars on the bar and followed the brothers toward the exit.

Stepping outside, I zipped up my windbreaker. The nighttime air was chilly but the lights of the casinos bathed the boardwalk in multi-colored warmth.

Zdenko patted his jacket pocket. "I need cigarette." He pulled out a pack and offered one to Nikolai.

Zdenko turned to me, "Smoke?"

"No."

He lit his brother's cigarette, then his own and said, "Smart, I hear is dangerous."

"The Surgeon General said it can kill you."

"Who is this General?" he asked.

"Some guy who worked for the government."

"These are special Russian cigarettes," Zdenko said "Very strong. Very good." He exhaled in satisfaction.

"You guys thought my bourbon smelled bad? Those things smell like you're sucking on sweat sox. Is this why you wanted to come outside—to smoke?"

"This is one thing I do not like about America," Zdenko said. "No place to smoke."

"There's smoking areas inside," I said.

Zdenko headed toward the alley between the casinos, and his brother followed.

"C'mon," Nikolai said to me.

They were ten feet in front and widening the gap. "Where are you guys going?" I asked.

Then I saw it.

The motion caught my right eye—the Shadow, materializing as a work-in-progress, half of nothing, yet moving above me. It floated from overhead to the casino marquee. In the next moment it dropped onto the boardwalk in front of me, standing between the two men and myself.

"Hey guys," I yelled.

Both men stopped and turned around, twenty feet ahead in the alleyway. They walked towards me and would intersect with the Shadow in a couple of seconds.

"What is that?" Zdenko asked.

I was stunned. "You see it, too?"

"Yes, but I am surprised to see one this late."

I looked at the Shadow, which wavered under the casino lights.

Zdenko said, "But we do not want the ride."

"What do you mean?" I asked.

"The rolling chairs they call them. This is late for any to be here. That man is too weak to push us, anyway."

I saw the man behind me, standing alongside the covered chair. "Anyone want a ride?" he asked.

"No, thanks," I said.

The residue of the Shadow faded into the moonlit night. I understood now. The brothers hadn't seen it. Of course, they hadn't. The Shadows were my private hell.

Zdenko elbowed his brother and Nikolai said, "Let's walk. We have something to show you."

Instead, I backed away from the alley, away from Zdenko and his brother—toward the door we'd exited from.

"That's my friend," I yelled, waving my hand in the direction of the casino entrance. "Gotta go. Sorry."

"Wait. We go with you," Zdenko shouted, as I reached the door first and hustled inside.. We go with you," Zdenko shouted, as I reached the door first and hustled inside.

Chapter Thirty-one

Keira drove me home from AC in the morning and went to visit her mother in North Wildwood. We agreed to meet later at my place.

I wasn't in my condo two minutes when the phone rang.

"Hello."

"Hi, Dave," Maggie said. "I called you yesterday but you were out and I didn't leave a message. I have to apologize again for that awful dinner party."

"I should be the one apologizing."

"No, the whole thing was my idea and I pushed you into helping. I don't know what I was thinking."

"Don't be too hard on yourself," I said. "I'm a big boy and I've seen worse."

"Then, you're not mad?"

"At you? Never."

"I'm relieved. No more detective work for me. I'll leave it to the real-life detectives and the Hollywood actors. Is Keira alright?"

"She's a rock, tough as they come," I said.

"I'm so glad. All that commotion and nothing to show for it. No confessions, no clues, except …"

"Except what?" I asked.

"Well, it's just interesting to see reactions the day after. Like Dennis, he stopped by to say it was a doozy of a party. Doozy was his word. Mr. Zdenko was also nice when he visited. Polite as always and we shared the leftover dessert. That man sure can put food away. He had two more slices of apple pie."

"Now you know what to get him for Christmas," I said.

"Mr. Jackson passed me in the hallway and said he didn't remember a thing. He did ask me if he was rude to Jetta because she was angry with him. I didn't want to say but he asked. I thought maybe he'd be upset, or remorseful, but he just kinda laughed."

"Did you hear from Jason?"

"Not a peep," she said.

"That's a good thing."

"I don't want anyone to be mad at me. My Harold always said I have a need to be liked."

"You are liked."

"As long as you're not angry, then I'm fine," she said just before we hung up.

It was late afternoon when I headed for the boardwalk. I made it as far as Curley's Fries, where I u-turned. I left the hardwood, and trudged on the beach, past the amusement piers, past the convention center. I turned my head away from the spot where Kate died.

The Crest Castle, a big fish in a little pond, blocked the remaining sunlight as I drew near. I entered the parking garage and smelled the cigarette smoke before I saw him.

"Hey you, where did you disappear to last night?"

He stood by the dumpster, smoking, and drinking from a beer bottle. A breeze ruffled his diminishing crop of gray hair. A wiry brush of dense stubble covered his face like Brillo.

"Oh, hi Nikolai. Last night, yeah, I was meeting a friend, remember?"

"Did you ever find him?"

"Yes I did."

"V will be glad to hear that. He thought you were hiding from us."

"Why would he think that?" I asked.

"I might've mentioned it to him."

Neither of us said anything for a few moments while he sucked deep drags on his black cigarette.

I gotta go," Nikolai said, stubbing out the butt on the cement floor of the garage. He then opened the door to a Range Rover, beer bottle in hand.

"It's against the law to drive with an open bottle of booze in your car." I said. "I wouldn't want you to get in any trouble."

He tipped the bottle to his mouth and guzzled the rest of the beer.

"Toss that," he said, handing me the empty.

Yes, sir.

I watched him pull out of the parking garage as I headed towards the elevator and the recyclables bin. I stumbled over a parking stanchion and fell to one knee.

"Shit." I noticed a rip in my favorite sweatpants. These were now garbage-bound. With a limp, I passed the parked cars and saw the Shadow. It sat on the hood of a pickup truck near the entrance to the elevator, a hint of legs dangling over the wheel well. Its featureless face appeared to be watching the ocean.

"What do you want?" I asked.

It didn't flinch.

I sensed this was the moment, the crossroads, an opportunity to confront them. I was destined to collide with Shadows at some point. I don't know how long I stood there, transfixed—determined to outlast it, force it to make the next move.

I heard a sound from behind me—a familiar noise, perhaps of shoes shuffling against rough pavement. However, when I spun my head, there was only the sight of the wide-open garage entrance giving way to the beach and the churning Atlantic.

I returned my gaze to the Shadow and saw it had dropped to the floor alongside the vehicle.

"What the …"

It slithered towards me.

I retreated a couple of steps. Its Shadow-arms reached for me. I moved back farther, brushing up against a metal beam when that noise from behind me returned.

Then my head exploded.

CHAPTER THIRTY-TWO

The Shadow spoke.

There were no lips to move, no voice to hear, but it spoke to me.

Come, it said. Follow me.

The Shadow World lay beyond The Great Darkness. I would learn about them. I would learn everything.

They were waiting for me.

"Those tubes look scary. Can David hear us?"

"We can't be sure."

I heard every word.

"As for the tubes, he needs the catheter for obvious reasons. This tube is for breathing and this one here is for intravenous nutrients."

"What's that one for, Dr. Montrose?"

"Please, call me Gail. We have something in common, you and me. We both like this guy."

"I'm glad you do. But, that other tube."

"We're dripping medicine to reduce the pressure on his brain."

"He doesn't even twitch or shift his body."

"You have to expect that."

"I'm worried."

"That's natural. His vital signs are good. This looks worse than it is. Dr. Patel assures me it's a low-grade coma and he should wake up soon."

No, I won't.

I reveled in the soft underbelly of the sky, above clouds that floated like popcorn below me. Then I flung myself loose.

A warm wind blew against my face. I was soaring, whirling, swooping. I dropped into a colony of seagulls, weaved my way in and out of their traffic, peeked down at the blue sparkling water and glided away from the sandy beach.

Free!

I could coast through a bed of clouds, outrace any bird, touch the sun, taste the freshness of raindrops, roll into loop-to-loops and figure-eights. I wondered why anyone would choose to be human, firmly glued to the ground, when they could be airborne above all the terra firma horrors.

I was content.

I was on a journey.

"What was he hit with?"

"Maybe a metal pipe or something like that. That's for the police to determine."

"Why would someone do that to David?"

"Robbery perhaps, though his wallet is right there in the drawer. You might want to hang onto it for him."

"No, Gail, not robbery. And whoever did this is still out there. I'm scared for him."

I have no fear.

Migratory birds flocked in formation, abandoning the cold for a distant warmth. I joined them for the thrill.

Where was that Shadow?

I veered off and drifted slowly downward, hung a right and caught a comforting breeze.

The Shadow cruised ahead in the distance. I increased my speed, though no manner of timekeeping existed here. I had a destination before me and all the time to arrive. I might reach the Shadow World today, tomorrow, or even yesterday.

There were secrets to reveal. The Shadow told me so.

The oceans below shimmered. They, too, had secrets.

I was going—

somewhere—

somewhere wonderful.

"How is he, Miss Donaldson?"

"Detective Cho, I didn't hear you come in."

"You were dozing, I believe."

"David's in a coma. They say he's going to wake up any moment."

"He looks serene, like he's having a sweet dream."

"I hope he is."

"Do you speak to him?"

"I've been talking to him nonstop—but nothing."

I hear a butterfly fluttering against the window.

Darling little creature.

Shouldn't you be leaving for a warmer clime?

"Such a shame."

"Detective, do you have any idea who did this?"

"We need to investigate further. I can tell you he was hit with a baseball bat."

"Oh my God."

"He's actually fortunate because the brunt of the impact was absorbed by a metal support beam he stood next to. As bad as this was, luckily it wasn't a direct blow. Otherwise…"

"How do you know it was a baseball bat?"

"It was recovered at the scene. The assailant must have panicked. The security guard showed up and the attacker ran off. Another hit would likely have been fatal."

"Did he see anything or hear anything else?"

"He was in the utility room when he heard the sound, likely the weapon connecting with the beam. The guard ran into the parking garage and heard footsteps running away. I'm sorry, Gail, but that's all I can confirm."

"What about the security cameras?"

"They're not in working order yet."

"If you have the weapon then you must have fingerprints."

"The attacker might have worn gloves."

The moon slipped away.

I continued on my mission. The Great Darkness, the portal to the Shadow World, my new home, lay ahead and the winds parted, allowing me to travel at hyper speed to the gateway.

The Shadow guided me upward. I watched the gray form blend into the camouflage of deep space. I climbed faster than any rocket and streaked across the dark void, chasing the Shadow.

To be one with the stars.

In that dark void, beyond any telescopic range, I saw the exquisite blackness rolling out before me.

Swallow me.

"David."

I want to be with them.

"David."

I heard something, drifting from an alternate universe. I accelerated, trying to escape the sound, which sapped my will. I couldn't be sure what it was but I sensed it was following me across the cosmos. Someone's voice?

The Shadow continued onward while I battled through the negative energy created by that sound.

Wait for me.

My wings tired. They had been invincible to the dangers of crossing the heavens. Now, wounded by a single voice, a single word.

"David."

I struggled in desperation—my efforts thwarted by a stronger counterforce. It was as if I had flown into a cluster of the most powerful storms.

I couldn't maintain my stamina.

The Shadow slowed and turned to me. This way, it said.

I descended through the atmosphere, gliding above the waters of the Atlantic, where the planet's mysteries were submerged under a dense blue veil.

When I saw the Shadow plunge into the sea I skimmed the surface hoping to discover whatever the ocean might reveal.

Tell me your secrets.

One thing I knew about secrets, you could bury them, but they always clawed their way out.

"Nurse. I saw his eyes blink."

"They opened?"

"Um, I think he's waking up."

"Mr. Farmer, are you with us?"

"David, it's me, Keira."

Sorry, but he's not here.

A foggy haze shrouded my memory. Something terrible had happened. I recalled an explosion—a stick of dynamite had been inserted into my brain and then detonated.

Dynamite? I should be dead.

"You're waking up now, Mr. Farmer."

In college, my roomie, Ed, smoked as much weed as the Colombian supply boats could transport. I wallowed in a constant state of second-hand smoke euphoria. I asked him why the drugs. Ed's answer was to quote F. Scott Fitzgerald, "His was a great sin who first invented consciousness. Let us lose it for a few hours."

Now I better understood those words, with my own tranquil non-existence in serious jeopardy of disruption. I longed for my new state-of-being to continue, continue for a glorious eternity.

I heard the voice repeat over and over again that name.

My eyes opened in reluctant increments until I was blinded by the overhead lights.

I closed my eyes.

Opened.

Closed.

My wings were worn-out, exhausted from the miraculous flight. I tried one last frantic maneuver to elude that voice, to discover all that the Shadows would reveal. They were waiting for me below the surface of the ocean. I dive-bombed into the water only to discover—

Down was up.

Wet was dry.

Death was life.

The sky turned white.

Not a sky—a ceiling.

I heard muffled voices and shifted my eyes as much as I could—enough to see Keira and Tommy. His arms were around her and they whispered to each other. He kissed her—maybe on the cheek. I blinked, blinked again, and they were still in an embrace.

"David." Keira pulled herself from Tommy and rushed to me. "You're awake, thank God." She sat on the side of the bed. "Tommy, go get the nurse," she shouted.

Keira bent over me and kissed the side of my mouth, avoiding the tubes. Tommy reentered the room. "You okay, buddy?" he asked from the foot of my bed.

I tried to process everything but it was too much, too soon.

"David, can you speak?" Keira asked.

I don't want to.

"David," said the voice that pulled me from my journey.

"What?"

"You're awake," she said.

"Where am I?"

"You're in the hospital."

"How long have I been here?"

"Last night and this morning."

Nurses hurried into the room. Keira and Tommy were ushered aside.

"What happened to me?" I tried to lift my head but a sharp pain invaded it.

"Mr. Farmer, lay still, please." A heavyset woman in rainbow-colored scrubs stood over me like Ali over Liston. She bent down, pressing her hands against my shoulders. "Don't try to get up. Dr. Montrose is just down the hall."

I closed my eyes.

The clouds were gone, the stars, the Shadow.

The secrets lost.

When I awoke again, Gail held a stethoscope against my chest. "Good, very good. I've got a call in to Dr. Patel. He should be here soon. In the meantime, I'm going to let your two friends stay for a few minutes. Then, I'll keep you company until your doctor arrives." She got up and touched Keira's arm. "Is that a deal?"

"Deal."

Keira wiped away her tears with a tissue as she returned to my side with Tommy.

"Do you remember anything?" she asked.

"What happened?"

"You got cracked on the noggin," Tommy said. "Someone tried to kill you."

Keira spun her head in his direction. "Tommy, I got this."

She turned back to me, sat on the edge of the bed and picked up my hand. "I don't know any other way to say this, but someone hit you on the back of your head with a baseball bat. It happened in your parking garage. You've been in a coma since they brought you in last night."

"Baseball bat?"

"Count yourself lucky," Tommy said.

Keira looked at him. "Tommy, please."

He flopped in a chair against the wall.

Keira said, "Detective Cho was here earlier. She thinks someone snuck up behind you. But you were apparently standing alongside a support beam when whoever it was took a swing at you. Instead of connecting flush—oh, that was hard to say—he must have hit a steel beam at the same time. So, thank God, it took most of the impact."

My memory returned in snapshots. The parking garage, someone speaking to me, a bottle of beer? A Shadow. A sound behind me.

Keira said, "I talked to you the whole time. I held your hand so tight I hope I didn't sprain any fingers."

I flexed my fingers and held them up. The heplock pinched the back of my hand. Keira gently returned it to the bed.

"You said Detective Cho was here?" I asked.

"Yes, and others. Tommy's been here with me. They think he's your brother. Maggie and Vedra Zdenko came together. And, oh, Dennis Slade stopped by. They were all stopped at the front desk."

"Dennis?"

"Yes. I went down to see him. I think he feels bad about the terrible things he said to you. And, naturally, Gail was in and out, helping to take care of you. Oh—and your agent called."

"Agent?"

"JJ she told me. She'd like you to call her back when you're feeling up to it."

That would be never.

I lifted my head again. "Tommy, you've been here the whole time?"

"We're best friends, aren't we?"

"Yeah."

"Keira phoned me and I came running," he said, getting up from his chair. "I'm glad you're back."

"Me too, I think."

Keira squeezed my hand. "Well, I'm glad."

Rejoining the conscious world was both good and bad.

I saw the positive side with vibrant clarity. The good was continuing my relationship with Keira. Her presence alone, sitting on my hospital bed, was more beneficial than any medicine they could shoot or drip into me. With Keira beside me, holding my hand, speaking in her soothing voice, I was no longer overwhelmed with the realization that someone tried to kill me.

Someone tried to kill me.

Oh, that was the bad.

Chapter Thirty-three

The following afternoon the hospital cleared me for release and Keira drove me home. We turned south onto Route 9 on the way to the pharmacy with my prescriptions.

"David, you're fortunate but the fact is you have a very dangerous enemy."

"Don't ruin my good mood," I said, pulling at the bandage on my head.

"Stop playing with that."

"I don't need the darn thing and it itches like hell."

"You can put up with it."

"I look like a war casualty with my head all wrapped. It's overkill," I said. "I've got a small wound in the back of my head. They didn't need to shave there, either."

"With what you've been through, this is what you're complaining about? A little patch of hair?"

"I like my hair."

"It'll grow back," she said. "And, in that bag, they gave you a smaller covering for when you start to heal."

I picked up the white plastic bag and glimpsed inside. A gauze-like dressing and a roll of white surgical tape were sitting on top of homecare instructions.

"As I was saying," Keira said. "We have to be careful. Someone tried to kill you, which means we watch what we do. No more biking all over the place."

"Yes, dear."

"Your balance is going to be off for one thing and I can drive you for another. But I'm more concerned about your attacker trying this again."

"Keira, there's no way I'm going to live in a bubble. The attack had nothing to do with my bike and it happened right where I live. I'll use caution but I'm living the rest of my life starting right now."

She punched me on my thigh. "You are stubborn."

"Keep both hands on the wheel," I said.

When we arrived inside my condo, Keira headed down the hallway. "I'm making your bed."

"Need help?" I asked.

"Relax, tiger."

I plopped on the sofa and assessed my situation. I had an array of horrors to consider. Murders, Shadows and JJ, a near-death experience, and the certainty this wasn't the end of my troubles. In the past, I ignored problems hoping they'd magically disappear. I looked the other way while JJ manipulated me. It was my pattern—to let the winds of misfortune blow me anywhere.

I couldn't allow that to happen again. Mark Twain said that if you wanted to change the future you had to change the present.

No time like now.

An ally would help—someone with Shadow experience. That requirement limited the roster of possibilities to JJ and—whom?

Other than my agent, I couldn't be certain who else knew about the Shadows, but I did have a guess—Nellie, my book reviewer. She'd come out of left field causing me to wonder if she was part of a grand scheme. JJ may have directed a behind-the-scenes production of bit players who never saw the big picture.

As an added clue, Nellie had formed the Phantoms Club in college and dealt with the paranormal. Thus, she offered experience. I added two plus two and hoped it came out four.

"Can I use your cell?"

"Sure. Who you calling?" Keira asked, handing me the phone.

"Nellie. The one who reviewed my book."

"Oh."

After Nellie answered, I introduced myself, she was quiet long enough for me to wonder if we were cut off.

"David Farmer, this is really you?" she finally said.

"It's me."

"I can't believe it."

"I'd like to see you."

"What, you don't say hi, how are you?"

Keira had been sitting on the loveseat but got up quickly, moved in front of me and whispered, "Ask her how she is—you're too abrupt."

Nellie asked, "Did you just say something?"

"No, my social coach told me I'm too abrupt."

Keira muttered, "You stink at this."

"Nellie, let me start all over. My friend, Keira, is here with me. That's the voice you heard in the background. How are you doing?"

"I could tell you I'm fine, but honestly, things could be a whole lot better. I live with Casper, my overweight cat, in a cramped apartment. My hair has gone white. I smoke too much and have sex too seldom."

"Oh, sorry to hear," I said.

"You asked."

"As for me, I live in Wildwood Crest. I want to talk to you about a great business opportunity."

Keira scrunched her eyebrows, and walked back to the loveseat.

"What's this opportunity?" Nellie asked.

"Tell you when you get here."

"Why can't you tell me now?"

I glanced at Keira and saw her staring in my direction.

"I don't want to go into details on the phone but let's just say you and I would make a good writing team."

Nellie hesitated. "Is this on the level? You are the author of *Shadows*, right?"

"That's me. And you wrote a rave review for The Times and I went on to milk the book until everything went to hell."

"Let's make sure I'm getting this. You're asking me to write—what—a book with you?"

"Yeah."

"Did you manage to save a few bucks from that first book to make this worth my while?"

"Very much so."

Nellie paused. "I guess it's worth looking into."

"Like I said, a big opportunity."

"Okay. I can take the Cape May ferry. The dock is practically at my doorstep."

"Good."

"I could walk on and you'd pick me up. Cheaper that way," she said.

"I don't have a car, do you?"

"An old van."

"You drive on and meet me at my condo, the Crest Castle on Ocean Avenue. Seventh floor. Number 7B. I'll alert the security guard. Can you come tonight?"

"Who's paying for the ferry ride?"

"Me."

"This is crazy. Of course I'll come."

"What was that all about?" Keira asked when I handed back the phone.

"You remember in the hospital when you told me my agent called? She wants me to write a book about the murders."

"And you agreed?"

"I'm considering it. Nellie can help me."

"I don't understand," Keira said. "You never mentioned you're even interested in writing another book. And I have no idea why you want this Nellie person to write it with you."

"She's a good writer."

"You invited her here tonight."

"Yeah."

"Why can't this wait? You're supposed to be recovering."

"You don't know JJ," I said.

"I know you need rest."

"I feel fine, except for this itchy bandage. Anyway, Nellie might not even show."

"Well, I'm supposed to be with Mom tonight," Keira said. "She's been a bit under the weather. But I can stay with you, or I'll just stop by later."

"No need to."

"I can bring food," she said.

"I've got frozen pizzas I can microwave. For now, I need to lie down."

"Okay, sure. Call me when you wake up, whether Nellie is there or not."

We kissed and Keira waved as she stepped into the hallway.

I was hungry and could use a drink, fresh air, but also wanted to meet Nellie without the possibility of Keira interrupting us. Any talk of Shadows had to be done away from her. We were too early in our relationship to give her reason to doubt my sanity.

I'd been thinking about Nellie for days and the attack on me provided a greater sense of urgency. I unraveled the bandage, crunched it up and dropped it in the bathroom wastebasket. I dug out the clean gauze and smaller dressing from the hospital bag and went to work.

I looked in the mirror. "It's showtime."

I picked up the handset and called Nellie.

"Hello," she said.

"Dave Farmer, again. Change of plans. Meet me tonight at the Crest Tavern on Pacific Avenue. GPS it. They have good food."

"Sure. I'm always up for a free meal."

"I checked the ferry schedule. Meet you around six. I'll already be there."

"So I recognize you—you still look like you did a few years ago?"

"No."

"Me neither."

I fished out my Exit Zero baseball cap from the closet and biked over to the restaurant. I had solid reasons for meeting with Nellie. She reviewed my novel with what I felt was unwarranted praise. I wanted to confirm it was *Shadow*-influenced. And, most importantly, assuming it was, maybe she had an idea how to fight them.

I sat at the bar with my bourbon waiting for Nellie to show.

I saw a dilapidated van pull into the side parking lot. I waved to Nellie when she walked in. She hadn't been joking about the white hair.

This could not be her.

Even though I never met the woman, I was amazed at her appearance. Nellie and I were both in our mid-thirties; however she looked twice as old. Her college yearbook photo, which I saw online, was of a confident young woman, her eyes wistful, the hint of a smile, an air of nonchalance and independence. This modern-day version didn't resemble the picture at all.

Her skeletal body offered a bony collection of sharp angles, which made her gait uneven as she walked toward me. Her black sweatshirt and blue jeans seemed flung on her coatrack frame, while Nellie's hollowed out cheekbones begged for food.

I slid off the barstool as she approached and I smelled the distinct aroma of tobacco.

"Dave Farmer, you have got to be shittin' me," she said, holding out her hand.

I was careful not to squeeze it too tight. I didn't want to harm the precious little flesh that draped her bones. "Hi—okay to call you Nellie?"

"You could call me Abigail, but that's not my name, so yeah, let's go with Nellie."

I removed a few singles from my wallet and laid them on the bar.

"This way," I said to Nellie, taking my drink and leading her to the last booth in the corner. I sat on the side against the back wall.

"You know, we're practically out on the street," Nellie said.

"So?"

"Are you in the Witness Protection Program or something?"

I smiled and motioned to the waitress.

"What can I getcha?" she asked.

"I'm good," I said, indicating my drink.

"Glass of water," Nellie said.

"You ordering food?" the waitress asked.

Nellie shook her head. "Not yet."

The waitress returned in a minute with the water and dropped a straw next to it.

"What have you been up to?" I asked Nellie.

"I told you the basics on the phone. Don't have any money. Don't have a job. Don't have a man. I know I don't look well. You think I'm ready for Social Security, don't you?"

I didn't answer.

She continued, "Not sure what to say, huh? I've got mirrors at home. But, I gotta say, you look good. You got that dimple thing going for you and your hair looks like a throwback to the sixties. You shouldn't try to hide it under the hat. And I can see you're in shape."

"Do you still write?" I asked.

"Seriously? I can't write for shit. You writing?"

"Afraid not," I said.

"That's a crying shame. You struck gold and didn't follow up. You could've written most anything and you'd have a built-in audience. Why didn't you?"

"So many reasons, so little time. For now I'm just going day-to-day."

"You mentioned you live in the Crest and it's a nice day-to-day place to call home. Since you made so much moola, I'm taking a shot that you're sitting smack dab on the Atlantic."

"I do live on the beach."

"Natch." She sipped her water through the straw. "Tastes funny," she said.

"You're in Jersey now—tainted water."

"Polluted water in New Jersey? Wouldn't expect anything else." She unwrapped her utensils and began scraping her fork with her index fingernail. "They got some taint on my fork, too." She placed the fork down and lifted her head. "Why did you call?"

"I have a question I've wanted to ask you for years."

Nellie leaned forward. "Bet I can guess what it is."

"Go ahead."

"It's that review I wrote. You want to know what I liked so much about your book."

"Bingo."

"I can tell you this. It was no masterpiece."

"Then why all the praise?" I asked.

"When my agent told me I'd be doing a review I was ecstatic. For The New York Times of all places. I was stuck in quicksand about to go under for good. No one bought my book. I had to make this review count. I wanted to nail the sucker. By the way, Slick, you see how that worked out for me—zero, zilch.

"Don't go thinking I disliked your novel. It had a certain quality, though I went a bit overboard. Hey, you owe me, don't you? I was a partner in your success."

"If your critique was professional, that should've been enough," I said. "Positive or negative you could draw attention by just writing it well. So, why the praise?"

"You ain't no Stephen King. If I beat the shit out of one of his books, then I guess some would take notice. But, a nobody criticizing a first-time novelist? Praising your work was a better option. And—to be honest— my so-called agent pressured me to make it a positive one."

"Who's your agent?" I asked.

"Mr. Nobody. The guy practically shit his pants when I was putting the review together—kept making suggestions—this word, that phrase. Probably selling used cars now. Anyway, I loved my name being attached to your book like I'd actually done something. That review was better than the whole fucking book I wrote. Oh my God, what a piece of shit that was."

I peeked at the other diners. "Nellie, could you watch the language while you're in here?"

"Jesus Christ, simmer down, will ya?"

I took a swallow of my waterlogged bourbon. "I have another question for you."

"Shoot."

"You said you went overboard on that review. Were you influenced by anyone—or anything?"

"Anyone—you mean like my agent?"

"Something like that," I said.

"No," she said, shaking her head. "You have something else on your mind."

"You answered my question. Your motive was to draw attention to yourself. Got it."

"Why don't you ask me what you really want to know?"

I hesitated.

"Spit it out," she said.

Here goes nothing.

"Okay. Did something happen in your life, something far out of the ordinary that influenced your review?"

"Let's try it this way—what are you *not* asking me?"

I strummed my fingers on the table. "That was it."

"Liar. You've got me wondering about you," she said. "Why am I here?"

"I heard they serve great chicken pot pies."

"I'm walking out and going home to Casper, I swear."

"Hold on a second."

The waitress returned and pulled out a pad from her pocket. "Ready to order?"

I pointed to my drink. "Refill on the Jack Daniels."

"A draft of Coors," Nellie said.

"Food?" the waitress asked.

"Later," Nellie added.

"Alrighty then," the waitress mumbled, walking away.

Nellie shook her head. "She's a charmer."

I stared at Nellie.

"What?" she asked.

"You want to know why you're here."

"It would be nice."

"Shadows."

Chapter Thirty-four

Nellie dropped her fork. It fell on the table's edge and toppled to the floor. She bent down and retrieved it, placing it next to her glass of water.

Neither one of us spoke for a few moments as Nellie fiddled with her spoon, turning it upside down, right side up.

"Shadows—I hate that word," she said.

"I see you know what I'm talking about."

"How do you think I got this white hair?" She snagged a few unruly strands, stretching them out farther.

"What happened?" I asked.

Nellie glanced over her shoulder. "Where the hell is my beer?"

"The bartender is giving it to her now," I said.

Nellie shook her head. "I had the feeling you were going to mention Shadows. Somehow I knew that's what this was about. But I still almost got a heart attack."

The waitress arrived with our drinks and set them in front of us. "You folks ready to order yet?"

Nellie turned her head to the woman. "We'll give you a wave when and if."

The waitress about-faced and headed to the kitchen. I doubted we'd ever see her again.

"I saw Shadows when I wrote the book," I said. "Then they went into hiding. Now, they're back."

"That's why you called me."

"That—and—do you know JJ, the agent?"

"I know she's a superstar."

"She's my agent," I said.

Nellie widened her eyes. "Josephine Janakowski is your agent?"

"Who? Oh, yeah. She doesn't go by that name."

"She's not cut out to be a Josephine," Nellie said. "I heard she's a barracuda."

"When's the last time you saw a Shadow?"

"When I reviewed your demented book. Though I get the feeling that if I hook up with you, that'll change."

"I need help," I said.

"And you ring me up. Thank you very much."

"I can pay you."

"Cash?"

"Cash."

"Now we're getting somewhere," she said.

"I'm in the middle of some bad stuff. Shadows, murders."

Nellie took a swig of her beer. "I'm not often on the Internet but a few days ago I bumped into something. There's been two murders here and you found both women. Kinda makes you a suspect, I'd guess."

"Two detectives interviewed me. They know I slept with one of the women and lied about it. They also discovered that years ago I bashed a guy in the head with a beer mug and he almost died. I plea-bargained my way into a mental institution."

"Beautiful. I'm sitting here with a murder suspect."

"Ssshhh," I said, holding a finger to my lips. "Your voice carries."

"I'm gonna carry it back to Delaware if I don't like what I hear."

"I'm not a suspect—anymore."

"You must've double-talked your way out," Nellie said.

I swirled my bourbon. "These two murders could be an opportunity for you."

"What—to be victim number three?"

"No way. I won't let that happen."

"I'll hold you to it."

"JJ phoned me the other day," I said. "She wants to capitalize on the serial killer concept—a true-life book, a movie perhaps, both probably. She said she's got contacts at HBO and could sell them a project. What do you think?"

"I didn't hear my name mentioned in any of that."

"See how this sounds—*David Farmer and Nellie Hagerstrom – The Wildwood Murders*."

Nellie smiled. "That doesn't sound too bad."

"We'd be 50/50 partners."

"You gonna put that in writing?"

"And sign it," I said.

"I just hope I live along enough to cash my first check."

"Don't you trust your instincts?" I asked.

"I sure do but I think I'm gonna try this anyway."

I leaned closer to her and said, "Okay then. Just so we're on the same page. I'll pay you—"

"Cash."

"—for teaming up for a book project on the murders. Agreed?"

"Agreed."

"And, we'll talk about the Shadows later."

"Where am I staying during all this? Hotels get expensive."

"You can stay for free at my condo," I said.

"No hanky-panky?"

"I'll be a gentleman."

"You don't have a jealous girlfriend, do you?"

"Keira's a sweetheart," I said.

"You guys tight?"

"If tight means we like each other, then we're tight."

"She doesn't live at your place, does she?"

"No."

"What's the next step?" Nellie asked.

"I throw my bike in the back of your van. You drive me to my condo and sleep in the spare bedroom. The ferry doesn't run this late, anyway. Hop one in the morning. Set up your cat so you can be gone awhile and then come back later tomorrow. We'll iron out the details."

She nodded. "I hope you're on the level. I can get pretty pissed if somebody's playing me for a jerk."

"I'm not playing you."

She extended her hand across the table. "Shake on it."

We shook hands.

"Do me a favor," she said.

"What?"

"When I leave tomorrow, don't get into any more trouble."

"That's not funny," I said.

"It's a joke, Mr. Serious."

"One more thing."

"What's that?"

"Try the pot pie," I said.

"What do I want with pie? I want a fucking burger."

CHAPTER THIRTY-FIVE

When I awoke the following morning, I checked the spare bedroom first. No sign of Nellie and the bed was made.

Her note sat on the nightstand. "You snore too loud. Talk later."

When Nellie and I arrived here after our dinner I was wiped out. Maybe combining the bourbon with pain meds wasn't a wise course of action.

Then I remembered—I'd forgotten to call Keira.

I grabbed the handset.

"Keira, it's me."

"I called you last night and couldn't leave a message. Clean out your voicemail, please."

"Sorry. I gotta figure how."

"Is your head feeling better?" she asked.

"Like it never happened."

"Good. Did Nellie show up last night?"

"Yeah, we went to the Crest Tavern. She was hungry."

"I'm glad you had something to eat."

"I had a chicken pot pie. Pretty good."

"I hope you didn't drink at the restaurant. Alcohol and oxycodone don't mix."

I know.

"I know."

"You and Nellie get along okay?"

"Yeah. We discussed writing a book together and she's all for it. On her next trip in we'll flesh out the details."

Keira hesitated. "She's coming back, then?"

"We want to get this thing rolling."

"Good for you. What are you doing today?"

"Going for a walk soon. After that, not sure," I said.

"Be careful. Maybe someone should go with you. I've got to be at the newspaper. Jimmy's off today."

"I could ask Jason to hold my hand but he might return empty-handed."

"I wish you would take this seriously," Keira said.

"I do. I'll call you later."

"Promise?"

"Sure."

There are only two seasons in the Wildwoods and Cape May—the tourist season and the off-season, as different as night and day.

The population swells ten times in the summer, as the tourists rub elbows with each other, jockeying for space on the streets and beaches, in the souvenir shops and restaurants.

During the summer, when the sun rises with a dazzling fury, the ocean teems with bodysurfers and swimmers.

I much prefer the off-season when all the visitors and snowbirds get out of my way. I travel the boardwalk without bumping into anyone, often without seeing anyone—like it's my own personal property.

But, not today.

"Mr. Farmer, is that you?" Faraday shouted, against the steady ocean breeze.

I weighed the option of running down the stairs onto the beach. Portugal loomed on the other side of the Atlantic if I had the stamina.

"Hi, Detectives." I pulled back the hood of my sweatshirt.

"I wasn't certain it was you under that hood," Faraday said.

"Friggin TV people are hanging around watching for me." I stared at him. "Somebody gave my name to the media."

"We'd like to talk to you," he said.

"I'm fine thanks—how are you?"

He started to open his mouth when Cho glanced his way. Then she turned to me. "You look well—considering what you've been through."

"Except for the lump on the back of my head, I'm good to go."

"I'm glad to hear it. You had folks worried," she said.

"Were you worried?"

"I was," she replied.

I smiled. "I was talking to Detective Faraday."

Both of them laughed.

"Do you have any idea who attacked me?" I asked.

"We'd like to speak to you about that," she said.

"You have a lead?"

Faraday answered. "How about the three of us get out of this cold wind and sit down for a chat? There's a little place we like," he said, pointing to a tiny restaurant nestled among a row of shuttered businesses.

No one greeted us upon entry. Cho accepted three menus from the hostess station and led us to a small round table in the corner. The restaurant could only accommodate a dozen tables and offered additional seating at a counter. The interior was bright with a 1950's Doo Wop theme, for which Wildwood was famous. I could almost hear Bobby Rydell singing *Wildwood Days*.

I noticed none of the tables were occupied. "You sure this place is open?" I asked.

As we sat down, Cho said, "They do great business in the summer. Their pork roll sandwiches are quite good."

"Are you guys following me?"

"We don't have to do that," she said. "If we need to see you, we will."

"What news do you have for me?"

"I can tell you we're making progress on the murders investigation. As a matter of fact, we found a clue on the pier."

"Today?"

She nodded.

"Good," I said. "If you find the killer you'll find the person who attacked me. They're all connected."

Faraday smiled. "You sure you're not a detective?" He opened his notebook and flipped to a blank page. I watched him write the date at the top.

"You probably have a voice-recording app on your phone," I said.

He glanced up without a word.

"Mr. Farmer," Cho said. "We'd like to ask you a few questions about the attack in your parking garage."

I glanced toward the counter area and saw a waitress talking to the only other customer in the eatery. "The service in this place could be better."

"Oh, that's my fault," Cho said. "They know me here and if I'm with someone they don't recognize they wait for a signal. Cho waved her hand.

The young waitress hurried to us. "Hi, I'm Melanie. Have you had a chance to check the menus?"

Cho said, "Detective Faraday and I will have the usual."

"Got it," the woman said. "Pork roll sandwich, well done, American cheese, and Coke. And you, sir?"

"The same. Sounds good," I said. "Bring the Coke first. I'm thirsty."

"Back in a jiff," she said, heading to the soda fountain.

Cho looked at me. "You and I spoke briefly at the hospital but you said you couldn't remember a thing. Do you recall anything since?"

"Yes. I'd been talking to Nikolai Zdenko just before it happened."

"What about?"

"I have no idea. For some reason I remember he handed me a beer bottle."

"For you to drink?" she asked.

"I think it was an empty. Yeah. He was getting in his car."

"And driving away?"

"Can't be sure."

"Mr. Farmer, do you think he might have hit you?"

Melanie brought our drinks in green sturdy plastic glasses. It wasn't bourbon but I took a couple of sips immediately.

"I can't see why he would."

Faraday asked, "Who do you think might have reason to?"

"I don't know."

"C'mon, Mr. Farmer, let us in on what you're thinking," he said.

"I don't trust half my neighbors. You can write that down."

I watched him scribble away.

"Detectives, do me a big favor. Figure out who did this before he tries again and my skull ends up halfway across the ocean."

Cho said, "The news people are practically camping outside your place and we've increased police patrols around the area. That should discourage any repeat attempt. Mr. Farmer, I want you to think back to that evening. Was there anyone else you recall seeing? Perhaps pulling into or out of the garage."

"We were alone."

"Prior to your talk with Nikolai Zdenko—as you were approaching from your walk, did you see anyone enter the parking garage, either on foot or in a vehicle?"

"No, I didn't."

"How about before your walk? Maybe you saw someone, spoke to someone?"

I thought for a few seconds. "One minor thing. Gail Montrose was in the hallway when I went to the elevator."

"Did you speak with Dr. Montrose?"

"We rode down together. She was on her way to work."

"What did you talk about?"

"She asked how Keira was doing."

"They're friends I presume?"

"Where are you going with this?" I asked.

"Did you see Dr. Montrose drive away in her car?"

"No, I headed to the boardwalk."

"Did you notice if her car was in its parking space when you returned?"

"Really? You think she could do this?"

"Do you?" Cho asked.

"Of course not."

Cho's eyes shifted in her partner's direction, but Faraday had already stopped writing and was eating his sandwich.

"I gotta get going," I said.

Cho reached across the table and offered her hand. "Thank you, Mr. Farmer."

We shook hands while Faraday continued eating.

"Thanks for the lunch," I said. "And Detective Faraday, just so you know, you've got a splotch of mustard on your tie."

Chapter Thirty-six

I had too many complications in my life, too many dangers. The list had Shadows at the top, JJ next and then the unknown assailant in the parking garage. The detectives weren't helping, either.

The sandwich churned in my gut. Maybe a drink would help to steady me. I checked my watch—almost one o'clock.

I stood there gazing out the glass slider as dense gray clouds darkened both the sky and the ocean roiling below me. Newspaper pages bounced along the deserted beach pushed by the gusting breezes.

I walked to the end table and grabbed the remote. The Weather Channel popped up on the screen. The crawl at the bottom indicated the Nor'easter was stalled, dumping rain on North Carolina, but the steering winds were aimed at the Jersey coast.

I called Keira at the newspaper.

"Thank you for calling the—"

"Keira, it's me."

"Hi, David. Did you go for your walk?"

"I didn't get very far with this wind kicking up."

"I'm glad you're home." she said. "You didn't see anything suspicious, did you?"

"No."

"See anyone at all?"

My two favorite detectives.

"An old man looking for shells on the beach."

"Okay, good. Are you staying in for the rest of the day?"

"I plan to," I said. "Keira, I want to ask your permission for something."

"Ooh, sounds intriguing. For what?"

"Well, you know Nellie's very interested in writing a book with me. She might be coming back tonight."

"So soon?"

"My agent has huge plans for this project."

"And you're sure you want to do this?" she asked.

"JJ talked me into it."

"And you said you want my permission?"

"I'd like Nellie to move in with me till we get the project off the ground."

I waited for her response.

"Keira?"

"I'm here. You really surprised me with this."

"If you don't like the idea, I'll—um …"

"David, I'd never stand in your way."

"This wouldn't change anything with us," I said.

"Depends."

"On what?"

"Does she look like Beyoncé?" Keira asked.

"Who?"

"Stunning singer and actress. Never mind."

"Now that you mention it, Nellie does resemble an actor."

"Who?"

"Cousin Itt of the Addams Family."

"Oh, that's mean," she said.

"I'm kidding."

Kinda.

"I should hope so." She paused. "Nellie likes the idea of collaborating with you, I guess."

"She's chomping at the bit to get started. She can really use the money and might take the ferry over later."

"That sure was quick," Keira said.

"That's Nellie for you."

"We'll talk later. I'm looking forward to meeting her. I might stop by after work."

"Good."

"I can change your bandage."

"Already done," I said.

"Oh, so impatient. Anyway, I bought you a gift."

"Cool."

As soon as I placed the phone down, it rang.

"Dave—my man," Tommy said. "How the hell are you?"

"Good, Tommy. You?"

"Jim Dandy. I'm just checking in. How's that bump on your head?"

"I'm fine."

"That was something, you getting clocked like that. Any idea who did it?"

"No."

"You must have pissed somebody off. You should watch your step."

"Thanks for the advice," I said.

"I'm serious. It wasn't robbery. Keira said they didn't take anything. That means someone wanted to hurt you."

"I get that."

"She also mentioned you had somebody in mind, maybe Cecily's husband?"

"You and Keira talk a lot?"

"No. Well, sometimes."

"Tommy, if you want to know what I'm thinking, just ask me."

"Gotcha. Maybe you shouldn't be alone. You know, in case that guy tries again."

"I've acquired a roommate."

"You don't mean Keira?"

"You introduced us. I owe you one," I said.

"I'm just surprised that I didn't know."

"Should we clear it with you first?"

"No, I—"

"It's not Keira. Her name is Nellie and if she makes it over from Delaware she might be moving in tonight."

"Who the hell's Nellie?" Tommy asked.

"She wrote the review of my book way back when."

"And you're so grateful you want her to move in. Generous guy."

"We might work on a writing project together."

"Wow," Tommy said. "If you change your mind, I'm here if you need me."

"What's the matter? Your wife and kids getting tired of you?"

"As always," he said. "I understand that your two detective friends have cops watching your building."

"Some media people showed up, too. There's a TV news truck across the street, and a cute reporter hanging around downstairs."

"I advise you not to talk to her."

"I'm laying low until they get tired and go home."

"Good idea," Tommy said. "If you need me just give me a holler."

I didn't want to drink.

Actually, I did want to.

Take another walk, Farmer.

I left the elevator and decided to stroll along the ocean and breathe the salt air. A brightly colored TV news truck was parked on the side street—a peacock logo painted on the van's side. A young woman with a microphone cradled in her hand paced in the parking garage, her brown hair ruffled in the breeze. A man held a video camera pointed at the ocean. I saw them both a moment too late. I spun back toward the elevator.

"David Farmer," she said, hustling to me. "Angela Prentiss, NBC 10 News. Can I have a word?"

"I'm not him." I tightened the hood against my head and adjusted my sunglasses.

"I'm sorry, sir. I thought you were." She motioned to the cameraman, hand slicing across her throat.

"That's okay, Angie," I said. "I know Farmer and he's a great guy. You want me to give him a message?"

"Um, sure. Could you ask him to come down for an interview?"

"Will do." I waved to her as I stepped into the elevator and she waved back. The cameraman smiled.

I hurried to the Maker's. The detectives, the news people, Tommy. And now this phone call I'd been avoiding—to Marcy. My ex-wife and I still cared about each other but I was the one saddled with guilt. I was the one who cheated. I was the one who ruined our happy family.

I poured an ounce. I passed on the ice and swallowed the bourbon in one fortifying gulp.

Marcy answered on the first ring.

"Hello, David?"

"Hi, Marcy."

"Are you alright?"

"I'm fine," I said.

"I was going to call you but with all that's happened I thought I'd give you a day or two and hoped you'd call me. Are you still in the hospital?"

"I'm home. It was no big deal. How much does Josh know?" I asked.

"I haven't told him anything. He uses his phone mostly for games and music. I read you were clubbed with something—is that right?"

"Where did you read that?" I asked.

"I saw an article online. CNN."

Busybodies.

"Oh."

"There's two murders now, and you found both bodies. Then you were attacked in your parking garage? Do I have that right?"

"I don't want Josh to know."

"I'm worried he'll find out—someone at school, maybe from a friend. People here don't really know much about us but Brian thinks Josh should hear it from me, just in case."

Brian.

"Brian, huh?"

"Don't you agree?"

"It'll scare Josh," I said. "And I don't care what your friend thinks. By the way, how is Kessinger?"

"His last name is Kessler."

"Oh, yeah." I inhaled deeply. "Do you really think it's best to tell Josh?"

"I don't want to frighten him, but I can word it better than anyone else."

"Is he there, now? I could reassure him."

"He's in town with Brian. Let me do it one-on-one. Are you okay with that?"

"I trust your judgment," I said.

"Thank you. I'll handle it. Now, please tell me—why were you attacked?"

"Some jerk hit me from behind. Police think it was a drug addict looking for money. I was hardly hurt at all."

"It's not connected to the deaths of those two women?" she asked.

"Just a coincidence."

"I'm worried," she said.

"You always were."

"To be fair, you gave me a few things to worry about."

"Touché."

"David, I don't want to bring this up, but I feel like I should."

What took you so long?

"What?" I asked.

"Are you seeing Shadows again?"

"Why do you ask?"

"I'm concerned about you. I'd hate for this to start all over again, for your sake."

"I told you not to worry," I said.

"Are you seeing them?"

"Absolutely not."

"Thank goodness," she said.

CHAPTER THIRTY-SEVEN

Reporters on the Weather Channel frolicked in the North Carolina puddles. They were a bit too cheery. Even when the weather guy lost his balance he laughed as he said, "Watch out, Brenda is heading north."

Nor'easters are a fairly common weather event for coastal New Jersey. The name is a derivative of northeastern, which refers to the spinning direction of the winds. They originate in the Gulf of Mexico, scoot across the Southeast and then up the coastline. Mainly they're rain events featuring winds approaching hurricane-like gusts.

I'd been through a few of them and didn't worry about my safety. The Crest Castle was constructed with the latest state-of-the-art materials, including special impact windows, rated as being able to withstand hurricane-force winds up to a Category 3. Flooding was a nonissue since I lived seven stories above the ocean and my bike was tucked and locked under the stairwell.

I needed to dump my trash down the hallway chute. Rule number one—look and listen. No sign of Dennis, so I stepped out of my condo and completed my mission. On the way back I heard a hissing sound. Maggie leaned out her door.

"Pssssst, Dave."

I walked over to her.

"Come inside, dear," she whispered.

When I was seated on the sofa she brought out an impressive crystal decanter, which was three-quarters filled with a golden liquid.

"Do you like my decanter?" Maggie asked.

"It's beautiful."

"Harold and I once cruised the Irish Sea and we purchased this nearly twenty years ago in Ireland. It's genuine Waterford right from the factory. It cost a pretty penny, I might add."

"I bet."

She held the decanter in front of her and tilted the contents back and forth. "The cognac glistens so nice against the cut glass."

"Looks almost good enough to drink," I said.

She poured a couple of ounces into snifter glasses, which she retrieved from the shelf of her china cabinet. The pour was done gracefully with a steady hand. I could envision Maggie perched upon a throne in a flowing robe, or waltzing in a ball gown, but not in a bathing suit playing shuffleboard on a cruise ship.

"This cognac is Courvoisier," Maggie said. "It was a favorite of Napoleon. He brought several crates for his exile in St. Helena." She handed me one of the snifters, "Pardon me," Maggie said, sitting on the opposite end of the sofa. "But I do so enjoy my simple pleasures."

We raised our glasses. "A toast," I said. "To Napoleon, a guy who knew how to exile."

Maggie smiled. "You have a way of putting things."

I sipped and swirled the cognac over my taste buds. "Hmm—excellent stuff. Maggie, you wanted to tell me something?"

"I must ask how you're feeling after the frightful incident in the parking garage. At the hospital, you were in a coma and I couldn't get in to see you. Mr. Zdenko and I were very upset."

"You mean V, and not his brother, Nikolai."

"Yes, V. His brother—I hate to say this—gives me the willies."

I nodded. "I'm not a big fan, either."

"Anyway, are you feeling alright?"

"I'm fine now," I said.

"I'm glad to hear that. Your lady friend Keira is so considerate. She called me with updates. Goodness gracious, you're going through a dreadful time, and I haven't helped one bit."

I laughed. "I had a lot of fun at your party."

"You had a fistfight with Jason."

"That's what I mean."

"I do hope you can patch things up with him," Maggie said. "He was so upset about that Kate woman. Do you find his behavior suspicious?"

"Obnoxious, for sure. Suspicious? Are you thinking Jason attacked me?"

"I wondered who you thought it was."

"I'm letting Cho and Faraday figure it out. In the meantime, I'm keeping my eyes open."

"Good. I was thinking—the person who attacked you used a bat. Does that put you in mind of our baseball player?"

"Maggie, let's you and I agree it's time for you to retire your detective's shield."

"You're right," she said. She took a tiny sip and smiled. "Your friend with the Phillies baseball cap is very polite. At the hospital, Tommy came down to say hi to Mr. Zdenko and me."

"That's nice."

"I feel funny calling a grown man Tommy."

"Once he actually does grow up, we'll call him Tom."

"You are a scamp," she laughed. "It's nice the three of you get along so well."

"The three of us? You mean me, him and Keira?"

"Yes. The other day I saw him, quite by chance, getting out of the elevator while Keira was about to get in. She'd just left your condo. They hugged and went down together."

"When was this?" I asked.

"The day Kate Bowman died. I was going to visit our library downstairs. You know, I didn't see your book there."

"Not surprised."

"I got to the library room and sat by the window flipping through one of the birders guides. We're lucky to be living in an area so rich with beautiful birds. The Cape May Warbler has the most gorgeous—"

"Maggie—you were saying?"

"Oh, yes. About that Kate woman—most unfortunate. She stood outside, staring up. At first I thought she was looking at the sky. But then I heard her shout your name. You must have been standing on your terrace. I couldn't understand what she said, although it was obvious she was quite upset."

You don't miss a thing.

I focused on the attractive decanter with its intricate pattern, mesmerized by the liquor sparkling inside.

"Is everything all right?" she asked.

I held out my empty glass. "Maggie, do you think Napoleon would mind if I had a few more sips of his favorite brandy?"

Chapter Thirty-eight

The more I spoke to my neighbors, the more I wanted to stop speaking to them.

After my chat with Maggie, I headed across the hall to my condo, to my bourbon. A new bottle awaited in the cabinet under the kitchen sink. It wouldn't be new for long.

I dropped a few ice cubes in a glass, tipped in a couple of ounces and thought Keira wouldn't approve. However, I assured myself I could stop drinking at this very moment. I drank daily but functioned well, paid my bills, maintained good hygiene and never collapsed stinking drunk in the gutter. Bourbon served a valiant purpose by smoothing the many ragged edges of my life.

I carried the drink onto my balcony where I eased into a beach chair. With the wind picking up, I was glad I wore a sweatshirt. I'd need to bring the chair inside before it went airborne.

The ocean was choppy, with Brenda targeting us from a few hundred miles south. A fishing boat chugged towards Cape May, bouncing in the waves, brown smoke puffing from its grimy smokestack.

Something moved out of the corner of my eye. For a brief moment I thought Shadow, but then saw a dive-bombing seagull gliding to the shore.

Shadows were ever-present on my mind and I wondered what happened to Doctor Sanderson, one of Rosewood's finest. He often assured me that we would solve my Shadows problem together.

When we last met, he said how powerful I was. "You control them. Never think they control you." He tapped his unlit meerschaum against the glass ashtray and then pointed the pipe stem directly at me, stabbing the air as he spoke. "Confront them; face the sons-of-bitches head-on and they will run away like scared rats."

His advice rattled around my brain and was still with me.

So were the Shadows.

Once again, a shape hovered a few feet away. This time it was the real thing. I gave the confrontational approach another try despite the failed attempt in the parking garage.

I stood to face the Shadow, but the thing floated over the railing, disappearing as it went. I searched left, right and up toward the gray clouds, but there was no sign of it.

I shifted my eyes to the ground and noticed a red Porsche parked on the side street by the parking garage entrance. The vehicle sparkled even with the cloud cover.

My doorbell chimed.

I turned and walked to the door. Through the peephole, I saw her standing in the hallway, a wide-brimmed crimson hat partially covering a shock of chestnut hair.

"Look who's here," I said, opening the door. "The Ghost of Christmas Past."

"Hi, sugar," JJ said.

I realized Maggie was probably watching and/or listening. I gestured and my visitor breezed in.

"Nice digs," JJ said, scanning my condo. "That view is absolutely fabulous. Not so fabulous is the fact you have no pictures on the wall, no curios anywhere. You're even giving simplicity a bad name. Hire an interior decorator."

"Is that why you're here?"

"Good to see you, too," JJ said, wrapping her arms around my neck. She kissed my cheek as an assaulting mix of floral and spice scalded my nose.

She struck a second time, kissing my forehead. "My poor baby. I read a nasty person struck you in the head. Is it all healed?"

"You should've called first," I said.

"I did call. You were over-the-top rude to me and I got the distinct impression you wouldn't be answering if I phoned again. So, here I am. Take my coat," she said, handing it to me.

"Plush."

"Pure Mongolian cashmere," she said.

"A herd of goats must've bit the dust for this thing."

She wore a jet-black knee-length dress. I couldn't miss the enormous ruby on her ring finger, which matched the gemstones in her dazzling gold necklace.

JJ had not aged. I didn't see one crease, one wrinkle on her face or neck. I might guess her age at thirty if I didn't know she was pushing fifty. She filled out the tight-fitting dress from her generous cleavage to her slim hips. Her long legs finally gave way to a pair of bright red heels. I had to admit—she was electric.

I draped her coat over a side arm of the sofa.

"You look prosperous," I said.

"A compliment? Thank you. And, may I say, you are dressed like a writer. You might want to ditch that ratty Pearl Jam sweatshirt. That band is so nineties."

"I assume you're still knocking them dead in the publishing world," I said.

"Well, I do have my own agency on Central Park West. I've got a corner office on the forty-third floor—"

"Where you can look down on all the peasants."

"Ouch, that wasn't very nice," she said.

I motioned to the living room. "Grab a seat."

She brushed past me to the sofa and placed her red Gucci bag on the cushion beside her. Then she removed her hat and carefully rested it on her coat. "Please tell me you can whip up a martini."

"I don't have any gin," I said, sitting down on one of the stools at the kitchen island. I swiveled to face her.

"You're twenty feet away. I don't bite," she said, winking at me.

"I'm comfortable here."

She laughed. "You sure don't look it."

"What brings you all the way from the Big City to little old Wildwood Crest?"

She flashed a cold smile and I felt its chill.

I remember first feeling that icy smile when we dined at The Four Seasons in New York after the publishing contracts were signed. She had reserved a table in the Pool Room, and Lobster Thermidors appeared with bottles of champagne. Overhead lights reflected off the water. We toasted and I wished aloud for a mega hit.

Be careful what you wish for.

That's when she smiled. "*Shadows* will be bigger than big," she had said, sitting under a branch of one of the indoor Japanese Maples. "Our book will be number one in no time."

I'm sure I flinched. "Our book?"

"It's both of us," she said.

"JJ, if there is no me, there is no book."

"Your manuscript dies on your hard drive without me. I make it happen. You have no clue what I did to get this deal done."

I actually had many clues at the time but didn't pay attention.

"Dave, hey, you listening?" JJ asked, interrupting my daydream.

"Yeah," I said. "I don't have any gin."

"You asked me what brings me here. Then—what did you do, blackout?"

"I'm listening. Those your wheels outside—the red Porsche?"

"Isn't it divine? It's the latest 718 Spyder."

"Matches your shoes and hat," I said. "What do you do when you wear white?"

"I've got a Lexus. What do you drive?"

"Cannondale M300."

"Is that one of the new BMW's?"

"It's a bicycle."

"Still the joker," she said. "What do you think of the HBO idea?"

"What idea?"

"We talked on the phone. I told you I would pitch a true crime project. Maybe a series."

"I said no, and it's still no."

"Stubborn. Fix me a drink. What do you have in that glass?"

"Watered-down bourbon—and there's a bottle of chardonnay somewhere," I said.

"Bourbon is fine. Two rocks."

While I was pouring her drink and refreshing mine, JJ rose from the sofa, sauntered to the kitchen and eased onto one of the stools. "Why aren't you glad to see me?"

"Because I'm sober," I said.

"C'mon, it wasn't that bad. We fought on occasion, but so what? That's the way it is with business partners."

"It was a rotten partnership."

"What did I do that was so terrible?" she asked. "I got half the country to read *Shadows*. Tell me what I did wrong and I'll apologize."

"I don't want any apologies."

I placed a glass in front of her and she lifted it toward me. "What should we toast?"

"To you leaving me alone," I said.

She swirled the contents, sniffed, and took a sip, letting it linger in her mouth. She followed that with another quick taste, and leaned around me to see the bottle on the counter. "Oh, Maker's. Try their barrel proof version—even better."

"JJ, before this goes any further, keep something in mind. I'm trying to live a quiet life."

"And failing miserably."

I pointed toward the sliding door. "See that?"

"What am I looking at?"

"We call it the Atlantic Ocean. That's enough for me. It's peaceful, calming."

JJ snickered. "So I saw firsthand. I parked my car and glanced up at what I thought would be your terrace and, lo and behold, there you were, serene, relaxing with a drink, captivated by the ocean. It was so darn adorable; I almost hated to disturb you."

"You sent the fucking Shadow?"

She shook her head. "I don't have that kind of power."

"Why don't you scoot on back to the city and take the fucking things with you?"

"You're being rude again." She slid the empty glass on the granite. "Refill, please. As for Manhattan, I'm staying at a B & B in Cape May and I'm here for as long as it takes."

"For what?"

"To get my way. As I told you on the phone, these murders are ripe for us. This kind of excitement never happens down here. And you're sitting pretty in the middle of it all. The average Joe wouldn't see the opportunity to cash in. But you and I, we're different."

Yeah, they're normal.

I refilled her glass. "I'm not writing another book."

"You didn't want to write the first one, either," she said. "At least you didn't want to finish it. You gave up. My fingerprints are all over those final chapters, remember?"

"I admit you helped me."

"Helped you? You gave me three quarters of a book. I brought the damn thing home."

"Good, then you write the next one."

"Remember what I told you on the phone?" she said. "That I had a brilliant plan?"

"Scathingly brilliant, as I recall."

"I'm honored you remember."

"It was too pretentious to forget."

"Wait til you hear my plan and you'll agree with my choice of adverb," she said.

"No, thanks."

"You need another drink. It might put you in a more receptive mood."

"Talked me into it." I picked up the bottle and added another ounce to my glass.

"Good boy," she said. "Now pay attention, I'm only going to say this as many times as necessary. We've got the perfect setup here—a Boston Strangler-type stalking his way through coastal Mayberry. We tackle this serial-killer angle first. You'll tell the world what it's like for you, a bestselling author with a checkered past, former big-city celebrity, now vegging out in the Cape May boonies. Then suddenly, disrupting your utopian existence, with the tourists gone home, the murders begin, under your very nose. It'd be a huge bonus if the police suspected you committed them. You with me, so far?"

"What did you say after good boy?"

"Everyone you know is a suspect and will get their own profiles. If it turns out the killer is one of your neighbors, well, how delicious would that be."

"I don't care," I said.

"It'd be a snap for you. No research needed. Just write the facts, and if they're too docile—embellish, improvise. You know what would be really sweet? If you screwed at least one of those women."

I stared at her.

"Okay, maybe you're celibate," she said. "You need a girlfriend. We've got enough here for a monster hit—a hit that will resend your name to stratospheric heights. When the accolades begin to subside—boom—then we strike with the next book, the follow up to *Shadows*."

"Two books you want? Even if I was crazy enough to agree, it'd take years to get done."

"With us working as a team—six months, a year at the outside. Anyway, Shadows have no concept of time—days, weeks, years—it's all the same. But my clock is ticking. I've got a bill to pay."

"What's that mean?"

"It means that after this first book we go full throttle into the *Shadows* sequel. We'll bang it out in no time. Both books will be on the bestsellers list simultaneously if we do this right. I'm giddy just thinking about it."

"Don't think about it," I said.

She sipped her bourbon and I noticed the lipstick stains on her glass.

"I've got the perfect title," JJ said, squaring her hands in front of her as though framing a picture. "The Off Season." She smiled and added, "The season is a little off, get it?"

"I got it. I don't want it."

JJ sighed. "What will I do with you? This is way bigger than the both of us. We're gears in a magnificent machine. Remember Professor Bradley Araway?"

What the fuck?

"At Seton Hall," I said.

"He recommended you."

My hand shook and I placed the glass on the counter before I dropped it.

"Those who can't do, teach," she said. "And, believe me, that boy definitely can't do."

"You're saying he recruited me?"

"I wouldn't put it like that."

"How would you put it?"

"I'm pro-active," she said.

"Damn, you have your dirty fingers in everything."

She held up her red-lacquered fingernails. "I'd never dirty these little beauties."

I thought about Nellie. "To get off the ground, though, *Shadows* still needed a favorable review from the Times. That was lucky, right?"

"Lucky? Oh, please," she said. "Have you ever heard of Robert Collier?"

"Another of your lackeys?"

"He wrote books on personal development almost one-hundred years ago. I follow his theory that if you don't make things happen, then things will happen to you. Now, no more chitchat. I'm not leaving Cape May until I have your signature on a contract."

"Get somebody else."

She shook her head. "It has to be you. You've got two things that make you the only man for the job. Talent—and the David Farmer name, which is forever connected to *Shadows* and whatever offspring we add to the franchise. C'mon, I want us to jump on this while we've got a thrill-thirsty audience just waiting."

"They have a long wait."

"You should be kissing my feet in gratitude," she said.

"This meeting is now officially over."

"Alright, sweetie. I'll go quietly. But, if you don't come around, I know where you live."

"Go," I said, motioning toward the door.

She stood and grabbed her coat. I helped her into it as she flipped her hair over the collar.

"Don't forget your hat," I said, handing it to her.

"You're so kind, sir."

"The hallway has ears. Don't make too much racket with those heels."

"I need a martini. I'm heading to Cape May and I hope to hell they have Hendricks at The Blue Heron. It's supposed to be the classiest B&B there." JJ pulled a business card from her bag. "Call me, or I'll show up here again—with steel-toed tap shoes and cymbals."

I took the card from her as we walked to the door.

"Bye," I said.

"If you're going to throw a girl out, shouldn't you at least open the door for her?"

I grabbed the handle, but hesitated. "I have a question for you," I said. "How do you know I didn't murder those women?"

She leaned over and kissed me on the cheek. "Darling, I'm hoping you did."

Chapter Thirty-nine

"I'm having second thoughts."

The longer I lived the more I expected curve balls. It didn't mean I could whack them out of the park but anticipating curves allowed me to at least put them in play. Nellie threw one from across the bay in Delaware.

"About what?" I asked into the handset.

"About coming over there, about the whole damn thing."

"You were just here a few hours ago. What happened since?"

"I got to thinking. You sweet-talked me about us writing a book together, my name on the cover you said. Wildwood murders. I ain't sure I believe it."

"Nellie, tell me the real reason," I said.

"You're inviting me into hell. The Shadows and JJ. And if the fucking Shadows don't get me you've got a serial killer."

"I won't let anything happen to you," I said. "Anyway, how many years has it been since you even saw a Shadow?"

"This morning."

Fuck!

"Seriously?"

"Floating above the Delaware Bay outside my ferryboat window."

"What happened?"

"Nothing," she said. "It was a warning and I ain't deaf."

I needed to be honest with Nellie, as well as myself. She said this was hell, and the Shadows were as close to hell on earth as you could get.

Another thing Mark Twain said—when in doubt, tell the truth.

"Nellie, suppose I be totally honest with you?"

"It's about time. Tell me why you want me up there and this time give me the straight dope."

I cleared my throat. "It's all about the Shadows. They were with me throughout the writing of my book. After it was published, they still bothered me. Then there were a couple of years when they didn't. Now, they're back in a big way. I've seen them on the boardwalk, in Atlantic City, Cape May—"

"Damn," she said.

"I can't be sure the Shadows will follow the storyline, but in my book they blocked out the sun over New York City. Likely an early step in world domination. That was JJ's idea. I intended for the book to be strictly fiction with the good guys winning, but JJ stuck her grubby hands in and changed the direction. Can the Shadows really do that? I don't know. One thing I do know is that I wouldn't have a clue how to stop them and I'm thinking you might."

"Why's that?"

"You headed up the Phantoms Club in college and investigated the paranormal. You've got the interest and maybe a similar experience. Then there's your review of *Shadows*, which I came to believe was influenced."

"Almost seems logical," Nellie said.

"And to make matters worse, JJ stopped by today in all her fancy glory."

"Jesus H. Christ! Did she say anything about Shadows?"

"Never did and still doesn't. She hints, infers, does everything but say it outright. Before she stepped into my condo, I saw a Shadow on my balcony. It's not a coincidence."

"What did she want?" Nellie asked.

"Two projects. A book on the Wildwood murders to get my name back out there to help create a demand for the sequel to *Shadows*. I'm guessing she wants the second book to further advance whatever malevolent goals they have."

"JJ said that?"

"No. I can read between the lines."

"She's like their emissary?" Nellie asked.

"I'm guessing there's some type of Faustian deal in place. She gets fame and fortune in return for paving the way for them. Plus, she looks like she's discovered the Fountain of Youth."

"Is JJ working with anyone else do you think?"

"It's not just her alone. You went to Seton Hall," I said. "The literature professor is part of an unholy network."

"You don't mean Araway."

"Him."

"You serious? The guy's a snot-nosed jerk."

"Connected to JJ," I said.

"That creep flirted with me after classes. One-on-ones he called them. Now I'm thinking he lost interest because I had no talent."

Neither one of us spoke for a few seconds.

"Nellie? Still there?"

"Did you mention my name to JJ?" she asked.

"No. Should I have?"

"Fuck no. I want to avoid that creature."

"We're agreed then?" I asked. "You're coming?"

"I just didn't want a snow job about us being a writing team."

"That still holds—but okay—I admit it's secondary."

"You did good with the straight talk," she said. "I know exactly how I fit in, even if you don't. You hit the fucking jackpot with me. Somehow, you stumbled onto the only person qualified to deal with this."

"I'm happy to hear that," I said.

"You have money, right?"

"I already said I did."

"I have a secret weapon," she said.

Holy shit.

"Am I paying for this weapon? Is that why you asked about the money?"

"You're paying to get my equipment out of a storage unit here in Delaware. I barely got room in my place for me and my Casper."

"Sure. What equipment?"

"Stuff I used chasing ghosts. The equipment's still good but I have to pay a few months back rental."

"Consider it done, but why do you want it?"

"I told you—secret weapon," she said.

"In a storage unit?"

"No, I always keep it safe with me. Thing is—I have to activate it."

"And the activator is in storage?" I asked.

"No. I have it."

"You've lost me."

"I bet that happens to you a lot," she said.

"What do I have to do to get you here today?"

"Before we hang up, I'm gonna give you the phone number for the storage place. You call them and pay the bill. Tell them I'll be there this afternoon to pick up my gear."

"Then you'll take the ferry over?" I asked.

"We never discussed all of my terms. You've got me walking into a fucking shitstorm."

"What do you want?"

"This isn't going to be an overnight-success story. I may be there for days, weeks."

"I realize that," I said.

"You pay all my expenses for as long as this takes, all my meals, my booze—and I'm warning you—I like my beer. Plus, whenever I need something, you pay for it. It might be best if you just hand over a credit card for me to use."

"Done. What else?"

"This murder book we write— you said we split profits down the middle. But, if there's no profits, or no finished project even, whatever, I still get paid, yes?"

"Yeah."

"And the sequel to *Shadows*, can I get in on that?"

"Nellie, if you can stop the Shadows, we'll write the sequel together."

"Cool. And I don't want anything to do with JJ. You're responsible for keeping her out of my hair."

"Is that it?" I asked.

I heard Nellie blow cigarette smoke.

"That'll do for now."

As we were talking, I one-fingered my way on the Internet checking the Cape May-Lewes Ferry schedule. "There's a four-fifteen from Lewes."

She read me the phone number for the storage place.

"We done?" I asked.

"I'll call you when I get close so you can meet me in the parking garage. Help me unload."

"Okay," I said.

"My stuff is expensive and I ain't leaving it in the van with all that's going on."

"We'll store it in my utility room. You bringing the secret weapon?"

"We'd have no shot without it," she said.

"Can I ask what it is?"

"Do you know what the word secret means?"

CHAPTER FORTY

I felt as if I'd lived three or four days in just a handful of hours.

No wonder I drank.

Later that afternoon, Keira called.

"Hi," I said.

"Everything alright?"

Nothing cognac and bourbon couldn't soften.

"Fine."

"Have you talked to Nellie? Is she still coming tonight?"

"She is," I said.

"Good. I don't want you to be alone. Mom's got a cold or something. As long as you have company I'll stay with her and drop by in the morning if she's feeling better."

"Okay."

I thought Keira hung up. As I was about to disconnect I heard her voice.

"David?"

"Yeah?"

"Are you sure you're alright?"

"Fine."

"Have you been drinking?"

"Maggie gave me a glass of cognac."

"Hmm. What time do you expect Nellie?"

"What time is it now?" I glanced at my watch and saw it was nearly five o'clock.

"It's almost five," she said.

"Nellie should be here—um—hour or so."

"Maybe I'd better I drive over and keep you company until she arrives."

"No, no. I'm fine."

"Okay," she said. "Call me later?"

"Yeah."

I napped until the phone rang. "What?"

"It's me," Nellie said. "Come down here. There's a couple of scruffy-looking characters in your parking garage. Hurry up; they're giving me the evil eye."

Two minutes later I stepped out of the elevator and hustled into the garage. I saw Nellie's van and bee-lined to it.

"Where are the people you mentioned?" I said as she lowered her window.

"You practically bumped into them."

I turned and saw Dennis smoking a cigarette, while Jason was alongside propped against the building.

"Who are they?" Nellie asked.

"Two guys who don't like me."

"Lovely."

"Let's wait a minute. Maybe they'll go inside," I said.

Neither of them recognized the van, which may be why they stared in our direction. When Jason took a couple of strides towards us, Nellie opened her door and hopped out.

"Hi," she said as I moved next to her.

"Who are you?" Jason asked.

I was about to introduce her but she beat me to it. "I'm Nellie." She walked to the back of the van and flung the doors open. Nellie ignored Jason and rummaged through the equipment.

I joined her and then noticed Jason had followed me.

"Farmer," he said. "What are you doing here?"

"I have a condo on the seventh floor."

He shook his head and focused on Nellie. "You're this guy's friend?"

She pulled herself from the van and looked at him. "He's my boss," she said, cheerfully.

Dennis arrived without comment, his foot rubbing out his cigarette butt on the concrete.

"Nellie," I said. "This is Jason. He lives on the same floor, and that's my next-door neighbor, Dennis."

"You're working for him?" Jason asked. "Is that what you meant?"

"Yep."

"Doing what?"

"Whatever."

Dennis said, "I think she's saying it's none of our business."

Jason smiled at me. "How's that head of yours?"

"It's okay."

"You must have a hard skull. It happened right about here, didn't it?" Jason pointed to a nearby beam.

We all stood silent for a few seconds. I reached into the van and lifted out a cardboard box when Nellie asked, "What's he talking about?"

"Tell you later," I said.

"Your boss got clocked with a baseball bat," Jason said.

"Why am I just hearing this now?" Nellie asked me.

"It was nothing. A drug addict."

Jason snickered. "You think some druggie mugged you? How much money did he get?"

I didn't answer.

"That's what I thought," he said.

A bolt of lightning zig-zagged over the Atlantic followed by a rumble of thunder.

"Big storm coming," Jason said.

I gazed toward the darkening horizon. "This isn't it. Brenda's 250 miles south. Not even a feeder band. For one thing, that lightning is coming out of the north."

Everyone stared at me.

"I watch the Weather Channel," I said, as Nellie leaned back into the van.

Jason said, "You can do it all, huh Farmer? You're a weather expert, you write books, you know where to find dead bodies …"

"Here, grab this," Nellie said, thrusting a long leather-cased item towards Jason's midsection. He stuck out his hands and accepted it in self-defense.

"What am I supposed to do with this, whatever it is?"

"It's a camera tripod. We're bringing it up to Dave's place. Just leave it outside his door and we'll take it from there."

"It's heavy and unwieldy," Jason said.

"That's why I gave it to you."

Dennis laughed but stopped as soon as Nellie handed him a hefty roll of cable bound together with large zip ties.

"Same destination," Nellie said.

She tucked a small PC monitor under her arm, jammed a mini camera in her jeans pocket, and led us to the elevator.

When we all got off on my floor, Jason bumped the tripod against the side wall.

"Watch that, dude. This stuff is expensive," Nellie said.

"Lady, I'm doing you a favor."

"Not if you break it you ain't."

"What is all this, anyway? You a photographer?" Jason asked.

Nellie looked my way but I offered no guidance.

"I take pictures of ghosts. Seen any?"

Jason and Dennis exchanged glances and Dennis said, "I guess she's telling us again to mind our own business."

A door squeaked from down the hall and Zdenko emerged from his condo. "I hear a lot of noise." Zdenko wore black slippers and red flannel pajamas. "I watch wrestling on TV and getting sleepy so I dress like this."

"Thanks for sharing," Nellie said. She maneuvered the monitor she held, freeing her right hand, which she extended towards him. "I'm Nellie."

Zdenko gently took her hand. "My name is Vedra Zdenko and now that I tell you—you must forget it." He smiled and bowed. "Call me V. I am from Albania."

"A gentleman, I see," Nellie said.

"I help you with that."

Zdenko reached out his arms and Nellie said, "Okay, chief."

"V," he said, taking the monitor.

I half-expected to see Maggie's door open but I guessed she was listening.

"Wouldn't it have been easier to leave all this in the van?" Jason asked.

Nellie cocked her head. "Sure. Then I could hang a sign on it, steal my shit."

"She is smart," Zdenko said.

Nellie stared at my condo door. "Open sesame." She turned to me. "Well, that didn't work. Got a key?"

"Oh," I mumbled, pulling the card from my jeans.

"Nice to meet you, Nellie. I'm done." Dennis said, placing the cable on the floor. He nodded to Jason, unlocked the door to his condo and went in.

"I've got to be out early," Jason added. "Farmer, grab this fucking thing before I poke my eye out." He handed the tripod to me and walked away.

"Thank you," Nellie mumbled to his back.

Zdenko said, "I help you bring all this in."

With the door now open, I guided him. "Follow me V; we're putting this in my utility room."

It required two trips but we dropped the gear between the water heater and furnace.

As V and I returned to the living room, Nellie said, "There's something else in the van, a green plastic laundry basket I want up here. It's loaded with stuff and has some weight to it."

"I'll get it," I said.

"No," Zdenko said. "Nellie, you give me keys and describe car. I take care."

Nellie handed him the keys. "It's the beat-to-shit dirty white van with the cracked front windshield. Lock it back up, please."

"Done," Zdenko said, exiting my condo.

I headed to the kitchen and grabbed the Maker's, which sat on the counter. "Nellie, what would you like? I have bourbon, a bottle of white, and more bourbon. We can get your beer tomorrow."

"Do you have something to mix with the whiskey?" she asked.

I opened the fridge. "Is Coke alright?"

"It'll do."

I placed the Maker's on the kitchen island and removed a can of soda from the fridge.

"You ain't kidding with that bourbon. It's a 1.75. "

"I'm a recreational drinker."

"What's that mean?" she asked.

"Not sure, but I heard somebody say that once and nobody flinched."

I got two glasses from the cabinet and placed them on the island. I dropped a couple of ice cubes in each.

"Two glasses?" she said. "What about the big guy—we're working him to death."

Dang.

"He's got a wrestling thing to watch."

"C'mon, Boss. Don't be a cheapskate."

Zdenko banged on the front door and Nellie ran to let him in.

"I thought you say this is heavy," Zdenko said. "Like feathers."

He rambled down my hallway.

I fixed Nellie a drink as Zdenko returned. "Take a seat," I said, motioning to the stools.

"What is that you drink?" he asked, handing Nellie the van keys and sitting next to her.

"Bourbon and Coke. Wanna try?" I said.

"Yes." Then he turned to Nellie. "Can I ask question? What is the stuff I carry?"

Nellie smiled. "Curiosity killed a cat."

"When this happen?"

"It's a joke, V. I doubt if it ever made its way to Albania."

"I like American sayings."

"I'm here to find a ghost," Nellie said.

"Why?"

"It's what I do."

"I help. I see a ghost in the staircase."

After mixing another drink, I said, "Here you go, V." I hoped Zdenko was a gulper and would polish his off quickly, then scoot on home.

"You saw a ghost?" Nellie asked. "And where's this staircase you mentioned?"

"I think he meant our stairwell," I said.

"Yes, I say wrong word," Zdenko said. "Two weeks ago, I see a ghost woman hanging from the railing—with rope around the neck. She is not there anymore. I could help look for her and your ghost. I have good eyes."

"No need for that," Nellie said.

He nodded and took a sip of his drink. "This is bourbon?"

"And Coke," I said. "Like it?"

"Need more soda."

"How did that wrestling thing end up?" I asked.

"Wrestling! I forget. They have big final and they all fight. I must go."

"Okay," I said as he jumped up from the stool.

"Thanks for helping, V," Nellie said.

"It is my pleasure, Miss Nellie. I see you tomorrow, I hope."

Zdenko hurried out the door.

I placed Zdenko's glass in the sink.

"Keep on the good side of that guy," Nellie said. "He's—" She started coughing, which quickly worsened to gagging.

"You okay?" I asked, turning around to face her.

"It went down the wrong pipe," she said, holding onto her glass. "I'm okay now."

I couldn't take my eyes off her.

"What are you staring at? Is my hair on fire or something?"

There was no fire. But I was concerned about the Shadow standing behind Nellie with its nearly invisible hands hovering above her shoulders.

Chapter Forty-one

The next day, I was in the kitchen making coffee when my roomie padded her way in with bare feet.

"Morning," Nellie mumbled. "Coffee." Her hair was a confused tangle, everywhere at once, twisting away from her head, ready to make a break for it.

"You don't even answer?" she said.

"Good morning."

I slid the coffee mug toward her. "How do you normally take it?"

"Black. I hope this ain't that decaf shit."

Cracks spread from her narrow eyes to the side of her face. I saw no evidence of makeup. Nellie's wide pale lips sat atop a square jaw.

A drab green sweatshirt covered her fragile upper body and flopped over a pair of tattered blue jeans.

She touched the empty bowl alongside the cereal box. "You better not be planning on feeding me Cheerios."

I smiled. "Nellie, you have a certain style going for you."

"I'm not a morning person, so watch your step."

"I've got peanut butter crackers."

"And?"

"Cheerios."

"Give me a pack of them crackers."

She reached into her pocket and her hand emerged clutching a prescription vial. She fumbled with the cap but it failed to rotate.

"Here," she said, pitching it in the air toward my shoulder where I speared it. "Open that, will ya?"

I pushed on the cap with a quarter turn, releasing it.

"What are you taking?" I asked.

"Alprazolam."

"Never heard of it."

"It's generic Xanax. Give."

I placed a bottle of spring water and the pills in front of her. "Why are you taking them?"

"I like the taste. What's the real story with you getting bashed in the head?'

"I already told you," I said. "It's a drug-related crime."

"Sticking to your fairytale, huh?"

"I—"

She held up her hand. "Don't bullshit me. Someone tried to knock your brains out. They failed. They'll try again. I ain't looking to get taken out by a stray bullet."

"It's not like that."

It is like that.

She blew on her coffee.

I thought I saw movement outside the sliding glass door. I tried to discern if it was the foggy mist or the Shadow from last night.

"What are you doing?" she asked.

"Going to rain any minute."

"When you're done checking the weather let's come up with a plan. I'm starving."

"I guess that puts food shopping up first."

Nellie shuffled over to the refrigerator and opened the door. "Nothing here worth eating." Next she checked the freezer. "Ain't much behind door number two. You are going to spend a fortune at Acme. Got pen and paper handy?"

"In that drawer," I said, pointing to the one by the fridge.

She pulled it open. "Bic pen, the old classic. Cool. Start writing," she said, pushing the scratch pad and pen on the granite surface.

"What?" I asked.

"Write down batteries—double A's, a couple of 9 volts. Ziploc bags. Got a tape measure in this joint? Of course not. Add that to the list. I want a roll of duct tape and chalk."

"Chalk?" I said.

"To use around furniture in case it moves. You getting all this?"

"Yeah."

"As for food, no need to make a list since we'll hit every aisle. Let's not get any more of these things," she said, getting up from the stool and tossing the remaining crackers in the trash.

"What about your equipment?" I asked. "What is that stuff in my utility room?"

"You wouldn't know if I told you."

"Try me. I saw a few ghost hunting shows on TV."

"Here goes nothing—EMF and EVP detectors, thermal scanner, infrared camera and thermometer, motion detectors, Bose headphones, 1080P resolution monitors. I got the whole kit and caboodle."

"Which one is the secret weapon?"

"None of them."

"Okay. What does all that stuff do?"

"I ain't giving tutorials just yet, but here's the basics. Ghosts are electromagnetic, meaning the energy they throw off causes a disruption in the magnetic field, and an EMF detector measures that. There's also a temperature change and that's where the infrared thermometers come in. When a ghost occupies a space it displaces the energy causing a cold spot, and a digital image shows on the meter's screen."

"Am I supposed to be writing all this down?"

"My equipment is expensive and, you can write this down, no one gets to play with any of it unless I say so."

"Gotcha. What does EMF stand for?"

"Electric and magnetic fields," Nellie said. "It looks like an old transistor radio but with a screen displaying a numerical gauge that detects ghosts before you see them."

"I love all this technical jargon. Nellie, I think I'm falling in love with you."

"What did I tell you about that?"

We stared at each other before she broke into laughter, ending with a coughing fit.

"Fucking cigarettes," she muttered.

"You never told me why you want to see the ghost in the Atlantus Tavern."

"I have unfinished business with Nancy."

"You know about Nancy?" I asked.

"Let's put it this way—this time I'm going to find her."

On the wall behind Nellie I saw a form taking shape.

"Hey, Boss," she said.

I didn't answer.

She snapped her fingers. "How are things in La-La Land?" she asked.

"Uh, okay."

"What are you looking at?"

"We have company," I said.

"One of them?"

"Yeah. But I don't see it anymore."

Nellie stood and looked around the room.

"It's gone," I said.

"What's that noise?" Nellie asked.

"I didn't hear anything."

"You must be deaf. It came from the hallway."

Nellie took a step toward my front door.

"Don't," I said.

"Don't what?"

Nellie continued to the door, and without hesitation, opened it wide.

Chapter Forty-two

"Oh my, how embarrassing." Maggie bent over cleaning up the mess on the hallway floor.

"Food!" Nellie exclaimed and immediately crouched down to help.

"Hi Maggie, what happened?" I asked.

"Dave, I'm so clumsy. I dropped the tray, but this nice lady and I have it under control."

Nellie looked over her shoulder at me. "Help, save the muffins."

I took one step into the hallway and slid on something that almost sent me flying.

"Nice going, Bigfoot," Nellie said. "You squashed a creampuff."

Scattered on the hardwood floor were a variety of muffins and pastries, with a silver serving dish upside down among them. The two women got the goodies back on the tray.

Maggie peered up at me. "They're fresh from Britton's Bakery and now..."

My neighbor's door opened and Dennis poked his head out. "You okay, Maggie?"

"Yes. I'm sorry for the commotion."

Dennis stared at Nellie and then me.

"Good morning," I said.

"Yeah," Dennis replied, and closed his door.

Nellie looked at me. "To him you say good morning."

I reached down and took the tray from Maggie. "Come in and have a cup of coffee."

"Right after I finish cleaning this up."

"I got it covered," Nellie said, rising to her feet. She held out a hand to Maggie and helped lift her from the floor. "I'm Nellie."

"I know," she answered. "I accidentally heard you last night."

Nellie turned to face me. *Accidentally*, she mouthed. "Get me some paper towels."

Maggie followed me into the kitchen and sat on one of the stools, shaking her head. After handing the towels to Nellie, I returned and touched Maggie's shoulder as I passed. "No harm done." I dropped a pod in the coffeemaker. "The hallway floor needed a cleaning anyway."

"You always make the best of everything," she said. "You don't rattle."

"Only when shaken."

Maggie laughed. "I feel better."

"Great. Why were you bringing the pastries?"

"I heard what Nellie said to the gentlemen last night. I want in."

Before I could think of a response, Nellie strode into the kitchen, munching on a round pastry partially covered with white icing.

"That's off the floor," Maggie said.

"Whole lot better than stale crackers."

Nellie plopped next to Maggie and held up her empty cup. "Garcon, more coffee."

"Just be a minute. By the way, this is my friend, Maggie. And she wants in."

"In what?"

Maggie said, "I heard you say you hunt ghosts."

"Did I say that?"

Maggie smiled. "I heard you say you take pictures of ghosts. I want to be involved."

"That's not a good idea."

"Why not?" Maggie asked.

"It's dangerous. Anyway, I've already got a couple of recruits."

I placed a mug of coffee in front of Maggie.

She said, "Thank you, Dave. I have a story to tell."

"Okay," I said, adding another pod to the Keurig.

"I have experience with the supernatural," Maggie started. "I saw a vision that would scare the socks off anyone. Many years ago my Harold and I stayed at the beautiful Caribbean up the street. It's that retro motel with a gorgeous blue sign and fifties music. We stayed there one night when our condo here wasn't quite ready. It was 3 A.M. and I'll never forget what happened."

"You remember the time exactly?" I asked.

"That's the hour of the dead," Nellie said. "Jesus Christ died at 3 P.M., so the Devil chooses 3 A.M. to unleash his demons."

"That's right, Nellie. You know such things," Maggie said.

"I'm a specialist. Finish your story, please."

"We were on the second floor across from their Cabana room. It was drizzling and I couldn't sleep and looked out my room's big window and—well, if I didn't have a heart attack then, I never will. Perched on the roof of their Cabana, sitting on top of that sign was something that looked like it stepped out from a horror movie—or more likely from hell, a giant devil-creature, reddish in color, huge pointed ears and a serpent's tail. I couldn't go hide under the covers because my feet were glued to the floor. I tried to call out to Harold but he always slept like a log and I couldn't speak above a whisper."

Maggie sipped her coffee as I pushed a mug to Nellie.

"Maggie," I said. "You don't have to finish telling us. It's too upsetting."

"Nonsense. I lived through it so I can certainly handle repeating it. The devil-thing stood up from the sign and floated through the air, over the ramp, the palm trees and swimming pool. I drew the curtains and sat at the table alongside the bed. Waiting. For what I don't know."

Maggie paused and Nellie said, "What happened?"

"There was no sound for maybe half an hour. I finally peeked through the drapes and saw only the rain. I opened the door slowly. The thing had gone but hoof-like footprints were imprinted on the outside carpeted walkway. The creature must've stood right at our doorstep."

Neither one of us spoke for a few moments.

Maggie said, "You believe me, don't you, Dave?"

I believe in worse.

"Of course."

"Nellie, that's why I could help you," Maggie said. "Whatever it is your hunting. I've got the strength to cope with it."

"I still don't think this is for you," Nellie said.

Maggie stared at me. "Dave?"

"I'm sorry, but Nellie is running the show and I agree with her."

"I could help plan. Do something."

"Let me get back to you on that," Nellie said, as she finished eating her pastry.

"If you don't mind, dear, let me have your phone number and I can call you if I think of any way I can help."

"Sure, Maggie." Nellie said and scribbled her number on a napkin and handed it to her.

The doorbell chimed and Nellie bounced off her stool and went to the door. I heard her say, "Don't tell me, you must be Keira."

"And you are—Nellie?"

"Yessiree. I'm here to chase ghosts and fill up Dave's fridge."

Keira carried a white plastic Acme bag, walked over to me and kissed my cheek. She whispered, "Chase ghosts?" She placed the bag on the counter and pulled out a toaster, bagels, butter and cream cheese. "Merry Christmas," she said to me. Keira then smiled at the two women. "How are you, Maggie?"

"Terrible. Dave and Nellie won't let me join their ghost-hunting team. Plus, I dropped pastries all over the hallway floor."

"You are having a bad morning," Keira said. "As for ghost hunting, you might be better off without it."

"You too, dear?" Maggie said. "Alright, I know when I'm licked." She got up from her seat, straightened her blouse, and strode towards the door when she pivoted to face us. "Nellie, I live just across the hall if you change your mind. Bye everyone."

Standing next to me, Keira said, "You didn't call me last night."

Crap.

"I forgot."

Keira nodded and slid onto the stool next to Nellie but kept her eyes on me.

"David, what is this about ghost hunting?"

I shook my head. "I'm not sure, either."

Keira raised her eyebrows. "Really?"

Nellie answered for me. "I haven't told Dave why I'm doing it."

"See?" I said to Keira.

"I'm ducking outside for a quick smoke," Nellie said, reaching into her pocket for a cigarette.

After Nellie closed the slider, Keira said, "I thought Nellie was here to write a book with you."

"She is. It was her idea to look for a ghost."

"But you didn't mention it. You don't always shoot straight with me."

"Uh—most of the time I do."

"David, I don't care if you dance around the truth with the detectives or your neighbors—fine. But not with me. I've already been through that with someone else."

Oh?

"You heard Nellie," I said. "She wasn't straight with me."

"I'm not going to split hairs. I made my point."

I looked at the balcony. Nellie was smoking, smiling, waving at me.

I motioned for her to come in. Nellie opened the door. "It's a tad chilly out there. Should I go hide in my room?"

"No, sit with us," Keira said. "I'm dying to know more about the ghost hunting."

"I'm looking for a particular ghost at a Cape May tavern," Nellie said.

"Nancy?" Keira asked.

"How'd you know?"

"I go to the Atlantus all the time. I head upstairs and always hope to see her. I took David there for lunch recently."

"Small world," Nellie said. "I tried to make contact with Nancy maybe fifteen years ago but I didn't know then what I know now. Maybe you and Tommy might want to help?"

Keira sneaked a sideways peek at me. "Yes, that sounds great. I'm excited. I've always had an interest in the paranormal. Mick, the owner, loves his ghost girl. Tommy and I know Mick pretty well."

You and Tommy?

Nellie said, "I met Mick when he let me do my half-assed attempt at meeting Nancy. It was an abysmal failure. I'm not sure he'd give me a repeat try."

"I think he would," Keira said.

"What do you think the chances would be for tonight?"

"So soon? Do you have your equipment with you?"

"Dave helped me carry it in last night."

Keira looked at me. "Did you call Tommy by any chance?"

"Not yet," I said.

"Let me do it," said Keira. "I have no doubt Tommy can get Mick to go along with this. They're long-time buddies and Tommy's there all the time. For Mick, it's great publicity, especially if we find Nancy."

"Wonderful," Nellie said. "You're the real deal, Keira."

"That's what I've been telling David."

CHAPTER FORTY-THREE

"Good news," Keira said. "Tommy just confirmed. Mick loves the idea and we can set up at the Atlantus tonight. He'd like us to wait until after his diners leave. The restaurant closes at nine and he'll shoo out any remaining bar crowd."

"Excellent," Nellie said.

Keira sat on a kitchen stool alongside Nellie. "This is so thrilling—I can't wait."

"Who's this Tommy guy?"

"He's the number one realtor in the area," Keira said. "Well connected."

"Already coming in handy," Nellie said. "I want to say a few words. I'm glad to have you both helping me but ghost hunting isn't fun and games. It's just the opposite—super dangerous. This won't be like those scripted TV shows Dave watches. Something unexpected will happen. Believe me; I've experienced some scary shit in my life."

"Nellie, I—"

"You don't listen well, do you, Boss? I have the floor."

Keira giggled.

"Continue," I said.

"I've chased ghosts and they've chased me. Years ago, a detached screaming head ran me out of an old hotel up in Lambertville. You see what I'm saying? It's not a one-way street. Sometimes when you find what you're searching for, the tables get turned. So, you pay attention and follow my instructions."

I raised my hand.

"Gotta go the bathroom?" Nellie asked.

"Are you done with your speech?"

"For now." She reached into her pocket and tapped a cigarette from the pack. "I need another smoke—tell you what, Boss. I'm not standing out there in the rain but I'll compromise. I'll do it over there by the sliding door, partly crack it and blow the smoke outside. You sit way over here. How's that?"

"You just finished a cigarette," I said.

"Your point?"

"Never mind."

"That's what I thought," Nellie said, walking to the glass door and lighting up.

"I wanted to ask if you plan on talking to Nancy," I said to Nellie from twenty feet away.

"I told you I have a gift for her."

"What is it?"

"Tell you when it's time."

"Nellie, you said your equipment is here?" Keira asked.

"In the back room."

"Great. When can I get a lesson?"

"You and Tommy come here early tonight, like six. That'll give me plenty of time to figure who does what. Then I'll give you all a crash course."

Nellie stubbed out her cigarette on the balcony floor and carried the squashed butt to the kitchen sink where she ran water over it. "There, all safe and sound."

Keira smiled. "Nellie, I know you're here to write a book about the murders."

"I am."

"But I'm wondering why you want to specifically find Nancy. There are many other ghosts in Cape May."

Yeah, how come Nancy?

"I have something she wants."

"That's cool," Keira said. "I'm so glad you're including me."

"I may need all the help I can get."

"Have you been ghost hunting in Delaware, if you don't mind me asking?"

"Keira," I said. "What's with the questions?"

"It must be the reporter in me."

"Relax, Boss," Nellie said. "I'm a big girl. All growed up. There's a restaurant, Crabby Dick's, which is part of the old Delaware City Hotel. Been there for like two hundred years. I tried to make contact with one of the resident ghosts but all I succeeded in finding were the best crab cakes I've ever tasted.

"That was years ago. I'm coming out of retirement you might say. The only thing I was doing back home was work, and that just went away. Do you know the name Harris Teeter?"

"The grocery chain?"

"That's them," Nellie said. "I was a cashier at their Millsboro store for five years. It wasn't a glamorous job but it paid the rent. They brought in self-checkout machines and I got the boot a month ago."

"That's terrible," Keira said.

"Me and my cat, we got nothing going these days. I'm glad your boyfriend called even though I give him a hard time—" Nellie looked at me. "—which will continue."

""Did you get all your questions answered?" I asked Keira.

"Okay, no more. I hope you're not offended," she said, turning to face Nellie.

"You'd have to go some to offend me."

"I'm glad that's settled," I said. "Should we celebrate with a drink?"

"You mean orange juice," Keira said. "It's not even eleven."

"I was kidding."

Keira smiled at me. "I apologize. It's just that today we all want to keep our heads clear."

"I always have a clear head," I said.

"Uh-oh," Nellie mumbled.

Keira said, "I shouldn't have said anything."

"You think I drink too much."

"David—"

"I never get drunk. You know that. I am absolutely, positively, not an alcoholic."

"I never said you were."

"You had no right bringing this up in front of someone else." I thumped the palm of my hand on the granite island, catching the corner of the tray sending two muffins to the floor.

"You happy now?" I asked Keira, tossing the muffins in the wastebasket.

"Far from it."

Nellie said, "Let me dare to weigh in on this sensitive topic. No alcohol for any of us if we're ghost hunting tonight."

"Really?" I asked her.

"Really. In case you didn't know, alcohol affects your judgment and response times. Are you shocked, Boss?"

"Like I said, I was kidding."

"Okay," Keira said. "I'm going to check on my mother now and I'll be back here by six. I'll try and get Tommy to commit to a time. He's not always prompt."

Oh?

"And Nellie," Keira added. "I'm sorry if we're off to a bad start with you."

"You kidding? This is good to see in case I ever lasso a guy."

"Bye," Keira said. She got up and kissed me on the cheek again. She left my condo without glancing back.

Nellie stared at me. "Very smooth, Boss. You two sound like you've been married for twenty years."

"This is none of your business."

"Gotcha."

"I have something to tell you," I said. "And I don't want you to get upset."

"I'm bracing myself," she said.

"Last night when we were talking ..."

"Spit it out, Boss."

"There was something standing behind you."

Nellie's mouth fell open. Her eyes widened. "Don't tell me it was a fucking Shadow!"

"Well—yeah, it was. But it didn't do anything."

"It could've choked me out with you in a ringside seat," she said.

"What was I supposed to do?"

"Something! Anything!"

"I'm sorry."

"You should've said that to Keira."

"Let's change the subject," I said. "Who else did you tell about the Shadows?"

"Tell who, what? I'm afraid of my own shadow?"

"I know what you mean."

"You haven't told Keira, right?" Nellie asked.

"Someday."

"You need to tell her, like immediately."

"I will."

"One more thing about the booze," Nellie said. "You need to be 110% sober tonight because you and I will be upstairs with Nancy."

I might've grimaced. "You sure you want me up there with you?"

"Totally. We're in this together."

Yes, Boss.

Chapter Forty-Four

"I'm wondering," I said. "When did you first notice the Shadows?"

"That's funny 'cause I was about to ask you the same thing."

We were silent for a few seconds before I caught on.

"Oh, you want me to go first," I said.

"Age before Beauty."

I smiled.

Thank God you're here.

"I'm not sure when I first saw them for what they were," I started. "In college, I ignored the couple of sightings. I drank a lot back then."

Nellie was about to speak.

I shook my head. "Don't say it. Years later, after Marcy and I were married, I exercised while writing my book to get the juices flowing. I was doing sit-ups and noticed my Shadow out of sync with me. I figured it was my imagination until it pulled itself from the wall."

"It's out there somewhere," she said.

"Except it doesn't follow me. Anymore." I raised my arms, moved them side to side. "Like magic—used to see it, now I don't."

"Fucking black magic," she muttered. "Mine's long gone, too. I don't miss it."

"The crazy thing is no one ever notices I don't have one."

"People don't notice them, not even their own," Nellie said.

I nodded. "Shadows can replicate themselves."

"How do you figure?"

"Because it's what JJ insisted I include in my book. She should know."

"Here's what I know," Nellie said. "They're all going to strike someday if we don't strike first."

"That's scary."

"Boss, your wife never had a hint they existed?"

"Marcy often caught me talking to them and I'd pretend to be working something out for the book."

"Good thinking," Nellie said.

"When I was in a writing frenzy they were scarce. Apparently, as long as I kept busy and following the program there was no need to intervene."

"You're saying they watched you?"

"I'm sure they did. If I just sat there in a funk they went into action, pacing the room, standing over me, passing through the windows, the walls. It was like a haunted Grand Central Station in my den, with these gray pulsing forms, some with body mass and even some with fang-like teeth."

"The easier to frighten you with," Nellie said.

"They left a message written in steam on the bathroom mirror when I was three-quarters finished with the book."

"You got one of those?" Nellie asked.

"You, too?"

She nodded.

"Mine read WE CANNOT DIE. I wiped it off and resumed writing, keeping the same plot trajectory. A day or two later a new message appeared—BUT YOU CAN."

"They have a way with words," Nellie said.

"The Shadows tracked the book's plot. Hell, the book was likely their idea from the get-go. My original intent was to conform to the basic formula of good conquers evil. They forced me to rewrite—they didn't like that direction."

"You were afraid not to."

"That—and then JJ stepped in."

"What happened?" Nellie asked.

"Her suggestions became demands. She basically wrote the ending. Then came one big blur—meetings with editors, publishers, publicists."

Nellie said, "I'm guessing I was part of that blur. That one stupid book I wrote was in the same genre so maybe JJ pulled strings to get me that gig. She probably thought I was an easy target to scare."

"It wouldn't surprise me. JJ controlled everything else. On my book tours, in every city, hookers showed up, blonde-haired bimbos drenched with cheap perfume."

"What—no brunettes?"

"Brunettes, redheads, all shapes and sizes—she was fucking with me. After I spent the night with one of the women I was late for a book-signing and JJ read me the Riot Act from New York."

"You're easy," Nellie said.

"Okay, your turn. When did you first see the Shadows?"

"Care to guess?"

"My book?"

"Let's get comfy." Nellie crossed to the living room where she slumped down on the sofa, lifting her feet onto the coffee table.

I followed her and sat on the other end of the sofa.

Nellie said, "I never knew those fuckers existed until the review. My galleys arrived with Shadows already built in."

"How do you mean?"

"I should've been suspicious when my agent told me the Times wanted me to review a book. Me, of all people. I thought how did the idiot swing this? It turned out he didn't do a damn thing. Someone called him. My twenty-twenty hindsight kicked in way too late."

"It was planned."

"Only took you how many years to catch on? There I was almost done reading your book and jotting notes. My agent's instruction about keeping it all positive faded away. I sprinkled in an appropriate dose of negativity."

"It didn't read that way," I said.

"That's because I revised it after all hell broke loose."

"A Shadow?"

"The damn thing appeared in one corner of the room and scrambled up my wall like a fucking spider. It crawled across the ceiling! I'd seen some shit in my life with the ghost hunting but this rocked me. As for my cat, Casper bolted toward the bathroom. That's what really ticked me off—that thing terrifying my little baby.

"The Shadow dropped to the floor and I was out of my living room in two seconds flat. I slammed the bathroom door and locked it. Casper squeezed himself behind the toilet. I started screaming—get the hell out of my home, leave us alone."

I recalled one of my first experiences with the Shadows; it scuttled across my ceiling, too. "That doesn't work," I said.

"No shit. Now, where was I? I'm in the bathroom and I'm thinking fuck it, this is my home. I open the door and charge out of there screaming like a banshee. I see two of them, two demonic spider-creatures morphing into a gray cloud and drifting through my wall."

Nellie plopped her feet onto the floor and rose from the sofa. She walked past me to the sliding door. "I need a smoke."

"Stand in the doorway like last time. Was that it for the Shadows?"

"I wish. The next day they show up again, human-like, quivering outlines. By this time, I know your book is possessed. I was tempted to chuck it in a dumpster."

"Why didn't you?"

"I had a better idea."

"Do you still have the book?"

"Well, about that," Nellie said. "It kinda fell into a metal washtub and then it kinda caught on fire and burned the fuck up."

"How did that happen?"

"It might've been the gasoline it was soaking in."

I smiled at her. "Did they leave you alone after that?"

"Hell no. I had to figure a way to get rid of the Shadows. So, I asked them."

"They talked to you?"

"Of course not," she said. "That day, after my shower, there was a message on the mirror written in the steam. ITS OUR BOOK—in big fat letters. I thought of giving up showers but I was afraid they would find a more gruesome way to reach me. I took their message to mean I'd better write a favorable review. I didn't need further prodding after their next mirror-message, which ripped my heart out."

"What did it say?"

"HERE KITTY KITTY."

Neither of us spoke for a few seconds.

Nellie said, "I went back to the drawing board, rewrote the bullshit review and never saw them again. Good fucking riddance. Years go by and then you call me."

"You sorry you're here?"

"They should be sorry—they fucked with the wrong girl."

While I was already certain the Shadows were real, I was grateful to share the experience with someone else. Dr. Sanderson wouldn't buy into them. Marcy never saw any. Kate didn't see the one enveloping her on the boardwalk. The Zdenko brothers didn't see it standing right in front of them in Atlantic City. As far as I knew for sure, it might've only been me and JJ.

At times, I almost doubted myself. Edgar Allan Poe was quoted as saying, "I became insane, with long intervals of horrible sanity." In my messy life, I couldn't distinguish the difference.

"So, you saw the Shadows at college and in your previous home," Nellie said. "What happened after you moved here?"

"I bought this place almost three years ago. Everything was quiet—no more sightings until Kate Bowman."

"Murder victim number two," Nellie said.

"Yeah. A Shadow crept up from the boardwalk and nearly swallowed her."

"What did you do?"

"I swiped at it and the thing went away. Kate believed me when I told her it was a bug. Another Shadow touched my bike on Ocean Drive sending me airborne into the marshes just as a car was about to run me over."

"Who hit you—the car or the Shadow?"

"Who knows? Soon after, I saw another Shadow at my door before it melted away. One in the Atlantus, my parking garage, my balcony, my bedroom, and then the Shadow standing behind you last night."

"Fuck," she said. "They're everywhere."

"That's why you're here."

Nellie shook her head. "Damn," she muttered, returning to the sofa. "Let's talk about something more cheerful. How come that Jason guy hates you?"

"I wouldn't call it hate."

"I wouldn't call it love," she said.

"He's always had something against me. I chalk it up to jealousy."

"Of what? Your run-of-the-mill looks or your sparkling personality?"

"A neighbor down the hall, Gail, told me Jason complains he works too hard and has little to show for it. His money is courtesy of his wife's family and she keeps him on an allowance of sorts."

"She has him on a short leash," Nellie said.

"Plus, he liked Kate who kind of liked me."

"And—did you like her?"

"I met her on the boardwalk and never got the chance to know her. Anyway, Jason and his wife may be on the outs. I haven't seen her in weeks. Who knows what he's thinking?"

"This doesn't explain why you don't like him," Nellie said.

"The jerk accused me of murder."

She laughed. "What did you say to that?"

"I took a swing at him. Maggie broke it up," I said.

"You have more adventures than Indiana Jones."

"Shit happens."

"And you think Jason was the guy who attacked you with the bat?" Nellie asked.

"He's a candidate."

"Who else?"

"Off the top of my head—Dennis Slade, Hot Rod Jackson, Nikolai Zdenko, a random criminal, Shadows—maybe even V."

"Doesn't anybody like you?"

"You do," I said.

"I get Slade, since you screwed his wife, and Jason maybe because of Kate and whatever else. Shadows? No. Who's Hot Rod and I didn't know V had a brother."

"Jackson's a former pro baseball player, lives on this floor, drinks too much." Then I pointed to my head. "Baseball bat—my skull. As for Nikolai, I sense a violent undercurrent there. Also, he and I were talking in the parking garage just before I got hit. These oddballs keep me paranoid."

"Maybe you're the oddball," Nellie said.

"I wouldn't argue that."

"How about that Tommy guy—could he have done it?"

Tommy.

"He's my friend."

"That's an exclusive club," she said.

"Thanks."

The phone rang and the Caller ID showed Keira's number.

"Hi, David, it's me. I'm going to stop by around 5:30 so we can go over whatever Nellie has in mind."

"What about Tommy?"

"He'll meet us at the Atlantus. Anything else?"

I'm sorry for arguing with you.

"No, guess not."

We said our good-byes.

Nellie stared at me.

"What?" I asked.

"Boss, can I tell you something?"

"No."

"You aren't exactly the warm-and-fuzzy type."

"Like you?" I said.

"I'm giving you good advice."

"Unsolicited."

"Your girlfriend is a keeper."

I know.

"What about tonight?" I asked. "Do you have it all thought out?"

"Not every step. I leave room for adlibbing."

"Just so you know, I'm a little nervous."

"Good," she said. "I'd worry about you if you weren't."

CHAPTER FORTY-FIVE

"Let's go shopping," I said.

We toured every aisle in Acme. I knew I was in trouble when Nellie grabbed a second cart. "Beer wagon," she said. It was soon loaded to capacity with two cases of Coors, a few bottles of wine, another of Champagne.

I exercised restraint by ignoring the whiskey section. "Nellie, do you think we're overdoing it on alcohol?"

"Storm's coming. The supply boat might not make it through."

The deli counter proved a main attraction for my roomie. Cold cuts, cheeses, potato and macaroni salads. Later, a carton of cigarettes found their way in.

With two carts filled to overflow, we checked out with enough provisions to feed every seagull in the Wildwoods.

As we pulled into a parking space at the Crest Castle, a large shape emerged from the building's door.

"What—is—that?" Nellie asked.

"Zdenko," I said.

"He looks even bigger out of his pjs."

"Hi, V," I said, stepping from the van.

"Hello, Mr. Dave. I see you are with Nellie."

Zdenko strode toward her and held out his hand. "I smell cigarette. I am smoker, too."

"Bad habit," she said, shaking his hand.

Zdenko nodded. "Smoking is bad for health. Dave said so."

Nellie started to step away from him. "I hear squeezing someone's hand can be bad for circulation."

He quickly released it. "I am sorry I hold tight."

"I'm kidding," Nellie said.

"Oh, you have sense of humor." Zdenko laughed and cuffed her shoulder. "Women in Albania do not have sense of humor."

"I hate to break up the fun," I said. "But we better get all this upstairs."

"What is it you have?"

"Piles of groceries and booze."

"Wait. I know." He lumbered into the building and reappeared pushing a luggage cart. "I save the day."

"You da man," Nellie said.

She swung open the back of the van and Zdenko leaned in, grabbing the cases of beer first. I tried to pitch in but he nudged me aside. "I do this. You both go."

"I can't let you do that," Nellie said.

"Miss Nellie. It is my pleasure. I lock your van."

Despite Zdenko's protest I picked up a bag of groceries while Nellie snatched two bottles of wine. As we entered the elevator, Nellie said, "That guy's a moose."

"I think he's got the hots for you."

"Oh, please."

"What's wrong with him?" I asked.

"For one, he'd crush me."

We were still laughing when the elevator opened to my floor. The sight of Jason squelched my good humor.

"Hi," I said.

"Farmer," he sneered. "Party time, huh?"

His voice softened as he said, "Hi, Nellie."

"Jason," she nodded.

"Excuse me," I said, sidestepping him.

"Have a nice day," Nellie said.

"You, too." He hesitated for a beat and then added, "Be careful."

I stopped and turned to face Jason.

"Go that-a-way, Boss," Nellie said, pushing me to my door.

After Zdenko wheeled our supplies into my condo, he began unloading the luggage cart onto the kitchen island, liquor first. "What, no vodka? Now I make joke."

"How about having a bite to eat with us?" Nellie said.

"I already eat chicken livers and cabbage. Last night you said you were the ghost hunter. What will you do when you find ghost?"

Nellie turned to me. "Boss?"

"We're thinking of writing a book," I said.

"Like the shadow book. This time about ghosts?"

"Yeah, maybe."

"Remember I told you I see ghost in staircase?"

"I remember."

"It was hanging with the neck. You could write in book."

"We'll keep that in mind," I said.

"Maybe I have a beer."

"I got it," Nellie said. She pulled a can from the case and handed it to him. "Sorry, it's not very cold."

"Just like old country. We drink it warm as long as it is beer." He downed a large gulp tipping the can more than halfway. "I have important question."

"What?" I asked.

"I want to ghost hunt."

"That's not a question."

"I help find ghosts. I have sharp eyes."

"We have enough help," I said. "Besides, you might scare them away."

His ever-present smile vanished. "I see."

"I was kidding."

"Ah." He turned to Nellie. "Dave say joke. I come?"

"I already have what I need. I'm sorry, V."

Zdenko nodded. He finished his beer with a final swig, crushed the aluminum with his left hand and dropped the mangled can on the granite surface, where it clanked, wobbled and died. The three of us stood in an uncomfortable quiet.

"Um, want another?" Nellie asked.

"See—I do you the favor. Now fits easy in recycles." Zdenko said. "I take cart downstairs."

"Thanks," she said.

"Bye, Miss Nellie."

After he left, Nellie pointed to the beer can. "He crushed it like it was a paper cup."

"I think he's disappointed," I said.

"Such is life."

As we stocked our supplies, I asked, "Your ghost gear—is it complicated?"

"Not for me it ain't. But, for you it'll be like a Rubik's Cube."

"I'll figure it out."

"Figure how to get your friend Tommy here."

"Keira said he'll meet us over at the Atlantus," I said.

"I don't like that. He'll be drinking. I don't want him fucking this up."

"Okay."

I walked over to the handset and tapped his number.

"Hi, Tommy," I said.

"Hey Dave, what's up?"

"You know we're ghost hunting tonight at Mick's place."

"I'm ready. Should be fun," Tommy said.

"We're meeting here at six and we'd like you to make it. Nellie wants to go over things, her equipment and stuff."

"I'd rather have a drink or two at the bar first."

Nellie walked over to me. "Well?"

I shook my head and she grabbed the phone.

"Tom, this is Nellie. Thanks for getting us into the Atlantus tonight."

"No problem. I'm looking forward to meeting you."

"About that," Nellie said. "I'm going to meet you here in Dave's condo at six."

"I planned on seeing you over there."

"That doesn't work for me. I'll see you here at six—and we're about to be cut off."

Nellie disconnected the call.

"Done," she said.

Keira showed up promptly at six while Tommy arrived ten minutes later, holding his Phillies cap in his hand.

"Hi, everyone," he said.

"You Tom?" Nellie asked.

"Yeah. Nellie?" He held out his hand to her. She left it hanging for a second and then accepted it. "We have a lot of ground to cover," she said. "Thanks for coming early."

"Glad to."

Tommy sat on one end of the sofa with Keira on the other. I sat adjacent to her in the loveseat while Nellie took the seat nearest the glass slider.

Our modest band of ghost hunters met among bottles of Coke, spring water, plates of cheese and cold cuts.

Nellie asked, "Can I get anyone some ice?"

"You wouldn't have a beer in the fridge by any chance, would you?" Tommy asked.

Keira spoke up. "None of us are drinking tonight. Nellie's rules."

"What kind of rule is that?"

"Alcohol and ghosts don't mix," Nellie said. "I need everyone alert."

I took a sip from my bottle of spring water. Tommy noticed.

"You?" he said. "Drinking water? Someone get a picture of this."

Keira said, "Tommy. We can all do without for a couple of hours."

He started to say something but stopped and nodded his head.

Some of Nellie's ghost-hunting equipment rested on the coffee table while the green laundry basket containing cables and meters were on the carpeting.

"Nellie," I said. "Could you outline your plans?"

"Aye aye, captain," she said, saluting with a crisp snap of her hand and then crossed to the center of the room.

Nellie made eye contact with each of us. "We're going to find a ghost tonight. Don't ask me how I know. I just do. But, this ain't gonna be a piece of cake. Even if it goes well, it's liable to get scary." She tugged at her white hair. "I used to be a brunette."

Tommy laughed.

"Yeah, except it ain't funny, Finch."

Tommy glanced in my direction, perhaps expecting help.

I shrugged.

Nellie continued. "I already know there's a ghost upstairs in the Atlantus. I visited the place years ago and failed to make contact with Nancy, the young girl who had that unfortunate fall from the second-floor window. Everybody with me so far? Finch?"

"Yeah, I know she's up there."

"Have you seen her?" Nellie asked.

"The owner, Mick—I think he has."

"And so will we," Nellie said.

"That'll make Mick happy." Tommy smiled. "Proof of a ghost in-residence—what a marketing coup." He bent over and grabbed a meter from the basket on the floor. "What does this do?"

Nellie stared at him. "Put that down, please. I'll show you when I'm ready."

"Sorry," Tommy said, peeking at me again.

Nellie watched as he carefully placed the meter on the coffee table.

"I'm no scientist but these instruments are products of the science community," Nellie said. "They don't come cheap and we need to treat them with respect."

Nellie introduced her gear. She explained their use and no one asked questions.

She picked up the meter Tommy held earlier. She pointed to my hallway and said, "In the back room, I have PC monitors and enough cable to stretch halfway to Cape May. I also have a camera tripod. I don't want to tell you how much that baby cost. No one will be allowed to use it other than me.

"Now, this little darling I'm holding is a Gauss Meter. It was invented by a German scientist and measures the strength of a magnetic field. It gauges the electromagnetic anomalies in an environment caused by a paranormal presence. The meter displays in number form any disruption. Just click the button, carry this thing into a room and walk in any direction checking the LED readout. A reading of .1 milligauss means there's no paranormal activity, and as you walk the area you might see it bounce around a bit—maybe to .8, still within normal range. But if it suddenly jumps to 3.5, well, that could mean something else."

"A ghost?" Keira asked.

"Perhaps. One thing is for sure; we'd take a closer look and compare that reading to others in the room. As much as the number values, we're looking for spikes. We'll have walkie-talkies so we can keep in touch."

"Time for a show-and-tell," Nellie added. I started to get up but she motioned for me to stay seated. "Keira, let's try this out."

"Super!" she said, almost leaping from the sofa.

Nellie gave the meter to her and together they walked to the front door and back across the room, stopping briefly near the kitchen, tinkering with a meter setting. They resumed and headed in my direction.

"Look at this," Keira said. "The reading went up to 1.2. Is that significant?"

"Not yet. I want us to try other areas to establish the range."

As they disappeared down the hallway Tommy and I looked at each other.

"Is Nellie on the level?" he asked.

"Why don't you ask her?"

"No, thanks."

After a few minutes, the two ghost hunters returned.

"Any activity?" I asked.

"Uneventful," Nellie said. "Well, there was one small item of interest."

"What was that?"

"Your razor scored mighty low. You might want to take it for a spin more often."

Chapter Forty-six

After Nellie outlined our assignments, Keira and Tommy helped us carry the equipment down to Nellie's van. Then they each drove off in their own cars. Keira wanted to check on her mother, and Tommy I assumed wanted to check out Mick's bar. We all agreed to meet 8:30 at the Atlantus. Nellie and I still had time to kill.

Nellie walked down my hallway and returned wearing a different sweatshirt—bright orange sporting the single word, "BOO!" in large black letters.

She perched on a stool at the kitchen island, and munched on veggies,

"Nellie, is now the right time for you to tell me about your secret weapon?"

"No."

I leaned against the counter next to the fridge, next to the bottle of Maker's. "Want a beer?" I asked.

"Yeah, but I'll hold off till after."

The phone rang and I answered it. "Hi—is something wrong? I'll be right there."

"Who was that?"

"Maggie. She doesn't sound good."

As we crossed the hallway, the door to Gail's condo opened and Jason stepped out, with Gail standing behind him. He fumbled with his belt and made the briefest eye contact with us before opening his own door.

Gail looked our way.

I nodded my head. "Hi."

"Have a nice day," she said, withdrawing inside.

"Who was that beautiful woman?" Nellie asked.

"Dr. Gail Montrose."

"I guess your pal, Jason, needed medical attention."

"He's married." I said.

"Aren't they all."

I was about to knock on Maggie's door when she opened it first. "Come in."

"Are you alright?" I asked as we entered.

Maggie wore a white terrycloth robe, which covered her body from neck to her pink slippers. "Please, sit. Can I get either of you a drink? I have white wine."

"No thank you, Maggie," Nellie answered, as we both took seats in the living room.

"I didn't like the way you sounded on the phone," I said.

"Oh, that. It was nothing."

"You were coughing and your voice was weak."

"I'm fine as you can see. It might have been a bad connection. As long as you're both here I have something to show you. Close your eyes," she said. "No peeking."

I shut my eyes and Maggie said, "Voila!"

I opened them. She stood in a purple velour sweatsuit while her robe now rested on the chair behind her.

"Huh? I mean you look very nice," I said.

"A woman needs an outfit for every occasion. This is my ghost-hunting outfit. Do you like it?"

"What do you plan on doing?" said Nellie. "Chasing the ghost?"

"Well, it is a jogging suit." Maggie executed a 360 so we could get the full effect. "I love these adorable white roses embroidered on the sleeves—don't you, Dave?"

"What do you mean ghost-hunting outfit?"

"I saw everyone taking Nellie's equipment into the elevator. I can put two and two together. Tonight's the night. All I have to do is put on my sneakers and I'll be all set."

"Wait a second. We already talked about this," I said.

"Yes, we did. However, I got to thinking. You need a person who brings something special to the party. I offer enthusiasm, confidence and a positive attitude. Don't you agree, Nellie dear?"

"I do," she said. Then she leaned toward me and added, "I'd rather have Maggie and bump Tommy to second-string."

I laughed. "You're something, Maggie. Okay. We'll leave around 8:15. Your sneaks—are they purple, too?"

"You have to ask?"

When we got back to my place I noticed movement outside my sliding glass door. Trying to distinguish a Shadow from the darkness wasn't always easy. Detecting motion was the easier job.

There was motion.

I walked to the slider and gazed out at the starless night. Below, the waves splashed against the beach, creating a constant din that drifted to my seventh-story home.

"You see something?" Nellie asked. "Not another fucking Shadow, I hope."

"I'm not sure what I saw," I said, backing away from the slider.

That's when it glided through the glass into the living room. Nellie picked up a bottle of wine and held it at her side. "Beat it," she said in a calm voice.

It disappeared.

"That works?" I asked.

Nellie strode down my hallway. I guessed where she was heading.

"Boss, you gotta see this."

When I reached the bathroom I saw Nellie staring at the mirror. I learned something new about the Shadows—they didn't need steam to communicate. There, on that mirror, was the proof. Written on the glass in blood-red lettering was a message, "DO NOT GO."

"I was wondering when we would hear from them," Nellie said.

"You were expecting this?"

"Only if we were on the right track."

That was the first sighting of the night.

At 8:10 I knocked on Maggie's door. She wore a gray jacket over her sweatsuit. "I wish my Harold could see me now."

"I'm sure he can," I said, not sure of anything.

Nellie interlocked arms with Maggie as we waited at the elevator. "Maggie, I want you to understand the seriousness of what we're doing tonight. It's dangerous."

"I'm not worried."

"I feel responsible for you. Once we're there I want you to do whatever I tell you."

"Of course."

We rode down to the parking garage and the elevator door slid open with a hiss.

They were sitting on the hood of Nellie's van. The first Shadow slid off and landed on the ground by the driver's door before melting through the frame of the vehicle, coming to rest in the back seat. Its partially-formed head turned and red jagged teeth showed in our direction. Above them two reddish circles stared at us.

"Do you see anything unusual?" I asked Maggie.

"Is that Nellie's van? I haven't seen it before but Harold and I once owned a Dodge Caravan much like that."

"She doesn't see them," Nellie whispered to me.

The second Shadow floated from the front of the vehicle and hovered a few feet before us. This pulsating gray-black mass was directly in our path to the van. Maggie moved forward and passed through it. She turned to look at me and said, "Hurry along, Dave, we don't want to be late."

Nellie unlocked the door, grabbed the inside roof handle and hoisted herself in. I stepped around the Shadow and caught up with Maggie, opening the front passenger-side door for her. Checking the back seat, I saw it was empty—yet I still hesitated.

"Hop in, Boss," Nellie said. She turned the ignition key to start the engine.

It growled.

It whined.

It went silent.

"Shit," Nellie said.

"Does this happen often?" Maggie asked.

"Normally this baby purrs."

I glanced at my watch when suddenly something banged on the window next to me. I almost dove to the floor.

"Need help?" Dennis Slade asked, brandishing a walking cane, which he had used to rap against the glass.

I rolled down my window and Nellie yelled across to him. "Do you know anything about engines?"

"I used to be a Teamster, so yeah; I know a thing or two."

He walked to the hood and popped it up. "Do you have any tools, Nellie?"

She twisted her body and tried to reach something on the floor behind her. "Boss, grab that metal box for me."

She jumped down from her seat and brought the tools to Dennis and then returned behind the wheel. After a few minutes Dennis shouted, "Try it now." The van kicked in on the first attempt.

"What did you do, Mr. Slade?" Nellie asked.

He slammed the hood and brought the tools to her. "I didn't see any obvious problem so I just tightened a few things. Somewhere along the line I got the right one." He leaned around Nellie. "Hey, is that you in there, Maggie? I didn't notice you before."

"That's all right, Dennis. We're going ghost hunting—want to come?"

What the fuck!

"You kidding? Maggie, you really believe in this stuff?"

"Doesn't everyone?" Maggie shifted her body to face him. "It's such a damp night for you to be out—you could easily catch a cold."

"You should be glad I came by."

"We are."

"Ever since I lost Cecily." Dennis paused and glanced at me. "Ever since that happened I do a lot of walking. Well, good luck in your— ghost hunting."

Dennis started to move away but Maggie wasn't done. "Thank you," she said. "By the way, that's a lovely walking stick. Is it new?"

"I got it a couple weeks ago—genuine Irish blackthorn." He brandished it out in front of him, as if prepping for a swordfight. "It's already come in handy."

Chapter Forty-seven

Many things occur in multiples of three. It's a common belief a famous person's death is followed quickly by two others.

Three—strikes you're out, blind mice, Musketeers—even Goldilocks had her three bears.

I should have seen it coming.

The Atlantus Tavern sits on a corner in the Washington Street Mall, the outdoor shopping area. The three-block-long collection of shops and restaurants is nestled in the center of Cape May. In the off-season, many of the businesses are closed, or remain open with reduced hours. After dark, the area is deserted.

Nellie parked behind the building, and Mickey Hatfield, third generation proprietor of a haunted bar and grill, opened the back door for us to bring in all the gear.

Keira walked outside with Tommy close behind.

Maggie passed them carrying two meters Nellie had given her.

Nellie handed Keira two cameras.

"Need a hand?" Tommy asked Keira.

"I'm good," she said, heading inside.

I removed the tripod from the van and handed it to Tommy.

"Careful with that," Nellie said to him.

"I think I can handle it," he answered, walking away.

"I got some cable for you on your next trip," Nellie called after him.

Nellie pulled on my arm "That guy's your best friend?"

"Why do you ask?"

"I'm not a big fan."

"How come?"

"He likes your girlfriend as much as you do."

"You're wrong."

You're right.

Mick had set up folding tables in the bar area and Nellie plugged in her two PC monitors. I didn't see any workers or customers in the restaurant. Tommy sat himself on a barstool and the owner poured him a beer, placing the mug on the varnished surface.

Nellie motioned to a chair in front of one of the monitors. "Maggie, this will be your station. Any action should happen upstairs but you'll have a ringside view. You'll also have this walkie-talkie so we can keep in touch. Please stay downstairs. Okay?"

"Got it," she said.

"Nellie," Tommy said from his barstool. "Have a drink with me."

She strolled over to him. "I asked everyone not to drink tonight."

"It's just a beer." Tommy said.

"Make it your last."

"You serious?"

"As a heart attack," Nellie said.

Nellie pointed to a shiny gray leather blazer draped over a nearby barstool. "Who belongs to that?" she asked Mick as I joined her.

"The only other customer—high-class woman, not my usual clientele. Still got a bit of her Martini left."

"Hendricks?" I asked.

"Yes," Mick said, scanning the restaurant. "Where the hell did she go?"

"I'm right here," a familiar voice said.

First came the Shadow in my condo warning us to stay put, then the parking garage, and now, completing the hellish trio, was obstacle number three.

"JJ, what are you doing here?" I asked, peering up the stairs.

"I went to the powder room," she said.

"You're JJ?" Nellie asked.

"In the flesh."

JJ's attire was more appropriate for sipping a nightcap at New York's Four Seasons. A black leather skirt was accented by a burgundy silk blouse. Her glossy black heels clicked on the hardwood steps as she made her way downstairs.

Without warning, she kissed me on the cheek. "Fancy meeting you here, Dave."

JJ then approached Nellie but she backed away and shook her head.

"I see you're the shy type," JJ said. "You'll get used to me. We're going to be seeing a lot of each other."

"That's not gonna happen," Nellie said.

JJ smiled at her. "Your novel was such a harmless book. But if I had been your agent …"

"I'd be rich and famous?"

"Well, you wouldn't be living in Delaware."

Keira inched closer to me and removed a tissue from her pocket. She dabbed JJ's lipstick from my face. "Your agent?"

"Former agent."

"Where are your manners?" JJ asked me. "How about a proper introduction?"

"This is Keira—that's JJ."

"Pleased to meet you," Keira said, offering her hand.

"Yes, I'm sure," JJ answered, barely touching Keira's fingers.

JJ surveyed the room, her false eyelashes curling upwards. "My, my, this is impressive equipment. Are all these people part of your little expedition?"

Maggie answered before I could. "We're ghost hunting."

"Isn't that quaint."

"Cut the phony chitchat," I said. "Why are you here?"

"Let's talk, just the three of us," she said, waving her hand in Nellie's direction. "I simply adore that sweatshirt."

JJ sauntered toward the dining room and we followed. She chose a table in plain sight of our group but far enough away to ensure privacy. She smoothed her blouse as she sat down. Her painted smile vanished. "They don't want you here."

"They?" I asked, taking a seat next to Nellie.

"They want you to leave and I agree—for your own safety."

"Sounds like a threat," I said.

"You don't want to challenge them." JJ leaned towards Nellie. "You do know what I'm talking about, don't you?"

"I dealt with them," Nellie said.

"They let you off easy."

"JJ," I said. "You came here to say something—say it."

I watched Nellie as she toyed with her cigarette lighter.

"You know what they're capable of," JJ said. "I'm here to help you. Forget this nonsense and I'll make you both fabulously rich. And save your lives in the process."

"Now, that is a threat," I said. "Time you hit the road."

"You speak to me like that after all I've done for you?"

"I barely survived the first go-round."

"Oh stop. If they wanted you dead you'd be six feet under long ago."

Nellie continued to play with her lighter, sliding it between her fingers, into the palm of her hand and back again.

I looked at Nellie. "Anything to contribute?"

"Let her finish. I'm about to be the richest lady on the whole fucking planet."

JJ continued. "Here's what I'll do. You two agree to write a book on the murders. I can bang out a contract in no time. The basics are already done—I just need to plug in some generous numbers. Add a detail or two. We can make it official when I hand you a check. I'd tell you how much you'll rake in but I can't count that high."

"No." I said.

"You're shortsighted. The book deal is a given but I'll aim higher. HBO. Their VP of Programming and I attend the same church. Before I drove down here, we lunched in the city. I outlined the basics and believe me there was huge interest."

"You go to church?" I asked.

"I'll go anywhere to get what I want."

"Is it getting cold in here or is it me?" I asked.

"It's friggin cold," JJ said, crossing her arms over her breasts. "Brrr."

"Nellie and I have things to do. Is your sales pitch over?"

"The moment you agree to sign a contract."

"I said no."

"I don't like this side of you." JJ placed her hands on the table, her lacquered nails strumming a frenetic rhythm.

"Nervous?" I asked.

She glanced back at Mick and our team. She leaned toward me and lowered her voice. "Take your friends out of here before they get hurt."

Nellie's eyes shifted from me to JJ.

I waited for Nellie to speak.

"Enough of this," JJ said. "You're wasting your time. I was just upstairs and I can tell you there are no signs of life, spectral or otherwise. Nothing except empty tables and chairs covered in two-inch dust. Pack up all this stuff and go home. What do you say?"

"I'll field this one," Nellie said, as she thumbed the lighter wheel and watched the flame dance. "What's your connection with them?"

"I help them—and they help me."

"In other words, they fucking own you."

"Say it anyway you like—it's very lucrative."

Nellie nodded. Both ladies stared at each other in momentary silence, the flame still flickering. Nellie then snapped the lighter closed.

"What are you so afraid of?" she asked JJ.

"Not a thing."

"Then why are you here?"

JJ smiled. "You think you'll survive this with some mumbo-jumbo bullshit? I know about your trip to Brazil."

Nellie laughed. "So, that's it."

"Brazil?" I said.

"You don't know about that?" JJ asked. "Nellie, shame on you."

"You really are scared," Nellie said to her.

"Of you? Not a chance."

"And yet, here you are."

Nellie still held the silver cigarette lighter. She exhaled on it and wiped it with her shirt. "Clean as a whistle," she said, returning the lighter to her jeans pocket.

She slid her chair back and stood up, keeping her gaze fixed on JJ. "We're done here."

Then Nellie looked at me and said, "C'mon, Boss—it's showtime."

CHAPTER FORTY-EIGHT

"Where did that woman go?" Mick asked. "Her martini is still sitting here."

Tommy said, "Their meeting must've gone wrong. She stomps over here like she's pissed. I say to her you okay? She goes mind your own business. Then she grabs her jacket and scoots out the door."

Nellie finished setting up the equipment downstairs—plugging in cables, getting the laptops up and running, testing the walkie-talkies, fiddling with the meters. Then she turned her attention to Maggie.

"How do you like these, Maggie?" Nellie asked, helping the woman with the wireless headphones.

"They'll keep my ears warm."

Nellie smiled. "There is a chill in here. It's a good sign. Here's your pair, Keira. The headphones will give you flexibility if you get up. There's a dial to adjust the volume. I'll try not to scream too loud if things go south."

Mick watched her. "Can I help?" he asked.

"Yeah. Don't give Finch anything else to drink."

"You got it."

"Mick, thanks for letting me take another crack at Nancy," Nellie said. "Years ago I wasn't quite ready. This time will be different."

"I'm rooting for you."

"Can you tell me anything else about her?" Nellie asked.

"You know the history, right? My grandfather rented the upstairs for a birthday party. Hot day. No air-conditioning and, of course, the window open. The radio, dancing, the Conga line, a woman lost her balance and fell into Nancy, sending her out the window. It wasn't a long fall, of course, but she landed wrong and broke her neck. If this kind of thing happened today, her family would own this place and I'd be sitting on a barstool, a regular like Tommy."

"When was the last sighting?" Nellie asked.

"A college girl, Lauren, waitressed here over the summer. Back at school now. She said Nancy stood in the window upstairs wearing a green dress."

"In the window?" Nellie asked.

"Lauren said it looked as though Nancy was stuck inside the glass. Doesn't sound possible, does it?"

Nellie shook her head. "A lot of things aren't possible—until they happen."

The room upstairs was dark and stifling. A musty odor invaded my nostrils. I had the nagging suspicion we weren't alone; something was waiting for us.

"There could be both ghosts and Shadows here," I said to Nellie at the top of the stairs.

"No chance of that."

"JJ doesn't make idle threats."

"She was bluffing. Shadows don't want any part of what's going down tonight."

"How do you know that?" I asked.

"Why do you think I didn't tell you about my secret weapon? I'm not tipping my hand."

"Finally, you can tell me what it is?"

"No."

"There's a light switch here somewhere," I said.

"Leave it alone."

We set up the tripod and camera in near darkness. "I'm proud of this baby," Nellie said. "It's got everything—swivel, tilt, thermal heat sensor. The auto tracker will follow me and transmit to the laptops, which is why I'd like you to stay off camera."

"I will."

"This is for you," Nellie said, placing a strapped object around my neck.

"What is it?"

"It's the infrared motion detector camera. You've got a thirty-foot detection range with a ninety-degree fan radius."

"Sounds impressive, but what do I do?"

"I showed you a few hours ago," she said.

"I thought I recognized it."

"You follow me with the camera. It'll signal with a flashing green light and then you aim it until the light turns blue. At that point it'll be recording. Got that?"

"Got it. Sounds like it kinda does the same thing as the one we just set up," I said.

"Redundancy is good. In case one doesn't get everything the other will."

"You got this all covered."

"There's an old saying—maximus praeparatus, then kick 'em in the ass."

"Who said that?" I asked.

"Nellie Hagerstrom, ghost hunter par excellence."

We rejoined our group downstairs and I grabbed a chair next to Keira.

"Everybody, listen up," Nellie said, clapping her hands. We all clustered together, except Tommy. He swiveled on the barstool to face her. Nellie pointed to him. "Finch, you're in the bullpen. Dave and I will be upstairs and if the shit hits the fan we may need you in a hurry."

"What—I don't have anything to do? I might as well have another brewski. Barkeep?"

"Let's hold off on that," Mick said.

Nellie pivoted towards Keira and me. "Keira, you're in charge down here. Stay with Maggie. Don't come up unless I call you," Nellie added, her finger poised over the walkie-talkie on her belt.

"Any final instructions?" I asked.

"Yeah. Sit tight while I get something out of my van. Be right back." She hustled out the back door.

"Lucky you," Keira said to me. "You get to go upstairs."

"I don't know. I see a bad moon rising."

Maggie walked to me from her chair, leaned over and gave me a hug. "Don't worry, Dave. I'll be down here, just a few steps away."

Nellie returned clutching a small pouch tied shut with a drawstring. The sack was pinkish and somehow organic. I didn't want to get any closer. She fastened the drawstring to her belt.

"What the hell is that?" I asked.

"My secret weapon."

"What is it?"

"A present for Nancy—the gift of death."

"It smells like pee."

"Then sniff in the other direction. Battle stations everyone," Nellie said.

She is the one.

Nellie climbed two stairs ahead of me.

"I don't want anything to happen to you," I said.

"What?"

"You might run into something unexpected."

"Relax. I'll handle it."

I peeked down the stairs. No one was visible and no one spoke. I did see Keira's right leg, her sneaker bouncing on the floor with nervous energy.

Nellie reached the landing first and I joined her.

I tapped her shoulder. "What actually happens when we …"

"Find her? Don't be afraid to say it."

"We find her—then what?"

"I deal with her and you continue to film. And don't knock that tripod over."

Nellie stood next to me and adjusted the starting read on the meter.

"You got the walkie-talkie?" I asked.

"Clipped to my belt."

"Okay, I see it, next to that other—thing. Is that what JJ meant when she said mumbo jumbo?"

"Boss, time to make like Charlie Chaplin and shush."

I haven't yet crossed over. Help me.

I held out my fist to Nellie, and with the glare from downstairs providing faint light, we fist-bumped. I whispered, "Whatever happens I'm grateful you're here. Thank you."

"You picked a hell of a time to get sappy. Just guard the stairs and fight the temptation to come to my rescue. If I want you I'll scream your name."

"Alright," I said.

She flicked a button on the Gauss Meter and the LED came alive.

I remained near the staircase railing while Nellie shuffled into the murky room. I heard a high-pitched beeping from the meter. The light on the tripod camera indicated it was in operation. I focused my camera on Nellie.

"Nancy?" Nellie whispered.

I saw her pause and listen for a response.

"Nancy?"

Hello.

Nellie turned to me. "Did you hear that?"

I shook my head. "Hear what?" I patted the Maglite buried in my front pocket.

As she passed by the bathrooms, Nellie said, ".6, .8, .9." She hesitated by a stack of chairs against the wall. "Nothing here." Then she moved to a few nearby tables. "Still .9," she said, shuffling toward the window. Here we go, just spiked to 2.3, now 5.7, and the temperature is dropping."

I heard a sound on the stairs behind me. Tommy was climbing up.

"What the hell are you doing?" I said, as I descended to meet him.

"I want to help. Move over," he said.

"Nellie told you to stay put unless she needed you."

"I can't just sit at the bar."

I grabbed his shirt as he tried to squeeze past. "Go back, you idiot."

Nellie screamed.

Tommy scrambled up the stairs with me trailing. He stopped as he reached the landing and I collided with him. I strained my eyes in the darkness and blinked a few times while pulling the flashlight from my pocket.

No Nellie.

"We're too late," Tommy said.

"Nellie!" I shouted, scanning the area with light. "Nellie!" I saw my breath in the air, realizing the sudden cold in the room.

"I saw her! I saw them!" Keira's voice. I glanced back as she arrived at the top of the stairs. I ran to her, catching her in my arms.

"Where's Nellie?" she yelled, panting as she struggled to get loose.

"I don't know."

"We have to find her," Keira said, shaking free and hurrying to the window.

"She's gone," Tommy said.

"You fucked this up," I yelled at him. "I was supposed to be with her."

"It wouldn't have made a difference."

"Keira," I said. "What did you mean you saw them?"

"On the laptop. Oh my God, it's freezing up here."

I tried again. "Can you hear me, Nellie?"

Tommy grabbed the camera from its mounting and headed down the stairs.

Keira said, "Let's go, David. You gotta see this."

Maggie was still positioned at the computer, her eyes wide with fear. "Dave, where's Nellie?"

"I wish I knew."

"Anybody know how to work this?" Tommy asked, holding the camera.

"Let me try," Keira said, taking it from Tommy. She pushed a button and a side screen popped out. "There's a way to transfer this so we can watch it on the laptop. I'm not sure how."

Tommy, Maggie and I gathered around that small screen, with me almost resting my head on Keira's shoulder.

"This is the moment before Nellie does her thing," Keira said.

In a few seconds Nellie came into view staring at her meter, walking slowly to the window. "Still .9," Nellie said. "Here we go, just spiked to 2.3, now 5.7, and the temperature is dropping."

I heard muffled voices followed by a garbled sound. Nellie's head turned.

"What's going on?" I asked.

"She hears you and Tommy," Keira said.

Nellie stood motionless. I sensed she weighed her options. She regained her focus on the window. A shaft of moonlight sliced through the room. Nellie approached and held out her hand as if bathing it in the warmth of that beam.

"Nancy," Nellie said calmly.

The moonlight shimmered with a golden glow. In that beam of light, I saw an outline—a white silhouette—vanishing in the same moment it became visible.

"Yes, it's here," Nellie said.

She untied the pouch from her belt and loosened the drawstring. She opened the pouch and it released a pinkish aura, which melded in a collage of pink, pale green and gold.

Nellie stepped into that rainbow swirl of colors. When she did, her face turned, as if to the camera, as if to me.

She smiled.

She screamed.

She disappeared.

Chapter Forty-nine

"What just happened?" Mick asked, "And where's Nellie?"

"Gone." Tommy answered.

"Shut up," I said. "She's not gone."

Keira looked at us from her seat. "Stop it, you two. We need to find her."

"How?" Tommy asked. "You saw what happened. Right there on the screen."

"We don't know what we saw," Keira said.

Tommy sat down on Maggie's seat.

Maggie's seat?

"Anybody see where Maggie went?" I asked.

"Oh no," Tommy said, glancing at the staircase.

I sprinted up the stairs shouting her name, but there was no response. Arriving at the top I headed for the window, where Nellie had disappeared into the whirlpool of colors just minutes ago. I walked through the last remnant of moonbeam and peered out the window to the pavement below.

No one there.

I turned and felt for my mini flashlight but I'd left it downstairs.

"Maggie?"

Nothing.

"Maggie?" I asked the darkness again.

"Dave, I'm over here."

"Where?"

"Dave." I followed the voice. Maggie stood in the corner against the wall.

"You all right?" I asked, reaching her.

"I think so. I tried to answer when you called but nothing came out."

I hugged her and she clung tight to me.

"I saw Nellie," she said.

"Where?"

"There." Maggie pointed a finger.

"You mean she was at the window?" I asked.

"No. She was *in* the window."

"Huh?"

"I went to her and she, well, she just dissolved."

"Did she say anything?" I asked.

"No, but her facial expression—I'll never forget it."

"I'm sure she was frightened."

"No, that's not it. She seemed—calm, maybe contented? I don't think she was scared. But I sure was."

I heard banging from downstairs.

"David! David!" Keira's voice.

I grabbed Maggie's hand and headed for the stairs.

"David. Nellie's here."

"Thank goodness," Maggie said as we descended.

Nellie sat at one the tables, her head buried in her hands.

"Are you alright?" I asked.

She nodded. "Yes—I'm very alright."

"Where did you go?"

"Someplace—" She hesitated. "Someplace wonderful."

"She pounded on the front door," Mick said.

Nellie looked at him. "Mick, what's your smoking policy?" she asked, while removing a bent cigarette from her jeans pocket. "My emergency stash."

"Be my guest," Mick said.

Nellie lit up and inhaled deeply, blowing out the smoke.

Maggie asked, "Nellie, what happened? I saw you inside the window."

"In it?"

"You were floating inside the glass."

Nellie shook her head. "That's a new one on me."

"You're so composed," Maggie said. "My heart is ticking way too fast."

"Me too," Nellie said, tapping her own chest. "Hey! Did we get all this on video?"

Keira said, "Maggie and I saw everything. You walked into the moonlight and you spoke to Nancy. There were colors, and then poof, you were gone."

"Cool. How about Nancy? Could you see her?"

"Well—I think I did," Keira said. "It happened so fast."

"I gotta see this," Nellie said. "Let me have the camera."

Keira handed it to her.

"Can we watch the video on the laptop screen?" I asked.

"After I work my magic," Nellie said as she sat in front of the computer. "This camera's loaded with an SD memory card." She removed a postage stamp-sized chip and slid it into a port on the laptop. "Just pop in this little guy, wait a few seconds till the computer sees it, key this, and—bang—open up. Easy as pie. We got slo-mo, stop action, anything we want."

Mick joined us and we all hunched over Nellie as the video displayed the empty upstairs room. Then Nellie came into view staring at the Gauss Meter.

"There I go, calling her name. Did anyone hear her respond?"

"No," Keira said.

"Anyone?" Nellie said, looking over her shoulder as we all shook our heads.

"Maybe there wasn't an actual voice but I heard it clearly. Okay, here it comes—the moonlight and Nancy. Oh—look at that!"

"Nancy?" Keira asked.

"Nancy. I wanna see it again," Nellie said.

"That flash of light?" I asked.

"Let's back it up—run in slo-mo and I'll pause it."

We watched as Nellie stepped into the moonlight again, her hand extended.

"You see that!" Nellie said, tapping at the still picture. "There she is. I can hardly believe it. My whole life I waited for this."

"It's a white splotch," I said.

"No," said Keira. "There's a greenish tint in the middle. David, look closer."

Nellie placed her finger on the screen and traced an outline. "That's her dress. Can you all see that?"

"No," I said. "I'm getting bleary-eyed."

"Me neither," Tommy added.

"I want to. Oh, I really want to," Maggie said.

Nellie pushed a key and the action resumed. "She asked me if I had what she needed. And there I am untying the pouch. I swear the pouch was alive in my hands."

"What is that thing?" I asked.

Suddenly Nellie shouted, "The Boto! Where's the Boto?"

"What's a Boto?" I asked.

"Oh, thank God," Nellie said, touching her belt. "It's here."

"That thing really is your secret weapon?"

The computer screen went dark.

"What happened?" I asked.

"I shut it down," Nellie said. "We're done here. Let's pack this gear and head back to your place."

"Wait a second," Mick said. "Nellie, I'm really glad you weren't hurt but what about Nancy and proving she's here?"

"That's the bad news, Mick. She's not here anymore."

"How do you know?"

"Nancy's waiting is over."

"Waiting for what?"

"For the gift I brought her."

Mick grunted. "Just my stupid luck. That girl was my meal ticket. Isn't she on the video?"

"Literally a split second. Nothing conclusive. Even our group here can't agree."

"No offense, but what do I get out of this?" Mick asked.

"Satisfaction for playing a role in one of the most significant events of our time. And I'll make you a copy of the video. You can run it on a loop in the bar if you like."

"It doesn't sound like anything I can take to the bank."

As we loaded the equipment in the back of the van it was near midnight and Nellie asked Keira, "Are you coming back to Dave's for the postmortem?"

"I wouldn't miss it. Be there right after I check on Tommy and Mick."

Nellie, Maggie and I climbed into the van. Nellie steered us through a light steady rain to the Crest. None of us spoke.

When she parked the van Nellie said, "Boss, bring that laptop with you. I got the camera. We can cart some of the other stuff up tomorrow."

When the elevator opened to our floor, Maggie immediately crossed to her condo. "I hate to miss your meeting but I'm exhausted and I'll need a sedative to calm my nerves. Nellie, thank you for letting me come along, and I hope someone will fill me in tomorrow."

I turned on the television as soon as we entered my condo. I flicked off the sound to the Weather Channel.

Keira knocked once on my door, let herself in, and saw the TV screen. A reporter in raingear stood knee-deep in water. "Turn that up," Keira said.

"The worst of the storm is over for the Outer Banks. We're still being hit with heavy rain. The winds are currently below tropical storm strength; however, the storm may intensify as it takes aim at the Mid-Atlantic States. Feeder bands are being felt as far north as New Jersey…"

I killed the volume.

"Darn," Keira said.

Nellie asked, "What are you two worked up about? If anybody should worry it'd be me. I got my sweet Casper in Delaware, a little too close to the water."

"I'm concerned about my mother," Keira said. "She lives with me and the bayside of North Wildwood floods and loses power too often."

"Oh, I didn't realize. I think we could all use a drink. Boss, let's get some booze out here."

Now we're talking.

"I'll help," Keira said.

"Good," said Nellie. "I gotta get this back in its home. Be right back."

Keira noticed the blinking light on my phone base. "Did you ever clear out your Voicemail?"

"Just like you asked." I pushed the button and a digital voice said, "You have two new messages. To hear your messages, press play." I did. "Message one, 'Remember, I warned you.'" The voice belonged to JJ. A chill slid down my spine.

"Message two, 'Mr. Farmer, this is Detective Cho. It's one-thirty in the morning. There's been an incident. We will stop by to see you before noon. Thank you.' End of messages."

Nellie approached us. "Who called?"

"JJ left a message. She said she warned us."

"Too late for her," Nellie said.

"There was a second message. Detective Cho wants to see me in the morning. That's today, I guess."

"Here?"

"Yeah. She said there's been an incident."

"We'll know soon enough," Nellie said. "In the meantime, I wanna tell you a story."

I corkscrewed open a bottle of Merlot. Keira selected three wine glasses from the cabinet.

"Keira," Nellie said, reclining on the sofa "No wine for me. Grab a can of beer from the fridge, will ya?"

"I got it," I said, walking the Coors to Nellie.

Keira poured two glasses of the red and carried them to the living room, placing them on the coffee table near the loveseat, where we both settled.

I stared at Nellie. "Well?"

"Anybody hungry?" she asked. "Should we munch on pepperoni or something?"

"Nellie, pleeeeease," I said.

"Keep your shirt on." Nellie swallowed a large gulp of beer. "The story of what happened tonight began two years ago along the Amazon River.

Frank, my older brother, works as a biochemist for a top pharmaceutical outfit and they sent him on a research assignment to the jungles of Brazil. Ever hear of a Boto?"

"You mentioned it at the Atlantus," I said. "Your secret weapon."

Nellie took a deep breath. "Fasten your seatbelts. I'm going to tell you some crazy shit about the world we live in. Strange thing is—it's all too real."

CHAPTER FIFTY

"Wait," I said. "You have a brother?"

"Yeah. He's an Einstein in the biochemistry world—that's his thing."

"And?"

"And," Nellie paused. "He wants my opinion. My brother, a fucking genius, asks me for my opinion." She took a swig of Coors and continued. "Frank traveled to the city of Manaus and was there for months doing research in the Amazon rainforest for his big pharma company. They wanted a new drug to treat immune deficiency disorders."

"Sounds exciting," Keira said.

"Too exciting. That region isn't for the faint of heart. He ran across a tribe of natives along the river and lived with them in thatched huts complete with spiders the size of your hand."

"Gross," Keira said.

Nellie nodded. "That wouldn't be for me, either. Still, I wasn't totally surprised when he called me and said, Nels, you should fly down here and see this. I'm like, no thanks—until he says the magic words."

"Free travel?" I asked.

Nellie flashed a be-quiet stare. "That's when he says he'd like my opinion. I would've flown to the moon."

"Opinion on what?"

"On what he witnessed. He knows I'm the expert on ghost hunting, you saw that, but also all things paranormal, the occult, voodoo—whatever's out there."

"Not to mention Shadows," I said.

Oops.

"Shadows are the ultimate Evil," Nellie said.

"What are you two talking about—shadows?" Keira ran her fingers through her blonde hair, and looked my way. "David?"

Nellie glared at me. "You should've told her."

"I was going to."

"Time for a cigarette," Nellie said, standing up. "Boss, give me a sign when it's safe to come back. I'm going to my usual smoking area."

As Nellie pulled on the glass slider, I tried to gauge the expression on Keira's face but found it difficult to interpret since she just stared straight ahead as though she didn't see me.

"I've been afraid to tell you—worried you'd run for cover. Ever since I began writing *Shadows* I've been seeing them."

She opened her mouth but didn't say a word.

"They've been plaguing me for years," I added.

"Shadows?"

"Not normal shadows. These do what they want, whenever they want. They're a separate kind of creature in a horror class all their own."

"Like your book?" she asked.

"Too much like it."

"David, you're saying the Shadows you wrote about are real?"

"They are real though I didn't know that when I started the book."

"What gave you that idea in the first place?" she asked.

"I'd been seeing them out of the corner of my eyes for months. Then I noticed they were out of step with me."

"What do you mean?"

"I walked down my street and one day it hit me. The thing was on the wrong side—between me and the sun—like I was its shadow."

"Oh my."

Oh my is right.

"I thought they weren't real. They couldn't possibly be alive. Now, I know different."

I hesitated but Keira said, "David, go on."

"When I was writing my book I'd take breaks and exercise. I noticed my Shadow wasn't following my motions. The damn thing pulled itself from the wall and moved around the room. I hoped it was my imagination. I remember trying to blink the Shadow away."

"It can walk?"

"Walk, float. They can pass through walls."

"Wait a second—there's more than one?"

"Nellie had a similar experience. So did JJ. I don't know how far-reaching this is."

"And what do they want?" she asked.

"My assumption is they plan to ultimately replace us as the superior species."

"Us?"

"The human race."

"Oh my God, David. Just like you wrote about."

I nodded. "They may be the next rung up the evolutionary ladder."

"You wrote that book—" Keira stopped for a second. "—as a warning?"

"I intended it as fiction. Now, it's more like prophecy. JJ changed the direction of my book. She's fronting for them, helping the Shadows for her own benefit, using me to help them."

"I'm not sure what you mean."

"JJ is on their side. She's been recruited and used me to inform people. Prepare them for the futility of fighting the Shadows and scare everyone into submission. All while she's getting rich. I'm still trying to piece this together and didn't catch on until recently."

"This is hard to believe," she said.

I felt sorry for her. I wanted to avoid this topic—maybe forever. But, like all bad things, ignoring them never works. "It is hard to believe," I said. "Yet, I'm living it."

She continued to look at me without speaking, perhaps questioning my sanity.

The lamp behind Keira cast her shadow on the carpeted floor. She studied it for a moment, then rose from the loveseat and sat back down. "My shadow seems normal."

"It is. Check out mine," I said, getting to my feet.

She glanced down. "You don't—"

"Mine's been AWOL for years."

"Is it possible I've been seeing these—Shadows—and not known it?"

"No. Only when your Shadow frees itself from you and not until the thing has a purpose."

"Have I ever been with you when you saw them?" she asked.

I peeked toward the balcony to check on Nellie. She was watching me, one step out the door, a cigarette dying in her fingers. I shook my head.

Not yet.

"Once, when you and I were in my bedroom and the doorbell rang—"

Keira grabbed my arm. "I remember that. You blocked me from seeing who was there. I had to practically shove you aside and the hallway was empty. I knew that was fishy."

"You were right."

"David, were you afraid I wouldn't believe you?"

Yes—and—

"Not just that," I said. "I loved you the moment we met. I never want anything bad to happen to you. It's safer if you never see them."

She smiled. "You said you love me."

We leaned into each other and kissed.

Nellie dragged the slider closed and came toward us, her hair stringy and dripping wet onto her orange sweatshirt.

"I didn't give you a sign," I said.

Nellie blew into her hands. "Your fucking storm is coming. I ain't waiting forever while you smooth over your blunder." As she moved past Keira, Nellie said, "How did he do?"

"We were just getting to the good part."

"I'm surprised there is one."

"Nellie, are the Shadow-creatures connected to the ghost hunting?" Keira asked.

"They are, though I haven't explained it to Dave."

Keira shook her head. "This is an awful lot to digest. But I'm game."

"First things first," Nellie said. "I need another beer." She headed to the kitchen and retrieved a Coors from the fridge. She also stopped by the paper towel rack and snagged a handful, tamping her hair.

I turned toward Keira and whispered, "I'm sorry for not telling you earlier."

She patted my hand.

Nellie crossed into the living room and flopped onto the sofa. "Back to the Amazon. Many tribes practice a religion called Macumba. They perform rituals for various reasons. Asking the gods for good health and prosperity is common. But two of their ceremonies interested me the most. The natives request the release of any souls of deceased tribe members trapped between heaven and hell. They also have a special ceremony to conjure an extraordinary power against evil."

"And what does that have to do with us?" I asked.

"Give me a minute." Nellie cleared her throat. "My brother's scientific brain has trouble wrapping its head around anything it can't rationally explain. Like I said, Frank tells me to fly down." Nellie looked at me. "Yeah, wise guy. He foot the bill."

I shrugged.

"Flying into Manaus was no problem. But the next leg—I squeezed into a two-person, sputtering hunk-of-junk bush plane, which barely cleared the treetops."

"That low?" Keira asked.

"I coulda reached out and grabbed a monkey. After we landed in a jungle clearing, Frank met me in a jeep for a bumpy ride to the village. I asked him what was up. He said he'd stumbled onto some voodoo-type stuff he didn't understand, but thought I might."

"Voodoo?" I asked.

"He was already buddies with the tribe's spiritual leaders. Hell, he even picked up some of their lingo. Frank brought a slew of drugs with him, including antibiotics and morphine. They saw him as a Medicine Man with more powers than they had."

"How does that—"

"Boss, listen and learn. The Macumba religion reveres a sacred white dolphin called a Boto. The tribes won't harm them but occasionally a dead one washes up and the natives harvest their organs. They hold a ceremony for the gods to trigger each organ's power as a weapon. The most powerful is the Boto heart. It's like their atom bomb."

"Where are you going with this?" I asked.

"I have one."

"A Boto heart?"

"In powder form. I never asked Frank how he was able to swing it but it must have cost him a gallon of morphine."

"You've got a ground up heart of a dolphin in that pouch you carry around?" I asked.

"Some of it."

Some?

"Where's the rest of it?"

"In the Morton Salt canister in my room," she said.

"I wondered why you brought your own salt."

"Don't touch it."

"No problem," I said, raising my hands.

Nellie continued. "Not just any old pouch, by the way. The natives stitch them from the skin of the Boto. Mine's been through the ritual—natives covered in feathers dancing their way around the pouch, which they sit on a mound of bones of departed loved ones. The natives chant to the gods to favor them by granting their requests."

"Did you see all this?" Keira said, her eyes wide.

"I wanted to video it but Frank said no way—or they'd be dancing around our bones."

"My God," Keira said. "What happened next?"

"A shaman went into a psychedelic trance by chewing on the resin from a special tree. Two things happened. One, the gods strengthened the Boto heart to defeat evil. Then, the shaman met deceased tribal members and shook the powder on them to release their imprisoned souls."

"And you know this how?" I asked.

"The interpreter told us what was taking place. Frank translated as best he could. What we witnessed was a purification ritual. The Boto heart became weaponized against the enemy."

"What enemy?" I asked.

"THE Enemy."

"The shaman told you that?"

"Yeah. It seems he saw an aura around my body. He judged me to be strong and pure of heart. The shaman said I could defeat the natives' main enemy Corpo-Secos, which literally translates to 'dry corpse.' He said these were shadowy creatures that haunted the Amazon basin and sucked the life out of many tribe members."

"Shadowy?" I asked. "You don't mean—"

"Yes, Boss. I'm sure they're our Shadows."

The three of us stared at each other in silence.

Nellie added, "The shaman said the Boto would be at its most powerful if blessed by an innocent child whose soul hadn't passed to its final resting place. He meant the soul would be trapped in the astral plane, stuck in limbo, and I could bring on its release. That's our Nancy."

"You sure about all this?" I asked.

"Don't be like Faraday," Nellie said. "This is the real deal."

"I just wondered about the coincidence. You hearing about Shadows in Brazil and them being here also."

"You think that's the extent?" Nellie asked. "I don't believe it for a fucking moment. We're not the only unlucky ones. I've read enough articles and seen enough news to make me curious as to which ones are Shadow-related."

"Shit," I mumbled.

"Damn straight. We're in the worst of it and we need to make this their Waterloo. My trip to the Amazon set me up and now I know what the hell I'm doing. I got the Boto blessed and Nancy enters heaven. It's the classic win-win."

"That's what you were doing tonight at the Atlantus," Keira said.

"Right." Nellie took another swallow of beer. "I admit I couldn't be certain Nancy would be receptive. She was. She's been waiting for this moment and told me so."

"I didn't hear anything," I said.

"You were too busy running down the stairs. So much for having my back."

"Tommy's fault."

"Whatever. Anyway, I felt extreme cold. I thought I'd literally freeze to death. The cold was followed by a flood of warmth and I felt comfortable and safe.

"I held out the Boto pouch to her and she touched it, blessing it. She knew what I was there for. Then I sprinkled some of the powder on my hand and blew it on her."

"What did she do?" Keira asked, leaning forward in her seat.

Nellie smiled. "Nancy displayed an expression of serenity I'll always treasure."

"Wow," Keira sighed.

Nellie bowed her head and I sensed she was composing herself. She looked up at us. "That's pretty much it, except I was suddenly outside the door of Mick's place."

"So, you've been hanging on to this Boto heart a long time," I said.

"Waiting for the opportunity."

"Then I called."

"I always assumed the Shadows would resurface, maybe pick up where they left off and you'd need help. I can add two plus two. I saw your mug on CNN's website and read the news regarding the murders."

"Lucky I called you," I said.

"The timing was right. I was mustering the energy to get to you. No offense, but you against the Shadows and JJ is an epic mismatch. With me, at least you have a fighting chance."

"David said JJ is on their side," Keira said.

"She's in league with the Shadows. As for tonight, JJ first tried to bribe us and when that didn't work she threatened us, proving we're on the right track."

"What do we do next?" I asked Nellie.

"We go on the offense. Nancy blessed the Boto heart and now it's locked and loaded."

"Is there a plan?"

"You have to ask? Details later. I think for now we're all a bit worn out. Let's get a few hours' sleep and then we'll put our heads together."

"Good idea," Keira said. "My brain couldn't take much more tonight."

"Yeah," Nellie said. "We hit you with a lot."

"One thing I'm sure of, though."

"What's that?" Nellie asked her.

"I'm glad you're on our side."

CHAPTER FIFTY-ONE

My bedside clock read 8:47 AM. I awoke with a jolt.

The jolt was Keira jabbing my side. "David, wake up."

My peaceful dreaming was interrupted by a dreamy reality. Keira lay next to me, propped on an elbow, hair disheveled, lips smiling and closing in. She kissed me and I smelled her morning breath—sweet.

"You naked?" I asked.

"Just my panties."

I slid closer to her, kicked back the covers and started to pull at my boxers.

"What are you doing?" she asked.

"Saying good morning."

"Not now." She gently nudged me away. "We have things to do."

She smiled and I knew I totally belonged to her.

I heard voices. I smelled food.

"What's going on out there?" I asked.

"Smells like Nellie's frying bacon and if I'm not mistaken, Maggie's here."

"When did this all happen?"

"Not sure. I was in and out of sleep and thought I heard a knock on your front door."

I yawned and rubbed my eyes. "I better take a quick shower."

"Let's save time," Keira said, heading for the bathroom.

"If it isn't Sleeping Beauties One and Two," Nellie said as we walked into the kitchen. "Just in time for breakfast."

My small kitchen table looked as it had seldom looked before. It was loaded with food.

The kitchen island had served as the site for virtually every meal. But Nellie changed that. A pile of bacon and a covered dish, which proved to be scrambled eggs, were surrounded by empty plates. Muffins rested on a separate dish and a carton of orange juice also awaited us. Maggie sat on one of the kitchen stools sipping from a mug of coffee.

"Hi, Maggie," I said.

"Good morning to both of you. I baked banana-nut muffins and thought I should offer them as my apology."

"For what?" I asked.

"I quit the team. No more ghost hunting. I'm still shaking."

Keira gave Maggie a hug.

"Thank you, dear," Maggie said.

"Okay," Nellie said. "Let's eat."

As I started for the kitchen table, I noticed Maggie taking a step toward the door. "Where are you going?"

"Home. I just stopped by to bring you the muffins. I already ate. Nellie filled me in on last night. I'm so impressed."

"Maggie, you sure you won't stay?" Keira asked.

"I am sure. Thank you, again," she said as she left.

"Dig in," Nellie said.

I managed to eat a forkful of eggs before the doorbell rang.

"What the hell," I said. "It better not be Cho and Faraday this early."

It was Cho and Faraday.

"Good morning," I said at the door.

"I assume you haven't heard the news," she said.

"What news?"

"May we enter?" Detective Cho asked, with Faraday looming behind her.

"Of course."

I led the detectives into the living room. Cho glanced at the kitchen. "I apologize for our timing. I see you have guests."

Keira rose from the table and spoke before I could. "I'm David's friend, Keira. Do you mind if I sit in?"

"I think it would be a good idea," Cho said, sitting on the sofa across from Faraday who settled into the nearby chair.

Keira sat next to me on the loveseat.

"How about the other lady?" Faraday asked, pulling out his notebook.

Nellie strode into the living room, crunching on a rasher of bacon. "I'm Nellie. Don't get up," she said to Faraday.

He smiled. "What is your full name, Miss?"

"Nellie Hagerstrom, also a friend of Dave's." Nellie sat on the remaining chair near Faraday.

"And you, Miss," Faraday said to Keira. "Your last name, please."

"Donaldson. I work at the local newspaper."

"Oh," Faraday said. "I've seen your byline."

"Are you aware of last night's fire?" Cho asked me.

"What fire?"

"The Atlantus burned to the ground."

I warned you, JJ had said.

No one spoke for a few seconds. I sensed Cho was gauging our reactions. Then she added, "Mr. Hatfield died in the fire."

That statement continued the quiet.

Finally Keira asked, "Mickey—dead?"

Cho nodded.

"Oh my God," Keira said. "What was the cause of the fire?"

"It's under investigation."

"I can hardly believe this," Nellie said to Cho.

"I understand you were all there last night."

"We were," Nellie said. "But, we had nothing to do with the fire. We all liked Mick."

Faraday peered up from his notebook. "When did you leave?"

"Around midnight."

"And how was the Atlantus when you left?" Faraday asked her.

"It wasn't on fire, I can tell you that."

"What were you all doing there?"

"I'm a ghost hunter."

Faraday snickered. "You were looking for a ghost in the Atlantus?"

"Yeah," Nellie said. "Is that amusing?"

"Did you find one?"

"I did—the little girl, Nancy."

Faraday shook his head.

"What's that, Stretch? You don't believe me?"

"Well, that puts you in a growing club of those claiming to have seen her."

"I did more than see her."

"How so?" Faraday asked.

"I set her free."

"What does that mean?" he asked her.

"You wouldn't get it."

"Miss Hagerstrom," Cho said. "I assume you have special equipment you use?"

"Yes, I do."

"Could any of it contribute to the start of a fire?"

"No," Nellie said. "And anyway, we took it all with us."

"By us, who do you mean?"

"Me, Maggie and Dave."

"Maggie Callahan?"

"Yeah," Nellie said.

"Did Mr. Hatfield help with loading it into your van?" Cho asked.

"We didn't need his help."

"What was he doing when you said your goodbyes?"

"Straightening up," Nellie said. "I saw him swabbing the bar with a towel."

Keira brought her hands to her face. "It's just horrible about Mick. I think I was the last to see him. Me and Tommy."

"His full name?" Faraday asked.

"Thomas Finch."

Faraday nodded. "Real estate. Seems to know everyone. Why was he there?"

"He's a friend of Mick's and helped get us in," Keira said.

"Where was Mr. Finch when you left?" Faraday asked.

"He got in his car as I got in mine and he drove off."

Faraday peered up as he was writing. "You saw him drive away?"

"I—I'm not sure. Okay, I remember waving to him from my car. I did leave before him."

Faraday stared at us. "Was there anyone else with you?"

"Oh, my agent was there for a while," I said.

"Is she the one with the Porsche?" Faraday asked.

"Yeah," I said, "Josephine Janakowski from New York City. You guys following me?"

"Why was she there?" he asked.

"To talk about a book project. She left a couple of hours before us."

"And you're doing business with her?" Cho asked.

"Not sure yet."

"Is she staying in the area?"

"The Blue Heron in Cape May," I said.

"Would you have her phone number?"

I slid open the end table drawer and retrieved JJ's business card. I read the number aloud.

"I think that's it for now," Cho said, rising from her chair. "I apologize for interrupting your breakfast."

"Detective Cho," Keira said. "You're obviously keeping tabs on David, so why didn't someone see what happened to Mick and the Atlantus?"

"Mr. Farmer is not under round-the-clock surveillance per se. But the officer who was assigned to him last night followed Miss Hagerstrom's van when she drove away from the restaurant."

The detectives left my condo and I felt confused. I had so many distressing issues for my tired brain to sort. Mick had just died violently, like too many others who came in contact with me.

"It's a fucking shame what they did to Mick," I said.

Nellie slammed her fist on the arm of the chair. "JJ's going to pay for that."

"He was my friend," Keira said. "Everyone liked Mick."

I regretted Mick's loss and felt guilty that I was also troubled by something else less important. It was what Keira said to the detectives. Me and Tommy. The last to leave.

Me and Tommy—one time too many for me to handle.

When was the right moment to mention this? Now, when so much chaos swirled around me? Or someday when everything might calm down?

Someday never comes.

"Keira," I said. "Can I talk to you alone?"

"Of course."

I turned to Nellie. "Could you find something to do for a while?"

"Ah, one of those private talks you both like so much."

"Nellie."

"Take it easy, Boss. I'll go finish breakfast and maybe I'll save you a piece of bacon."

"Come on," I whispered to Keira. We walked into my bedroom. I closed the door and sat on the bed with Keira alongside.

"What's bothering you?" she asked.

"I don't know how to say this. I'll just blurt it out. You and Tommy."

She stared at me. Her eyes glazed and she tried to blink the tears away.

"I am so sorry," she said.

"Whatever it is, just tell me."

Before I collapse.

"I feel terrible," Keira said. "What you must be thinking." She dabbed her finger at a tear. "Tommy and I were married."

Maybe my mouth fell open. I can't be sure.

"We divorced nearly four years ago," Keira said. "We're friends now, which we seldom were during our marriage."

"Why didn't you tell me?"

"I always wanted to. At first, it was just too weird. My ex-husband introduces me to a prospective boyfriend. That's crazy, right?"

I didn't answer. I couldn't.

"I feel like a hypocrite after saying you're not always honest with me. I wasn't trying to hide it from you but there's so much happening in your life. The two women murdered, you nearly getting killed in the parking garage, Nellie living here, the ghost, the fire, and tonight you tell me about the Shadows. You don't give a girl much of a chance."

"How long were you married?"

"Almost two years. He's an alcoholic and had an anger issue he's dealt with."

"You sure you don't love him anymore?" I asked.

"I like him. I love you."

Thank you, Lord.

"You said he was an alcoholic?"

"That hasn't changed," she said.

"That's why you're on my case about drinking."

"So far, I've been easy on you. I'm not looking the other way like I did with him. I care about you too much."

"I am so relieved." I took a deep breath and released it. "Okay, I'm cool with this. You know I was married and have a son and that didn't throw you."

"We both had other lives before we met. Our future is what's important."

I leaned over and hugged her. We kissed.

"You're fine then?" Keira asked.

"I've got a hundred and one things to worry about, yet here I am—the happiest guy in the world."

Chapter Fifty-two

Just as we finished breakfast I heard a thump coming from the wall. "What the hell?"

"You must have some big mice," Nellie said.

I stepped into the hallway and heard loud voices coming from Dennis's condo. I rang the doorbell. The voices subsided and Dennis opened his door.

"Oh, it's you," he said.

"Everything okay?" I asked.

"None of your business."

"I guess that's it then. Sorry to bother you."

As I was about to turn away, a strong voice sounded from inside the room. "Dave, how are you my friend?"

I leaned in. "Fine, V. And you?"

What the hell are these two doing?

"I am good."

Dennis stood directly in front of me and said, "I need you two in here like I need a hole in the head."

"Come in," Zdenko said.

Dennis snorted but backed up a few strides and I entered. Zdenko, clad in his red leather jacket, stood by the sofa.

"Guys," I said. "Everything all right?"

Dennis spoke first. "How the hell could anything be all right with my wife dead and you two bastards standing in her home?"

"I go for walk. He bumps me in elevator," Zdenko said. "I say we go inside and be quiet."

"Didn't work," I said.

Zdenko pointed. "He push me against wall."

"So I heard," I murmured.

"You and him," Dennis said to me, with a snarl. "You both screwed Cecily."

Zdenko grunted. "He accuses I have sex with his wife. I try to calm him but he threatens me. I do not take this."

"You're just lucky I don't do something about it," Dennis said.

"See? That is threat. Maybe I tell police."

"Go ahead. I bet you don't even have immigration papers."

Dennis moved a stride towards Zdenko and the giant man stood his ground.

"Stay away or I send you through wall," Zdenko said.

I stepped between them. "Hey, stop this stuff. Someone could get hurt."

Me.

"I know this," Dennis said. "A few days before she died, Cecily left here without her jacket. She didn't go for a walk. I never heard the elevator. I never heard the door to the stairs. Cecily didn't leave this floor. And later, when she comes home, what does she smell like? Cigarettes. Same as you, V."

"I am not only smoker. Jason smokes. Baseball player, too. Whole world is smokers." Zdenko looked at me and spread his arms. "Yes?"

Dennis said, "Why are you talking to him? I'm right here, asshole."

"In Albania people who call names—"

"Fuck Albania," Dennis shouted.

Zdenko cocked his arm with a closed fist, his knuckles ready for action. He stepped toward Dennis and I blocked him. Zdenko pushed and I staggered backwards, falling across the coffee table, which tipped over. Two decorative glass dolphins crashed to the floor shattering on impact.

"Cecily loved those things," Dennis exclaimed.

Zdenko bent down and swallowed my hand in his. He started to hoist me up but I felt my upper arm muscles ready to shred.

"Whoa! Stop," I screamed. "I may need this arm." I struggled to my feet, rubbing my shoulder, the same one that absorbed the landing in the marshes off Ocean Drive.

The front door to the condo opened and Nellie rushed in. "What's going on here?"

"Nothing," I said. "I lost my balance."

"Nothing? Sounds like Moe, Larry and Curly working a new bit."

Keira followed her and stood in the doorway. "David, are you all right?"

I nodded. "I'm fine." I waved my hand and she retreated back into the hallway.

As she left, Maggie arrived. "Gentlemen, stop this behavior at once."

Behind Maggie I saw Jason approach and squeeze past her, a toolbox in his hand.

Hail, hail, the gang's all here.

"What are you three idiots doing?" Jason asked, removing his bush cap. "Farmer—I might've guessed you'd be involved."

"Party's over. Let's go, Boss," Nellie said.

"Everybody, clear out," said Dennis. "Except these two. I'm not finished with them."

Jason whispered to Maggie. "Come on. I'll walk you home."

Nellie stared at me. "Boss?"

"Be there in a minute."

"Okay. I'll give you three minutes and then I'm coming back."

"I like her," Dennis said.

"Marvelous," Nellie muttered as she walked out, letting the door close behind her.

"There is nothing I hear from you," Zdenko said to Dennis.

"You'll listen to what I have to say."

Zdenko folded his arms, glaring at him. "Be fast. There are things I do."

"Cecily didn't give a shit about either of you," Dennis said. "Now she's gone and one of you killed her. When I find out which one I'll take care of it my way."

I didn't flinch but Zdenko unfolded his arms and reached into his jacket pocket.

Uh-oh.

His hand emerged holding a cigarette. "I need one," he said. "Hurry and make your say."

Dennis said, "At least Farmer admits what he did. But you, you overgrown piece of shit, you don't have the balls to admit the truth."

"Say anything like that again, you will regret," Zdenko said.

"Don't threaten me. One day your sorry ass just might disappear."

I thought Zdenko might take another run at Dennis.

Instead, Zdenko smiled at him and formed his index finger and thumb into a gun. He aimed it at Dennis. "You have big mouth." Zdenko stomped his way out the door and tried to slam it shut but the pneumatic device prevented it.

Dennis and I were alone. The door seemed a long distance away.

"Get out," he said.

"You had twenty seconds left," Nellie said when I entered.

"It was nothing. I got accused of murder again and Zdenko tossed me like a twig."

Keira took a stride towards the door. "I want to talk to them."

"I did. It's over."

"Why did Mr. Zdenko attack you?" Keira asked.

"He didn't. He went at Dennis and I got in the way. Let's talk about something else."

Keira and I parked on the sofa. Nellie stood at the glass door and slid it back a foot or two. "Mick," Nellie said. "He was murdered because he helped us." She lit a cigarette.

"We know how it happened," I said.

Nellie grunted. "Yeah, JJ. We're going to avenge Mick's death."

"What do we do?" Keira asked.

"Your boyfriend and I are going to pay JJ a visit."

"Oh, I don't like the sound of that," Keira said to Nellie.

"We owe her."

"Not today with the storm," Keira said.

Nellie gazed past the balcony into the pounding rain. "This does look ugly. Put on the weather," she said.

I grabbed the remote and switched on the TV, which was already set to the Weather Channel. A woman bundled in weather gear and holding a microphone leaned against the fierce wind on a beach, her other hand holding a rain hat in place.

"I'm Megan Winslow and I'm standing, well, trying to stand, here at the Jersey shore in Wildwood Crest as everyone here awaits the arrival of Brenda. Her winds are nearing tropical-storm force and the rain has increased in intensity." She scanned her eyes left and right.

"Wildwood Crest?" Nellie said.

I saw Megan wave her hand.

"Sir, could I speak with you?" she shouted. "I'm Megan Winslow with the Weather Channel."

A man huddled alongside her.

Nellie said, "Hey, isn't that—"

"Yeah, it is," I said.

"Can I ask your name, sir?"

"Jason."

I noticed his hat was firmly tied under his chin. He appeared anything but happy.

"You're the only person I've seen," Megan said. "Where are you going?"

"My job," he said, raising his gray toolbox. "I'm securing the pier rides."

"The storm is arriving today."

"That's why I'm securing the pier rides."

"I meant should you be working in this weather? It's dangerous."

"Lady, I've been doing this for many years and I'm not afraid of a little rain and wind. Now, if you don't mind, I've gotta go."

Jason crossed in front of her and trudged away.

Megan's hat flew off. "Oops. Back to the studio."

"Jason was kinda gruff," Nellie said to me.

"I'm glad to see he's rude to other people, too."

I hit mute. The station cut to a split screen showing the desolate Wildwood Boardwalk on one side across from a radar image of a circular mass of red, orange and yellow.

"Brenda sure is colorful," I said.

Nellie shook her head. "Let's see how much you like her when she rips the roof off this building."

My phone rang. I picked up the handset without checking the Caller ID. "Hello?" I asked.

"It's lucky you didn't stay for the midnight buffet."

"Fuck you."

"Not by you, sweetheart," JJ said.

I hit the speaker option so Nellie and Keira could hear.

"Did you have to kill Mick?" I asked.

"I didn't kill him—you did."

Nellie ripped the phone from my hand. "You're a dead woman," Nellie said calmly. She disconnected and placed the handset in my outstretched palm.

"You gotta stop hanging up on people," I said.

"You gotta stop being so wishy-washy."

"What do we do next?" I asked Nellie.

"You'd be lost without me, wouldn't you?"

"If you say so."

"We have contracts to sign, don't we?" Nellie asked.

"Okay—but we need a plan."

"Leave it to me."

"I've been meaning to ask you," I said. "Can we actually kill Shadows?"

"I don't come with guarantees."

"I wasn't—"

"David killed Goliath with a measly slingshot," Nellie said. "Well—we've got our own David and the Boto heart is a superweapon. I can't promise it'll kill the Shadows but I do know this—we're going in with guns blazing. At the very least we can put a big dent in their plans."

"Don't do anything until after the storm," Keira said, grabbing her coat. "I'm going. I don't want my mother to be alone. Call me later."

"Will do," I said.

"Are we agreed?' Keira asked. "We'll deal with JJ after the storm."

I nodded.

"Nellie?" Keira asked.

"Ditto."

I walked Keira to the door. "I love you," I said, kissing her firmly on the lips.

"I love you, too," she said.

"Drive carefully."

I stood in the doorway as Keira headed toward the elevator. Then I ducked back inside—a few seconds too soon.

CHAPTER FIFTY-THREE

"Maybe you shoulda walked her to the car," Nellie said.

"Now you say that?"

"I've got a bad feeling."

I rushed out the door hoping to catch Keira. As I approached the elevator, I heard a scream coming from the stairwell.

I yanked the door open. "Keira!" Leaning over the railing I saw Keira's jacket on the stairs far below.

Keira shouted, "Dav—"

Her voice cut out and was followed by a scuffling of feet—a thud—a moan.

"I've got a gun!" I yelled as I raced down the stairs, my hand sliding along the metal railing. A door slammed on a floor below me.

On the first-floor stairs, I sprinted past Keira's jacket on my run to the bottom landing. She laid face-up on the cold cement near the wall by the parking garage entrance. Her handbag was alongside with its contents spilled. Keira's blouse was torn at the collar and a trickle of blood visible on her lips.

Please, God, please.

"Keira! Keira!"

I knelt down, lowered my head to her breast and listened to her heartbeat.

"Keira."

She groaned.

Her eyes fluttered—then opened. She tried to speak but coughed instead.

"Don't try to talk," I said.

Her eyes shifted from side to side. "What—what happened?"

"Can I sit you up?"

"Yeah." She started on her own and I helped prop her back against the wall.

"You're going to be alright."

I hope.

Her pocketbook was within reach on the floor and I saw a small pack of Kleenex. I grabbed the pack, pulled a tissue and patted the corner of her mouth.

"I'm bleeding?" she asked, sweeping her tongue across her lips.

"It stopped."

She cried and hugged me before turning her head towards the stairs.

"We're alone," I said. Looking for confirmation, I looked around the basement. My bike stood chained under the empty staircase, while folding chairs balanced against the far wall. The door to the parking garage was shut.

She squeezed my hand. "Did you see him?"

"I didn't see anyone."

"David, he was crushing my throat."

"Who?" I asked.

"I don't know. He came at me from behind."

"We need an ambulance and the police," I said.

"I heard a door open, maybe the first floor? He was on me quick and I tried to pull away. My jacket came off. He gripped the back of my neck and his other arm wrapped around my throat. Then …"

"Then, you got him good." I said, noticing the blood on her long fingernails.

"Yes. Yes I did! I clawed him and he let go. I was going to run into the parking garage but he shoved me against the wall."

"Bastard. Do you know where he went?"

She shook her head. "Back up the stairs maybe—the parking garage? I might've blacked out."

"Did he say anything?"

"Nothing. David, Is my face a mess?"

"No, you're beautiful as ever."

"Seriously."

"You've got a cut on your lip and a small scrape on your cheek."

"Help me to my feet," she said. "I want to go back to your place."

"You up to it?"

"I don't want to stay down here."

I wedged my arm under her shoulder and lifted gently. "We need the police and EMTs to check you out."

She nodded.

"Your phone is in your pocketbook?"

"I'll get it," she said.

"No. You catch your breath." I bent down and picked up the scattered contents and put them back in her bag. I moved a few items around. "The phone's not there."

Keira took the bag from me and her hand came out with a cellphone. "In a side compartment."

"Are you okay standing here for a minute?" I asked.

She leaned on my shoulder as I tapped in 9-1-1. I provided my name, address and a few details.

"Keira, why didn't you use the elevator?"

"There was a sign saying it was out of order."

"What did the sign look like?"

"Um, it was scribbled on a sheet of white paper. Why?"

"The maintenance crew uses an orange preprinted placard," I said.

"Are you saying—?"

"It was phony. Let's try the elevator now."

"Okay. Ooh, David—one more thing I just remembered. He's a smoker. I smelled it all over him."

I caught movement on the upper wall and saw the lights flash above the elevator.

6-5

"Someone's coming down," I said.

4-3

"David," she whispered, gripping my arm.

2-1-B

I stepped in front of her.

The door hissed and Vedra Zdenko emerged. His red leather jacket was open to a green flannel shirt. He smiled when he saw us.

"Good morning, Dave and Miss Keira." He removed a glove from his right hand and extended it toward mine. We shook.

"You like my driving gloves?" Zdenko asked, sliding the one back on his hand. "Genuine Italian leather—like not wearing glove at all."

"I thought the elevator wasn't working."

"It is working." He angled his body to get a better view of Keira. "Are things okay?"

"No," I said.

"I see rip in Miss Keira's shirt. There is cut lip and blood on her hand."

"She slipped on the stairs."

Zdenko peeked behind him. "Oh. You call ambulance?"

I felt Keira's body waver as her fingers dug into my shoulder. Zdenko immediately pushed me aside, while scooping Keira up into his arms in one motion. All that was missing was the big "S" on his chest.

"Open elevator," Zdenko told me.

"Mr. Zdenko, I'm fine," Keira said.

"Call me Z. It is Z best name. That is joke to cheer you."

"You can put me down."

"You need rest. You need doctor."

I covered the electric eye with my hand and the elevator door remained open as Zdenko carried her in. I pushed the seventh-floor button.

As the door slid wide I saw Nellie standing there.

"Oh my god—Keira! Are you okay?"

"Miss Keira needs to lay down," Zdenko said.

"Boss, you call 9-1-1?"

"Yeah, and left a message for Cho, too."

Nellie went to my door. "What happened?"

"She fall on stairs," Zdenko said, as he rushed her to the sofa, laying her down. He removed the same black glove again and stuffed it into his jacket pocket as he knelt beside Keira. Her neck rested against the sofa's arm but Zdenko reached and grabbed a pillow, sliding it under her head.

Another long reach and he latched onto the other pillow, settling it under Keira's feet. "I need cool compress. Antiseptic. Someone make Miss Keira cup of tea."

"I already have tea made," Maggie said.

"Maggie?" I said, looking up.

"I heard all the commotion and dashed over. Let me get her a cup of chamomile. Be back in a jiff."

"Nellie," I said. "I've got a first aid kit in my bathroom under the sink. And there's clean washcloths."

"Where is ambulance?" Zdenko asked.

"Be here any minute," I said.

Nellie returned a moment later with the kit and removed the compress, and tried to hand it to me. "Take this while I heat some water," she said.

"Good idea, Miss Nellie," Zdenko said, as he intercepted the item and ripped at the pack like a Grizzly tearing apart a salmon. The compress fell into his hand and he draped the cloth over Keira's forehead. "This is instant kind, is very cold and reduce swelling."

"Can I help?" I asked him.

"Yes, give me that."

I handed him the first aid kit.

He rummaged his massive fingers through the contents and found what he was searching for. "Aha!" he said. "Antiseptic towelette. You have good kit, Dave."

"All this isn't necessary," Keira said. "I feel fine."

Zdenko smiled. "Ssh. Patients not know what is good for them."

Maggie arrived with the tea and placed the cup on the end table on top of a napkin she brought with her.

Zdenko raised his head toward the kitchen. "Where is hot water?"

Nellie brought in a small bowl of water. "Here you go, Doc," Nellie said to Zdenko, handing the bowl to him.

The big man chuckled. "Yes, I am doctor, to a degree. To degree I do not have one." Zdenko laughed again. "Laughter is best medicine," he said to Keira.

She managed a weary smile. "What's the hot water for?"

"Wash bruises, wash face, hands."

Zdenko dabbed Keira's mouth. He picked up her hands but Keira took the washcloth from him. "I can do that," she said.

Two EMTs entered my condo and hurried to Keira. Zdenko hesitated, then stood and backed away. "She fall on stairs," Zdenko said. "If you need help I am here."

Keira began to sit up but one of the men asked her to lie still.

"Do you know where the police are?" I asked one of the EMTs.

"There's two cops downstairs and a tall guy with a notepad."

Nellie and Keira looked at me.

Faraday.

The EMT added, "The tall one said he'll be right up. Says he knows the way."

"That he does," I muttered.

I hooked Zdenko's arm and guided him toward the glass slider.

"Let's give them breathing room," I said. We stood silent for a moment as seagulls dive-bombed under the cluttered gray sky.

"They do that because storm comes," Zdenko said.

"Huh?"

"Seagulls need more food to ride storm away."

"Makes sense."

Zdenko turned his back to the shrieking gulls and watched the medical techs with Keira. "I do not understand," he said.

"What?"

"Miss Keira fall down stairs. Yes?"

"Yeah."

"You asked ambulance man about police. Why are police here if it is accident?"

"Well, I guess so much has happened they're interested in everything."

He shook his head. "No, that is not it. You made call. If there is danger I should know. I protect her."

"She was attacked by someone," I said.

He gasped. "This is terrible thing. We find this person and I deal with him."

"You bet we will."

He stared at me a moment. "Dave, why did you lie?"

"It wasn't a lie. I was just being cautious about saying she was attacked."

He nodded. "Oh. Cautious."

We were silent for a few seconds as I gathered my thoughts. "V, I want to thank you for taking such good care of Keira."

"She is fine woman."

"I know." I hesitated, still not certain how to proceed.

"You have question? Say."

"I don't want to offend you," I said.

"Say."

"With this storm I'd think everyone would hunker down."

"What is hunker?" he asked.

"Staying put. You were on your way to the parking garage. You had keys in your hand."

He reached into his jacket and dangled a black-on-red keychain in front of me "These? Albanian flag—two-headed eagle is sign of strength."

"So, where were you going?"

Zdenko glared at me. "That is unusual question. At Maggie's party, baseball player say you ask questions because you are writer. Jason says you are nosy. I defend you because you are friend."

Now what, Farmer.

I tried again. "I'm just thinking about the fortunate coincidence of you being in the stairwell right after she was assaulted. That's all."

Zdenko lowered his head. He inhaled a deep breath. "I do not like this. I go now."

Zdenko pulled the glove from his pocket and over his fingers. He tightened the fit by interlocking his fingers one by one and driving each gloved hand into the other, keeping his eyes fixed on me. "You step over line."

He turned and walked to my front door bypassing everyone without a word.

"What was that all about?" Nellie asked me as I rejoined the group.

"I pissed him off."

"Natch—your specialty."

One of the medical techs helped Keira to a sitting position.

"How is she?" I asked him.

"Her vitals are good. She's made it clear she doesn't want to go to the hospital. I recommend she see her regular doctor as soon as possible." The EMTs collected their supplies and headed out the door.

I sat on the sofa alongside Keira. "I wish you would've let them take you."

"I really am fine."

"And you think I'm stubborn. Where's Maggie?" I asked.

"Home. She said to call her later. By the way, what happened with Mr. Zdenko? I wanted to thank him."

"I took care of that."

"Good." Keira touched my arm. "You know—I hesitate to say this but ..."

"What?" I asked.

"Mr. Zdenko, he smells like cigarettes."

He sure does.

"I wanted to check his hands for scratches but he never removed his left-hand glove. I was half tempted to pull the darn thing off."

"Seriously?" Keira asked. "Mr. Zdenko?"

I was about to answer when I noticed Nellie staring at me. "Are you saying you think he attacked Keira?"

"I'm not saying he didn't."

Chapter Fifty-four

I glanced toward the kitchen cabinet, where my bourbon waited for me.

Bad idea.

"Buckle up," Nellie said. "We're flying at warp speed for the next couple days."

"How's that?" I asked.

"We're gonna take care of business—the Shadows first and then we'll set our sights on the serial killer."

"Oh, is that all?"

"If we do nothing, we're going backwards," she said. "We haven't really talked much about the murders. Let's do that now. We'll start with this—you think Zdenko attacked Keira?"

Before I could say a word, Keira said, "Not Mr. Zdenko—I don't believe that."

"Sherlock Holmes's approach was to eliminate the impossible," I said. "Then, no matter how improbable, whatever remains is the truth."

"And what possibilities have you eliminated, Sherlock?" Nellie asked.

"That's my problem. I don't trust anyone—not Zdenko, not his brother, Jason, Dennis, and the ballplayer. Hot Rod—why keep a name like that? His playing days are long over and he stunk anyway. I don't even know his first name."

"Whoa, Boss, come back to Earth."

"Nellie, do you have thoughts about who the killer is?" I asked.

"I'm chock full of thoughts. Most people lead complicated lives. Their brains get all cluttered. Not me. Fortunately, I have no men to deal with and I've got a wonderful cat giving me all the apathy anyone could ever need. So, my brain has time to ponder life's mysteries."

"We don't have all day," I said.

"The same neighbor murdered the two women, ambushed you in the parking garage and attacked Keira."

"You sure?" Keira asked.

"I've connected the dots. The murders are a definite. The attack on

Dave because he's the link between the two women and the attack on you because you're Dave's friend."

"Oh. That sounds logical," Keira said.

"Yeah, but which neighbor?" I asked.

"You've got great suspects right outside your door," Nellie said. "I'll start with Jason. He has a huge chip on his shoulder and is mad at the world, even with people he doesn't know. We saw him snarl his way through the interview with the weather girl. Did you know his wife and kids have been gone for over two months?"

"I didn't know it was that long. They're visiting her mother."

"Visiting? It's like they forgot where they live. And you've got Cecily's body washing up by that pier with the big rollercoaster. You said it yourself; he's always doing maintenance on that ride. Add to that his jealousy of your friendship with Kate…"

"Way ahead of you," I said.

"Then there's your neighbor, Dennis. You screwing his wife—definitely not kosher. Unfortunately for him, he's stuck living next to you. Can't blame the guy for hating you. He almost smashed a punch bowl on your head."

"He was on the other side of the room."

"Lucky for you," Nellie said. "Then we've got Jackson whose first name is Dashonte, which might explain why he sticks with the nickname. Even his current girlfriend, Jetta, doesn't call him that. She goes with D-Man. And Jackson's still got baseball bats as mementos of all the curveballs he's missed."

"Where do you get this information?" I asked.

"He's not a fan of yours. He's got you pegged as an elitist and thinks you're rude and condescending."

"That's bullshit." I turned to Keira. "Right?"

"I still love you," she said.

"Boss, have you ever pissed Jackson off?"

"We had a few dicey moments at Maggie's party but I rallied and bonded with him. We did a secret-handshake thing."

"That's lovely," Nellie said. "All of our suspects, by the way, are smokers. Jackson's been trying to kick the habit and ever since Jetta moved in, he's not allowed to smoke in his own condo. He ducks outside on the balcony—like yours truly."

"Almost done?" I asked her.

"You impressed?"

"You didn't tell me anything of importance. All I learned was Jackson's first name and I already forgot it."

"Doesn't say much for your attention span."

"I asked you before—where are you getting this info?"

Keira answered instead. "That's easy. Maggie, right? "

"It wasn't like pulling teeth," Nellie said. "Ask her a question and stand back."

I smiled at Nellie. "What did you and Maggie think about the Zdenkos?"

"Ah, Vedra Zdenko, our gentle giant from Albania."

"And his Neanderthal brother."

"Maggie does not like Nikolai at all. She's scared of him."

The doorbell rang and we all glanced in that direction. Nellie hopped out of her seat. "I got it." She returned with Faraday trailing. "Hey guys, our second favorite detective."

"Good morning," he said.

Nellie pointed to the chair alongside the sofa. "We saved your seat."

"Thank you, Miss Hagerstrom." Faraday sunk his hand into his jacket pocket and slid out his little spiral-bound pad. He flipped the pages before coming to a stop.

Keira and I moved to the sofa while Nellie dropped on the chair next to the detective.

"Weather is getting worse," Faraday said. "The island's going to take on a lot of water."

"I need to get home," Keira said to him.

"Where's home?"

"North Wildwood, right off the bay. My mom's there alone."

"That part of the island will be underwater," Faraday said.

"I was going there—when—when this happened."

"I won't take much of your time. Before I forget, the CSI boys have the crime scene and they'll be hanging on to your jacket. I'm driving up island and I'd be glad to give you a lift. I'll get my Captain to assign a uniform to keep an eye on your house."

Keira nodded. "Thank you."

Faraday clicked his pen. "Miss Donaldson, the EMTs provided me with a health status. I'm glad you're doing so well. I notice the blood on your right-hand fingers. The assailant?"

"Yes," she said.

"I'm pleased you didn't wash it off."

"A neighbor almost did."

"Excuse me?" Faraday said.

"Vedra Zdenko—you know him?"

"I do."

"He literally carried me to the sofa and tended to me until the EMTs arrived. He patted the cuts on my face but I wasn't going to let him touch my hands. I assume there's DNA."

"Very good." Faraday reached into a pocket and extracted a sealed yellow paper bag. He opened it and removed a vial, a wooden stick, nail clippers, a pair of surgical gloves and a cotton swab, which he used to swipe under Keira's fingernails.

"Looks like a mini laboratory you got there, Stretch," Nellie said to him.

A brief smile crossed Faraday's lips. "I came prepared. In addition to the swab I'd like to cut a couple of your fingernails, Miss Donaldson."

"I'm sure David will pay for a manicure."

"I always thought you used plastic baggies," Nellie said.

Faraday shook his head. "Plastic doesn't allow the evidence to breathe—can cause moisture contaminating the sample. When I get back we'll freeze this in the lab and hopefully have someone there to process it. Trying to find an immediate match is contingent on the assailant's DNA being on file." Faraday turned to Keira. "What time did the attack occur?"

"Um—I—I don't know."

"Approximately."

"Half an hour ago," I said.

Faraday glanced at me, checked his watch and made a note.

"Why were you in the stairwell?" Faraday asked Keira.

"I was going to see my mother."

"I mean why didn't you take the elevator?"

"A sign said it was out of order."

"Detective," I interrupted. "Keira said it was a handwritten piece of paper but the maintenance guys use preprinted cards. I assume it was a fake."

Faraday wrote quickly, stopped a moment, and looked up at Keira. "Tell me exactly what happened, please."

"He grabbed me from behind and—my jacket came off and I ran down towards the basement door."

"Where exactly did this occur?"

"Um—on the stairs past the first-floor landing. I saw the number one on the door. I remember that." Keira took a deep breath.

"Relax, Miss Donaldson," Faraday said. "We're all on your side."

Keira showed a brief, weak smile. "He grabbed the back of my neck and his other arm wrapped around my throat and I couldn't catch my breath ..."

"Which hand grabbed your neck?"

"I don't—um—his right hand. And then his left forearm came across my throat."

"What did you do?"

"I really dug my nails into him—oh my God."

"You're doing a great job," Faraday said. "Did he say anything?"

"Nothing."

"A sound, any sound—perhaps when you scratched him?"

"Well, he grunted."

"Could you better describe that?"

"Like he was surprised and mad at what I did. That's when he pushed me into the wall." She sniffled and I slid myself over and held her hand.

Nellie pulled a couple of tissues from the box on the coffee table and handed them to Keira.

"I know this is hard," Faraday said. "Just a couple of more questions. What happened after he pushed you?"

"That's when I heard David yell something. I might have blacked out for a few seconds."

Keira fumbled with another tissue and blew her nose.

I picked up the story. "I came running down the stairs—"

"Mr. Farmer," Faraday said, looking at me. "I'd like Miss Donaldson to continue." He turned back to Keira. "What's the first thing you remember after you were pushed?"

"David kneeling next to me and saying my name."

"Did you actually see Mr. Farmer coming down the stairs or exiting the elevator?"

"No. Like I said, I was out of it. Why?"

I stood up and walked to the detective. "Why?" I said. "Because he thinks I might've done this to you." I pulled up my sleeves on both arms, extended and rotated them.

"Satisfied?" I said to him.

He nodded.

"Need my DNA?" I asked.

"Already have it."

I headed back to the sofa and sat alongside Keira. She placed her hand over mine.

"Let's continue," Faraday said to Keira. "After Mr. Farmer arrived, then what?"

"Mr. Zdenko stepped off the elevator."

"How much time passed from your attack to Mr. Zdenko's arrival?"

"Uh, I don't know."

Faraday shifted his attention to me. "Mr. Farmer?"

"Five minutes."

"Did you see or hear anything on your way down the stairs?" he asked me.

"As soon as I opened the stairwell door I screamed I had a gun and heard someone slam a door below me. I assume he left this stairwell to use the elevator or stairs on the other side of the building."

Faraday jotted in his pad. "Did you actually have a gun?"

"No."

Faraday smiled and returned his attention to Keira. "Can you tell me anything about the clothes he was wearing? Did you see his arm perhaps or hear a sound the clothing made?"

"No, I didn't—wait a second—my hand touched part of his jacket. Leather maybe. Or it could've been a smooth fabric like a heavy nylon."

"Was it wet or dry?"

"Dry, I think."

"And, how about his height?"

"I felt like he leaned over to put his arm around my throat. Maybe because he was on the step above me."

"Anything else to add?" asked Faraday.

"He's a smoker. I smelled that clearly."

The windows rattled and we all looked toward the ocean.

"Here it comes," I said.

Faraday snapped the pad closed. "That'll do for now. Miss Donaldson, if you're ready I can drive you."

Faraday slipped the pad into his pocket and the four of us headed to the front door of my condo. Nellie got there first. She opened the door as Faraday approached.

"Thank you, Miss—"

"Call me Nellie."

As I passed the coatrack I grabbed my windbreaker and helped Keira into it.

"Thank you," she said.

I kissed Keira on the lips. "I love you. We'll talk later."

"Isn't that sweet," a voice said in the hallway.

Jason.

He stood next to Dennis and both were near the stairwell entrance, which was now cordoned off with yellow and black caution tape. Jason wore a weather-beaten gray slicker and his customary bush cap, while Dennis adjusted his blue sweatshirt.

"Mind your own business," I said to Jason.

"Anything you say."

"I saw you on TV," I said. "You told the weather lady you were headed to the pier."

"Yeah. And I'll be heading there again, if that's okay with you."

"Forget something?" I asked.

"Like you said—mind your own business." Jason glanced at Faraday. "Okay to use the elevator?"

"Yes. There'll be an officer downstairs."

"See you later, Den." Jason said, stepping into his condo.

"What's with the crime tape?" Dennis asked.

"There's been an incident," Faraday said. "I don't want anyone in that stairwell."

Dennis peeked at Keira who was standing partially behind me "I see you've got a cut on your face, Miss. Somebody hurt you?"

"Yes. I, um …"

"Don't say anything else," I said.

"At it again, Farmer?" Dennis asked.

"Not me—maybe you."

Dennis stomped in my direction. "You son of a bitch."

Faraday stepped between Dennis and me. "Get back, Mr. Slade."

"What are you—defending him?"

"I don't want any trouble."

"Now I've heard it all," Dennis said. "A guy like you protecting a guy like him."

"What's that on your wrist?" Faraday asked.

"What?"

"That bandage."

"What about it? I was slicing up a salad for lunch and the knife slipped."

"I'd like a closer look." Faraday took a stride forward.

"This is crazy. You're treating me like a criminal."

"Mr. Slade, would you have any objections to rolling up your sleeves?"

"You've got the guy," Dennis said, pointing to me. "He killed Cecily."

"We've already covered that ground with you. We're investigating your wife's murder. Now, for the last time, do you have any objections to my getting a closer look at that cut?"

"Don't that beat all," Dennis said, while tugging at his sleeves. He peeled off the bandage and held out his arm for Faraday. "See?"

The detective inspected the wound. "Would you mind if I got a picture of that?" Faraday asked, producing a cellphone from his coat pocket.

"Go ahead."

"The picture would help substantiate your account."

"My account? That's rich."

Faraday moved in for a close-up. "Thank you, Mr. Slade."

Dennis rolled down his sleeves and walked toward his condo. He stopped, and turned his head. "Keep an eye on that guy—he's dangerous."

Faraday shrugged. "Sure."

"I was talking to the women."

Chapter Fifty-five

"Now what?" I asked Nellie when we stepped back into my condo.

"Call JJ. Tell her we wanna see her."

"Where? When?"

"Cape May in that B&B where she's staying. When? Right now."

"Will your van even make it there with this rain?"

"That baby's seen some shit. It's stormproof."

"We haven't prepared anything," I said.

"We're gonna cram." She went down the hallway to her bedroom and returned a few seconds later clutching a yellow Acme bag. She placed it on the kitchen island. She reached in the bag and slid out the Morton Salt canister.

"That's it?" I asked.

"That's it."

"You got a lot left?"

"Enough. We're taking it for a ride," Nellie said. She opened the refrigerator and pulled out the bottom crisper.

"What the hell?"

"Keeps better cold," Nellie said, now holding the Boto pouch.

"That thing was in my fridge?"

"Under the celery."

"Thanks for telling me," I said.

"I figured it was the last place you'd stumble across."

I took the phone from the counter and called JJ.

"I knew I'd hear from you," she said, answering on the first ring.

"You must be psychic."

"I assume Nellie is there?"

"Yeah."

"I'm not happy with her," JJ said. "Nellie called me a dead woman."

"She's such a kidder."

"I guess you've come to your senses and want to partner up with me."

I don't think so, bitch.

"Maybe."

"You and I can hammer out a great deal. We always did work well together."

I laughed. "That's how you remember it?"

"You were the talent and I stayed behind the curtains."

Pulling my strings.

"I'm talking Nellie into meeting with you," I said.

"Want me to help convince her?"

I glanced toward the window. In the shifting gray light beyond the balcony I sensed movement. "Hang on," I said, cupping the phone. "Nellie, do you see anything out there?"

"Like what?"

"Shadows," I mouthed.

Nellie eased off the stool and walked to the sliding door. "Nada."

"Seeing Shadows, are you?" JJ asked me.

"Just the storm."

"You sure you can tell the difference?"

Nellie approached me, her hand outstretched and her fingers motioning. "The phone."

I handed it to her. "No hanging up." I leaned against the kitchen counter.

"JJ," Nellie said.

"Nellie Hagerstrom, alive and well."

"You know what I'm thinking of doing?"

"I can't imagine," JJ said.

"Paying you back for killing Mick."

I wrenched the phone from Nellie. "I'll take it from here."

JJ was in mid-sentence. "I'm back," I said, interrupting her.

"Oh, what happened to Nellie?"

"She's gotta pee. So, we're good to drop by and talk things over?"

"The sooner the better."

"This afternoon," I said.

"Dave, I want you to know that Mick wasn't supposed to get hurt."

"I'm sure you're heartbroken—I mean if you had a heart."

She hesitated. "You don't understand. I don't get to pick and choose."

"You're at the Blue Heron. What room?" I asked.

"204. Go up the stairs—"

"I'll find it."

"I have the contracts sitting on my hard drive. I can easily amend them after an old fashioned give-and-take. You remember the first one we had at McSorley's?"

"I'm not going down memory lane with you."

"Fine. Let's sign an agreement even if we don't dot every i and cross every t. I'd like to have something in my hand when I make my pitch in New York. HBO is hot for this project."

"I'm not promising anything."

"When can I expect you and Nellie?"

"Are the Shadows there?"

"Hopefully we won't need them."

I looked at Nellie, who was staring at me with no hint of a smile.

"We'll be there in an hour or so."

"Fabulous, darling. It's like old times."

I disconnected and Nellie said, "You were too easy on her."

"We want her thinking a deal is possible. Gives us the element of surprise."

"Makes sense, I guess. I thought you might be going soft."

"JJ's responsible for Mick's death," I said. "That means so am I. Mick was a good man. No—I'm not going soft."

"Glad to hear it—because this may get ugly."

I opened the cabinet door and pulled out the bottle of Maker's. "Want a drink?" I asked.

She nodded.

I handed Nellie a tumbler of two ice cubes and poured an ounce or so of bourbon.

We raised our glasses. "To the Shadows—fuck 'em," Nellie said. She downed half the contents and winced. "This stuff is seriously wicked."

"You should sip it."

"Better I should dump it."

"Nellie, you don't plan on killing JJ, do you?"

"We're going after the Shadows. If there's collateral damage, so be it."

"But, so I understand, the Boto stuff wouldn't kill her, would it?"

"It might just make her face fall off. Why?"

"I'm not murdering anyone. Regardless of what any of my neighbors might believe."

"And if she gets in the way—are you going to politely ask her to step aside?"

I sat down at the small table in the corner of the kitchen and swirled the ice in my glass. "I'll do pretty much whatever it takes."

Leaving her unfinished drink on the kitchen island, Nellie moved toward me and sat across the table. She pulled a pack of cigarettes from her pants pocket. "I want one, and I ain't in the mood to get blown off your fucking balcony."

"Do what you want."

She produced a lighter from the same pocket, lit her cigarette, and sucked the smoke deep into her lungs before releasing it.

"Are we okay discussing our strategy out loud?" I asked.

"What do you want to do—use mental telepathy?"

"The Shadows might be listening."

"Even if they are, they have no clue what this is all about."

"So, what are we doing?" I asked.

"Here's the way I see it playing out. We get there, do some basic schmoozing, and then you continue with that kumbaya-partnership charade. She'll be so giddy she won't be paying any attention to what I'm doing."

"Which is what?"

"I'll be scoping the premises. If I see any Shadows, then bang, they're getting a snootful."

"What'll happen next?" I asked.

"The Shadows will either sputter and die or—they won't."

"Is there a Plan B?" I asked.

"Uh-uh. I don't expect to need one."

I waved away the smoke. "Getting back to JJ, if we eliminate the Shadows she'll be alone. We sic Cho and Faraday on her for the fire. That's enough vengeance, don't you think?"

"I feel responsible for what happened to Mick. I won't be satisfied till JJ is toppled from her ivory tower, and crawling through the filthy back alleys with rats gnawing at her toes."

"Remind me never to get on your bad side."

Nellie rose and turned on the sink faucet holding her spent cigarette under the running water. "If JJ makes a move to stop me then you make your move. Do anything to keep her away from me. Anything. Got that?"

"I'm not killing her," I said.

"Is that the only song you know? Just keep that woman the fuck off me while I'm busy."

My glass contained only melting ice cubes. I was thinking refill and looked toward the counter. "Where did the bottle go?"

"Back where it belongs." Nellie said. "I'm keeping you sober. You might come in handy if things go sideways."

She picked up the Morton canister and carefully poured some of the powder into the Boto pouch and tied it off. She then placed it in the Acme bag. "Can I trust you to hold this till the time comes?"

Yikes.

"Sure. What happens if the Shadows don't show themselves?"

"If they get bashful, we ratchet up the proceedings."

"What's that mean?" I asked.

"You get physical with her."

"Physical?"

"You want me to draw you a diagram? Grab her by the throat. Wave a fucking knife around. The Shadows will come out of the woodwork."

"I'd probably end up stabbing myself," I said.

"As long as you don't stab me."

CHAPTER FIFTY-SIX

Nellie and I stood at the seventh-floor elevator waiting for it to open. I'd been staring down and wasn't expecting anyone to step off.

"V—oops—I thought you were your brother."

"I'm not him," Nikolai said, shaking water from his jacket collar. "It's pouring out there."

"No kidding," Nellie said.

"Nellie, this is Nikolai, V's brother."

"So, you're Nellie," Nikolai said. "Vedra likes you. I don't know why."

"Let's keep it that way," she said.

Nikolai touched his front pocket and dug out a cigarette. He lit up while glaring at me. "You accused my brother of hurting your girlfriend. That's wasn't smart."

"He misunderstood," I said.

"No, he didn't."

"I'm sorry if I offended him."

"Sure you are." Nikolai inhaled a long drag on his cigarette.

"I've been meaning to ask," I said. "That night we were talking in the parking garage."

"What about it?"

"I got attacked right after that."

"So I heard."

I waited a couple of seconds. "Did you see anyone else out there?"

"No."

"Alrighty, then."

I pointed to a no-smoking sign on the wall. He raised his middle finger in its direction and dropped the cigarette to the floor. "Have a nice day," he said, heading toward his brother's place.

Nellie stamped out the butt. "Delightful man."

We rode the elevator to the basement and I hesitated at the area where I found Keira.

"That's where she was?" Nellie asked.

I nodded.

She gently put her hand on my elbow and steered me into the parking garage.

Fortunately, it wasn't high tide. Rain swept across Ocean Drive from the Intracoastal into Cape May Harbor as Nellie's windshield wipers fought the downpour. Gale-force squalls pounded her van as we splashed our way past the marshes, moored fishing boats and shuttered restaurants.

When we crossed the bridge entering Cape May, the sea roiled to our left threatening the popular Lobster House, which would likely be inundated with flooding waters in a few hours.

We drove by the Victorian hotels, whose vibrant colors were softened by the density of the rain. The streets were abandoned.

"There it is," I said. "That's where she's staying."

The white-painted spires atop the blue B&B almost swayed in the howling gusts. Nellie parked directly in front and we raced up the wooden stairs.

No one was at the front desk.

"I feel like a drowned rat," Nellie said, patting her hair, and then stopping a second later. "Aw, fuck it."

"Yeah, who cares?"

"I see why they call it The Blue Heron," Nellie said. Various paintings, mostly those of the graceful birds decorated teal-colored walls. A strong scent of lilac drifted in the lobby. Silk flowers sprung from baroque vases.

"She's on the second floor, room 204," I said, leading Nellie up the creaking stairs.

"Just keep a strong grip on the bag. Without that powder we might as well go in with a peashooter."

We right-turned at the top of the stairs, right-turned again and found JJ's room tucked in the corner. I knocked on the door and waited a few moments. I knocked again.

"JJ?" I said.

Nothing.

"JJ."

"What was that?" Nellie asked.

"What?"

"That sound from downstairs."

"Anyone there?" I yelled, leaning over the railing.

No response.

Nellie twisted the doorknob. "It's not locked."

I heard a rumbling noise coming from the stairs and snapped my head around to see the Shadow rising towards us.

"Open the door," I said.

Nellie pushed it and JJ stood near the window smiling at us. "Come on in."

I bumped into Nellie as we almost fell into the room. The door slammed behind us.

JJ wasn't waiting out the storm out in sweats, but this was the dressed-down version. She wore gray slacks with black ankle-high boots rimmed with silver fur, and a plain white blouse sporting an orange brooch in the shape of a winged dragon. Her reddish-brown hair flopped to her shoulders.

"What's the matter, Dave?" JJ laughed. "You look like you've seen a ghost."

"Uh-uh. One of your friends."

"They won't bother us. Take a seat."

An antique writing desk sat by the window with a single chair on one side and two chairs across from them. A Victorian-style sofa, with tufted cushions hugged the wall to my right flanked by floral-embroidered matching chairs. To our left was the archway to the bedroom where I spotted a four-poster bed.

The desk held neat stacks of papers in front of each chair. Orange Post-it Arrows stuck out from pages indicating where signatures were needed. Mont Blanc pens rested in their open boxes alongside.

JJ pulled out a chair and sat down, her back to the window, the angry ocean barely visible across the street. We sat opposite her and I placed the yellow bag on the floor between us.

"What's all this?" I said, waving my hand over the papers.

"Duh—it's why you're here. I'm not schlepping my way back to New

York empty-handed. However, before we start, I'm intrigued by that yellow bag you're toting around."

Nellie said, "My favorite rain hat. I was afraid Brenda would swipe it from me."

"Let's get this over with," I said.

Nellie propped her elbows on the table. "Yeah, let's."

"Of course," JJ said. "In front of you are contracts ready for your signatures. I'm sure you'll find the terms amenable."

Nellie ignored the contracts and surveyed the room.

"What's this?" I said, trying to keep JJ's focus on me.

"What are you referring to?"

I jabbed my finger at the first page. "This shows us as equal partners. I'd need more than a third regardless of whatever project we agree to."

"What do you think, Nellie?" JJ asked.

"I'm with him."

JJ shifted her eyes back to me. "What would you propose?"

"Forty-five, forty-five, and ten for you."

"You're kidding, I assume."

"Nope."

Yep.

"Without my connections you two are dead in the water. I'm the only one who can get you a fabulous deal. Books, documentary, movie—it's all me."

"It's all us, you mean," I said.

"I provide the clout."

"Then you get fifteen percent."

"I'm insulted you would even suggest that."

"I didn't think you were the sensitive type," I said.

Nellie rose from her seat and headed toward the bedroom.

"Where are you going?" JJ asked.

"Bathroom."

"Second door on your left."

As Nellie stepped into the bedroom, JJ glared in that direction. "What's she up to?"

"She pees a lot," I said.

JJ leaned toward me. "It's time we address the 800-pound gorilla in the room."

"Great idea. What are you talking about?"

"You have experience with the Shadows. Your friend, however, is out of her league."

"You clearly don't know her," I said.

"She's a loose cannon and will jeopardize our project."

"This isn't her first rodeo. The Shadows threatened her when she reviewed my book. They weren't very nice."

"You get used to them." JJ stared over my shoulder. "What's taking so long?"

"I could go chase her but that wouldn't be gentlemanly."

Nellie rejoined us, strolling back to the table and sitting down.

"Did you find what you were looking for?" JJ asked.

"Yeah. Toilet was right where you said."

"Which one of you sicced the detectives on me?" JJ asked. "They paid me a visit. That little lady is tenacious."

"She doesn't like it when people do bad things," I said. "Cho already knew about you. Police saw your Porsche cockroach parked at the Atlantus."

"Spyder," JJ said.

"Whatever. She'll pin the fire on you. Only it won't be just arson."

"Dave, stop being so disagreeable. It's not productive."

JJ looked at Nellie. "Did you find your ghost last night?"

"Sure did."

"I suppose it burned up, too."

"You wish," Nellie said.

JJ dropped her pen on the table. "Okay you two; I want to nail this down before I need a goddam boat to get to the Parkway."

"Goddam?" I said. "You didn't used to take the Lord's name in vain."

"What—you're Mormon all of a sudden?"

"I'm wondering if God made the Shadows."

"Why not? It's the same God that brought us cancer, and dished out a nasty brew of atrocities all over the world."

"The Shadows are the worst atrocity," I said.

"They can be very useful if you understand their capabilities."

"And limitations," I added.

"There may not be any. But I can tell you this—they're evolving just as the human race did. In time, their powers will increase exponentially."

"Unless they're exterminated," I said.

"What makes you think they can die?"

Nellie touched my arm. "My turn, Boss." She shifted to JJ. "Even Superman had his kryptonite."

JJ laughed. "This is real life, Hagerstrom."

Nellie tapped her fingers on the table. "Where did the fuckers come from?"

"Like any other species, they evolved."

"From what?"

"Us. They developed the power to materialize from a mere silhouette copy to their own independent being."

"How'd they manage that trick?" Nellie asked.

"You'll have to ask them."

"How many are there?"

"Enough for now—soon to change."

"Why pick on me and Dave?"

"Because certain people are more useful to the cause—though in time every Shadow will break away from their host."

"I won't allow that," Nellie said.

JJ sighed. "This is getting tedious, although I'd love to see your precious rain hat."

"You will. What's the purpose of your almighty Shadows?"

"Seriously—you have to ask?"

Nellie raised her voice. "What's their fucking purpose?"

"Advancing their species," JJ said. "They're babes feeling their way. Once they mature—once they learn how to harness their powers, they will have dominion over all of us."

Nellie shook her head. "I don't think so. They barely scared my cat."

"You were lucky."

"I burned the book and the Shadows ran away like little girls."

"Their business with you was concluded. Now, we're closer to the transition."

"Transition," Nellie said. "That's what you're calling it?"

"Call it whatever you want."

"And what exactly is your role?" Nellie asked.

"A bit of everything—emissary, facilitator, PR Manager of sorts."

"Flunky. Traitor. Murderer."

"Sign the contract," JJ said.

Nellie picked up a pen and rolled it back and forth in her hand. "I asked you a minute ago why Dave and I are so fucking important to them. Your answer was weak."

"You are exasperating," JJ said. "You both have talents I don't. We want to deliver an effective message. Prepare everyone for what's coming. Dave's first book gave a hint but the next one will be much more explicit. It'll be real. The Shadows will turn the skies black."

"What good is a planet of dead people to them?" Nellie asked.

"They don't want mankind going the way of the dinosaurs."

"Yeah," I said. "They'd have no slaves."

JJ smiled. "You're catching on—finally. The Shadows will demonstrate their power on a smaller scale. Maybe take out New York City. Maybe Cape May County. It'd be a test run, a sneak preview of things to come if there's a lack of compliance."

I stared at her. "What the fuck have you turned into?"

"I've always been a pragmatist. Number one, none of us has any choice. Think of it as the natural Darwinian evolution of species. This would take place with or without me, which leads to number two; I want to be around when it happens. The three of us are going to enjoy a privileged life at the top of the food chain."

"I'm betting you don't even make it through today," Nellie said.

"What—"

"You need to answer for Mick."

"That was an accident," JJ said.

Nellie snickered. "You're about to have an accident. Go, Boss."

Now or never.

I lunged at JJ, flinging my body across the desk, reaching for her neck. The chair fell backwards against the windowsill as we tumbled to the floor.

"Get off me," JJ shouted.

I heard a rumbling sound as if a window opened inviting the storm inside. It was the same sound I imagined when I wrote Shadows, the muffled cacophony of lost souls wailing in a forsaken choir.

"Dave!" Nellie screamed. "Help me!"

I released my grip from JJ's throat and jumped to my feet.

Nellie's fragile body flailed amidst a cluster of Shadows, her arms lashing in all directions. The black pulsing mass swallowed her and she disappeared—

—then reappeared.

The roaring din increased as I headed toward the Shadows, toward Nellie. Her mouth was open now and she screamed, but the noise in the room drowned out her voice.

I couldn't make out a word but I saw where she pointed.

CHAPTER FIFTY-SEVEN

The water is warm and soothing.

I never learned to swim. Mom didn't know how and my father was a hard-working man with little time for fun.

Yet—I'm swimming alongside Keira. She is stunning; it doesn't matter we are underwater. Her hair, despite the ocean, is yellow silk; her eyes are diamonds. She bobs, swirls, performs a loop-de-loop under the rippling surface.

She is a mermaid.

We head to the barrier reef knowing they are waiting for us. We love each other and nothing can change that—this is our Kingdom. She is the queen and I am her mate. Our daughter swims with us.

She is a water nymph.

Her name is Nancy. Yet, I can't recall who named her or how old she is. These are things a father should know. I really must ask Keira.

"Davey!"

The water is turbulent today although I'm not certain if this is unusual. Keira's tail propels her ahead of me but I'm rallying and freestyling in her direction. Keira's wiggling motion—it is practical. It's sexy.

Our daughter hitches a ride on the fin of a white dolphin and whisks away only to return and plant a kiss on my cheek.

"I'm helping Mommy," she says, and is off again.

Fish of every shape and color dive under us, dart left then right. Keira and I are following the blue-colored fish, their scales morphing to black at the tails.

"Keira!" I yell.

She turns and smiles. She rarely speaks; each word is measured. I sense that when we arrive at the reef our world will change. Something bad will happen. I see it in her face.

Her arm motions in my direction.

"Slow down!" I say.

She laughs, spins a 180 and swims to me.

"Slowpoke," she says.

"Davey!"

My mother is calling me.

Mom has a booming voice and when she stands on our front porch shouting my name, the whole neighborhood knows it's dinnertime. Her voice canon-blasts across the streets, through the trees, into the park, wherever I am—over, under or through any obstacle.

"Davey!"

Keira glances over her shoulder and sees I'm lagging again. She stops and treads water until I join her.

"I'm worried," I say.

She raises a finger and touches my lips.

Her casual touch forges a passageway direct to my heart—a warm sizzle of affection finds its way. One finger with so much power.

The water darkens. The turbulence increases. I fight to maintain my course.

Suddenly, we are alone. No fish anywhere—nothing but a dark void closing in on us. I start to swim back but Keira grabs my arm.

"I need you," she says.

Those words should ease my fear.

They don't.

I can't pull free even if I want to. She is stronger than I am.

"Davey!"

I'm coming, Mom.

"Let's go home," I say.

Keira tugs at me, scuffles with me. I push her away.

She is upside-down.

She is spinning in a whirlpool.

She is no longer a mermaid.

She is no longer Keira.

"Dave, give me that."
Nellie?

I am consumed by a black Shadow-mass that clogs my lungs. My vision is hindered, my eyes stinging. Nellie is there—next to me—her body whirling—now vertical, now horizontal.

Then I remember.

I had pulled myself off JJ and sprung up to see Nellie thrashing inside the Shadows. She'd wasn't able to grab the yellow bag in time and pointed for me to get it. I gripped it at the same instant the Shadows sucked me inside.

Nellie's fingers clutch my arm with strength impossible for anyone with her frail body.

"It's too late," she moans, as she drifts further from me into the murkiness.

I look down at my hand and see the bag, its loops wrapped around my wrist. I pull out the Boto pouch realizing what has to happen, but fumble with the drawstring.

"What are you doing?" JJ asks, sounding more amused than concerned.

There, inside that small pouch is the powder Nellie kept under wraps for years—waiting for this exact moment.

"The Shadows will let you go if I tell them," JJ says.
I got this, JJ.

I gasp for breath and a burning sensation assaults my throat. Reeling in a vortex, I battle for control of my movements. The Boto pouch moves in my hand and I drop it and—worse—have no idea where it goes.

Then, a delicate voice whispers to me, "Here." I blink the fog out of my eyes as a petite shape glides away from me.

Somehow the pouch is now sitting in my unsteady hands. The string is untied exposing the contents to the maelstrom. I don't have to do anything. Inhuman screams fill my ears as the powder churns like a pink tornado.

The screams fuse together and become a thunderous roar, which increases rapidly to an unholy crescendo.

JJ shouts, "Stop that!"

I see the terror on her face—both hands now cover her ears.

Just when I think my own eardrums will rupture, the Shadows cease their collective wailing and a dazzling lightshow unfolds. Pinks, greens and silvers fill the room, the colors like shooting stars ricocheting off the walls, the floor, the ceiling.

I am watching all this happen from within the diminishing haze and comprehending little. It is there in front of my eyes, yet my brain is unable to make sense of it.

I just want this to end.

The noise subsides and the colors vanish as the black Shadow-mass fades to pale ash and dissipates.

Nellie and I tumble to the floor.

I'm grateful Nellie is alive. More than alive—she's smiling.

"What the hell was that?" JJ asked.

"A souvenir from Brazil," Nellie said.

I took inventory of my body. Legs fine, arms good. A fleeting thought entered my head and left in a flash—Keira had a stranglehold on my arm. I notice my shirt is torn.

Keira?

Underwater?

I struggled to my feet. Nellie did the same, placing her hand on my shoulder for support. We both checked the room knowing what the other was looking for.

"Are they gone?" I asked her.

"I—I think so—yes."

"What have you done?" JJ cried.

"The impossible," Nellie said.

I willed my hands to stop trembling. I turned to confirm the Shadow-cloud was history. No sign of it. The empty pouch lay near my feet. I reached down to see if any powder was still inside. "All gone," I said, handing it to Nellie.

"More back at the ranch if we ever need."

"Did you see anyone else in there with us?" I asked.

Nellie's eyes widened. "No. You did?"

"A little girl in a green dress."

"Oh—my—God."

JJ walked into the bedroom and stood there before heading toward the hallway door. She flung it open. She stepped out into the hallway—stepped back in. She lowered her head. "I can't feel them anymore."

Nellie slapped my shoulder. "Holy shit—it fucking worked!"

I saw chairs overturned, a lamp lay shattered on the floor and papers were strewn everywhere—so much for JJ's neat piles of contracts.

"You keep a messy place," I said to JJ.

"I don't understand what just happened. What was that stuff?"

"I could tell you," Nellie said, "but then I'd have to kill you."

"Whatever that pink fairy dust was, don't think this is over."

"It's over," I stated.

I hope.

"Damn," JJ mumbled. She scanned the room, cocking her head as though listening for something, anything. She stood beside a table lamp casting a shadow. "It's dead—useless."

"Yeah," Nellie said. "Just like the whole fucking plan."

"No," JJ said. "They did it once and they'll do it again—next time stronger than ever. Species find ways to adapt."

"You don't give up," Nellie said.

JJ smiled. "Wait a second. This still works for us. One side scores a surprise early-round victory but the enemy reforms and the battle rages on."

"Us?" I said. "Did you just jump sides?"

"I'm always on the winning side."

Nellie shook her head. "Go back to New York. Stay the fuck out of everybody's way."

Then I heard Nellie's ringtone, *Who you gonna call? Ghostbusters!*

Nellie moved an upturned chair and bent down into the clutter, emerging with a phone to her ear. "Slow down, I can't understand you." She looked at me. "I think it's Maggie."

I snatched the phone from her. "Maggie, you okay?"

"Dave," she said. "Jason went into the elevator. He's got a gun with him."

"You saw it?"

"I saw him slip something in his pocket. It's a gun, I'm sure."

"Maggie, calm down."

I heard her inhale, exhale. "Mr. Zdenko, V, knocked on my door."

"What did he want?"

"He asked where you were."

"I'm not following this," I said.

"He said to let you know Jason is going to kill Keira—at the boardwalk pier where Jason works. I'm getting dressed now."

"Absolutely not! Stay home."

"I don't know what to do." She hung up.

"Let's go!" I shouted at Nellie. I shoved her phone into my pocket, yanked her arm and scrambled to the door. We flew down the stairs.

"Where are we going?"

"Wildwood. Maggie said Jason is going to kill Keira."

"What?"

As we climbed into the van, I said, "Drive as fast as this thing can go. I'm calling Keira." I punched her number.

"Keira!" I yelled into the phone.

"This is her mother."

"Put her on the phone, please."

"She's not here. Who is this?"

"Dave Farmer. Where did she go?"

"Oh, Mr. Farmer. She forgot her phone when she ran out of the house—to—meet you."

"Where?"

"I don't know. Keira was very upset and told the caller she'd be right there. I guess she wasn't speaking with you?"

"No, she wasn't."

"I'm worried," she said.

Me, too.

"I know where she went. Call you later."

"What was that about?" Nellie asked.

"Can't this crate go any faster?"

"It's not a fucking submarine."

Chapter Fifty-eight

"That was Keira's mother?" Nellie asked me.

"Yeah. Someone phoned Keira and told her to meet me, I think at Adventure Pier."

"Who called Keira?"

"I'm not sure."

"You're confusing me," Nellie said.

"Maggie told me Zdenko said Jason's going to kill Keira."

"Still not getting it," Nellie said.

We nearly hydroplaned as we approached the bridge to Wildwood Crest. "Watch where you're going," I said.

"The storm is trying to dump us into the fucking harbor."

Arriving in the Crest, I plotted our route. I'd pedaled these streets often and noted the flooding patterns in case I ever got ambushed by rain and high tide. Ocean Avenue stretched parallel to the ultra-wide beach and the water rarely crossed that expanse.

In addition to mapping our present path I developed a second plan— to keep Nellie safe.

"Turn right at the light," I said. "Then make a left on Ocean Avenue and stay straight to the boardwalk past Convention Hall."

"What do we do when we get there?"

"Working on that now." I made another call. "I'd like to speak to Detective Cho or Faraday."

"Who's calling?"

"David Farmer. It's an emergency."

"What is the nature of the emergency?"

"Murder. Tell them to go to Adventure Pier, the one with the big rollercoaster. Jason Bell is there and he has a gun. Tell them I'll be there, too."

I finished the call and placed Nellie's phone in the center console.

"Keira's car!" I shouted. Her blue-and-white-striped Mustang was parked in one of the lots near the boardwalk. "Pull over by that Jag." Keira's car was dwarfed by the red Jaguar XJ.

"Zdenko," I muttered.

"What?"

"That's Zdenko's car."

"Why is he here?"

I mulled the possibilities. "Go back to my place and get my gun," I said.

"No way! I'm helping you."

"A gun would help me."

"Where is this gun?"

"In a safe in my bedroom closet, side shelf. The code is 8987. Also, check and make sure Maggie is okay and stays put."

"I don't know about this," she said.

"Go!"

"You're gonna be in trouble without me."

I know.

"The cops will be here soon." I opened the door of the van as the wind fought me every inch of the way.

Nellie looked at me and I motioned for her to leave. "Be careful, Boss."

I half-skidded my way up the slick ramp leading to the boardwalk and the moment I stepped onto the hardwood a gust of wind nearly sent me airborne. To my right, I saw the murky outline of the Convention Center and in front of me at the distant end of the pier was The Great White coaster. Its skeletal body stretched 110-feet high overlooking the Atlantic, which now swallowed most of the beach and thrashed against the pilings.

"David!" The voice came from my left.

"Keira, where are you?" The wind blasted the rain sideways, stinging my eyes. I shielded them with my hands.

A running figure slammed into me. Her arms were extended and she wrapped them around me.

I pulled Keira into a storefront entrance and we bumped against the closed metal shutter. We hugged, partially sheltered from the fierce elements.

"David, thank God you're alright."

"Why are you here?"

"I got a phone call. He said you were injured at this pier."

"Who said?" I asked.

"I didn't recognize the voice."

"Did it sound like Jason?"

"It was deeper."

"Any accent?"

"None," she said.

"Why didn't you check with Nellie to see where I was?"

"I don't have her number."

"I want you to go home," I said.

"Only if you go with me."

"Suppose—"

"No. We're staying or leaving together. Where is Nellie?" she asked.

"I sent her to the condo to get my gun."

"You don't have a gun."

"I know. I called the police." I removed my rain jacket and handed it to Keira. "You've only got a sweater. Put this on."

"Thanks. I ran out of the house."

I held her tight against my side, my arm curled around her shoulders.

"Who parked in the lot first, you or Zdenko?" I asked.

"What do you mean?"

"Zdenko's Jaguar is parked next to your car."

"What's he doing here?"

"I can guess."

She squeezed my hand. "David, I don't like this."

A bolt of lightning slashed across the sky followed by an explosion of thunder.

"Damn, the storm is on top of us," I said.

"I'm here, too," a voice sounded from behind Keira.

"Detective Cho," I said. "You got here quick."

"I live a few blocks over." She wore a dark green slicker, its hood protecting her head. In her hand was a service revolver, the barrel pointed at the ground. "I understand Jason Bell is here with a gun."

"Someone called me and said David was hurt," Keira shouted, trying to be heard over the constant torrent of rain.

I leaned toward Cho. "Maggie Callahan said Jason has a gun. Vedra Zdenko told her Jason was going to kill Keira. I know that's confusing."

"I'm pretty sure I know what's going on. Backup is on the way," Cho said, peering over her shoulder. "The flooding may delay—"

I never heard the gunshot.

Cho slumped to the cement of the storefront. I pulled Keira down covering her with my body, bracing for the next bullet.

"What happened?" Keira yelled.

"Oh my god! Are you alright?" I asked Cho.

"I've been—shot."

A dark splotch spread from under Cho's jacket over her left shoulder. Then I spotted the weapon lying next to her.

"Can you get up?" I asked.

Cho's body trembled. "Help me to my car, please."

"Take her," I said to Keira. "Call for an ambulance."

"What about you?" Keira asked, wedging her arm under Cho's other shoulder. I used the opportunity to pick up the gun and slide it into the front pocket of my sweatshirt.

"I'll wait here."

"No—"

"Get her to safety," I screamed.

I followed them for the first few strides trying to block any possible bullets. I watched them struggle down the boardwalk ramp and then I turned toward the pier.

It was time for me to end this. Nellie was the Voodoo Queen, the Ghost Whisperer, all things occult. But I wasn't helpless. I would make killing the murderer my business. I owed it to Cecily Slade, Kate Bowman and Keira.

I owed it to myself.

"Farmer!"

The male voice faded to a whisper in the wind as the sound reached me—from the direction of the rollercoaster. I stared at the hulking structure; it stared back through the mist like an enormous T-Rex awaiting dinner.

I strode forward onto the waterlogged boardwalk.

"Watch the tram car, please."

What the fuck?

Emerging from the haze, the iconic blue and yellow tram cars steered directly at me, with Shaky Sam at the wheel. My first thought was that death had been kind to him. The shakes were gone. As he approached, I heard my old landscaping boss shout, "Get to work, young man!"

Seated in the car behind him were Cecily and Kate, both waving their arms. Kate shouted, "Hi, Davey! See you later!"

I wiped my eyes and refocused. In seconds, the tram cars would collide with me.

Too late—I stood mesmerized. Shaky Sam's steady aim was true and he crashed into—no—through me. I felt a chill ripple along my spine. I spun in time to watch the three of them disappear into the storm.

"Farmer!" That voice again coming from the pier.

I advanced without thinking twice. If I did, I might've reversed course and left it to the police. I staggered forward against the wind and kept my right hand firmly in my sweatshirt pocket, fingers gripping the butt of Cho's gun. The gales pushed me side-to-side. I could picture myself lifted from the pier and tossed into the seething ocean.

The Merry-Go-Round creaked to my right and I ducked behind one of the wooden ponies. I glanced toward the street for any sign of flashing lights and listened through the storm's rage, hoping the voice would again call out.

Fuck it.

I stepped into the open and ran to the giant coaster where I heard sounds—a scuffle, muted voices, a gunshot.

Chapter Fifty-nine

The rusted chain gate to the Great White rollercoaster lay on the ground. I scanned the pier and the dormant rides, searching for possible shelter, not from the nor'easter, but from whoever was lurking about.

Zdenko was somewhere close and possibly Jason.

I saw no immediate place for me to hide except within the underbelly of the mammoth structure itself—a gloomy network of beams and cross braces.

I stepped inside the gate and paused as I reached the imposing thrill ride. Standing before its labyrinthine supports, I strained my eyes to see through the drenching downpour.

I wasn't alone.

Cho's revolver rested inside my raincoat's pocket and provided a certain measure of comfort. I never fired a gun in my life but had confidence I'd figure things out.

Point and shoot.

"Did you see him?" a voice shouted from inside the metal-and-wood jumble. Zdenko emerged from the darkness wielding a pistol and walked towards me.

"See who?"

"Jason." Zdenko yelled. "He is murderer."

"I've got a gun," I said, pulling out Cho's revolver.

"Give me that!" His giant paw swiped at the weapon and sent it skittering over the edge of the pier into the savage waves.

"What the hell—"

"You lose gun," he said. "I do this myself."

Zdenko wheeled and fired a round into the rattling tangle of supports—and fired another.

"Stop shooting!" I screamed.

I heard a groan but it was difficult to be sure with Brenda on the rampage. Zdenko took a stride forward heading into the coaster. I grabbed at him and caught his jacket sleeve but he yanked his arm free.

I wasn't sure whether to follow him or stay put.

I stayed—my heart pounding.

Seconds passed as I awaited Jason or Zdenko.

"Help me." A shape stumbled from within the framework. I recognized the hat and ran to him, as he grabbed a strut for support.

"What happened?" I put my arm under his shoulder.

"Bastard shot me," Jason stammered. He leaned against me. "Call the police."

"They're on their way."

"Get me out of here."

I tried to walk while propping Jason upright but he collapsed, dragging me with him—the side of his face falling into a large puddle. I lifted him clear of the water, and knelt beside him.

He opened his eyes and murmured, "He'll kill us."

His eyes closed.

"Jason." I felt for a pulse.

"Jason."

He was gone.

"He is dead?" I heard Zdenko ask.

I turned and saw him sitting on one of the crossbeams. He cupped his hands, attempting to light a cigarette. "Fucking storm," he said, flicking the unlit cigarette away.

"What happened?" I asked.

"Come closer and I'll tell you."

I don't think so.

"You shot Jason," I said.

"I should get a medal."

I backpedaled, bumping into one of the braces.

"Where you going?" he asked.

"The police are coming."

He smiled and shook his head—calmness covered his face. "They won't be here in time for you, my friend."

No accent!

Shit.

Zdenko reached into his pocket and pulled out a gun. "I have something for you."

The bullet struck the steel beam alongside me. The echo stung my eardrums.

"What are you doing?" I shouted.

"Finishing the job I started when I whacked you with the bat." He smiled again. "Damn if you didn't move at the last second, you lucky bastard."

Stall for time.

"Why would you want to kill me?"

"I loved Cecily, and you slept with her. Because of you, she's dead."

"She loved Dennis," I said.

"He's a stupid old man."

"She slept with him every night—probably had great sex."

"No!" he roared. "She stopped that. She only loved me."

"Cecily loved everyone. Dennis told me she was a sex addict."

"We were going to get married. I was taking Cecily to my place in Paris."

"Not your beloved Albania?"

Zdenko laughed. "Albania is no place for a classy woman like Cecily."

"I thought you loved your home country," I said.

"Farmer, you're a gullible idiot."

"I'm gullible? There wasn't a chance in hell Cecily would marry you."

He stared at me. "I'm going to enjoy killing you."

I glanced towards Ocean Avenue—hoping for the cavalry. "Why did you kill Jason?"

"I didn't like his fucking hat."

"What did he ever do to you?" I asked.

"Wrong place, wrong time."

"You didn't have to kill Kate."

"I wanted the police to think you killed both women since you were the obvious link. Turns out the two detectives were smarter than I thought."

"Kate's only mistake was in liking my book," I said.

"I read your book—it was junk. Enough talk. Time for you to go away."

He fired the gun and I flinched, feeling a thump to my left leg. It took a moment to realize the bullet struck me mid-thigh. Blood didn't gush as I might've expected. A burning sensation ran the length of my leg as a gray circular stain spread on my jeans in the teeming rain.

I felt woozy and slumped against one of the pillars.

"Hey, Farmer, you okay?" Zdenko asked cheerfully.

"Stop this before it's too late," I said.

"It's already too late for you." Zdenko raised the weapon and appeared to pull the trigger. I didn't hear a sound. He repeated the firing motion.

"Fuck," he said, staring at the object as though it betrayed him. He hurled the gun at me. It flew past my shoulder.

"The police are here," I said. "I see the flashing lights."

Where the hell are they?

He turned his head.

"Liar," he mumbled, coming toward me.

I imagined my neck in his arms, bones yielding to his monstrous strength. Diving off the pier was out of the question. If the impact didn't kill me, the water would. Fighting Zdenko was also pointless—a guppy versus a shark. But ...

I punched him.

My fist connected with his cheek as he jerked his head.

He snickered. "Cecily hit me harder than that."

I kicked him with all the force my good right leg could muster. My shoe found its target between his legs. He groaned as he dropped to one knee.

Unfortunately, the kick caused me to lose my balance and I fell, landing on my side.

"You son of a bitch," he grunted.

Zdenko wheezed and struggled to his feet while I managed to get to mine. Staggering, he shambled with outstretched arms and a menacing sneer.

Fucking Frankenstein!

I sidestepped and hobbled into the rollercoaster's guts. In the windswept rain, he trailed me. I searched the ground looking for something to use and spotted a rumpled canvas cloth. I dragged it aside and saw Jason's open toolbox. A hammer sat atop the tools.

Thanks, Jason.

I lifted my new weapon and felt comforted by the heft it provided. I limped onward, ducked under a crossbeam and slid behind a vertical support.

Zdenko shuffled in my direction singing, "Zip-a-dee-doo-dah, zip-a-dee-ay. My, oh, my, what a wonderful day."

I waited for him to get in striking range.

"Farmer?" He took another step—then another one.

I lunged swinging the hammer at his head. He raised his arm as the hammer crashed against his left forearm.

"Ooowwwww!" he screamed.

I headed deeper into the maze hoping for a place to hide, though that strategy hadn't worked for Jason.

Crap. Nothing.

I started climbing. Jason once told me that years ago a teenager attempted this difficult feat for a thrill. He gave up. I was no kid but I was motivated.

I wedged my good leg between the slanted intersections of two crossbeams and pushed myself up. I grabbed the beam overhead and hoisted up further. A pattern suggested itself—straddle a horizontal beam, then shimmy up a diagonal brace to the next one. Repeat.

"Goddam you son of a bitch," he yelled. "I think you broke my arm."

"Next time I'll break your skull."

I heaved my body between two more beams and edged higher. The metal braces were slippery but I wrapped my arms around them and scooched upwards a few inches at a time.

I saw that Zdenko managed to begin his own ascent. He was heavier but stronger and had the advantage of two good legs.

"Where you going, Farmer?"

A dead end.

The top of the structure loomed near—the wind raging with added fury at this height.

Then I saw the emergency vehicles—strobes flashing in the parking lot declaring the arrival of the Wildwood PD. I just needed to stay out of Zdenko's reach for another few minutes.

The entire coaster shook and I wondered if Jason had fully buttressed the Great White. A continuous creaking sound warned me the whole thing could topple like an erector set.

I paused to peer down at Zdenko. He struggled but his foot managed to slide into the same wedges of metal-to-wood that aided me. His eyes peeked up at me like two penlight rays in a dark room. I was scared but I detected something that tempered my fear. He was scared, too.

He gulped a deep breath and made steady progress. "Ah, that's better," he said, to my disappointment.

Zdenko's right hand snared my left foot, provoking a new level of pain in my leg.

"Where will you go now?" he said.

I kicked his hand and he released his grip.

"The police are here," I shouted.

"So what. I'll throw you off. You're a dead man whether you land in the ocean or on the pier."

"They'll shoot you down," I said.

"I'll jump after I toss you. I was a champion diver and swimmer in college."

"You won't make it through the storm."

"The current will carry me and I'll find a spot. The cops won't find me. But they'll find your body—right where you found Cecily."

He stretched his arm and slapped at my ankle. I wriggled away. On one of these attempts he would snatch my leg with enough force to send me flying into the storm

Zdenko grabbed my foot. "Gotcha!"

His strength was too much and I was too fatigued. I slid toward him, toward my death like that shark hunter in *Jaws.*

I checked the pier below where the police now gathered.

Then I heard a familiar voice alongside me.

"Hi, Mr. Farmer."

Oh my God!

I jerked my head toward the voice.

"I can't see you," I said.

"I have something for you to remember me by."

She pressed a tiny object into my hand.

"You once said you liked it," she added.

A second later Zdenko screamed, "Let me go."

Suddenly, my feet were free from his grasp. I saw the big man in full panic. Zdenko flailed one arm wildly—battling an invisible force while the other arm tried to maintain his hold of the beam.

His voice trembled, "But—you're dead."

I heard a clear response. "You would know."

I squinted, trying to see the struggle.

He punched and kicked at the air, swung his arm and shrieked, "No! No!"

He didn't fall straight down.

Zdenko's body drifted sideways before gravity took charge and dropped him into the churning cauldron below. A wailing cry trailed his free fall.

My senses sought to confirm his merciless landing. The swirling winds and the deafening Atlantic virtually sealed my eyes and muzzled my hearing.

Zdenko was gone.

I clutched a strut with both hands and laid my head against a wooden brace.

Chapter Sixty

Nellie and I defeated Shadows in Cape May. I successfully battled a maniacal killer in the Wildwoods. Here in the off-season these were supposed to be the quiet months.

Following the incident on the Adventure Pier, the nor'easter soon finished its local onslaught and set sail for the open seas.

Days later, Detective Daiyu Cho and I recovered at the hospital in Cape May Court House. My gunshot wound wasn't serious. The bullet whizzed through the outer edge of my thigh, missing the femoral artery, and got lost in the storm.

If this were the movies, cowboys would call it a flesh wound.

Detective Cho wasn't as fortunate. Surgery repaired her fractured clavicle and she would miss a couple months of chasing bad guys.

I limped along the hallway, clad in my pajamas and robe, to the private room where Cho lay propped up in bed. Her left arm rested in a sling; an IV dripped into her vein. Faraday sat in a chair on the opposite side of the room paging through a newspaper.

I leaned on my cane and tapped the IV. "Vodka?"

"Still the wise guy," Faraday said.

Cho glanced at him.

Faraday chuckled. "Don't worry. I kind of like him." He rose to his feet, folded the newspaper and placed it on the rolling tray within easy reach of his partner. He headed around the bed and toward the hallway but stopped next to me.

"One question," he said. "Did Zdenko fall on his own or did you push him off?"

"Neither."

He shrugged. "Whatever."

Keira and Nellie stepped into the room.

"If it isn't my favorite too-tall detective," Nellie said.

"Miss Hagerstrom, a pleasure." Faraday extended his hand.

"You have got to call me Nellie. That's all there is to it."

They shook hands. "Alright—Nellie."

Faraday smiled at Keira. "How are you, Miss?"

"Keira—I'm fine."

"Get a load of this," Nellie said. "One big happy family."

Faraday laughed. "I was just leaving."

Nellie shook her head. "Not yet, Stretch. We've got ground to cover."

A nurse ducked her head into the room. "This is a Trauma Unit. There really should be no more than two visitors. Ms. Cho, can I do anything?"

"Yes. Could you give my friends more time? Also, please have someone bring in a couple of chairs."

"Of course," she said. "I won't watch the clock, either."

"Nellie," I said, "Did you notice how Detective Cho handled that? You can catch more flies with honey than with vinegar."

"Got no use for flies," she said, sticking her tongue out at me.

Faraday returned to his seat. I sat in the one other chair and motioned for Keira to sit on my lap.

"Behave," she said quietly.

"Mr. Farmer, it's nice to see you getting around," Cho said.

"Can you call me Dave?"

"Let me work on that."

"I hope you feel as good as you look," I said.

"I feel well enough to miss being on the job."

Get-well cards lined up across the ledge of the window behind Faraday. Vases of colorful flowers rested on a small table.

A young man in blue scrubs arrived with additional chairs. I waited for him to leave and then asked the question I'd wanted to for some time. "Did you both seriously think I was the murderer?"

"You didn't help yourself by lying to us," Cho said. "First when we asked if Cecily Slade was ever in your home and you played that semantics game with us."

"Yeah, Farmer. That wasn't nice," Faraday said, smiling.

"Then, after Kate Bromwell was murdered," Cho continued. "You weren't forthright about your upcoming meeting with her on the boardwalk."

"The truth can make you look guilty," I said.

"Lies make you look more guilty."

"You played him well," Nellie said. "Diner cheesecakes, pork roll sandwiches, keeping him relaxed while you were warming up the hot seat."

Cho laughed. "We realized he was innocent. Vedra Zdenko was our main target after the second murder." Cho shifted her gaze toward me. "If you recall, I mentioned we found a clue by the convention center where Miss Bromwell died."

"You never said what it was."

"We do that sometimes," Faraday said.

"It was a cigarette butt," Cho continued. "A Sobranie Black, very popular in Europe, and rather unusual to find here. We were on alert when speaking to him though he never smoked in our presence."

"So, how did you know it was his?"

Faraday laughed. "Once in a while we get lucky. First time we saw the guy we were canvassing the floor and there he was carrying a red trash bag to the hallway chute. We filed that bit of info," he said.

"Then what?" I asked.

"One of our undercover guys fished out Zdenko's trash bags from the utility room dumpster and we came across the discarded black and gold box. We were about to bring him in when the storm hit."

"You knew he did it?"

"Dai, you want to field that?" Faraday said to his partner.

Cho swallowed a sip of water through her straw. "We couldn't be certain he was guilty, but were confident enough to bring him in for questioning and see where that goes. It took us too long to get the DNA results from Miss Donaldson's injuries. That match would've sewn it up."

"Did Zdenko have a criminal past?"

"Yes. The night before his death the State Department responded to an inquiry we'd made. Mr. Zdenko has definite ties to the Albanian Mob."

"Like the mafia?" I asked.

"Worse," Cho said. "They're butchers without regard for human life.

We're currently trying to locate his brother, Nikolai, who remains a bad actor with them."

"He's not at Zdenko's place?"

"No. We also checked his apartment in Atlantic City. He may have gone underground—perhaps back to Albania."

"Not good," I said. "I'll be looking over my shoulder with this guy on the loose."

"We're cooperating with the Feds and hope to have word soon."

"Are you allowed to tell me when you do hear something?"

Cho nodded. "I'm sure we can find a way."

"Good. I want to sleep at night."

"Sleep well. We also have an officer stationed outside your room."

"I didn't see anyone."

"The officer is not in uniform," Cho said.

"If he needs a home, I'll take a boarder."

"Whoa. You're not getting rid of me that easy," Nellie said. "I could get used to the view from your balcony."

"Whom did you suspect?" Cho asked me.

"At first, I figured Dennis for my one-nighter with Cecily. Keira steered me away from him."

"I sensed it," Keira said. "Despite Mr. Slade's animosity, he's a good man. He loved his wife and mourned her death. Living next to David hindered his grieving progress. Jason, on the other hand, was harder to figure."

"Jason got pissed at me," I said. "Kate was a sweet woman. Jason liked her and was overprotective. He noticed me and Kate talking a couple of times on the boardwalk. The last time she confided she was being followed. I didn't know what Jason was capable of, especially with his family missing in action. He told Maggie they were staying with his wife's mother."

"They are," Nellie said. "Jason's wife filed for divorce."

"How do you know?" I asked.

"My amazing deductive skills. Oh—and I scoped out the public records."

"Why didn't you tell me?"

"I have to tell you everything?"

"Here I am wondering if he frightened them away—or worse."

"Relax. I only found out yesterday."

"And then there was Zdenko," I said.

"Excuse me, David," Keira interrupted. "But that man had me totally fooled."

"Me too. He put on a good act. He killed Cecily and Kate, and went on behaving as though nothing happened."

"What made you suspect him?" Cho asked.

"It's going to sound crazy."

"No kidding," Faraday said, drawing another glance from Cho.

I paused for a couple of seconds and then went all in. "Shadows. A Shadow, appearing like a watered-down version of Zdenko, was at my door one morning."

"Oh boy," Faraday muttered.

"One other time, a Shadow jumped between the Zdenko brothers and me in a boardwalk alley in A.C. I think the Zdenko brothers intended to kill me there. If I was sharp, I would've put two and two together sooner. It almost cost Keira her life. The attack in the stairwell—when Zdenko conveniently popped up out of nowhere—that was the clincher for me."

"Why do you mention shadows?" Cho asked.

I hesitated. "Nellie will fill you in later, right?"

"Whatever you say, Boss."

"Getting back to Zdenko," Cho said. "He was jealous of you—being with Mrs. Slade?"

I nodded. "That night on the rollercoaster he claimed he and Cecily were in love, moving to Paris and I spoiled their plans. Killing Kate was meant to throw the blame on me since I could be connected to both women. When that didn't work, he tried to kill me and then Keira."

"And then you again," Cho said. "Mr. Zdenko was quite determined."

"He phoned me and said David was injured near the pier," Keira said. "I didn't recognize Zdenko's voice. He sounded very different without the accent. I get the creeps thinking he used me to lure David there."

"He disguised his voice," I added.

"How about him hitting you with a baseball bat." Keira said. "You never told the detectives the rest of the story."

"Oh?" Faraday said.

"Here goes. Zdenko reached a boiling point when you guys didn't arrest me for the murders. In the parking garage, I saw a Shadow sitting on the hood of a car. It slid off and took a step. So, I backed up at the moment Zdenko swung at my skull, mostly connecting with a beam."

"A shadow?" Faraday asked me.

"A Shadow."

He shook his head. "Farmer, you oughta write a book."

Nellie answered before I could. "Funny you should say. We're going to give it a whirl. Your character is the cynical detective who doesn't believe a cotton-pickin' thing."

Cho stifled a laugh. "She's got you pegged."

"On the other hand, you allow for the paranormal, don't you?" Nellie said to Cho.

"Well—In Jakarta I did see an apparition in the Casablanca tunnel. A massive cemetery was relocated for the tunnel's construction. Spirits are said to haunt the area. I'm certain what I saw was a ghost. I rarely tell that to anyone. Too many people like Artie." She smiled at him. "Maybe that's what makes him such a great cop—his innate cynicism."

Cho turned to Nellie. "These shadows you refer to, are they ghosts of some sort?"

"No," Nellie said. "They're a whole other breed of horror."

"Yet, Mr. Farmer indicates they helped him?"

"They protected him because they had a long-term sinister use for him—something that should scare the shit out of all of us. It's a lot to explain right now. Next time."

"That should be most interesting," Cho said.

"Excuse me, Detective," Keira said. "This morning I spoke to Thomas Finch. He told me the police found Zdenko's body."

Cho cleared her throat. "Mr. Finch has good sources. The Coast Guard discovered the body late yesterday near Rehoboth beach in Delaware. Mr. Zdenko's neck was broken and his face was—rather disfigured."

"Revenge," Nellie said.

"What do you mean?" Faraday asked.

"I'll explain it when you take me to dinner."

"What?"

"You're not married, are you?"

"No."

"How'd I guess?"

Faraday shook his head. "Nellie, I've got a question for you."

"Shoot."

"How did you ever get involved in this supernatural stuff?"

"Well, you don't go to school for it. I was born with the gift—even went to Brazil to see some wicked voodoo firsthand. There ain't no one like me."

"You're going to tell me about the shadows?" Faraday asked.

"Yeah, over a thick juicy ribeye and a bottle of red."

Faraday nodded. "I know just the place."

"I knew I'd wear you down," Nellie said. "You don't know how close we came to being overrun by these things—and how it could still happen. That's why Dave wants me to hang around, don't you?" Nellie winked at me.

"We'd drive each other nuts."

"Don't I get a say in this?" Keira asked.

"I don't see a ring," Nellie said, smiling at Keira. "That means he's up for grabs."

"Detective Faraday," I said. "Earlier you asked me how Zdenko came to fall from the coaster."

"You didn't answer."

"It wasn't the storm and it wasn't me."

"The guy slipped on his own," Faraday said.

"No. Kate Bowman. She was on the boardwalk that night and later up there with us."

Saying this out loud caused even me to question my sanity. Memories of Rosewood returned and I could hear Dr. Sanderson reassuring me I was cured.

Okay, Doc.

"Continue, please," Cho said.

"When I stepped onto the boardwalk, I saw Kate as clearly as I see you. And later, when Zdenko was about to fling me into the ocean, she pried him off the beam. I know what that sounds like but it's all true."

Keira leaned over and kissed me on the cheek. "You can believe anything David says."

Please, Lord. Don't ever let me screw this up.

"You're saying a dead woman pulled Zdenko off the coaster," Faraday said.

Nellie answered before I could. "Let me take it from here. I can say this in lingo even Mr. Nonbeliever might understand. Death isn't necessarily the end of the line. If someone dies and there's unfinished business, their spirit can exist in an astral plane. With me, so far?"

"Nope."

"It's gonna be one long, long dinner," she said. "While Kate might've seemed the shy-type, Zdenko messed with the wrong gal. When the time came, she struck."

The only sound in the room was Cho's monitor chirping away.

Then Faraday broke the silence. "I know that all of you buy this, but it's too bad there's no tangible proof."

"Yeah—too bad," I said.

I reached into the pocket of my robe and pulled out my show-and-tell item. I peeked at my hand and saw the blue seahorse pin that Kate always wore on her jacket. The seahorse's pink eye stared back. I once told her I liked it. On top of that rollercoaster Kate placed the pin in my hand just before she grabbed Zdenko.

I closed my fingers and slipped the pin back inside.

As the three of us walked into the hallway, I put my arm around Keira.

"You guys make a cute couple," Nellie said. "I gotta get me a boyfriend." Nellie then elbowed me in the ribs. "Uh-oh, Boss."

A woman leaned against the nurse's station. The nurse behind the counter pointed in our direction and the woman turned, beaming at us.

I wasn't expecting to see her today, tomorrow or perhaps ever again. But—there she was, sporting a black pantsuit and blazer with a red silk blouse. She was out of place in this building, in this town.

Crap!

"Hello, partners," she said.

"What are you doing here?" I asked.

JJ's heels clicked on the tiled floor. I smelled her perfume as she approached and hugged me.

"Silly boy. I'm here to see how you are."

"I'm fine. Thanks for coming. Bye."

She clasped her hands. "Fabulous news! Your friend Tommy just sold me a beachfront condo in that new development in Cape May."

"The North Beach Project?" I asked. "Those are going for millions."

"Ooh, I know. Isn't it sinful?"

Nellie and Keira didn't say a word.

"I—I don't—"

"Cheer up, Dave. We're practically neighbors."

Stephen Heck is retired from a career in distribution management. He and his wife, Janice, live just outside of Cape May and Steve is working on his sequel to *The Off Season*.